The cover design and interior illustrations are
by the Author. Photographs are by the Author, the
collection of the Author's Grandfather and from
public domain sources

The Navy SEAL Photo on the cover
is Courtousy of the United States Navy

The Blackwater Shaft

By

R. Blair Savage

For Marilyn

2017 by R. Blair Savage

2nd Edition

R. Blair Savage

Boynton Beach, Florida

rbsavage1@gmail.com

I dedicate this work to my 8th Great Grandfather, Thomas Savage of the Jamestown Colony's settlement on the Eastern Shore of Virginia. A remarkable man, he is my most ancient, proven Savage ancestor.

The Lord called him in 1654/55.

Acknowledgements

I want first to thank my beautiful wife, Marilyn for putting up with me for 38 years and going along with some of my foolish ideas. I am blessed.
I want to thank several people who I trusted to preview this work and give me their honest opinions of the content. I love these folks and appreciate them as family and friends.

Marilyn Savage
Tawnia Mazzulo
Trina Honer
Tracy Zuccaro
Tricia Savage
Tamara Savage Clay

Dennis & Karen Carter
Bob & Nancy Engstrom
Jerry & Margo Perry
John & Linda Stocker

Introduction

Hopefully this book will be found of interest by the general public, but I particularly hope it is of interest to my daughters, my grandchildren, their children and those who follow. Why? Because I want them to know a little bit about how my father, paternal grandfather; and I think possibly my paternal great, grandfather, spent a good part of their working lives in the coal mines of West Virginia.

My maternal grandfather was a timberman, a vocation also explored a bit herein.

I was born and spent my early years in a grimy coal mining camp in West Virginia during the mid-1930's and early 1940's. I was sixteen when my father worked his last of 31 years in the mines. As far back in those 16 years as I can remember I was afraid that my dad would not come home one day; that an explosion, a fall, methane gas, or a dozen other calamities would take him from us. I listened to the stories told by my father, my grandfather and my uncles about the hazards of mining. Some of those true stories are intertwined within these covers, including a description of No. 1 Hill, along Scott's Run, where I was born.

This is a story about several generations of two coal mining families in the coal fields of West Virginia. One wealthy and one poor. The wealthy family was blessed with a huge tract of land. Officers in the revolutionary war received large tracts of "bounty" land as a reward for their services. If that land was rich in timber, water and minerals, it could provide a comfortable life, as it did for our, Robert Dawson, an officer who received 20,000 acres. Dawson's son inherited the land; as did His son, and His son, and so on over the course of more than 200 years.

The second family is typical of most poor souls who struggled to eke out a living by working the Appalachian coal mines, but in our story, these two families somehow, come together.

Our story will take you back through time as it touches on events in the lives of several generations of these two families. Random events and specific actions taken by the Dawson men over the course of the 100 years following the Civil War have a dramatic impact on the lives of present day Dawson's as they face extreme danger at the hands of foreign extremists.

This is a story about a part of American life of which relatively few people are aware; the hardship and danger of mining coal, particularly in the first hundred years of this industry in America. There are a few twists and some suspense found between these pages, but overall, this is a story about people.

As you read this you'll find that in telling the story I drift between past and present tense. This is because I developed such a close tie with the imaginary Dawson's I feel as though I was a part of their story and was there, with them. So, pardon me if I say "is" when you feel I should have said, "was", or, "has" instead of, "had". I could have made corrections before sending this off to the printer, but in so doing I feel I would have lost a part of me, and the Dawson's. This story is fictional. Names of certain places mentioned herein do exist in reality, but may have been placed in another location. For example; there was a small coal and limestone mining community along Decker's Creek in Preston County, West Virginia. It was called, Cascade and it was there that my parents met in 1923. The community was still active when I was a boy, but today there is no trace of Cascade.

The headwaters of Decker's Creek are near Athurdale in Preston County, West Virginia, where my family lived for a few years; a time when we were not living in a mining camp and the air was fresh. Decker's tumbles and cascades from 1800 feet elevation at the headwaters to 800 feet where it enters the Monongahela River at Morgantown. When I was a boy the creek was yellow from acid drainage brought on by mining operations. But today, Decker's is being brought back to life by a conservation effort began in the late 1990s and spearheaded by the "Friends of Decker's Creek". As a boy I pictured Decker's as it must have been before coal mining began there; a pristine flow of cascading water splashing and spraying over huge boulders as it plunged toward the Monongahela, so as I envisioned Decker's in times gone by, it became Cascades Creek in our story.

There is a Blackwater River near Davis, West Virginia and that is where I borrowed the name. The river is named for amber-colored waters which plunge over a 60 foot fall and then twist and tumble through an eight-mile long gorge. The "black" water is a result of tannic acid from fallen hemlock and red spruce needles.

Cast of Characters

The Dawson Family
By Generation

1. Tom Dawson – Wife, Elizabeth
2. Robert Dawson - Wife, Lucretia
3. Alex Dawson - Wife, Sarah
4. Nat Dawson - Wife, Alice
4. Ben Dawson - Wife, Marilyn
5. Cole Dawson – Son of Ben

Other Principal Characters
In approximate order of appearance

Commander Pell — Navy SEAL Leader
Angelo Valentini — Coal Miner
Nicola 'Nicki' Valentini — Angelo's Daughter
Jaime Siebert — Nicki's Friend
Jim Ryland — Mine Supt.
Kip Ryland — Jim's Son
Cass Parker — Mine Supt.
'Cormorant' — Sleeper Terrorist
Yasin Ganji — Iranian CMI Agent
Capt. Jeremiah Slade — Op Cen. Commander
Gen. Bruce Maddox — Chairman, Joint Chiefs
Adm. Arland DeWitt — Navy, Joint Chiefs
Rear Admiral Thomson — U. S. Navy
Robert Burke — U.S. Senator from WV
Adam Bucklew — President of the U.S.A.

The
Blackwater
Shaft

Chapter 1
Danger Above
Danger Below

August 15, 2002, 9:23 P.M.

Near the Small Town of Cascade, West Virginia

As the divers enter the water, Civilian Cole Dawson takes the lead position, Lt. Commander Linden Pell takes the number two spot on the safety line and the seven remaining Navy SEALS are spaced about eight feet apart on the nylon line. The water, which had years before filled the flooded coal mine, had first appeared to be as black as the surroundings in the cool, dank, abandoned coal mine, but as the divers go under, they find it to be crystal clear. The beams from the lights mounted above their heads cut through the water with no resistance, although there's little to see except for the twin rails that extend beyond the reach of the light, rails that seem to journey forward into infinity, leading him where, Cole Dawson wonders, to the old airshaft or to his death?

Even through his dive suit, Cole can feel the chill of the water's 50 degrees. Not nearly as cold as the water had been when, many years before, he made that early spring dive to the old submerged bridge in Cheat River, but still pretty cold. Behind him, he can feel the mild tugs on the safety line. Sometimes very distinct, as though from the man just behind him, other times subdued, from one of the divers further back, diminished by the hands in between.

Cole feels a twinge of trepidation in this lonely place. He tells himself he's not frightened, just apprehensive. He's made short dives into caves in the tropical coral waters of the Caribbean, but never far enough that, if he had an equipment failure he could not have made it out of the cave and to the surface in a free ascent. Here, in the abyss of the mine, were his equipment to fail, he'd have to rely on one of the SEALS to let him buddy-breathe. This is also the first time he's used a rebreather instead of compressed air. There seems to be a taste to the air, or gas, as the SEALS call it, which is different from the compressed air to which he's accustomed. Sort of a metallic taste, or a chemical that he

can't identify, but he feels fine and shakes the thought from his mind. He estimates they've traveled two
hundred yards since they entered the water. He periodically notices the side entries off the main haul and assumes they should be approaching the first ventilation control door, or trap door, as it was called by the miners.

Abruptly, Cole remembers why he's here, why he's risking his life in this dark water within the bowels of Laurel Mountain. He's here because of the woman that he loves more with every beat of his heart. In anger, he clamps his teeth hard on his mouthpiece. If he doesn't make it in time, if things go bad, if she dies, how will he handle that? How will he handle her absence if it were final, forever?

Suddenly, he feels a sharp yank on the safety line. He stops and turns. The SEAL leader, Commander Linden Pell gives a "slow down" motion with his palm down. Cole realizes that, as the thought of his beloved being harmed tore at his insides, he must have been kicking faster and faster. He gives Pell a thumbs-up and returns to a smooth, rhythmic kicking stroke as he and the other dark forms glide through the blackness of the mine, their lights giving little reflection from the dark walls.

Cole's thoughts return to the woman who has come to mean more to him than life itself. After all those years that she was lost to him, now that they've found each other again, is he about to lose her for good? He's determined to not let that happen.

Gradually appearing out of the gloom, Cole sees the outline of the first trap door. As they get closer he's surprised to see that the condition of the wooden door and surrounding framing is in perfect condition. He had wondered whether the wood would have decayed and fallen away, but it's perfectly preserved after all these years. The door is in the open position and Cole and the SEALS swim through without delay.

As they continue, Cole feels a calmness settle over him. He realizes his actions have a distinct purpose and having purpose has always been critical to his temperament. He

3

needs purpose, a direction, and a goal. He needs to feel accomplishment, to be challenged, and he certainly has a challenge before himself now.

With the calmness comes a more thoughtful, curious attitude. He directs his lights to the overhead electrical line, the copper cable that fed power to the low-slung locomotive which the miners simply called; "the motor". The motors hauled the long trains of tram cars which carried the ancient black rock to the outside. Behind Cole, Pell directs a powerful handheld spotlight into a passing side-entry, which leads into another section of the mine. Cole wonders how many tons of coal the Dawson men removed from this old mine. They created miles and miles of labyrinth and innumerable chambers. Where did all the coal go? In earlier times it was used to heat countless homes, fired the boilers of steam ships, was baked into coke for the steel mills and fired the boilers of the electric power companies. How much coal?

With roughly two hours of swimming before him, Cole settles into a rhythm as his thoughts continue on the history of the mine. He recalls the story told to him by his grandfather, Alex Dawson; the story about the early history of the Dawson family, the discovery of coal on Dawson land, the years of building the timber, coal and construction businesses. How old was he when he first heard the story, perhaps ten, maybe twelve? They sat on the old porch swing at Grandpa's home as the old-timer began the story about Cole's great, great grandfather, Tom Dawson.

"Yes sir, Cole, my boy," Grandpa began, "My Granddaddy, Tom Dawson was a real man, a man's man, if you know what I mean. Why, when he wasn't much more than a boy, he goes off to fight in that nasty war between the North and the South. In no time at all he's in the thick of it, fighting those confederates."

A hint of a smile creases Cole's cheeks, even with his mouthpiece in place, as he recalls how, when Grandpa would tell his stories, he would drift back and forth between present and past tense and his voice would modulate with enthusiasm; "And after one of those scrapes with the Rebs, Granddad and his buddies have them on the run, when a rebel sniper took aim and" --

Chapter 2

Ambushed

May, 1864

The Mountains South of Winchester, Virginia

Young Tom Dawson urges his mount to give him more as they plunge through the woods. It's warm in the mountains of Virginia and his mare is tired, the ginger usually found in her step not present this evening. Tom's unit, Company E of the 6th West Virginia Cavalry, had been in a hard fight near Winchester that morning and is now moving southward, through the forest, looking for retreating confederates. The mare's coat is splattered with mud that would have dried by now was it not for the lather that wets her body. It's been a warmer than normal May and this day is hot and she has worked hard.

The young man on her back looks even younger than his twenty-four years, and his 185 pounds was normally an easy load for the mare, but not this evening. His light brown hair is almost blond and catches glints of the sun as it bounces off his shoulders. He's a good-looking man with angular features and a strong jaw. The mare has been carrying him several days now, without a break, and the mountains that split Virginia from West Virginia are steep and rugged. The year before, there was no split between these two states. There was no West Virginia. There was only Virginia, where the grand American adventure began two hundred and fifty-seven years before, at Jamestown. Virginia, which once reached to the west and the north further than a man could ride in three months. Virginia, which again felt the inevitable knife of history carve another chunk from her bosom, and the cartographers of the period enjoyed the added business.

The new dividing line, that separates the two Virginias, zigs and zags through the rugged mountains, at times opposing the ridges and valleys and at times following their northeast, southwest persuasion. The new line meant money in the pocket of the cartographer, but unbelievable emotion in the minds and hearts of those mountain families split by the pen and ink. On the Virginia side they were Confederate, but most of the West Virginians remained with the Union. Some families had sons on both sides.

The mare is not in the least aware of these heartaches. Her thoughts are much more fundamental in form. She wants rest. Her great heart is pounding and her breathing seems terribly restricted by the thing that the man fastens around her body and which seem to attach him to her. Her legs are tired and her hooves sore and still he pressures her to give more.

As he rides, Dawson's one good hazel eye scans the forest ahead. He has learned from this war to always be questioning his surroundings. His other eye is hidden under a black patch and beneath a heavy scar that angles upward across his forehead. An even six feet when standing, Dawson sits tall in the saddle, broad shoulders anchored to an erect back. There's no slouch to this man. Powerful legs grip the mare's body.

The company of cavalrymen is spread out as they move through the hardwood and hemlock forest looking for rebel stragglers. If they can take some prisoners they may gain valuable information about confederate movements.

Although the riders have found no rebels, they have found the woods to be alive with signs of spring. The mixture of oak, poplar, beech and maple, on the hillsides, are well along in issuing their canopies of green, which the hemlocks along the streams have continued to provide throughout the winter. The forest floor is a colorful array of wild flowers. The vivid yellow of the Touch-Me-Not, the differing hues of the Blue Bell, the virgin white of the Trillium all blend with greens and browns of the wooded carpet. Where some of the riders pass under the hemlocks, along the slow-moving section of a crystal-clear stream, huge umbrellas of skunk cabbage provide haven for a hundred tiny life forms. Nearby, a cousin of the smelly skunk cabbage, the Jack-in-the-pulpit, seems to stand at attention as heavy hooves smash into the soft carpet of moss and rotting leaves.

Suddenly, the large, brown eyes of the mare that carries our young soldier become more alert as the rider prods her down a steep embankment. She knows that he wants her to move faster to get a good start for the steep climb up the other side of the small gully. She gives him the burst that he asks for, lunging down the side of the gully, jumping the creek at the bottom and urging her aching legs to carry them both, horse and man, up the other side. Half way up the bank, her front hooves strike loose shale and she goes to her knees.

Quickly recovering, she bolts upright again, but even as she does, a rifle shot drowns out the noise of her hooves in the shale. Dawson feels a hard thump on the calf of his left leg, then searing pain. He slaps the mare on her flank, urging her upward and forward. She goes down again. Dawson knows he's been shot and he needs to find cover before the shooter reloads. The shooter must be using a muzzleloader. With a repeating rifle he would have gotten off a second shot by now. Dawson pulls hard on the reins, trying to get the mare back on her feet. She tries, but he's pulling so hard, so hard that it hurts. She raises her great head to try to relieve the pressure. She finds solid footing under her hind feet. She raises her head higher. Dawson yells and pushes on her neck. She paws at the air in a desperate attempt to maintain her balance. She feels a fire and terrible pain in her side. She's confused and frightened, exhausted and hurting, and her normally powerful rear legs collapse as she falls backward.

Dawson knows the mare is going down and he's, in all likelihood going to be caught between horse and earth unless he dismounts fast. Even before he realizes it, his feet are out of the stirrups and on the mare's rump, and as she falls away, quartering to the right, he tries to push off to the left, but his wounded leg gives way and he fails to clear the animal.

As the mare falls backward, Dawson is catapulted through the May air. He tries desperately to position himself to land on his hands and feet so that he can roll and cushion the impact, but his attempt fails and he plunges to earth backwards, landing on a log at the edge of the creek. The impact is brutal, but he never loses consciousness. For a brief instant he feels no pain, just confusion and anger, but only for an instant, then the pain is upon him and it's wicked. His leg is throbbing from the large hole left by a 50-caliber lead ball, and there is excruciating pain now welling through his lower back and upper rib cage. He tries desperately to catch his breath and winces at the effort. He landed on the log in such a way that the breath exploded from his lungs. His diaphragm was momentarily paralyzed. The mare lays close by, making wheezing noises. She raises her head and looks at him. Her large, frightened eyes seem to plead for help.

Now, only seconds after the shot, his breath slowly returning, Dawson realizes the sniper will soon have his piece reloaded and will try for a finishing shot. He figures that, since the shot came from his left, his fallen mare, to his right, could provide cover if he could get behind her. Dragging his bloody leg, tortured by the pain in his ribs and back, he crawls to the far side of the mare. He sees the butt of his Sharps carbine, still in its scabbard, sticking out from under the horse. As he pulls on the carbine he realizes that, if the shooter is up the hill, looking down at him, even the horse will not provide enough cover.

With the rifle pulled free, he's about to strike out again for the protection of a large boulder when another shot thunders down the gully, this time from behind. From the direction of the first shot he hears something crashing and tumbling down the hill. All is quiet for a moment, then, from the direction of the second shot, Dawson hears a sound, a voice calling, "Tom, you alright?"

With his breath regained, Tom Dawson shouts back, "Yeah, I'm hit, but I think I'm okay, that you Matt?"

"Yeah, it's me, but stay low for a spell, that son-of-a-bitch may still be alive."

Up the gully a short distance, a soldier on horseback appears from the trees. He moves his mount along the stream, carefully past Dawson, looking for the confederate. He finds him in a tangle of brush, thirty yards down the gully. He's dead.

Within several minutes, a number of Corporal Thomas Dawson's comrades surround him. His best buddy, Matthew Davis, explains how, at the sound of the sniper's shot, he called out to Tom, but got no answer. Then, he headed his mount down the gully looking for him. He saw the Reb in a tree up on the hill just as he was finishing reloading his caplock and was ready to send another ball Tom's way. Matt raised his own rifle and, shooting from the saddle, killed the Reb with a shot into the center of his chest.

Dawson looks up at his friend and in a husky voice acknowledges the deed performed. "Well, Matt Davis, you saved my life, I sure owe you one."

"No you don't, we're just even. You saved my neck on Droop Mountain, or have you forgotten already? If you hadn't come back for me you'd still have a good eye."

Dawson struggles to find his voice again. His leg is on fire, his ribs feel like he must have busted some and his back hurts bad.

He pulls himself along the mare until he reaches her head, which he cradles in his arms. "Bess old girl, I sure was asking a lot of you, let's get your saddle off and see how bad you're hurt. Matt, can you give me a hand here."

"You just slide outta the way and let me tend to her, Tom."

"Anyway, hell, Matt, I do still have a good eye - and it's my shootin eye. If I'd lost my shootin eye then I'd say you weren't worth it, but I'd trade my left eye for you any day, ol buddy." Then he grimaces in pain as he continues; "Damn, this leg hurts, and no I haven't forgotten, I never will. I expect I'll always remember every single man I've killed in this war, whether I want to or not, but that rascal didn't die easy and it was my own fault that I caught his blade in my eye. I shoulda made sure he was dead before I rolled him over." He tries to shift the injured leg and scowls at the hurt. "But, I learned from that experience - learned not to take too much for granted."

Another soldier arrives with a medical pack and starts working on Dawson's leg. As he does, he looks up at him and asks, "Tom, why do you suppose that Reb took a shot at you? He knew there was a bunch of us giving them a chase and that we'd soon be all over him"

"I been thinking about that, Okie. I figure that Reb fell way behind his buddies, saw me, wanted my mount, thought he could knock me off and then get away from you guys by hi-tailing it south on my horse. But, he made two mistakes; first, he shot my horse, not a very good marksman, I'd say; and second, he got himself lined up in Matt's sights."

Matt turns from the mare and grins; "Heck, Tom, that slug only went in her about half an inch, I can feel it. Soon as Okie gets you fixed up we'll get that ball outta her and he'll have her back on her feet. After going through your boot, your leg, a couple layers of leather, her blanket and her hide, that ball was about spent. And I betcha that Reb didn't put a full load of powder in his piece; he was probably running low. And the young fella looked kind of ragged, clothes kinda tattered, probably didn't have much to eat the past couple of weeks – I feel kinda sorry for the boy."

Dawson spent several weeks, recovering from his wounds, in a camp hospital near Clear Spring, West Virginia, where he remained until he was well enough to join his Regiment again. Before the war ended, he and his good friend, Matt Davis, fought side by side in two more major battles and many minor skirmishes. But Tom lost his friend. In the final days of the war, he and Matt were cut off from their own unit and joined up with General Phillip Sheridan's cavalry. Tom was at Matt's side, at the battle of Appomattox, on April 9th of 1865, when the aim of one of Lee's exhausted, desperate, emaciated, hungry, but accurate marksman was too good, and the ball tore away Matt's throat. It seemed incongruous that Matt would fight so diligently throughout the war, only to lose his life just hours before Lee's surrender.

Chapter 3

Coal

April, 1871

Cascade, West Virginia

When Tom Dawson had arrived home, after the war, he was older than his years; older and wiser. He had returned to his home in Cascade, in the northern part of West Virginia, formerly Virginia. The small town, situated in Cascades Creek Valley, was founded by Tom's Great Grandfather, Robert Dawson. Now, at age 31, with a wife and two children, Tom manages the family lumber operation. His land, 8,000 acres, has been in the family since 1785 when it was part of a twenty-thousand acre tract obtained by Robert Dawson in a trade for a Maryland land grant which he had received for his service as a high ranking officer in the Revolutionary War.

Tom's father, who inherited a quarter of the original 20,000 acres, bought an additional 3000 acres from an uncle who left Virginia for the gold rush in California. The various Dawson family members, who remained on their inherited land, prospered from timber, sawmill and grist mill operations.

Tom had spent three years fighting in The War of The Rebellion, or, the Civil War, and held the rank of Sergeant when he was discharged. He recovered from his wounds without any long-term affects other than the loss of sight in his left eye, but, although physically able, he was having a hard time dealing with the emotions of losing several of his family and friends, including Matt Davis, to the war. He was especially hard hit by the loss of two older brothers, who he had learned to lean on since his father's death in a lumbering accident, at a relatively young age.

With the loss of his brothers, and a sister who died during childhood, Tom and his mother were the sole owners of the entire 8000 acres, which surrounded the town of Cascade. They also owned much of the real estate within the town limits.

Tom married Elizabeth Stevenson, a beautiful, green-eyed

girl of 29. He married Liz as soon as he got home from the war. They had been sweethearts when he went to war and she was there for him when he returned.

Now, early on this April morning, Tom, who lives just south of town, saddles his horse for a ride down Cascades Creek, through the village of Cascade, then further downstream to check on one of his timbering crews. There had been heavy snows during the first half of March and as the April showers have set in, there's still a foot and a half of snow remaining on the mountains.

The gentle rain has been light, but steady over the course of several days and the melting snow, coupled with the determined rain, soon spawned numerous cascades, which plunge down the steep hollows and tumble into Cascades Creek. These cold and clear waters swell Cascades, which flows generally southwest, then breaks through Laurel Mountain and flows west into Big Sandy Creek which flows south into Cheat River. The Cheat, joined by other swollen streams will transform into a thunderous dynamo. At Point Marion, across the border in Pennsylvania, the Cheat joins the Monongahela and their combined volume surges into a mighty partnership with the Allegheny at Pittsburgh. One to two months later, via the Ohio and the Mississippi, these mountain waters will flow through New Orleans and into the Gulf of Mexico.

Dawson's men had been spent three days waiting for the rain to subside, when a group of them came to him to ask if they could move down into Cranberry Bottom, where the slopes were not so steep, and do some cutting, the logs to be hauled out later when the ground dried a bit. When the timber crews were not working they were not paid and few could afford to stand idle for very long.

Knowing that the rain and soft ground would slow his men and raise his cost, Dawson none-the-less agreed to the plan. He knew his men and he knew their needs. They were a hard working group with families to support. When he needed something extra, they gave it, so he told them to go to Cranberry Bottom and have at it.

And now, on this drizzling morning, he rides down Cascades Creek to see how the crew is doing at Cranberry Bottom. Riding along the northwest side of the creek he comes to the place where Little Pine Run empties into Cascades. Little Pine was normally a small brook that one could jump across with ease, but this morning, it's raging down the hollow, which it has spent eons gouging out of the shale and sandstone.

The normally quiet brook is now a torrent as it enters Cascades and Dawson doesn't want to gamble on crossing it at this point. He follows it through wispy hemlocks, branches heavy with rainwater, up the hollow, looking for a place where he might, more safely, get across. He's been up the trail that follows Cascades many times, but has never had the occasion to take this little detour up Little Pine.

It's a narrow hollow that the stream has cut through the rock as gravity relentlessly pulls it toward Cascades. The water normally carries tiny specks of sand along with pebbles and small shards of jagged rock. This morning, with the tremendous force that falling water can expend, it carries larger and heavier rocks that pound, scrape, scratch and abrade the base rock over which it flows. Over millions of years, the result of this abrasion was a slow, but ever so sure, formation of the steep sided hollow.

Dawson begins to feel the dampness form inside his black rubber slicker, which is effective at keeping the rain out, but not too efficient at letting air circulate around his body like his old military poncho did. That poncho kept him warm and dry many times during the war. More than once he had quietly thanked Mr. Goodyear for the shelter it provided.

His leg and back give him pain this morning. Damp weather does that to his old wounds. The water drips steadily from the brim of his hat, creating tiny flashes as particles of morning light are captured and focused through the tiny prisms. Up ahead, he sees an area where the hollow broadens, spreading the water over a wider basin, making it shallower and less rambunctious; a place where he can get across without his horse losing its footing. As he guides his horse through the larger rocks and starts across the stream, his attention is drawn to the rock wall beyond the opposite bank. It's black!

He urges his horse up the bank, over a large, decaying log and through the hemlocks until the horse stands in front of the black, rock wall. He's never seen rock like this. It's of the deepest black, and portions that are smooth have a deep luster and a bright, softly shining surface. As he sits astride his horse, the top of the black rock wall is roughly eye level. There is a sharp demarcation between the top of the black layer of rock and the grayish hard rock above.

He dismounts, takes his pocketknife and presses the blade into the rock. It's relatively soft; he can easily carve a small channel through it. The unusual stone captivates him. He squints his one good eye and looks closely at the channel, which his knife engraved. For a moment he's mesmerized by the whole scene. Then, abruptly, it hits him! He's looking at what must be an eight to nine foot layer of solid coal.

When he had returned from the war he heard reports that coal mining operations near Fairmont and Morgantown were anticipating increased business with the growth of the railroads. Up to now, coal was mostly used locally for heating homes. But, one of his buddies in the cavalry told about the need for baked coal, what did he call it? Coke, that's it, coke, in the steel making mills up in Pittsburgh.

A dozen thoughts diffuse through his mind. The Baltimore and Ohio railroad is only ten miles to the north, and only one mile beyond the northern border of the Dawson land. If they could use coal for heat in Morgantown, then why not Baltimore? Why not Chicago? Why not barge it down the Monongahela to Pittsburgh and the steel mills? Why not indeed!

A short time later, Dawson took a job at a mine near Fairmont to learn coal-mining operations. With the help of a family friend he persuaded the mine owner to work him in the mine for a while so that he could learn, first hand, all the operations involved in the extraction and processing of coal. On his 40th day in the mine, he received a critical part of his education. An explosion rocked the mine, killing thirty-seven men and boys and closing the mine temporarily. Dawson himself narrowly escaped the fate of the dead miners. At the time of the blast, he was driving a mule, hauling coal from the mine and, luckily, had just exited the portal when the blast

occurred. He later learned that a father and three of his sons were included in the thirty-seven souls lost in the disaster, something that was not at all unusual, multiple family members dying in a mining disaster.

Seventy-four miners, who were not killed by the explosion, escaped the mine before being overcome by the smoke and carbon monoxide released by the blast and resulting fire. Dawson helped with efforts to rescue another 12 men who barricaded themselves in a side entry to escape the fumes.

With the Fairmont mine closed, Dawson signed on at a mine near Morgantown. Over the course of three months he worked at a variety of jobs, all the while maintaining a journal which outlined the methods used in the extraction of coal. He made sketches of the various tools and equipment and recorded his ideas as to how some of the operations could be simplified and the equipment improved. He also took measures to determine the sources where materials, tools and supplies could be purchased. Items such as rail, drills, blasting powder and caps, coal cars, head lanterns, etc. He learned that the mine superintendent, Jim Ryland, had fought in a couple of the same battles as he, during the war, and the two men had numerous conversations on the subject.

Dawson found Ryland to be a likable and interesting fellow. He was a ruggedly handsome man of medium height, but with a stocky body that gave him a powerful look. He had serious blue eyes, light hair, oval face and a mustache which looked too finely trimmed for his weathered face. And Dawson couldn't help noticing that he walked with a trace of a limp, a peculiar hobble, as though there were something wrong with his knee.

After one of their battle discussions Ryland gave Dawson some background in coal mining history. And as the days went by, he continued to share his knowledge of the mining business.

All of Dawson's questions were above board. Ryland knew of Dawson's plan to open his own mine and he found nothing surreptitious or covert in Dawson's manner. The two men became good friends. Dawson was a quick study and after he had what he felt was a firm grip on the mining, processing and shipment of coal, he thought he could do it; and perhaps do it better and safer.

In the summer of 1872 Tom Dawson gambled his resources to build a coal-mining complex. He built ten miles of railroad from Little Pine Run to the B & O Railroad's main line west of Terra Alta. The first nine miles followed down Cascades Creek, on Dawson land, and the final mile of right-of-way was purchased with a $500.00 down payment and a promise to pay 50 cents per carload of coal for five years.

While the railroad was being built, construction was begun on the mine facility. A tunnel was started at the face of the coal layer in the side of Laurel Mountain. The tunnel would proceed on a level course into the mountain and the coal. A mine with a level entry was called a "Drift" mine.

Two other types of entry were commonly used to get at coal, "Slope" and "Shaft." A slope mine had a tunnel entering the earth at a downward angle to get at a layer of coal a short distance below the surface. A shaft mine used a vertical shaft to get at coal located deep below the surface. While efforts were under way to open the mine tunnel, a coal chute was built to transfer coal from mule powered mine cars to the breaker house where chunks of slate and rock would be removed. Other chutes and hoppers were constructed to transfer the coal to railcars.

A few days before the first coal was cut, Tom Dawson had a visitor. It was his friend, Jim Ryland. Dawson was directing a group of men who were constructing a water tower for the company's only steam engine when Ryland rode up on a beautiful chestnut gelding. With all the noise from the building project, Dawson doesn't hear the horse and rider come up behind him.

Ryland had recognized Dawson's broad shoulders and erect stance from a hundred yards out. He calls out, "Does any man here know where I can find the ugliest man in Preston County, goes by the name of Dawson?"

Dawson instantly recognizes the voice and whirls around. "Well I'll be damned, Jim Ryland; you old son-of-a-gun." He quickly covers the six steps to Ryland's mount and holds up a welcoming hand. "How are you, you homely excuse for a coal miner?" As the two friends shake hands Dawson notices that Ryland's left eye is swollen and blackened. The two continue small talk as Ryland steps down from the gelding, but as he does the gelding spooks when one of Dawson's men throws a bucket from a scaffold where he's working. The bucket makes a loud clatter which startles the horse just for an instant, but it's enough to catch Ryland off balance and his bum leg buckles under him. He goes to the ground in an ungainly heap and ends up on his butt looking up at Dawson with a sheepish grin. Dawson chuckles as he reaches down to give him a hand. "You are a sorry looking son-of-a-gun, Jim Ryland. That's one hellacious black eye." As he pulls Ryland to his feet he continues, "And by the way, I always meant to ask, did you hurt that leg in the war?"

"Hell no – wern't nothing that glorious. A damn mine mule kicked me in my knee once when I wasn't looking."

"A mule kicked you! Why I'd be ashamed to admit it, Jim. Come on, you need a drink of cool water." As Dawson led him to a shade tree where a bucket of water sat on a bench, Ryland queried, "Alright, since we're gettin personal - what the hell happened to that eye of yours? That happen in the war?"

Dawson's hand automatically goes to the eye patch to assure it's properly positioned. He's always concerned that it may slip out of place and expose the damaged eye. "As a matter of fact, it did. And it happened because I was stupid." He reaches for a dipper, dips it into the bucket and hands it to Ryland.

"How's that - the being stupid, I mean?" Ryland returns.

Dawson scowls, "Well, we were fightin the rebs up on Droop Mountain, that's down state about a hundred miles or so. We were in a brief retreat and I lost track of my buddy. I went back, looking for him. He was hit in the hip, not real serious, but it must have hit a nerve, or something, and he couldn't use either leg. He'd found cover behind a log and was trying to reload when two rebs rushed him and got his piece. They were arguing over whether to kill him, or take him prisoner. That's when I came along. The two were standing side by side, one of them aiming his piece at my buddy. I fired at the one who was about to shoot my buddy, and I'll be damned if they didn't both fall - the ball went through the first and lodged in the neck of the other. Well, I ran up and found them both lying there - thought they were dead. I found out later that one was, and one wasn't. After I took care of my buddy, I leaned down to roll over one of the "dead" guys to see if he had any papers on him. That's where the stupidity comes in. The guy wasn't dead. He slashed me with the biggest damned knife I've ever seen. I took the knife off of him and finished him off with it, but he had got me good, so I've been old one-eyed Dawson ever since."

Ryland sat on the bench shaking his head. "That's a helluva story, Tom. How'd your buddy make out?"

"Oh, he recovered fine from that wound, but he didn't make it home. We lost him at Appomattox."

"That's too bad, Tom. Hell, he made it all the way to Appomattox and then got killed; that's a son-of-a-bitch!"

Dawson didn't reply right away, just stared at the ground for a long moment before he responded. "Well, what brings you to these parts, my friend? And what in the hell happened to you - that ol mule kick you in the face?"

"Well, to the first question, I'm looking for a job," Ryland quips, almost in a joking manner, then, "and as for the second, the black eye, well, it kinda goes along with why I'm looking for the job, I guess."

"What happened, you get caught in the hayloft with the owner's daughter?" Ryland shoots back. "Well, something like that, except, twasn't his daughter, twas his wife."

Dawson looks astonished. He thought of Ryland as an honorable man. "Go on, Jim, are you serious?"

"Yup, dead serious. I never intended for it to happen, but it did. No excuses, she made it awful easy and I hadn't the power to resist."

Dawson shakes his head. "Well I'll be damned, I will be damned."

"So, anyway," Ryland continues, "The old man found out. He took a swing at me and I had been feeling so guilty about the whole thing, well, I didn't even duck. I could of, I mean, hell, he wasn't that fast, I saw it coming, I just didn't duck, I took it. I guess I figured I deserved it. So, anyway, that's why I'm looking, so whatta ya say mister coal operator, you got a place in these digs for another hand?"

"I sure as hell do. You must have been sent here by an angel from heaven. I'm the only man here who has any idea of how to dig coal, these guys are all timber men, and I still have a hand in the timber business, so I've got more on my plate than I can handle."

A relieved smile spreads across Ryland's face. "I'm willing to do anything, Tom, work at any job; I just thought you're one guy I'd like to hook up with."

"Well, it would be a pleasure to have you as a part of this outfit. How much do I have to pay for a good mine Super?"

"Oh, I didn't have in mind being your Super, I wouldn't want to take anything from one of your men. I just thought maybe you could use a good Foreman."

"Well, I can, but I'm in dire need of a good Super. Hell, Jim, as I said, none of my men know anything about the coal business. I figured I'd have to teach everyone from scratch, and hell, I'm a novice myself."

"You're wrong there, my friend. You picked up more about

mining coal in a few weeks than most men do in a lifetime."

"I don't buy that, but I can't argue with a mad man. Whatta ya say, will you be my super? Like I told you, I think an angel must have sent you."

"Well, I wouldn't quite call her an angel, but it was a woman that caused me to be knocking on your door."

And with that, Jim Ryland became the first Superintendent for the Dawson Colliery Company and the coal mining operation got off to an exceptionally good start under the cool-headed guidance and innovative methods of Dawson and the team-oriented management style of Ryland.

Chapter 4

Coke

Cascade, West Virginia

In late autumn of 1873 a healthy and vigorous baby boy was born to Tom and Elizabeth Dawson. They named him, Robert, after his great, great grandfather, the founder of Cascade. As the boy grew, so did the Dawson Colliery Company. Tom Dawson started a coking operation with a string of fifty coal baking ovens and supplied the sought-after product of coke to the busy steel mills in Pittsburgh. After only two years, fifty more ovens were added, in order to meet the needs of a growing country, which demanded more products made of steel.

By the time young Robert Dawson was a teenager he had a fair grasp of his family's business. He had been just a small boy when Tom Dawson first introduced him to the operations of the coal mine and he often traveled into it with his father. He developed into an intelligent and enterprising young man and when he finished high school he attended West Virginia University at Morgantown. There he studied business and a relatively new program, mine engineering. As he grew into manhood, Robert was a good looking fellow, a little leaner than his dad, but a stout man.

The people of Cascade prospered because of the Dawson mining and timbering operations. The war had taken a number of her young men, but the mountain families were hardy and stoic and life moved on in the small town. When Robert Dawson completed his studies at Morgantown he returned to Cascade, eager to become an important part of the mining business. He jumped into the job with both feet, incorporating new business ideas in administrative and financial functions. He also put his engineering degree to good use by improving methods in the mine, on the tipple and in the coking operations.

By 1899 Tom Dawson was less involved with the mining end of the business and developed a renewed interest in his timber operation and state politics. For years he had many friends at the capital in Charleston and was a close personal friend of the governor. He had no plans for holding office himself, but had a keen interest in influencing the state legislature. So, while he spent more time in the timber operations and politics, young Robert Dawson, now assigned the job of Mine Engineer, regularly suggested more changes to operations, but even beyond that, started recommending policy changes that conflicted with Jim Ryland's philosophy of management.

Tom Dawson sensed the problem and offered to move Ryland up to the General Manager position, but Ryland didn't feel qualified. So, Dawson, placing too much importance on the college education of his son, moved Robert, at the young age of 26, into the General Manager slot. Tom remained as President and Chairman, but he allowed his son a relatively free hand in the mining end of his broad business base, while he occupied himself with his other interests. With the Dawson rail line tied into the B & O main line, his businesses had ready access to markets for coal, coke and lumber and healthy profits were being made on each product.

To the chagrin of mine superintendent, Jim Ryland, the young and eager Dawson made a number of changes that tended to take the company's management style along authoritarian lines rather than the more humanistic, team approach that had been initiated in the early days by Ryland and which had dramatically helped the business prosper. As is often the case when a young person is given too much authority too soon, Robert relied too heavily on his authority rather than gaining respect as a leader. This management style would handicap him throughout his career.

On a cold and blustery December morning, Robert Dawson entered Jim Ryland's office, a small building which sits between the tipple and the mine portal. As he enters, wind howls through the open door, flinging chunks of snow into the room; snow that the wind had plastered onto the exterior of the door. Pieces of the snow land on the small pot-bellied stove that provides heat to the Spartan quarters, and it sizzles and pops, flinging small water droplets onto the papers which crowd Ryland's rickety desk, and Ryland hurries to save the papers from the wind. Satisfied that he's accomplished that, he looks up at young Dawson, who stands impeccably dressed in his expensive Pittsburgh suit and overcoat, his tie sporting a conspicuous diamond. If one were to look closely at the diamond's gold backing, they would see the engraved initials, R.D. "What can I do for you?" Ryland says, without feeling.

Dawson brushes snow from his sleeves. He appears hesitant, fidgety, anxious, tense. He has never developed a feeling of comfort with Ryland, who seldom agrees on the need for change. Ryland insists many of the changes have a negative impact on the men, and ultimately, on the welfare of the business itself.

"Jim, I've come over to see if you've implemented my new directive on prices for the miner's supplies."

"That's a pretty steep increase, Mr. Dawson, ten per cent. You know, sometimes I think it's a mistake to require the miners to furnish their own powder and squib's. I can understand requiring them to supply their own tools, but the supplies needed to blast the coal and the oil to light their lamps, well, it just seems like those things ought to be supplied by the company like they used to be."

Dawson scowls. "Then I take it you haven't instituted the new prices." Ryland doesn't answer.

"Well then, is this something I'll need to do myself?"

"No, I'll handle it, Mr. Dawson, but I wish you would reconsider the ten percent. How about five percent now and another five next year?"

Dawson removes his gloves, pockets them, and holds his hands over the little coal stove. As usual, Ryland is resisting his policy changes. He tries a different tact, turns more cordial. "Jim, why do you insist on calling me, Mr. Dawson? You've known me all my life. It used to be, Bobby. Now, it's Mister. Why is that?"

"I guess, cause you're the General now."

"But you never call dad by anything other than, Tom, and

hell, he's the top dog."

"It's different. Your dad and I were friends from the beginning, even before I worked for him. And, he's still my friend." Dawson pulls his gloves back on. A pained expression pervades his face. "Do I take it from that, that I'm no longer your friend?"

Ryland relents. "Hell, Bobby, of course you're my friend, you're Tom's boy, how could you not be my friend? But damn it, boy, you've got different ideas than I'm used to. Different thinkin on how the mine oughta be run, and how the men oughta be treated. And the men hardly know you. Hell, all of them always knew your dad, could talk to him any time. He was available, and they didn't have to go through me. You don't want to have direct contact with them. You want them to go through 'channels' and I'm not comfortable with that way of operating."

Dawson stiffens his back. "Well, that's the way modern businesses are run, Jim. It's 1899 and we need to have standards. We need to take this business into the new century with up-to-date operating procedures."

"We seem to have operated a pretty good business up till now, and provided damn good jobs for the men in this town."

"But we can do better. If we can improve our profit margin we'll improve the long-term outlook for the business."

"Yeah, but what about the long-term outlook for the families of this town? If you keep raising the cost to the miners how does that improve their lot in the long haul?"

"Jim, if we don't make a profit, there will be no long haul."

Ryland gets up from his chair, opens the door to the stove and throws in a couple of lumps of coal. As he does, he says, "Sounds like you're telling me we aren't making a profit now."

Dawson hesitates before he replies. "No, I didn't say that, we are making a profit, but it could be better."

Ryland isn't buying it. He doesn't have access to the financial accounts, but he has a pretty good flavor for the health of the business and his read is that it turns a pretty good margin. He sits on the edge of his desk, crosses his arms, and gazing at the red glow on the sides of the little cast iron stove, offers, "Maybe it's time I step aside and let you put someone in this slot who can make you a better profit. I've put a little money away over the years, I expect its time I hang it up, do a little huntin an fishin."

Dawson didn't expect that. He doesn't want to lose Ryland's experience, but, on the other hand, with a younger man as Superintendent, a man who would give him less resistance, he could more easily implement his perceived improvements. Cautiously, he inquires, "You think you have enough savings to see you through a retirement?"

Ryland rubs his chin, looks thoughtful. "I'd get by."

Dawson jumps on the opportunity. "Do you think Kip is ready to take your place?" Kip Ryland, Jim's son, is a Foreman and has been an understudy to Jim for some time. Kip is a smart and easygoing young man, and Dawson figures he can easily wield influence over him.

Ryland raises an eyebrow. He hadn't really considered retirement before this moment, but if Dawson is willing to put Kip into his spot, then maybe -- "Kip's still kinda young, but he's got a good head and the men respect him. I suppose, if I was available to give him some advice now and then, he'd be up to it."

"Then, how about you acting as a consultant? I'll pay you a monthly retainer to be available as needed. No schedule, just be on call when Kip or I need your help."

Ryland purses his lips, thinks for a moment, then replies slowly, "Let me think on that for a couple of days, maybe talk to your Pappy about it, and you can think about how much that retainer might be."

Dawson smiles broadly, "Fine, I'll put some thought into that, and I'd like to discuss it with Kip. That okay with you?"

"Yeah," Ryland says, "but I wanna tell him first."

Later that day, Ryland walks across the complex of mine buildings and rail facilities to the building which houses the general offices of Tom Dawson's varied businesses. He finds

Tom in his office dictating a letter to his secretary. He sticks his head in the door, "Tom, Got a minute?"

"Jim! Hell yes, come on in. How ya doing?"

"I'm doing alright, I guess. I don't want to interrupt, but there is something I'd like to discuss when you have time."

"I've got time right now." Dawson turns to his secretary, "Violet, why don't you finish that up for me, you know what to say." Violet nods and leaves. He turns back to Ryland. "What's on your mind, Partner?"

"I'm thinking about retiring, Tom. Bobby says he'll pay me a retainer to be available as a consultant, and I think I might take him up on the offer. I didn't want to give him an answer without passing it by you."

Dawson leans back in his chair, looks hard at Ryland. "The boy gettin to ya, Jim?"

Ryland hesitates. He and Tom have always been straight up with each other, but he doesn't like the idea of being critical of Tom's family. Dawson reads him well. "Yeah, the boy's gettin under your skin, I guess I expected that."

"He's still young, Tom. But he certainly has his own ideas about running the mine. I guess I'm just behind the times."

"Hogwash, you're not behind any times, you're just older and have more sense; it's too bad Bob can't see that and take advantage of it. You should have taken me up on the offer of you being the General. Damn it Jim, you certainly have the capability to do it until Bob gains more experience."

"I appreciate you having that confidence in me, Tom, but I don't have the education for the job. I'd just get in Bobby's way."

Dawson frowns, "You sure you don't want to stick it out? I can talk to the boy."

"Naw, don't think so."

"What about something else, in timbering maybe? I can always use a hand there."

"To tell you the truth, old friend, I think spending some time without an alarm clock, huntin an fishin for a year or so, may just add several years to my life. After that, maybe I will want to putter around in the woods, or sumthin. And who knows, maybe Bobby will want to use me for a little consulting. I figured he just wants to get me outta the way, but I may be wrong."

"Fair enough, then. I'll see to it that your consulting fee is what it oughta be."

"That's not why I came here to talk, Tom."

"Hell, I know that!" Dawson says as he takes hold of a watch fob and pulls a pocket watch from a small pocket at the waistband of his trousers. It's a gold Longines with a brook trout engraved on the front cover. He flips open the cover and glances at the face of the watch. "Tell you what, it's time we get outta here, let's go over to the Inn and have a drink to celebrate huntin an fishin."

As it turned out, Jim Ryland did do a lot of trout fishing in Cascades Creek during the spring of 1900, and he found it to be mighty pleasurable.

Later that summer, the Baltimore and Ohio carried a beautiful, auburn haired young lady from Richmond, Virginia to Tarra Alta, West Virginia. From Tarra Alta, she took a coach to Cascade. Her name was Lucretia Barton and she had come to spend the summer in the tranquility and coolness of the mountains, away from the heat and humidity of Richmond. She stayed with her aunt, and one day, while joining her aunt at dinner with the Dawsons, she was introduced to Robert. He was smitten by her beauty, and her sophistication, and he courted her throughout her summer stay. Lucretia was captivated by his charm and fell hopelessly in love with him. The two were together every minute that Robert could get away from the business. When Lucretia, or, Lu, as he called her, returned to Richmond, Robert continued the courtship through the fall and winter, with frequent rail trips to that city. He proposed on New Year's Eve, promising his love and devotion for the next hundred years. They were married in a lavish ceremony, in Richmond, in the spring of 1901. Through that year and the next, Lucretia Dawson had difficulty adjusting to life in the small town of Cascade, but she did so, and in later years she would be instrumental in bringing an additional touch of culture to the small town in the mountains. The following year she and Robert became parents of a healthy baby boy. They named him, Alex. Unfortunately, Lucretia sustained injuries from giving an arduous breech birth and two years later, during her second pregnancy, she miscarried. She was never able to conceive again.

Chapter 5

A Dangerous Business

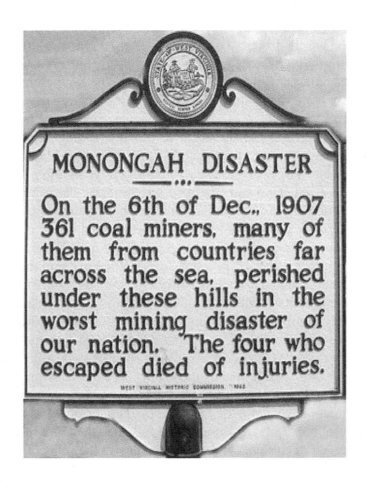

MONONGAH DISASTER

On the 6th of Dec., 1907 361 coal miners, many of them from countries far across the sea, perished under these hills in the worst mining disaster of our nation. The four who escaped died of injuries.

WEST VIRGINIA HISTORIC COMMISSION. 1963

The farm of Tom Dawson

On a mild summer evening in the mountains, the exquisitely sweet smell of locust blossoms is in the air as old Tom and Elizabeth Dawson sit on their porch swing, slowing drifting forward, backward, forward, backward. His right arm is around her shoulder and his left hand clutches hers. They talk softly in the twilight. Before them the mountains stretch into the purple distance.

Their farm overlooks Cascades Creek, upstream and several miles southeast of the village of Cascade. The front entrance of their home faces the creek, which tumbles over massive boulders a hundred yards away, down a sloping lawn. Beyond the creek, to the northwest, a few rolling foothills set the stage for the green magnificence of Laurel Mountain to provide a spectacular view. For a few years after they were married, Tom and Liz lived just south of Cascade, but they eventually built another home further up the Cascades as the town grew and Liz became interested in breeding horses.

Their home is large, but not huge. It's post and beam construction and is wrapped in chestnut planks and stone. There are barns, stables, various out buildings, and quarters for three farm hands standing three hundred yards down a lane that follows the creek. A shiny black 1921 Oldsmobile Model 46 Seven Passenger Touring Sedan sits in a garage recently built beside one of the stables. It's the Olds top-of-the-line series with the heavy V-8 engine.

The quiet conversation of Tom and Liz is interrupted as they notice a horse and rider approaching. It's their grandson, young Alex Dawson. He dismounts, throws the reins over a rail, and as he walks across the lawn he calls out, "Hi Gramps, hello Grandmother, you two look like teenagers, sitting there holding hands like that."

"Sometimes we feel like teenagers," says Elizabeth, as the young man comes up the steps. "And your Grandfather is still my beau, so I guess we can hold hands."

Tom offers, "What your Grandmother means, son, is that sometimes my old bones don't hurt quite as much as usual, and I'm able to chase her around some." Elizabeth blushes and fakes a smack at Tom's cheek.

Alex leans to his grandmother and kisses her cheek. She's delighted to see her only grandchild, who lives with his parents, Robert and Lucretia, on a 500-acre farm a half mile down the road. Alex always visited often before he went away to school. Tom and Liz also have a daughter who lives, with her husband, on another 500-acre tract beyond Robert. The daughter has no children and since the only child of Robert and Lucretia is Alex, it's probable that he will ultimately inherit the entire 8000 acres of Dawson land.

"Well," Alex continues, as he takes a seat in a comfortable old rocker, "I think it's fabulous that you still feel that way about each other."

"Why aren't you downtown having fun with the rest of the young people, Alex?" Elizabeth queries. "Now that you're home from school for the summer you mustn't spend all your time working at the mine and hanging around with old folks, didn't they teach you anything at that university?"

"Actually, I'm learning quite a lot, Grandmother, and I've made a lot of good friends. And Morgantown has a lot of action going on all the time."

"Well," Elizabeth continues, "Your Gramps has invested a lot of money in the University. I hope you can profit from it."

"I have already, and the mining school is just completing a new lab. Next term we'll have the most up-to-date mining college in the world. The mining school has really progressed since dad was there."

"Well, that's very nice, Alex, but you haven't told me why you're not in town enjoying some time with your local friends."

"Oh, I've had something on my mind, Grandmother, and I, well I thought maybe Gramps could help me with it."

Old Dawson removes his arm from around his Elizabeth.

"Why sure, Alex, what is it?"

"Well, it's, uh, well, maybe we could take a little walk down by the creek, Gramps? But, I hate to interrupt you and Grandmother, you both look so comfortable."

"Not at all, Son," Tom says as he slowly rises from the swing. "Sweetie, would you excuse us men for a little while?"

"Certainly, but Alex," Elizabeth says, as she gets up from the swing and walks toward the door, "You must promise to visit with me for a while before you leave. I've got some blackberry cobbler left over, it's your favorite."

"You betcha, Grandmother. We won't be long."

As the old man got up from the swing he reached for a cane, which leaned against the porch rail. Now, placing part of his weight on the cane, a barely perceptible grimace hints of pain in his lower back, a reminder of the fall from his horse on that day in May, so many years ago. "Damned arthritis," he grumbles, "I sure don't feel like a teenager tonight, boy."

"Gramps, how old are you? I forget." Alex asks as they walk down the steps.

"Just add 62 to your age, Alex. You're 20, right?"

"Yes sir, 20. So tell me, Gramps, how old does one have to be before he doesn't want to do it anymore?"

The old man feigns confusion. "Do what?"

The boy grins sheepishly. "You know what I mean, Gramps."

"Is that what's so all-fired important, you want to know about my sex life?"

"Naw, that's not what I came over to talk about, I just happened to think of it when you complained about your arthritis and after seeing you and Grandmother holding hands."

"Well, I guess your mind is right smack dab where mine was 62 years ago."

The older Dawson pauses by a large oak, leans his cane against it, raises his hands to adjust his eye patch, then, looking hard at the boy with his one good eye, grumbles, "New patch, the damn thing isn't broke in yet, keeps sliding off to the side." Even after all these years, Dawson is still self-conscious about anyone seeing his damaged eye. "Well, let's see, what's the question? Oh yeah, how old - how old? Well, I'll tell you this much, boy," and a sly grin curls at the corners of his mouth, "if you want an answer to that question you'll have to ask someone older than me." And with that they both giggle like little boys.

Arriving at the creek, the older Dawson eases himself down on an ancient, weathered bench and the boy straddles a nearby boulder. The tumbling waters of the creek kick stabs of starlight into the growing darkness. A bat flutters by on silent wings, looking for an early meal of helpless moths.

"Well, what's on your mind, son?"

The young man halfheartedly kicks at a rock and waits a long moment before speaking. Old Dawson waits. Finally, Alex speaks. "It's Dad, Gramps, he won't let me work in the mine, says it's too dangerous. He has me working on the tipple. Shucks, if I'm studying mine engineering, and if I've got a shot at running the mine one day, well it just makes sense for me to start getting experience inside. Besides, if it's too dangerous for me, then what about the men who go in every day, why isn't it too dangerous for them?"

Tom leans forward on his cane and ponders the boy's question. He thinks an awful lot of his grandson. Sometimes he wonders if he doesn't think more of Alex than he does his own son, Alex's father, Robert. He sees more of himself in Alex than he does in Robert. Alex is more sensitive to the needs of others, more understanding of one's weaknesses, more forgiving, compassionate, considerate, all traits that Tom Dawson feels to be high qualities in people. Unfortunately, he sometimes finds those characteristics to be less than conspicuous in Robert.

He finally responds. "Alex, do you think a coal mine is not a dangerous place?"

"I guess there is some danger, Gramps."

"Son, do you know how many men have been killed in the Dawson mine since I started it 48 years ago?"

"No, I don't Gramps."

The old man takes a deep breath and sits upright on the bench. He reaches for the fob to his pocket watch and pulls the watch from his pocket; flips open the face, and studies the watch for a moment before continuing. "It's almost ten after eight, Alex. It was just a little after eight o'clock one morning in 1872 that I lost my first man to the hazards of coal mining. He was a boy, maybe a year older than you, just a boy."

Tom sits quiet, gazing at the tumbling water. Alex shifts his position on the rock, but says nothing. He's aware of the emotion in his grandfather's demeanor. When Tom speaks again, it's almost a whisper, a raspy whisper. "He was by my side. We had just started opening the portal to the mine a couple days before. We weren't in more than ten feet. I was working right alongside the boys, instructing them in undercuttin and blasting. A big chunk of the roof fell. The boy was crushed under three tons of rock. Another man got his leg broke. We got the rocks off the boy pretty quick, he was still alive, but he didn't last. He died there in my arms. Had blue eyes, vivid blue eyes, had white rock dust around them. I brushed it away. A lot of blood came out of his mouth and ran off his chin, onto my shirtsleeve. I'll never forget the colors, Alex, the blue eyes, the bright red blood, on a young face white with rock dust."

Alex swallows hard. He has never seen his grandfather in a mood like this. He adores this man, his strength, his courage, his wisdom. It hurts him to see the hurt.

Tom continues, "Twenty-three."

"Twenty-three what? Gramps."

"Twenty-three men and boys killed in my mine since that first boy, Alex. Twenty-three. And that's just in the Dawson mine, Lord knows how many other West Virginians have been killed during that time. There was 39 down in Newburg in 1886. Eighty-four in Stewart in 1907. Another 361 in Monongah in 1907. Fifty-one at Lick Branch in 1909." He pauses to take a deep breath, and then continues with his grisly history lesson, "One hundred and eighty-one in Eccles in 1914. Hundred and twelve in Layland in 1915, and that's just the big ones, no telling how many were killed by the ones, twos and threes, and how many thousands have been maimed for life." Alex says nothing, just watches his grandfather's eye in the dim light.

"Yes boy, it's a dangerous business, a God-awful dangerous business."

"But Gramps, this is 1922 and things must be improving as we get more experience and develop better methods. They teach mine safety in my engineering classes and if we apply that teaching we should be able to make things a lot safer, don't you agree?"

"Oh I agree that we could make it safer if every man would apply good safety thinking, Alex, but unfortunately, in the real world not every man has your degree of motivation."

"Well Gramps, don't you think it's our obligation, as a mine owner, to give them that motivation?"

It's dark now, but Tom looks hard at the boy and even in the darkness Alex can sense the penetrating eye. He doesn't back away. "What do you say, Gramps, isn't it our responsibility?"

The old man is proud of the boy's perseverance, and his young idealism. He rises from the bench, pushing up with his cane and starts walking toward the house. Alex walks beside him. "Well," Tom says, "I've heard your side of the story. Tomorrow I'll get the other side."

Alex is taken aback. "But, there is no other side, Gramps."

"Oh, but there has to be, Alex, there has to be. There are at least two sides to this story, maybe more."

"But I've given you both sides; mine and dad's."

"No, you've given me your side and what you think to be your dad's side, son. There's a difference. Your dad has his reasons. I'd like to hear them before I take up for you."

Alex scuffs his boot in the ground and says, rather dejectedly, "Aw, I guess that makes sense, Gramps."

"Now, are there any other sides to this story - how about your mother, she have an opinion?"

Alex is surprised at the question. "Anything concerning the mine, she always goes along with dad, you know that. But if she knows you're on my side, that'll make a difference with her. She worships you, Gramps."

Old Tom harrumphs as he clears his throat over the obvious compliment. "Well then, she does have an opinion, right? Now it seems we have three sides to this little drama. Are there any more?"

Alex hesitates, then replies, "Aw, I guess Kip has some thoughts on it."

"And what are those?"

"Well, he always goes along with dad too, you know that."

"No, I don't know that, Son. Do you think there's a problem there?"

"No, I'm not saying that Kip's not a good man, he is. It's just that, well, it seems like it's hard for him to go against my dad, you know, stand up for his own ideas."

"Well, your dad is the head buck."

"Yeah, I know, but sometimes I think he ought to listen more to his men, you know what I mean, Gramps?"

Tom ponders the comment and question before he answers. "Maybe I do, Alex. I'll talk to your dad in the morning." Then he takes a knurled hand, rustles the boy's hair and good naturedly challenges, "Now, do you understand how there's usually several sides to every story?"

Alex grins, "Yeah, I get the message, Gramps, I get the message."

"Good, now let's go have some of your grandmother's cobbler."

The rest of the summer of 1922 Alex worked inside the mine and got a firsthand appreciation for what coal mining was all about. It was quite different than the impressions he had garnered while growing up and accompanying his father around the interior of the mine and the operations outside. It was a dangerous and dirty business and he vowed that one-day he would make it better.

Chapter 6

A Double Barrel Breather

The following October, on a cool and overcast morning, the aroma of breakfast bacon is still in the air as Tom Dawson pulls on a jacket in preparation for a ride, by horseback, up Cascades Creek. One of his men has his horse saddled and waiting by the back porch. At eighty-three, Dawson is still lean and fit and rides regularly, but Elizabeth worries each time he rides out. She puts a hand on his arm as he buttons the jacket. "Tom, why not skip your ride this morning, it's cool out and it looks like rain."

"Horse feathers, Liz, I've ridden in the rain a hundred times, I'll have my slicker with me. I want to ride up to the forks of Cascades, it's just a few miles up, we're timbering there. You know, Sweetie, it's been fifty years since we first timbered that tract and that area around the forks grows timber mighty fast, why some of the oaks in there are bigger than two men can reach around."

She pulled his jacket tight and buttoned the top button. "Well, you be careful Mister Dawson, you're not as limber as you were fifty years ago."

Before he's out of sight of the house, the rain starts. He pulls his slicker from a saddlebag and hauls it on over his jacket. The slicker is split up the back for riding and it covers his legs down to his boots. His hat is broad brimmed and the oiled felt sheds water as well as the slicker. He's comfortable and contented as he rides. At 83 he still sits straight and tall in the saddle.

A short time later, he's a mile above his farm, riding in a drizzling rain, along the south side of Cascades. He's anxious to see how the timber crew is doing. It reminds him of another rainy day over a half century before when he was riding along the creek in a drizzle to check on his crew at Cranberry Bottom, the day he discovered the coal.

Across the creek, on the north side, runs the dinky track, a narrow-gauge rail spur for hauling logs down to the sawmill. A small steam engine, called a Dinky, is used to pull the train of cars loaded with logs.

An hour has passed and the rain has let up as Dawson nears the area where the timber crew is working. Suddenly, he hears men yelling up ahead. He urges his mount into a light gallop to see what the commotion is about. He soon sees several men up to their butts in the water, on the opposite side of the creek, where they surround a huge log that has obviously rolled off a rail car, as it was being loaded from a ramp on the far side of the car. Through the commotion Dawson can hear a man screaming, "It's sliding down, it's pulling him under!"

Dawson urges his horse across the water to the men. From his higher vantage point he clearly sees a man under the log, two men at his side, holding his face above the water. The huge log continues to slide further into the stream, pulling the man with it. In another instant his face will be below the water. The man screams; "Guys, do something, don't let me drown!"

Dawson can't understand how the man is even alive with such a large weight on him. He quickly surmises that rocks under the log and some buoyancy from the water must be keeping the full weight off the man. Dawson yells to one of the men, "Randle, who is it? Can't you pull him out?"

The man turns, surprised to hear Dawson's voice. "No, Tom, we can't budge him, it's got his legs pinned tight and the damned thing is shifting! It's Virgil Cutlip!"

Dawson grabs his shotgun from his saddle scabbard and jumps from his mount into the creek. He slips on the rocks and goes under as his body convulses from the icy cold water. Cascades is always cold. But in an instant, in spite of the fast current, he finds footing and breaks to the surface. Coughing and sputtering, he automatically reaches his left hand to assure that his eye patch is still in place, then, moving the same hand to the fore-piece of the shotgun, breaks open the gun, and drops out the shells. He then jerks off the fore-piece and removes the barrels. He thrusts the barrels toward the man he called, Randle, and yells, "Give him these to breathe through and one of you hold his nose." He turns and yells to two men on the bank, "Hank, you and Buck get a team down here in the water, and you others grab some pivies, we're gonna roll that log off his legs!"

Hank and Charlie run for a team of six large Belgium's which stand calmly by as all the yelling and commotion continues.

Before the accident, the huge workhorses were dragging the logs to the loading ramp. Other men run for cant hooks, or spike-peavys, the tools used to roll and move logs.

As the huge log again slides further into the water, Virgil's head goes under. He has his mouth wrapped tightly around the muzzle end of both barrels of the 16 gauge shotgun. One man holds Virgil's nose closed and another struggles with his footing while trying to hold the breech end of the barrels in the air.

Shortly, Hank has the team in the water. Both men and horses have difficulty standing on the slippery rocks of the fast moving water. Tom Dawson repeatedly falls. The water is ice cold and his body is already racked with waves of shivers as hypothermia sets in. The men quickly have a chain around the log and hitched to the harness of the Belgiums. Dawson yells, "Don't drag it, all of you get your spikes in it and roll it as Hank gets the team going."

With considerable splashing, thrashing and yelling, several of the men jam the spikes high on the log, then tilt the handles, engage the hooks and pull hard on the handle to roll the log as the team tries to gain footing on the slippery rocks.

Hank yells at the lead horses, "Giddup, Blackie! Haw, Goldie! Git, git, git, git!" The men pull hard on the "hooks" as the oak monster slowly begins to move and roll away from Virgil's legs.

There was little question that Tom Dawson saved the life of young Virgil Cutlip that day. Only one leg was broken, and besides some cuts and bad bruising, the lad was in pretty good shape. Old Doc Howell did a masterful job of setting the bone in the broken leg. For years after, the people of Cascade claimed that Virgil Cutlip could suck the bluing off a double-barreled shotgun without any effort at all.

Yes, Tom Dawson saved the boy, but it cost him. At eighty-three it's difficult for the respiratory system to battle pneumonia. Tom Dawson was a fighter, always had been, but this fight would be his last. With Elizabeth and his family at his side, Tom died five days after he saved young Cutlip's life. People came from all parts of the country to the funeral of Tom Dawson. The Governor and several members of the house and senate were there. Mine owners from West Virginia, Maryland, Pennsylvania, Ohio and Kentucky came, as did several representatives of West Virginia University. And of course, the whole town of Cascade crowded outside the church. Tom Dawson was a respected and loved man in those northern hills of the Mountain State, and his memory still lingers.

Chapter 7

Don't Take Out That Timber

July, 1925

Dawson Mine #1

Kip Ryland, the current mine superintendent at the Dawson mine, and son of old Jim Ryland, stands in the small building that serves as his office, talking to one of his "Straw Bosses," Charlie Walters. "Charlie, I want you to take young Dawson and pull timbers out of 36 West. We've got all the coal that we can get out of that panel and there are some decent timbers in there. We can make good use of them over in 42 east. Alex needs the experience and on something as tricky as pulling timbers I want him to be with someone who knows his stuff."
"I dunno, Kip. Do you think the boy is ready for something like that?"
Alex Dawson, now 23 and home from college, has been assigned to a one-year hitch laboring in the coal mine. Alex has been on the job for a couple of months and has worked on a variety of jobs. Kip Ryland knows the boy well.
"Charlie, that boy has been learning about the mine from his dad for most of his life, and from me and guys like you for the past two summers, yeah, I think he's ready. But, like I said, it's tricky, we both know that, so don't let him take any chances."
"Whatever you say, Kip, where is the boy?"
"He's been working with Russ Weaver, bonding rail over in 42 east, you can find him there. Russ doesn't need him; he's just been giving him training in welding bonds."
Two hours later, Charlie Walters and Alex stand ankle deep in black water. The illumination from the carbide lamps on their hard hats cause eerie shadows to dance throughout the large "room" of the coal mine. Except for the sound of rubber boots sloshing through the water there was no other sound to be heard. Over two miles from the portal there is little opportunity for extraneous noise. Because this area has been worked out and abandoned it has not been ventilated for awhile and before the two men entered the area they

adjusted the ventilation doors to flood in fresh air. The safety lamp carried by Charlie gives no indication of gas and he considers the air safe. In the labyrinth of a coal mine, a series of large doors, called trap doors, are situated to direct movement of fresh air toward the working faces or any area of the mine where men are working. The fresh air is supplied by huge ventilation fans.

It's a cool 55 degrees in the mine, as it always is, summer or winter, but the men are perspiring. They remove the coal dust soiled coats that they wore into the mine that morning. Although the rail has been removed from the section where the timbers are to be pulled they still had rail to within a hundred feet of where they now are working. At the railhead they left a motor, trailing three cars, on which they will haul the recovered timbers to 42 east. As Charlie speaks, his words echo through the dank and tenebrous chamber. "Alex, I'll get a couple of lanterns going to give some more light, then we'll start knocken-um out over to the left there. Now, like I told you coming over, I'll take out two or three to show you how it's done, then you take over and I'll carry-um to the cars."

Alex Dawson's carbide lamp signals a nod of agreement. "O.K. Charlie, but let me help you with the lanterns."

With the area lighted, Charlie moves to a timber, and after carefully looking over the roof above it, he gives the wooden post several hard licks with a ten-pound sledgehammer and the timber falls away. After performing the same procedure on two more timbers, he hands the sledge to Alex. "O.K. boy, your turn, take out that one, there," pointing to the forth post in the line.

Alex takes the hammer from Charlie's hand while thinking, "If he calls me 'boy' one more time I think I'll use this hammer on him instead of those timbers." He splashes through the water to the designated timber. Before he lifts the hammer he carefully studies the roof section being supported by the soon-to-be-claimed timber. Although he has been working in the mine for only a few summers, in his youth he had been in the mine many times with his dad.

Robert Dawson taught him about mine procedures, including important safety issues, one of which is the condition of the roof of a mine. Somehow, Alex is just a little restive with the appearance of the roof in this area. He gives the timber a few raps with the hammer, moving it several inches to one side, and then listens. He hears nothing to indicate that the roof section over this particular support is giving way, so he gives it a final sharp blow and it falls with a splash. He continues the same process with two more supports and as he removes them, Charlie carries them away. As he steps back to his fourth timber he hears an almost imperceptible sound.

The natural result of removing support timbers is often a collapsing roof, but normally it's a slow process and is usually associated with sound of movement in the rock, not always, but usually. Also, the timbers are removed in such a pattern that the workman is under the roof section still being supported until the timber is removed and thus somewhat protected from any falling rock. However, there are times when the roof can fall immediately after a timber is pulled.

Alex decides to leave the fourth timber in place and moves to another section of the "room" to begin another pattern, but before he starts, Charlie returns. Seeing that Alex has moved, he shouts, "Hey boy, how come you left the section where we started?"

"I'm not too comfortable with the roof in that area, Charlie. I think it's unpredictable and the few timbers there are not worth the risk."

"Here now, boy," responds Charlie, "Go ahead and take-um out in that section, the roof looks good to me."

Alex looks hard at the older man. He knows that Charlie Walters has more than twenty years of experience in the mine, and he doesn't think he would be careless enough to let the mine owner's son get hurt, but he stands his ground.

"Charlie, I know you've been in the mine a long time, and you certainly wouldn't mean to do something to get us hurt, but I've been around long enough to have seen a few of your friends go to meet their maker long before they were ready,

49

and I don't think that roof section is stable enough, so, I'm not taking out that timber. Besides that, some of these timbers are pretty old and the entire roof may come in. I'm not gonna risk my life to save a dollars worth of timber."

"Well boy, I think I know a good roof when I see one, and your dad says we need to save all the posts that we can, gimme that hammer." Alex hands him the sledge hammer and backs away, steaming over the fact that Charlie continues to call him, boy, and further, because his dad would give orders to salvage rotten timbers, but he holds his tongue.

Charlie moves to the original timber in question. Alex turns his head to direct the light from his lamp toward the area behind him. He wants to assure himself that he has a good mental picture of his position and his escape route should the roof come in. He turns back toward the timber as Charlie strikes the first blow. The timber does not want to move.

Alex cautions, "Charlie, there's a heavy load on that timber, I don't think you ought to take it out!"

There is no response from the Straw Boss. Another blow and the timber budges. Several more blows and the timber falls. Charlie turns towards Alex and is about to speak, when he pauses, his mouth framing a word, but the word never came. In an instant he's buried beneath tons of rock as the roof comes in where the suspicious timber had stood a moment before. As quickly as that section of the roof collapsed there is a "wave" of falling roof as the old timbers snap like twigs, and the wave is moving toward Alex. Even before he turns to run he's enveloped in a thick cloud of dust which is moving before the pressure front caused by the collapsing roof. He runs blindly toward his "mental picture" of his escape route and as he runs, falling rock tears at his back.

When Robert Dawson learned of the death of Charlie Walters and the near death of his own son, he issued orders that Alex would no longer be working inside the mine, but Alex has developed a measure of independence and is now ready to stand toe to toe with his father on the issue.

He finds Robert in his office, a place the older man rarely leaves. Robert is studying the monthly financial statement when his son knocks at the door.

"Who is it?"

Alex opens the door. "It's me, Dad, can we talk?"

"Of course, Alex, come on in. I guess I know what's on your mind, don't try to dissuade me, I'm firm on this, Lord knows Lucretia would kill me if you were to get hurt inside."

"Mom's not the issue here, Dad," Alex says as he plops down in an old chair next to his father's desk. The furnishings in Robert's office have been the same for forty years. They were well worn when Tom Dawson turned the office over to Robert. A spendthrift, Robert is not. He's a good man, a good father, a good husband and a fair businessman, but he has never been quite able to grasp the critical understanding of how to run a dynamic business, of people and how they are motivated. He's not the businessman that his father was.

Shoving his papers aside, Robert rises from his desk and slowly walks to a dingy window that looks out across the blackened buildings of the mine complex. "She may not be the issue, but you're her only child, Alex. When she lost her second child and was rendered incapable of having another, well, I'm afraid you were given a great burden. Your happiness is her happiness, Alex. Your well-being is her well-being, I dare not do anything to challenge that."

Alex shifts uncomfortably in the old chair. "Dad, you have it all wrong. Sure, Mom loves me, I know that, but her life revolves around you, not me. She lives to please you. If, one day, you go before her, I'm afraid I'll not be able to fill the void."

Robert is quiet as he continues to gaze out the window. Alex continues, "Dad, I need the experience inside. If you want me to run this operation one day, I need to know the real guts of what's going on, and if I'm to be effective at keeping this mine a money-making venture, well into the future, it's going to take the right mix of education and experience. I've got the education; don't shortchange me on the experience!"

His father throws a glance over his shoulder. "What more do you need, you've spent two summers and another two months inside, you'll have a good Super and good Foremen to run the mine for you one day, you'll need to spend your time managing the money and sales."

"Dad, I learned something critically important from Charlie Walters just before he died. He told me about your desire to economize on old timbers. Well, those old timbers, that you wanted saved, cost Charlie his life and almost cost me mine. You're not aware of small, but important details like that because you don't spend time with the men and you don't listen well enough to your Superintendent. That's why I want to get more time on the inside under my belt, to get to know more about what the miners think and feel. That's where the real knowledge about coal mining is. I think old Jim Ryland knew that."

The mention of Jim Ryland jerks Robert around from the window. "What do you know about Ryland's thinking on running a coalmine? The man's been dead for five years."

"Dad, I used to have some good talks with old Ryland. When I was a boy I'd sit and listen for hours as he talked about mining. He loved it, Dad, and when he talked about the old days I could tell how important the men were to him, and how he'd ask their advice. He said that if you really want to know what makes a coal mine run you gotta listen to the engine, and that the men are the engine. I've not forgotten that."

Robert's ears turn red at the thought that his son would think that Jim Ryland would know more than he about running a coal mine. His voice rises as he feels the need to defend himself. "Well what else did mister Ryland have to teach you about mining?" he shouts, with an emphasis on "mister."

Alex is bright enough to know that he has touched a sore spot and he backs off. He wants to say more. He wants to talk about how Gramps used to talk about mining. How, when Tom Dawson and Jim Ryland together would tell tales about their days in the mines he would be riveted to every word, and how much he respected and missed his grandfather. But now was not the time. Instead, he falls back to a more strategic position.

"Dad, I'm not implying that Ryland was the best Super in the world, just that I think he had a good idea about getting involved, and that's what I want to do. I want to be a Foreman and then a Super before I move up front. If, one day, I'm the General Manager, I want our people to respect me for my knowledge and my methods, not for my name."

Robert's temper cools a bit. He's not normally one to fly off the handle, he prides himself on that, and usually maintains an even temperament. Embarrassed about his flare-up over the mention of Jim Ryland, he begins to come around. "Alex, I hear what you're saying. Let me think on it for the rest of the day, and I'd like to discuss it with your mother this evening."

Alex knows he has won. His mother will worry, she always does, but he feels she'll be on his side on this one.

By September, with three months in the mine under his belt, Alex has gained more experience than most new miners do in several years. This is because he has been assigned to just about every job in the mine, and he's very quick. Ed Jacobs, the mine electrician, was amazed at how quickly Alex grasped the fundamentals. One day he said, "Alex, boy, you're gonna be able to run this mine in your sleep!"

Alex was embarrassed. "I don't think so, Ed. I may pick up on the fundamentals quickly, but it's the nuances, that have taken you years to learn, that I will only get if I spend the time on the job that you have."

Ed looked confused. "What's a nu-onz?"

"You know, Ed, the little tricks that you've learned, like, the tricks of the trade."

"Oh, I getcha. Yeah, I guess you're right. Some of those nuonzes I learned the hard way. Yeah, hard experience is the only way, and that takes time, Alex. In the mine it's the kind of experience I call, "asshole puckering." But you've got nothing but time in front of you, boy, and you'll get "asshole puckering" experience soon enough. You're going to run this mine real good someday."

"I hope so, Ed, I hope so," Alex laughs, "But I don't know if I'm exactly looking forward to the kind of experience you're referring to."

Chapter 8

Get Me Some Air

October 1925

Cascade

The summer of "25" was a difficult period in the coal mining industry. There was a heavy movement toward unionization of the mineworkers and there were sporadic episodes of violence at some mines around the state, but so far Cascade has avoided serious conflict. Tom Dawson had always been fair and generous to his work force, but Robert Dawson, during his tenure, has tightened up the organization and is more distant from the workers. The Super and the Foremen run the mine with little day to day input from Robert.

Now that the miners at Cascade are under heavy pressure from the union's attempt to organize them, Alex is concerned about the scuttlebutt he hears. Some of the younger miners have been talking union and he spends a large part of his time convincing them that a union is unnecessary, that the Dawson's will provide all that a union mine will, and more.

He assures them that they will always have a direct line to him to air their grievances or suggestions once he's in a management position. He further assures them that he will be the arbiter on any disagreement they may have with a Foreman or the Super. For the time being, at least, the younger men adopt a wait-and-see attitude and the union threat is avoided.

On a sunny morning, as the maples are taking on a vivid red and the beeches a scintillating yellow, Alex drives the short distance from his apartment, in Cascade, to the mine complex. As his Model T Ford slowly passes the parking area, on his way to the main fan house where he has been working with a maintenance crew, his father is walking from his own car. He waves at Alex, motioning him to stop. He yells: "Alex, can you come into the office? I've got something to discuss with you."

"Sure, Dad, let me run on up and let the crew know, then I'll be right there." A few minutes later Alex taps on his father's door and walks in. Kip Ryland and Robert Dawson look up from a large blue print of the Dawson mine. Kip shows a warm smile and greets Alex, "Hi, young feller, how's the repair on the fan house coming along?"

"Really good, you've got some mighty good boys in that crew, Kip."

"Don't I know it?"

Alex takes off his cap and throws it on a chair, "What's up, Dad?" His father points to a spot on the map: "Alex, the mine has penetrated three miles underground. We have tunneled under Laurel Mountain and under Gap Mountain and the forward working faces lie below the floor of Blackwater River Valley, which, as you know, is situated on the far side of Gap Mountain. Back in, let's see, I think it was 1905, when the mine was about one and a half miles in, and under Laurel Creek Valley, we sunk the Laurel ventilation shaft down to the mine. I don't recall, son, have you been over to the Laurel fan since you've been working, I know you were there with me when you were a little shaver."

"Yes, Dad. As a matter of fact, I worked with the maintenance boys over there a couple of weeks ago, repairing a damaged fan blade."

"Good, then you've got a pretty good handle on our ventilation system. I know you've spent time working on the main fan. Well, about 1-1/2 miles is the maximum distance the Laurel fan can provide adequate ventilation and since we've now penetrated the coal seam another mile and a half beyond the Laurel fan, Kip tells me we're beginning to have some dead air at the forward faces. We need to put in another fan."

Alex nods. He's well aware of the latest engineering models for mine ventilation and knows that the rule-of-thumb of a 1-1/2 mile max distance is just that, a rule-of-thumb. It can vary dramatically depending on several factors. He asks, "I assume we'll sink a shaft down from Blackwater. How deep are we at that point?"

"Sixty feet," Kip offers. The older Dawson resumes, "Alex, I'd like you to Engineer the new fan facility and oversee the construction." Alex is ecstatic, "What? Dad, that's great. I've been dying to get to do a new project like that, gosh, this is great!"

"Good," his dad says with a broad smile. "But, you understand that you'll be working for Kip, and he has final say on the design and build."

"Of course, Kip is the boss," Alex says, with a smile directed Kip's way.

"Well, mister designer, you best get started, I'm gonna need air damn soon," and with that, Kip playfully shoves Alex's cap on his head and pushes him toward the door.

Alex gets started on the new project immediately. After doing a measurement of air flow at section 45, the location for the new fan and laying out a proposed plan for the future course of the mine, Alex begins calculating the air volume needed to provide good ventilation at the lowest cost. As the airshaft and the fan increase in size, the cost escalates exponentially. His task is to ascertain not just the optimum type and size of the new fan, but also the cost to operate it. He settles on a Jeffery squirrel cage fan, eighteen feet in diameter and six feet wide, to be operated by a 200 horsepower electric motor turning the fan at 800 revolutions per minute. He determines that a sixty-foot deep airshaft will require a diameter of 12 feet. The fan will push fresh air down the shaft.

With his calculations complete and fan model determined, he begins designing the shaft, foundations for the fan and the fan house. The airshaft will reach 60 feet from the floor of Blackwater Valley down to the main entry air course. The earth and rock will be stabilized with walls of reinforced concrete four inches thick. A steel ladder is to be mounted on the side of the shaft to allow the shaft to be used as an emergency escape route from the mine in case of fire, explosion, or gas. The shaft will sit below a building which will house the Jeffery fan, motor and accessory equipment.

A huge duct will conduct the forced air through the floor and down the shaft. The air intake will be above the roof with a four-inch mesh screen covering the mouth of the intake duct,

It takes the Jeffery Fan Company three months to manufacture and ship the new fan and by the time it's delivered in January, Alex has the shaft completed and the open structure ready to accept it. Within another three weeks the fan is installed and tested, and the building closed in. Alex and his crew hang a large sign over the door. In large red letters. It reads, BLACKWATER FAN, Dawson Colliery Company. That done, the men celebrate by busting a bottle of homemade whiskey on the corner of the building. That evening, the celebration continues at a watering hole on the outskirts of Cascade. All the crew agrees that they and Alex have done a fine job on the project. The praises and raised glasses continue well into the night.

Chapter 9

Number 1 Hill

Glen Haven, West Virginia

December, 1934

It's a gray March day on Number One Hill. Many bare trees dotting the slopes are not void of leaves simply because they're dormant in Wyoming County, in southern West Virginia, but because they're dead. Some species of trees do not survive on the hills above the mining camps on Trout Run. From a small house; a crude house, weathered and darkened from the incessant coal dust, comes the unmistakable cry of a newborn. The baby has strong lungs, an attribute that will be of advantage in what will ultimately be a family of eight. Number One Hill was so named by the coal company that had carved Number One Mine into the base of the hill. The Headley Coal Company, of Glen Haven, West Virginia, owns several coal mines along Trout Run. The Run, as the creek is called by the inhabitants in the various mining camps along its banks, is a dirty, yellow-orange color and is so acidic that no marine life can be sustained beneath its surface. Trout Run, as is the case with many streams in the mine fields of the Appalachians, is polluted with the acid, sulfur and other chemicals and minerals disturbed by the mining operations.

It is in a coal company house, on the hill above these colorful, yet lifeless waters, that Angelo Valentini is born. Glen Haven is not what one would normally picture when the descriptive word, *glen* is used. No, one would no doubt picture a quiet, green valley with a sparkling stream tumbling over polished stones with a moss-covered log here and there. The Scottish describe a glen as a deep, narrow valley in the Highlands. That's a pretty good description of what West Virginians typically call a *Hollow*.

Back in the early days many of the Appalachian coal miners were of Scotch-Irish extraction and many mining camps were named Glen-something; most of them being in a hollow which would eventually lack much greenery and would have a putrid creek running through it.

Glen Haven is certainly no kind of haven. The coal company houses are crudely constructed, un-insulated and heated with a single "pot belly" coal stove. There are open sewers and privies, which drain into the waters of the creek. Living along the Run in the thirties, when Angelo is born, are about 3000 people. The great depression has dealt the coalfields of West Virginia a serious blow. Two thirds of the miners, on the "Run", are out of work and in some parts of the state almost half the population is on relief. Malnutrition and typhoid fever are widespread and medical service is hard to come by. A writer for an eastern newspaper describes the Trout Run mining camps as, "The damnedest cesspool of human misery I have ever seen in America."

As unhealthy as the creek is, the children still swim in it. They have little choice as to how to find fun and recreation, so they do the best they can with what's presented to them. A short way up the creek from the house where Angelo is born, a slag dump, or gob pile, burns and gives off noxious smoke and gases. The slag dump is where the mining companies pile the slate and poor-quality coal that's sorted, in the breaker, from the good coal. From the pressure of the weight of the huge mound the slag spontaneously combusts and smolders continuously. The resulting gases kill most of the vegetation on the hills above and downwind of the dump.

Angelo's is one of the few white families on Number One Hill. His neighbors are a mixture of white and black. The whites are an assortment of European extraction, English, Scotch, Irish, German, Italian, Polish, Etc. But, whether white or black, German or Pole, all are desperately trying to eke out a living under extremely trying circumstances. Even though the "Colored" are required to attend a different school, Angelo never thinks anything about their differences. He plays with blacks, eats in their homes and never thinks for a minute that they are any different from him, other than the fact that they are dark and he is light. His momma and poppa never speak in a negative way about any race. They have friends of all types. Race is not much of an issue in the coal camps. It's a poor existence, but there's a lot of love in the Valentini family to compensate for the hardship.

Angelo will ultimately be a coal miner like his own father, Nicholas, son of an Italian immigrant who came to America in 1902 at the age of twelve. The immigrant family had nothing but empty pockets and a willingness to work hard. At that young age, twelve, the little Italian boy went to work in the coal mines with his own father. Nicholas himself entered the mines at the age of fourteen, and Angelo will be only sixteen years old when he first starts working in the mine. This will not be his plan - his plan will be to escape the mining camps. But sometimes life doesn't heed our plans.

It was hot on that morning, during the dog days of summer, when Nicholas Valentini almost looked forward to going into the mine to find coolness. As he sat on the hard surface of the coal car, as the man-trip took him to the working face of the mine, he thought about the conversation he had with Angelo, the evening before. They talked about what courses Angelo would study in high school and how hard he would study in hopes of earning a scholarship to West Virginia University, or another state school. There would be no sports scholarship; the schools in that part of the state didn't have much of a sports program, so if there was to be a scholarship it would have to be an academic one. Even if Angelo would only finish high school he would be the first Valentini to do so. *But he must go to college; he must get out of the mining camp,* Nicholas vowed to himself. *Tonight, I will have a long talk with my boy. He must get away from here. He must have a better life.*

But, there will be no further talks between Nicholas Valentini and his son, Angelo. There will be no more talks between Nicholas and any other living person, because Nicholas Valentini is a bonder, and later this day, as he touches his welding electrode to the rail, the electrical arc will ignite lingering methane gas, and at the age of forty,

Nicholas Valentini will go to meet his maker. And instead of finishing high school, Angelo Valentini, at the age of sixteen, will go to work in the mine to help support the family.

One of the few things left to Angelo, when his father died, was a tattered and worn copy of a newspaper that the little twelve-year-old Valentini immigrant, Angelo's grandfather, had found on the day he arrived in America in 1902. The little immigrant boy kept the paper, promising himself that he would, one day, be able to read it. By coincidence, the paper contained an article on coal mining. The piece was written by an old Pennsylvania miner:

"I'm twelve years old, goin on thirteen," said the boy to the boss of the breaker. He didn't look more than ten, and he was only nine, but the law said he must be twelve to get a job. He was one of a multitude of the 16,000 youngsters of the mines, who, because miners' families are large and their pay comparatively small, start in the breaker before many boys have passed their primary schooling. From the time he enters the breaker there is a rule of progress that is almost always followed. Once a miner and twice a breaker boy, the upward growth of boy to man, breaker boy to miner, the descent from manhood to old age, from miner to breaker boy, that is the rule. So the nine-year old boy who is "twelve, goin on thirteen," starts in the breaker. He gets from fifty to seventy cents for ten hours work. He rises at 5:30 o'clock in the morning, puts on his working clothes, always soaked with dust, eats his breakfast, and by seven o'clock he has climbed the dark and dusty stairway to the screen room where he works. He sits on a hard bench built across a long chute, through which passes a steady stream of broken coal. From the coal he must pick the pieces of slate or rock.

It's not a hard life but it's confining and irksome. Sitting on his uncomfortable seat, bending constantly over the passing stream of coal, his hands soon become cut and scarred by the sharp pieces of slate and coal while his finger nails are soon worn to the quick from contact with the iron chute. The air he breathes is saturated with the coal dust, and as a rule the breaker is fiercely hot in summer and intensely cold in winter. In many of the modern breakers, to be sure, steam heating pipes have been introduced into the screen rooms, and fans have been placed in some breakers to carry away the dust. But, however favorable the conditions the boy's life is a hard one. Yet it's a consistent introduction to what is to follow.

The ambition of every breaker boy is to enter the mines, and at the first opportunity he begins there as a door boy, never over fourteen years of age and often under. The work of the door boy is not so laborious as that in the breaker, but is more monotonous. He must be on hand when the first trip of cars enter in the morning and remain until the last comes out at night. His duty is to open and shut the door as men and cars pass through the door, which controls and regulates the ventilation of the mine. He's alone in the darkness and silence all day, save when other men and boys pass through his door. Not many of these boys can read, and if they did it would be impossible in the dim light of their small lamp. Whittling and whistling are the boy's chief recreations. The door boy's wages vary from sixty-five to seventy-five cents a day, and from this he provides his own lamp, cotton and oil.

Just as the breaker boy wants to be a door boy, the door boy wants to be a driver. When the mules are kept in the mines, as they usually are, the driver boy must go down the shaft in time to clean and harness his mule, bring him to the foot of the shaft and hitch him to a trip of empty cars before seven o'clock. This trip of cars varies from four to seven according the number of miners. The driver takes the empty cars to the working places and returns them loaded to the foot of the shaft. They are then hoisted to the surface and conveyed to the breaker where the coal is cracked, sorted and cleaned and made ready for the market. These boys, are in constant danger, not only of falling roof and exploding gas, but of being crushed by the cars. Their pay varies from $1.10 to

$1.25, from which sum they supply their own lamps, cotton and oil.

When the driver reaches the age of twenty he becomes either a runner or a laborer in the mines, more frequently the latter. The runner is a conductor who collects the loaded cars and directs the driver. The laborer is employed by the miner, subject to the approval of the superintendent, to load the cars with the coal, which has been blasted by the miner. As a rule he's paid so much per car, and a definite number of cars

constitute a day's work, the number varying in different mines, averaging from five to seven, equaling from twelve to fifteen tons of coal. The laborer's work is often made difficult by the water and rock, which are found in large quantities in coal veins.

Each laborer is looking forward to becoming a miner in the technical sense of the word, that is, the employer of a laborer must have had two years experience in practical mining and be able to pass an examination before the district board. If he passes he becomes a contractor as well as a laborer. He enters into a contract with the company to do a certain work at so much per car or, yard. He blasts all the coal, and this involves judgment in locating the hole, skill in boring it, and care in preparing and determining the size of the shot. The number of blasts per day ranges from four to twelve, according to the size and character of the vein. He's responsible for the propping necessary to sustain the roof. According to the law, the company operating the mine is obligated to furnish the miner the needed props, but the miner must place them at such places as the mine boss designates. Most of the boring is now done with hand machines. The miner furnishes his own tools and supplies. His powder, Squibb paper, soap and oil he's compelled to buy from the company, which employs him. His equipment includes the following tools, a hand machine for drilling, drill, scraper, needle, blasting barrel, crowbar, pick, shovel, hammer, sledge, cartridge pin, oil can, toolbox and lamp. As a rule he rises at five in the morning and enters the mine *shortly after six. In some cases he's obliged to walk a mile or more underground to reach his place of work. He spends from eight to ten hours in the mine. Taking three hundred days as the possible working time in a year, the miner's daily pay for the past twenty years will not average over $1.60 a day, and that of the laborer not over $1.35.*

His dangers are many. He may be crushed to death at any time by the falling roof, burned to death by the exploding of gas, or blown to pieces by a premature blast. So dangerous is his work that he's debarred from all ordinary life insurance. In no part of the country will you find so many crippled boys and broken

down men. During the last thirty years over 10,000 men and boys have been killed and 25,000 have been injured in this industry. Not many old men are found in the mines. The average age of the miner is 32.

It's an endless routine of a dull plodding world from nine years until death, a sort of voluntary life imprisonment. Few escape. Once they begin, they continue to live out their commonplace, low-leveled existence, ignoring their daily danger, knowing nothing better.

Nicholas Valentini would read this particular article over and over to his young son and he would tell him, "Angelo, boy, this is just like it is, and it's no life for a man. You must do better than your poppa, and your grand poppa, and your great grand poppa. You must never go into the coal mine, Angelo, never go into the coal mine."

But, it didn't work. Nicholas was killed and five days later, Angelo entered the mine where he would work for the rest of his life.

Chapter 10

Along Trout Run

Fortunately for Angelo, a few years after starting to work, he met and married an alluring, dark eyed Italian girl who also grew up in a mining camp, a couple of miles up the run. They met at a missionary youth center, which had been established by the Methodist Church. Her name is Theresa, and to Angelo she is a lifesaver. She gives his life a meaning and purpose that he has not felt before.

Angelo and Theresa start their life together in the blackened mining community along dirty Trout Run. The town of Glen Haven, if it can be called a town, is referred to by the miners as a camp, a name long used in coal mining parlance. It was undoubtedly coined in the early days of coal mining when common housing for the miners was canvas tents.

Any newcomer to the camp along Trout Run would chuckle at the name of the creek. Once the home of native brook trout, a brookie has not survived in the stream for fifty years. Government controls don't permit the kind of contamination found in the creek, but it seems to persist unabated in this remote area of the southern mountains.

The camps along the Run have little more than the necessary services to sustain a simple life. There are, of course, the coal company stores where the miners are able to purchase their daily needs of food, clothing, household appliances, gasoline, etc. They make their purchases with "scrip." In the early days of coal mining the mines were usually located in remote areas of the mountains, a distance from the business centers where banks were readily available. This made it difficult to maintain a ready supply of real currency, so the mine owners began paying the miners with the owner's own currency, which was called, scrip. No doubt the mine owners had another motive for the use of scrip; the miners could only spend it at the company store. This, of course, gave the mining company another source of profit. So it is, under these trying conditions that Angelo and Theresa Valentini try to eke out a living and start a family.

Theresa worries every day that her husband will not come home, that black damp or an explosion will take him from her. Angelo worries about Theresa, that this is no life for a beautiful young girl. But they each go on, hoping that their love for each other will overcome the fears and frustrations.

Angelo tried to keep Theresa from learning about the mine accidents and deaths that happened too frequently in the mountains, so he did not spend the money to get the Charleston Daily Mail newspaper, but all the wives knew of each and every soul who was lost; the word moved up and down the run quickly.

It was on a cold November morning that word came of an explosion up in the Kanawha River area. Word was that 43 men were killed outright and 76 were trapped. The trapped men had barricaded themselves in a section some distance from the explosion. They quickly fashioned a wall of boards and clothing to try to seal themselves from the afterdamp. Their brave action worked for a while, but eventually the afterdamp seeped through the men's barricade. Afterdamp is a toxic mixture of gases left in a mine following an explosion. It consists of carbon dioxide, carbon monoxide and nitrogen. It is the high content of carbon monoxide which kills by depriving the men of oxygen. When the bodies were later recovered a few notes were found scribbled by one of the men, an Italian fellow by the name of Cappanelli, only recently arrived in America. The first note read; "At peace with God." The second, assumed written sometime later, was not quite as clearly written, it read; "Dear Mary, tell father I was saved." And finally in lines fainter and quite irregular; "We do not feel any pain. Try to stay in the U.S.A. Love to the kids. R. Cappanelli."

As Theresa reads these words she begins to softly weep, but soon her tears begin to flood as she pictures Angelo sitting in the dark mine writing a last note to herself. In that moment she vows to not have children. Children who will most likely grow up without a father.

Angelo found her still sobbing when he arrived home that evening. "Don't cry my Sweet. I heard the news too. But that explosion was in a mine known to be gassy and our mine here is not like that," he lied.

It took weeks and much comforting for Theresa to recover

from the tormenting vision she had of Angelo sitting in the black place with the stub of a pencil in his hand. But, she did recover, and she slowly put from her mind the idea of not having children.

Chapter 11

Explosion

November, 1951

Cascade, West Virginia

It's been twenty-five years since Alex Dawson completed his Blackwater fan project. The forward workings of the mine now extend over a mile past the Blackwater airshaft and the faces of the eastern side entries have penetrated the coal seam another half mile. In all, five square miles of the seam has been mined-out during Alex Dawson's tenure. These have been relatively good years for the Dawson mining business. The timbering business has also flourished. A couple of years after the fan project, Alex had married a lovely lass from Garrett County, Maryland, by the name of, Sarah Casteel. Two years later, a son, Benjamin was born, and two years after that along came Nathaniel. In 1941 Alex had tried to enlist in the Army, but the government said his management of the coal mine was too important to the country's war effort and wouldn't accept him.

Young Ben Dawson is now 21 and in his senior year at the College of Mining Engineering at West Virginia University. His brother, Nat, at 19, is a sophomore in the engineering school. Alex Dawson has foreseen the need for heavy government investment in infrastructure which suffered during the war, and to better position the family businesses, plans the addition of a construction division. As a result, he suggested to Nat that he study Civil and Electrical Engineering to prepare himself to start up such a business.

It's a cold, wet and dreary November morning in the mountains. The cheery colors of autumn have faded and the mountains have taken on a grayish cast, accept for splashes of brown, where the oaks still cling to some reluctant stragglers, and chunks of deep green, the winter shade of the hemlocks.

A light rain falls as Alex sits in his office staring at the month ending financial statement. Outside his window, a sputtering column of rainwater falls from a broken gutter. His father, Robert, walks in. The older man, still spry at the

age of 78, none-the-less carries a cane to help with his balance. Without speaking, he walks quietly across the room and lowers himself
into a comfortable chair in the corner. Alex continues to study the figures and seems unaware of his father's arrival. After a minute and no acknowledgement of his presence, Robert, sensing a troubled feeling on the part of his son, finally speaks, "You look like you lost your best friend, son."

Alex looks up, genuinely startled, "Oh, hi Dad. Yeah, I guess I'm not in the best of spirits, I don't like the way the numbers are going."

Robert leans forward, his hands cupped on the top of his cane, "I heard we lost the contract with Eastern Power and Light."

Alex leans back in his chair and stretches his arms, "Yep, Consolidated underbid us by a buck-twenty-five a ton. Every day it gets harder to compete with the big operators. With the co-ops being formed downstate and the strip mining in Ohio getting more efficient with those monster drag lines, I'm having to bid darn close to our variable cost in order to win any contracts."

"Are costs staying in line?" Robert asks.

"Yeah, our variable cost, as a per cent of sales, is holding fairly steady, but our fixed overhead remains the same, and with the decreased volume of business to spread it over, the net result is awful skinny profits. And as I've been trying to tell you the past several years, we need to invest in new, more reliable and efficient equipment if we're going to compete, otherwise, we're going to need to dip into other reserves to keep the mine operating."

The older man scratches his chin and ponders his son's words. He absentmindedly reaches for his watch fob and pulls a gold pocket watch from a vest pocket, a watch with a brook trout engraved on the front cover. He flips open the cover and stares at the face of the watch for a long moment, then offers, "Well Son, I don't think we ought to be spending a lot on new equipment when we have less than five years of coal left."

Alex smiles, "Is that a magic watch that tells you when the coal is gonna play out?"

His father grins sheepishly as he snaps the cover shut, with a click. "I guess that's an old habit of mine, looking at my watch when I'm studying on something. No, it's not a magic watch, but it's a special one."

Alex leans forward in his chair and with a soft kindness in his voice, says, "I know it is, Dad, it was your dad's watch."

"Yes, and it's a good watch. It's a Longines. Dad paid a pretty penny for it. Bought it in Baltimore in 1888. You know it's solid gold and has a 21-jewel movement. Has his name here inside the cover, Tom Dawson. Course you know that, I'm just rambling on like an old fool."

"No, you're not rambling, Grandpa was a special guy."

"You know, he was a special man, Alex, and this may sound foolish, but I miss him. I'm 78 years old and I miss my dad, I miss him a lot, even more so lately, for some reason."

"I miss him too, Dad."

"I always intended on passing the watch on to you, Alex, but what would you think if I left it to Ben? He's always admired it so, I kinda always had it in my hand when I'd tell him and Nat stories about their great-grandpa."

"Dad, I think that would be a wonderful gesture, would mean a lot to Ben."

"Yes, I think so too. Course, I'll have to come up with something for Nat, can't leave him out, can I?"

"Nope, you gotta leave something special for Nat too; you're his hero, Dad."

"Well, I'll have to think on that, I mean, what I could leave for Nat." With that, Robert stands, slips the watch back in its place in his vest pocket and says, "Like I was saying, I don't think we ought to be spending a lot of money on new equipment with little more than five years of coal left."

Alex has had this discussion with his Dad many times before and the older man's lack of understanding of how mining machine technology has dramatically increased since the war ended, has him frustrated.

"Dad, I understand your feelings, but since the war ended,

all those engineers that had been working on tanks and planes have been shifted over to automobiles, construction equipment and mining equipment, among other things. Today's new cutting machine design gives five times the output of our machines, and the men are constantly fighting to keep our old machines running. The only thing keeping us barely in the ball game is the depth of experience of our guys; they somehow seem to keep this old equipment operating."

"Maybe the new machines are better, Son, but if we buy new machines today, in five years they wouldn't be worth anything, because within those five years, as you say, there's going to be even more advancement in new cutting machine design."

"But Dad, in five years they would save ten times their cost."

"Maybe they would, maybe they wouldn't. Nothing is certain, Son."

"I respectfully disagree with you, Dad, one thing is sure certain, we're going to continue to lose orders if we don't modernize our equipment and improve our productivity so that I can quote lower prices and still make a profit."

"Well, maybe you just need to get a little more work out of the men."

Alex hangs his head in frustration. At 78 years of age his father has not kept up with mining industry technology and it's hurting the business. Although Alex has the main responsibility for managing the mining operation, his father still holds the "bag of marbles" in that he has majority interest in the company stock, and as such, his approval is required on major acquisitions. For the past several years his refusal to spend adequately, on new equipment, has placed the mining company in a perilous position.

The following morning, it's still raining as Daniel "Collie" Collins runs to catch the man-trip as it's heading toward the main portal of Dawson Mine #1. The motorman stops the string and waits for Collins to climb aboard. Swinging one leg over the side of the coal car, which has been converted to carry miners, then, the other, Collins slides down heavily onto the oak plank bench. At the head of the string the motor revs again and the cars, in ordered sequence, clash against their couplings.

Collie leans back against the cold steel of the mine car and lets out a deep breath. Next to him, his friend, Jerry, moves a bit to give the late arrival a little more room on the cold plank. As he does, he speaks to Collie without turning his head. He has his

collar pulled tight around his neck to keep the rain out and does not want to disturb the seal between collar and neck. "You're running a bit late this fine morning, Collie my friend."

The rain has added to the drowsiness that Collie feels this morning. He has not slept much during the night and it was hard enough to crawl out of bed at 5:30 in the morning, even with a full night's sleep. But Collie had not had a full night's sleep for two weeks now, not since the new baby had arrived. "Aw Jerry, I'd give me mothers own holy bible for just one night of good sleep, this blessed little baby of ours has had the colic from the first day and I'll be switched if it ain't the truth that he and his poor mother are about worn out."

Jerry pats his friend on the knee. "I know just what you're a going through, Daniel Collins, and you and yours surely do have my sympathy, but you hafta look at it this-a-way; the little shaver will soon be well and you've got tomorrow to catch up on your sleep. I'll tell the good reverend why ya ain't in church."

"I suppose you're right, Jerry. Now don't talk to me anymore, and wake me when we get to the drop off, oh, I forgot, the Super stopped me on the way out of the lamp house and asked if you and I want to undercut by hand today. It seems our cuttin machine broke down last night."

Jerry doesn't answer, just nods. Collie is the unspoken leader of the two and Jerry usually goes along without questioning him. As the man-trip enters the mouth of the mine the men willingly trade the cool morning rain for the relative dryness inside. The mine always feels damp, but the men are accustomed to the dampness and this morning consider it more comfortable than the rain.

Collie lowers his head to his chest and prepares to doze as he sucks in a breath of the dank air. A coalmine has a unique smell, unlike any other place. It's a cool, moist, oily, metallic, acidic, and earthy kind of smell. In some coalmines, with high sulfur content, one can also detect an odor reminiscent of rotten eggs. But Collie has no awareness of the various odors; his senses are too accustomed to the taste of the mine to notice.

Twenty minutes later, and four miles into the mine, after dropping miners off at a couple of side entries along the way, Collie is shaken awake by Jerry as the man-trip grinds to a stop at entries, 64 East and West.

As the two men exit the man-trip, Jerry asks, "Which side we gonna work, Collie?"

"Uh, west." Then, Collie pauses, which side did Cass tell him to work? He knew he told him specifically to work either the east or the west section, which was it? Damn! If he had been more awake! Oh well, he thinks, what difference could it make? "Let's take the west, the first rooms just about broke through, might as well finish it."

As they prepared to get started, Jerry, uncharacteristically, protests, "Jesus, Collie, I'll be damned if I can understand why it's you and I that's gotta cut by hand, hell, why can't they put a couple of the greener guys on it? We ought to have first dibs on another cutter-loader."

"Hell, I don't know, Jere, I have a hunch Cass plain forgot about it until the rest of the guys were on the man-trip and I just happened to come along late."

"Well, it kind of pisses me off, Collie, that the company is too damn cheap to buy some new cuttin and loadin machines."

"Those things ain't cheap, Jere, and if you want to know what I think, I think the company is having trouble competing against the big boys and money is a little tight.

The way I see it, the Dawsons have always treated us fair, and if I can help out by doing a little work with a pick, well that's okay by me."

Jerry was quiet for a while as the two continued their walk toward the face, then he mumbles, to himself more than to his comrade, "Well, I guess."

Jerry was angered by the fact that digging an undercut with a pick-ax was replaced by electric powered cutting machines years before. The machines replaced backbreaking pick and shovel work. Even before the mines were electrified there were steam operated machines, in a few of the bigger operations, used to undercut the face, replacing the old method of a miner lying on his side while hacking out an undercut with a pick. The more he thought about it, the more he stewed. But, he would not go against Collie's decision.

So, a few minutes later, Daniel Collins and Jerry McCabe start working at the face of room #1 in Section 64 West. Their task is to hack out an undercut, drill holes in the face above, place explosive charges in the holes, and blast down the coal.

These two relatively young men have neither high aspirations nor great ambitions. They both would be satisfied with a simple life in the mountains of West Virginia, steady work at the mine, hunting, fishing, drinking beer with good Irish friends, and raising some kids. But fate has determined that even a simple life is not in store for them. Instead, the final minutes of their lives are ticking off.

Collie will not be there when his new baby gets over the colic. He will not be there to comfort the wife and kids of his friend, Jerry, and Jerry will never again stew in silence over one of Collie's decisions.

Serious accidents involving a number of people are seldom caused by the act of a single person. They usually happen because of a series of unique and random events, seemingly unrelated acts and decisions that join together to form a chain that leads to a catastrophic climax. When such a chain of events occurs, it's difficult to point a finger at any one individual. It would therefore be unfair to later say that

Collie Collins was the one person responsible for the deaths of 23 men.

Had Collie's baby not had the colic, had Robert Dawson not been so stubborn about spending money to upgrade the equipment, had the cutting machine not broke, had Collie not been running late that morning, had the super not bumped into Collie at the lamp house, and had Collie not been drowsy and less alert, perhaps the explosion would not have occurred.

No one will ever learn for sure what actually caused the explosion, that there was methane gas in section 65 just behind the face of room #1, off entry 64, that, when Collie's charge of dynamite went off it blew through the wall into section 65 and ignited several thousand cubic feet of gas, that the pressure front of the primary explosion of the methane gas caused coal dust in this and other sections of the mine to "dust" into the air, precipitating additional and much more powerful explosions and fire. No, no person would ever know exactly what events triggered the tragedy.

Alex Dawson was shaving when the phone rang. He kept a phone in the bathroom because it was not uncommon for him to get calls early in the morning. When he picked up the phone it was Cass Parker, his mine Superintendent, on the other end, "Alex, we've had an explosion!"

"What! Jesus, Cass, how bad?"

"It's, it's a bad one, Chief! Real bad, and I'm pretty sure we've got fire."

"Did anyone get out?"

"Yes, thank God, some of the boys got out, 20 made it out through the main portal and I believe others got up the auxiliary fan shafts, I've sent men over the mountains to those shafts to find out. I don't know yet how many got out, but we're sure there are some still inside, and from first reports it doesn't look good for them."

"Do you know which section?"

"Not yet."

"Have you started putting together a rescue team?"

"No, I wanted to call you first."

"Well, Lord, Cass, Get on it! I'll be right in."

As Alex throws on some clothes he asks Sarah to call his father, Robert Dawson and let him know there was an explosion at the mine. "Tell him I'm on my way, and I'll see him there."

Sarah put her hand firmly on her husband's arm, "Alex, please don't take any unnecessary chances." She knew it was a useless request, but she had to ask it for her own peace of mind."

As Alex neared the mine he saw a tremendous column of thick, black smoke hurling heavenward. As he pulled his truck into the mine complex he saw his father, with a large group of miners, watching the smoke pouring out of the mine portal. Robert lived closer to the mine and the old man had been in his car within minutes of the call from Sarah.

There were also a number of women present, wives of the miners who had entered the mine that morning. The women had responded to the continuous blast of the steam whistle that broadcast the message always dreaded in a mining community, DISASTER!

Cass Parker was shouting directions to several of the men as Alex walked up. Cass was pale, his eyes reflected fear and sweat ran down his temples. Alex pulled him aside, "Cass, what's the situation?"

Robert Dawson also approached as Cass began, "Hi, Chief, hi Mister Dawson, well, from what the fellows told me, the explosion probably occurred somewhere the other side of Section 60. That makes sense, we're working at faces in 63 East and West, and, uh, well, I asked Collins and McCabe to work in 64 East this morning."

Alex looked puzzled? "64 East! Cass, wasn't it in 65 where we found gas a couple days ago. I thought you bratticed off 65 and planned on pulling back and holding off work in 64 until you made sure air was moving better through 65?"

"The gas was limited to 65 West, Chief, and we did brattice it off. I told Collins to work by hand in 64 east."

81

Alex was taken aback, "By hand! But, Cass, do you think it was smart to blast coal when gas was evident in the vicinity? Why by hand, for God's sake?"

Cass groaned. He suspected from the beginning what caused the explosion; that perhaps his instructions were unclear to Collins, and Collie went into a north room off of side entry 64 West instead of East. If Collie's blast at the face broke through to the gaseous section 65, no, God no! He didn't want to admit it, even to himself.

Now, faced with the possibility that it was his mistake that caused the tragedy, Cass turned defensive. "Well, shit, Boss! We had two cutting machines go down again last night, and the one that Collins would have taken over this shift is wedged into the face. I've got to get the coal out one way or another, so I asked Collins if he and McCabe would cut by hand until we get his machine going. You know what kind of shape these machines are in, I've been asking you for better equipment, hell, you know as well as me that we've been just limping along the last several years cause the old man, here, won't loosen the purse strings, so what am I supposed to do?" As soon as he said it, Cass regretted his words, but the anguish he felt for his men inside the mine overcame his normal diplomacy. Ordinarily, the men referred to Robert Dawson as, "The Old Man," with esteem. But on this occasion the normal respect was absent in Cass's voice.

The blood drains from Robert Dawson's face. Already badly shaken from the tragedy, he sags against his son, grabbing his arm to keep from going down. Alex quickly gives the old man support and leads him toward the lamp house as he continues the discussion with Cass.

"But, Cass, Why 64 East?"

"Because there's smooth base rock in there and I thought Collie and McCabe would have an easier go at shoveling, and hold on, we don't know yet what really happened."

Alex understood exactly what Cass was saying and could not strongly disagree with his logic. He leads his father into the lamp house where he finds a chair. He sits the old man down. Cass had followed them in. "Mr. Dawson, I, I didn't mean what I said, I'm, I'm, Jesus, Mr. Dawson, I'm just out of my head!"

The older Dawson, his face a deathly pale, looks up at Cass. "No, Cass. No, you're right. It's my fault, my fault." His words trail off as he says, "It's my fault, all those boys, and I've killed them."

Alex squeezes his Dad's arm, "Get that out of your mind, Dad, you would never have done anything to harm those men, you know that. And we don't know yet what happened, or where."

Robert Dawson suddenly stiffens, gets up from his seat and shouts, "Cass, where's your rescue team? I'm going in with them."

Cass and Alex respond at the same time, "No!"

"Oh, yes. I head this outfit, I call the final shots, I'm going in to help those boys!"

Alex knows it would now be useless to argue with his father. He turns to Cass and says, "Get masks for him and me, I'll take him in behind the team."

"Hell, Alex, we don't know if we can even get a team in there."

"Well, let's find out, Cass, let's find out."

Just then, a miner bursts into the lamp house. It's the man Cass had sent over the mountain to check on possible survivors at the two auxiliary fan shafts. He's breathless, but sputters, "Cass, 101 men made it out through the fan shafts!"

Once Cass and Alex get the man calmed down they learn that 43 men escaped up the Blackwater airshaft and 58 men made it out through the Laurel shaft. With the 20 who made it out through the main portal there is a total of 121 survivors. Seventeen men are missing.

Alex asks, "The men who are unaccounted for, where would they have been working this morning, Cass?"

"Two of my foremen are among the missing, so I can't be positive, chief, but I think I have a rough handle on it. As I said earlier, I sent Collins and McCabe to 64 east. Most of the guys were working at faces in 63 east and West. Uh,

Bartelli and Sadowski were supposed to be rock dusting in 62 west. Let's see, Hanley and Cooper were to be replacing some bonds in the entry to 63 west. Stiles and Allessi were repairing cable in the main haul around section 47.

"Alright," Alex says, "It seems obvious the problem occurred between the Blackwater shaft and 65 west. Let's see, the shaft is off the main haul at entries 45. We need to assume that the men in the room where the explosion occurred are dead. The men in other sections between 45 and the fire have a chance, if they were able to seal off their sections to stop encroachment of fire, smoke and gas, we need to operate under the assumption that men are alive in those sections between 45 and 65. Let's keep the fans running. That might keep the main air course clear of smoke, depending on how doors are set, of course any number of doors may have been blown out, but we'll gamble on that. I know that the air coming back down the main haul will feed any fire, but men still alive this side of the fire will die from smoke if we shut down the fans and they can't seal themselves off. Cass, what do you think?"

"That sounds good to me, so far." Cass responds.

Alex continues, "And I think our best bet is to go down the shaft at the Blackwater fan, it's this side of the problem, it's pushing air down, and once we're down there and have the problem located we might be able to manage trap doors to put the airflow in the most favorable direction."

"Ok Chief, but I think we also ought to send some men down the shaft at the Laurel fan and some through the main haul, to look for survivors."

"That's true, Cass, but keep in mind that once we start changing air doors around Blackwater it may affect airflow between Blackwater and Laurel. The fans are moving a hellava lot of smoke out of the mine and any fire is going to follow the air. If we divert Blackwater air toward the far sections without knowing how the doors are set on this side of it, we may put the other teams in trouble."

"Alright, I see what you're saying, we could possibly pull fire into the main air course behind the other teams."

"That's what I'm saying, Cass. It's a gamble, but I think any men who had a chance of making it up the Laurel shaft, or out through the main haul, did it. Anybody still inside must be on the other side of Blackwater."

"Ok, Chief, I buy into your plan."

"Good, let's do it." Alex turns to his Father. "Dad, since you insist on going in, I'd like you to stay close to me. We're going down the Blackwater fan shaft; it's a long way down that ladder, you up to it?"

"You kidding, boy? I'm in better shape than you." Robert Dawson had been silent to this point, listening to the younger men who better know the current workings of the mine. He now becomes more involved. "Cass, have you contacted the regional mine inspector?"

"Yes sir, I did that soon as I called Alex, that is, I called his office. He's at Masontown, they're trying to get hold of him."

"Good," responds Robert, "If we're going into the mine we need to have someone designated to meet him here when he arrives. Make sure that this contact knows precisely what our plan is."

"I'll make sure of that, Mister Dawson."

Alex continues, "Cass, who are you putting in charge here, while we're attempting to get into the mine?"

"I hadn't thought about that, Alex, I guess Pete Hollis, he's my second-best Foreman, I'd like to have Tanner go in with us, and Albergetti can take the three guys into the main haul."

"Ok, then let's get at it," Alex responds.

Twenty minutes later, after speeding over Laurel and Gap Mountains to Blackwater, the rescue team of twelve men, plus Cass, Alex and Robert, converges on the Blackwater Fan House. Entering the house through a sliding door located between the fan and the shaft, the men have to brace themselves and hold on to a handrail to keep from being blown down the shaft. Fighting the continuous blast of turbulent air, Cass, Alex and Robert lead the group down the ladder, 60 feet to the darkened mine below.

At the bottom there is no light, the electrical system knocked out by the explosion. The lights from the men's hard hats light up the mine with dancing beams. With the rush of air now diminished as the current spreads through the labyrinth of the mine and reacts to the normal frictional loss of speed, the men no longer fight to maintain their balance as they did in the shaft and fan house.

Alex shouts, "There's no smoke coming down the air course, so the doors are obviously set to move air toward the face. Let's get moving."

The men proceed as a group up the main haul, toward the far reaches of the mine and the area where they suspect the explosion occurred.

After no more than 200 feet they see an orange glow ahead, obviously from fire. Cass is the first to react, "It doesn't look good, Chief, we've got fire already and with this air flow it's going to be spreading fast."

"Let's get a closer look," responds Alex, "The air is moving toward the fire."

Twenty more steps and they feel heat radiating from the flames. Another twenty steps and they see the fire, 300 feet ahead, the coal which forms the walls, or, ribs, of the mine, burns furiously and flames from the ribs form one solid mass, creating a monstrous, orange hole in the earth. Temperature at the center of the flame front exceeds 2000 degrees.

"Cass," Alex shouts, "I didn't expect to find fire this soon, we're a long way from section 60, if we have fire all the way from here to 60 there's no way anybody could be alive on the other side."

"I think you're right, Chief. What do you want to do?"

"I'm not sure, there's no way we can get that fire out short of flooding the mine and that would take days. What do you think?"

Cass is silent for a moment, and then speaks with a tone in his voice that betrays his lack of hope. "We could shut down the fans, that would slow the fire, but then the smoke would fill up the mine in this direction and kill anybody this side of the fire."

"I think you're right. Even if there are men alive on the other side, I don't think we have any chance of getting to them. There's no way we can put down that fire."

Robert Dawson, feeling unimaginable guilt, screams at Alex, "We have to get in there, Alex, there may be men sealed off in side entries between here and the fire."

"But why would they seal off this side of the fire, Dad? If they were on this side they would have had a clear way out."

"That assumes they knew where the explosion was, they may have thought it was this side."

"But this side is all rock dusted real good and they know the main haul shouldn't have gas."

"Damn it, boy! Who knows what goes through a man's mind under such circumstances, we have to at least check out as many side entries as we can get to."

"Alright, Dad, we'll get in as far as we can and check the entries. But, I'd feel better if you stay back."

Robert starts ahead, "Nonsense, I'm going to check."

Cass leans close to Alex, "Chief, I don't think there's a chance in hell of any men being between here and the fire, and besides, there could be a chance there's also fire behind us."

"How's that possible, Cass?"

"Well, there had to be a big explosion to give us fire all the way from 60 to here, I figure there was a primary gas explosion, followed up by a big coal dusting which then went off. That could have been a big one, maybe causing multiple dust explosions between here and some point on the other side of Blackwater, we didn't check down that way and who knows, if the wrong air door is closed there may be air coming this way and pulling fire from the other side of the shaft.

"That makes sense, Cass. You take the guys back out, I'll go a ways with Dad to humor him. He's not thinking clear, feels he's responsible for all this."

Jim Davis, one of the rescue team, has overheard most of the discussion between Alex and Cass. He steps up to Alex, "Alex, I been with your Dad too long to let him go in there on his own, I'll go with him."

Before Alex can respond the rest of the team steps forward, demanding that they, too, go on.

"Alright," Alex exclaims, "Let's do it this way, six of you guys go with Cass to assure we have a safe back track, six of you come with me and Dad, but I gotta tell you guys, this is not a smart move."

Davis says, "Let's get going, Alex, Mister Dawson is getting too far ahead of us."

Alex trots swiftly, the six miners following, to his father's side. "Dad, you can't take the blame for this, let's get out of here while we can, there's no way we'll find anybody alive in here."

Already feeling intense heat, Robert holds a hand in front of his face to shield it. "I've gotta try, Son," he says.

They reach the first side entry. The trap door is open. "No one's sealed this," Alex shouts.

As they prepare to try for the next side entry they hear a call from behind. It's Cass. "Alex, hey Alex, there's fire coming the other way, let's get out of here!"

"Ok, boys, let's go, Alex shouts." He takes his father by the arm, "Dad, let's go."

His father pulls away. "You go ahead, Son, I'm gonna get my men , they need my help, I gotta get them out of here."

"Dad, they're goners, there's nothing we can do, let's get out while we can."

The old man stands fast, his suddenly frail form outlined by the orange glow behind him. "I'm going for my men, I got them in trouble and I'm going to get them out."

Alex is dumbfounded. He grabs his father in a bear hug and shouts to Jim Tanner, "Tanner, give me a hand with this old fart!"

As Tanner comes to the aid of Alex, one of the other men, a huge Polish immigrant, Art Dombrowski, also steps forward. Each of them grab a leg of the struggling and cursing Dawson, and with Alex, they carry the old man back towards the airshaft and safety. Some of the other men go ahead of them, while the others bring up the rear.

As Alex, Tanner and Dombrowski shuffle along the tracks with old Dawson, Alex trips and goes down heavily, smashing his right knee into a rail. He curses at the searing pain and his own clumsiness. In the confusion, Tanner and Dombrowski release Robert Dawson for an instant, to attend to Alex. In that brief moment the crazed old man breaks away and runs back toward the fire. Several men run after him, their headlamps disappearing into the glow as they chase the old man down the haul way.

Alex yells, "Dad, come back, men, don't let him do it, stop him, stop him!" He tries to get to his feet, but his right leg will not support him and he goes down again, this time his left foot catching under a rail and wrenching his ankle. He's now totally helpless. Tanner shouts to Dombrowski, "Art, get Alex out of here," and he starts after the men who are chasing Robert Dawson.

Meanwhile, Cass can be heard yelling at the top of his lungs, "Alex, Alex, let's get the hell out of here." Dombrowski, with arms the size of railroad ties, picks Alex up, slings him over his shoulder, and runs toward the shouts of Cass. Alex, totally overcome with concern for his father, pounds Dombrowski's back with both fists, trying to get him to stop, but the giant ignores the fists and the shouts, he intends to save Alex Dawson and Art Dombrowski.

As Dombrowski approaches the entry to the airshaft he sees the form of Cass silhouetted against an orange glow like the one Dombrowski left behind minutes before.

Cass shouts, "Who's there -where are the others?"

Dombrowski answers, "It's me, Boss, Dombrowski, and I've got the big boss."

Alex yells as he bounces on Dombrowski's broad shoulder, "Cass, get me off, I've got to go for my dad!"

Cass shouts over the protests of Alex, "Art, where are the others, what happened to Alex, where's Mister Dawson?"

Dombrowski moves quickly past Cass, toward the base of the airshaft, shouting as he goes, "Old man was heading for fire, the other guys, they run after him, the big boss busted legs, I'm getting him and me the hell outta here."

As Art Dombrowski climbs the ladder with Alex, Cass hesitates for a minute, struggling with the thought of old Dawson, Tanner and the others trapped by the fire, but by now the heat and smoke are unbearable and he also moves to the ladder. As he climbs, he tries to sort out in his own mind, just what happened to Robert Dawson and his men.

At the top of the shaft Cass quickly exits the fan house, anxious to be in the open. Once outside, he hurries to Alex, who lies sprawled on the ground beneath the looming Dombrowski, his face contorted with pain from his injuries, and anguish over the obvious death of his father. Cass drops to his knees beside his boss and his friend and pleads, "Chief, what the hell happened down there, where are the others?"

"They're dead, Cass, all dead. Dad led them to their deaths."

Cass is incredulous. "What! What do you mean? How? Why?"

The men, who were with Cass, and preceded Dombrowski up the shaft, surround Alex, also anxious to know what happened to their friends. He lifts himself on one elbow and struggles to find the words. "Dad insisted on going down the main haul to check the side entries for signs of survivors. We tried to stop him, but I busted myself up and in the confusion he broke away. Tanner and the others ran after him. I'm sure they could not have made it back to the shaft, nor would I if Art here had not carried me out. Dad was out of his head, Cass, totally out of his head. He thought he was responsible for the explosion."

Cass groans, now feeling that he's responsible, because of his inadvertent chastisement of old Dawson. "Jesus, Alex! It's my fault, and I laid the blame on him! Holy Mother of Jesus!" Seeing Cass so distraught, Alex briefly forgets his own emotion as he puts a strong hand on Cass's shoulder and tells him, "You're not to blame, Cass, get that out of your head."

Chapter 12

Drill Baby, Drill

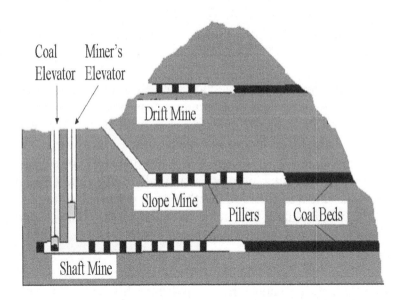

March, 1952

Morgantown, West Virginia

On a cold and windy afternoon, young Ben Dawson, now in his senior year at WVU and only two months from graduating, is in the engineering library studying geology reports and information on coal discoveries in various areas of West Virginia and Pennsylvania. As a result of his research he speculates that there may be another layer of coal under the Dawson family land, but at a greater depth. Since the explosion and closing of Mine #1, he has dreamed of starting a new mine and has a hunch that a thicker seam of coal lies deeper beneath the Dawson land.

Last year's loss of 23 men, in the mine explosion, touched a far greater number of Cascade families than just 23. A total of sixty families lost one or more loved ones. There were uncles, brothers, fathers, nephews, cousins and grandfathers included in those lost. The tragedy was devastating to the small town. Making the loss almost unbearable to many was the fact that the bodies of their loved ones were not recovered. The fire in the mine burned unabated for several weeks until the mine entrance was sealed with concrete and the mine allowed to flood. Without the pumps running, the water accumulated and rose to quench the flames and glowing walls of what must have certainly looked like the worst kind of hell.

The coalmine itself became the burial chamber for the 23 men. When one cannot honor and bury his loved ones it's difficult to find closure. Robert Dawson's widow, Lucretia, had a particularly difficult time. She insisted that her Robert was alive and would be home at any time. Each day she called Alex at his home to find out if there was any word from his father. Alex could not convince her that her beloved husband would never return. After the memorial service, even he had slipped into a depression that haunted him through the winter. His mine was closed, his men were out of work, so many families were mourning, some of them without their breadwinner. It was hard for Alex to accept. He made sure that none of the widows went without, and he provided work in the timber operation for most of the miners. He told them he could always find trees to cut. Those men not laboring in the woods, he put to work upgrading the rail line, replacing ties, packing new ballast and clearing undergrowth from the right-of-way. He figured if he could keep the men busy for a year, or two, he might get the construction company on line ahead of schedule and use many of them in that business. Nat was still a couple of years away from graduating, but he had friends that he could rely on to provide structural engineering assistance. Still Alex worried, still he hurt, and still he mourned.

The next weekend, Ben visited home and discussed with his father his theory that another layer of coal lays beneath their land, at a depth of 200 to 300 feet. Alex came alive with interest for the first time since the explosion and he and Ben decide to have some test drilling done.

Several days later, early on a brisk March morning, with snow in the mountains, Ben had Jack O'Rear, one of the mine Foremen, on a vintage company bulldozer cutting a road and clearing and area for a drill rig to sink a test hole. Jack had his little son, Teddy with him and Ben thought it fitting that young Teddy would be a part of a new adventure. Ben positioned the site for the test hole a quarter mile south of the sealed portal of the discontinued Dawson Mine #1.

Three days later he, Nat and Alex stand by as Hank Dalton, a real "up the hollow" West Virginia mountaineer and owner and operator of the drill rig, starts his machine and punches mother earth with a six inch drill bit. Hank removes a pouch of chewing tobacco from a coverall pocket, takes a huge pinch and shoves it inside his cheek. He then smacks the super-structure of the rig and yells; "Drill baby, drill!"

Through alternating layers of shale, sandstone and limestone, Hank made thirty feet the first day.

The following day being the Sabbath, the drilling was halted for the day and Ben and Nat returned to school at

Morgantown. Although he didn't expect to find coal for a week or more with a drill rate of roughly 30 feet a day, Ben none-the-less made his

father promise that he would call them immediately if the drill brought up coal. During the next several days the drill continued at the same pace, just under thirty feet per day. On the following Saturday morning, the seventh day, Ben and Nat are home again to watch the drilling. As they hang around the drilling rig with their father, the two young men find him in better spirits than they've seen for a long time. Alex asks Ben, again, about the expected depth of the coal. As Ben is about to reply, they hear a yell from Hank Dalton; "COAL!"

From a depth of 180 feet a lustrous black substance is spilling onto the floor of the rig. The Dawsons try hard to contain their excitement. It may just be a thin bed of coal, not worth pursuing. But the drill twists deeper and deeper, continuing to lift the black rock from what was once the floor of an ancient bog. The thrill mounts as the drill moves much quicker through soft bituminous coal. Two feet of coal, three feet, four, six, eight. In one hour of cutting through the soft coal the drill penetrates ten feet before it again hits rock. Nat yells, "YE-HAA." Ben is beside himself. He yells at his father, "Dad, a ten-foot seam, and it's great looking coal! Can you believe it?"

Alex is elated. He has not felt this level of excitement in years. He wishes his grandfather, Tom Dawson, could be here right now, and suddenly, he's curious that the thought of Gramps would enter his thoughts now. Why Gramps? Why not his father? He thinks it must be because Gramps was the first to discover coal on Dawson land, and it was he who started the coal operation in the beginning, so it would only be fitting that he should be here, if only in thought, to experience the rediscovery. He finally answers Ben, "Son, it's hard to believe, and I'm mighty proud of you for what you've done. You've just made a tremendous contribution to the families of Cascade."

A huge grin flashes across Ben's face. It's a handsome face, deep set, dark eyes, a strong jaw, straight nose, and angular features. His dark eyebrows accent his sandy colored hair, just like his younger brother's. He cannot contain his enthusiasm. "So Dad, what's the next step? How soon do we get started on a design?" Alex leans back against the railing of the drill rig. He rubs his jaw, a sign that he's thinking hard. "Well, son, I think we need to give some thought to bringing in some outside help." Ben's smile fades. Alex continues, "Now hold on, I know you're all fired up, and I know you and I certainly have the capability to design a shaft mine, even though neither of us have had any experience along those lines, but we need to get an operation on line fast and I need to get my men to work. The thing is, I'm not sure that we have the resources to build a whole new facility on a fast track basis."

Ben protests, "But, Dad, I don't think we need a complete new facility. I think we can use the existing tipple to start, maybe replace it in the future with a more modern design, we just need to move the coal to it with conveyors instead of by rail. We can sink the main shaft right in front of the old portal to minimize the distance to the tipple. All the service buildings and powerhouse will work as is. The only major design and build effort will be the main shaft, head frame and elevator, and the airshaft and fan. And, we can use our own men for a good part of the work. Come on, Dad, let's do it."

Alex moves from his leaning place and surveys the surrounding complex. "But, we don't have the equipment to dig the shafts, Ben, we'd need a big clamshell."

"We can rent one, Dad, or, better yet, we could buy one and sell it after the job is done. We'll spend a lot less than if we hired a big engineering company."

Alex weakens and says, "Your enthusiasm may be clouding your thinking, Ben." He turns to Nat, who has been quiet throughout the exchange between his brother and father. "Nat, what do you think."

Nat has been squatting beside the fresh coal, examining a handful. Nat looks a lot like Ben, some say not quite as handsome, others say he's the better looking of the two. He's not as serious as Ben. He's more fun loving and outgoing, but he's exceedingly clever. It feels good to have his father ask his opinion. He straightens up, and turning to his father, says, "Dad, I know you'll just think that Ben and I are young and foolishly aggressive, but I think Ben makes some good sense for a change." He glances at Ben with an ornery grin, the grin is returned, then he goes on, "We could bring in the big boys. It would cost us a bundle, and yeah, it would get us started sooner, but if we do it ourselves, and we use your men, I think they'll buy into the deal a lot stronger and feel more a part of the action. Now, this is not my thinking, it's Ben's, he's been talking about it all week, and I think he's got something."

Ben jumps in, "But Dad, these are your ideas, about involving the guys and making them more a part of the action. You've always talked about it, but Grandpa always undermined any efforts you made along those lines, he was too autocratic. But you're the final authority now, you can do what you want, you can manage in your own style."

Alex nods. He's impressed at what seems to be some real wisdom coming from his boys. And he knows they're right, it's his turn to set the tone for the Dawson Colliery Company, it's his turn. He turns back to Ben. "Well, maybe you boys can teach your old man a thing or two, let's do it."

The summer of 1952 was a busy one for the Dawson men. Ben and Nat assisted their father on the project on weekends before summer break. Of course, Ben graduated in May and was now officially an engineer. He was proud.

The entire project took the balance of 1952 and a good part of the following year. It was June, 1953 when the first ton of coal was brought to the surface of Dawson Mine #2. Many of the existing facilities from the old mine were used, but rebuilt and brought up to modern design standards. All in all, it was a very successful project.

Before the new mine got into full swing, Alex Dawson decided to have a meeting of his entire work force. On a Monday morning, they meet in the Cascade school auditorium. Alex stands at a microphone before the men. He is strangely nervous, hands sweaty, a catch in his throat. He has never had this problem. He has stood before groups of his men a hundred times. But, he has never had them all together in a somewhat formal setting like this one. There is a lot of shuffling of feet and murmuring in the large hall. He clears his throat, and speaks. "Men, I wanted you here today to get your thoughts on an idea that I've been kicking around for a while." His voice grows stronger as he proceeds; "With the start of a new mine I think it's time we Dawsons come up with some new thinking. As you know, we've been in the mining business for a long time. In 1785, my ancestor, Robert Dawson, the man my father was named for, acquired this land. He cut timber, built mills and founded the town of Cascade. My grandfather, Tom Dawson started mining coal here in 1873. Most of you men come from families who have worked for the Dawsons for several generations. A lot has changed in the mining industry since the opening of that first mine. Changes in the market for coal, changes in equipment, in methods, in relations between you and management."

"There have been numerous mergers and consolidations in the coal industry that have created huge companies with a whole lot of capital. Today these big coal companies are making it awful hard for us smaller operators to compete. I believe that we can compete, but it's going to take a different way of running this business than we've done in the past. I believe it's going to require a whole different style. An approach that means more involvement on your part; that means more listening on my part and on the part of all the management people. It's going to require a whole new way of thinking about how you're compensated."

At the sound of the word, compensation, a definite murmur rolled through the hall. Stan Hunter leans toward the man sitting next to him and whispers, "What's comsenpation?" His neighbor replies all knowingly, "That's your paycheck, Stan, your paycheck."

"Oh," Stan says, aloud.

"I want you to be involved in such a way that you share your ideas, your innovation. Let's face it, you know more about the detail, the everyday, real, down in the dirt workings of the mine, than any mine owner. If we can all be a part of the action in making Cascade #2 a more efficient and profitable operation, then we can beat the big boys and we can all prosper. So, here's what I want you to think about." Alex places a large pie chart on an easel to his right. Pointing to the chart he resumes. "I propose that any profit made from this operation be distributed as shown on this chart. Thirty percent divided among you fellows, the foremen, supers and administrative folks, in the form of a bonus at the end of each year. Fifty per-cent reinvested into the business in the form of capital improvements, that is, new equipment, modern, more productive and safer, and twenty percent to me and my family to pay us a return on our investment and our risk of that investment."

Turning from the pie chart, Alex continues. "Now, all this assumes that there is a profit. If there is no profit, then there is no bonus and there is no business. That's it men, in a nutshell. Any questions?"

There is no sound other than shuffling feet and a few whispers.

"Men, I know you've got questions and I'm staying here until they are asked."

An older man in the front row speaks. "Alex, are you serious about this, what's the catch, ain't never been a coal operator give a man any part of a profit; you been sneaking back into the cave where ol man Bolyard keeps his shine?"

A howl goes up throughout the auditorium.

A generous smile spreads over the face of Alex Dawson. "No Ramsey, I haven't been into the shine, at least not yet, I'm dead serious."

From the back a man shouts, "Hey Alex, how much money is 30 percent?"

"Well Charlie, that depends on how much, if any, profit we make. Let me put it this way, Suppose we sell a thousand dollars worth of coal. And suppose that after all expenses we clear 10 percent, or one hundred dollars of that thousand dollars. Then, thirty dollars of that hundred would be split up by all company employees, fifty dollars would be spent on equipment and improvements, and twenty dollars would be retained by us owners of the company. Of course, the government will take a chunk of your bonus just like it takes part of your paycheck, and it will take a big chunk out of us owner's share of profits."

"You mean we get thirty dollars and you only get twenty?

"Yes, Charlie, that's the deal, but keep in mind that the fifty dollars we plow back into the business means the business is more valuable and if any family member cares to sell all or part of his, or her share it could be more valuable."

"Does that mean that you might sell the company?"

"No Charlie; no plans to do that, no family member is permitted to sell a share to an outsider, but a member may want to sell to another family member and that's permitted."

Charlie rubs his chin for a moment, and then scoffs; "Ben, it sounds like the damn government is getting a big chunk of that hundred dollars - from all of us!"

"That's a fact of life, Charlie."

A young man, relatively new to the company, raises a hand.

"Go-ahead," says Alex; then adds, "You're Stan Hunter's boy, aren't you?"

"Yes Sir Mr. Dawson. Now don't get me wrong, my Pa says you're a good man, and, and you and he go back a long way, but, er, how do we know how much profit is made?"

"What's your name son?"

"Jim, sir."

"Well Jim, in the first place, I'm not Mr. Dawson, I'm Alex. Mr. Dawson was my father. Secondly, to answer your question, how do you know how much profit there is? That's easy, you look at the books, and Jim, that was a very good question and it took balls to ask it."

Jim sat up straighter in his chair and there was a murmur of agreement that the young man did have balls.

"But we don't know how to read them numbers, Alex," piped up Jim's dad, Stan Hunter.

"Then you can hire an accountant to do it for you, Stan"

"How much would that accountant cost? Stan asks."

"Well, not a lot, Stan, when you spread his cost among the group."

An old timer, in a horse voice cackles, "Alex, it sounds like you wouldn't make enough profit to make the business worthwhile."

"Now hold on Charlie, I'm not in this business just to be charitable. Let's look at it this way; suppose you guys are real, real good at what you do. Suppose you come up with some ideas which would save the operation some money, and it occurs to you that each dollar of that money goes into the profit pool, and that 30 per cent of it would find its way into your pockets. Now, don't you think that maybe, just maybe, you'd start thinking real hard about how you can do your job better? Suppose we operate so efficiently that we can sell our coal at a lower price than the big boys and as a result, get more business. And suppose we make two hundred dollars profit instead of one hundred. Then the company's take would be forty dollars instead of twenty dollars and you have made me twice as much money."

It takes a while for this to sink in. There is considerable commotion as the men trade thoughts on just what it is that Alex is proposing. Stan Hunter again asks his neighbor, "Chester, is Alex saying that we would be making a lot more money?"

Again, Chester shows his exceptional financial aptitude by saying, "It sounds like it depends on how smart we are and how hard we want to work, Stan."

"Oh," Stan mumbles. He begins to get a hint of what is going on. He thinks; "I can work smarter. Hell, I've got lots of good ideas to talk about if it will put more money in my pay envelope."

The same thought begins to spread through the auditorium. A large, redheaded man stands up in the third row and asks, "Alex, does that mean, if you get twice as much, then we would split sixty dollars instead of thirty; twice as much bonus?"

"That's right, McNamara, you're getting the idea," Alex replies.

There is a loud buzz throughout the auditorium as the men talk over what they have just heard. Suddenly, McNamara stands up again and shouts, "What are we waiting for boys, let's get out of here, we've got bloody coal to mine."

Alex shouts, "Hang on men, hang on. I've got one more important thing to discuss. Sit down. Mac, Ed, please sit down. Men, let me say one more thing."

The group slowly winds down. Alex proceeds, "There is probably not a man in this room whose family has not, at some time in the past, lost a family member to a mining accident. Lord knows many of you lost family in the explosion. Well, we can't operate that way anymore. Aside from the human misery at the loss or maiming of a loved one, I'm convinced that a safe mine is more likely to be a profitable mine. I want you men to put together what you believe to be the most effective form of a safety committee, and I suggest McNamara head it up, but who heads it up is your call, and I want the safety committee to recommend what portion of our capital investment goes toward improving safety. Now, we're getting ready to run a brand-new mine. Let's make it the safest and most efficient mine in the country." At that, a cheer went up that rattled windows across the street.

Over the course of the next few years the new shaft mine proved to be a substantial success. Suggestions on how to improve methods and safety poured in from the miners. The operation was profitable from the very beginning and each year the miners enjoyed a bigger bonus than the previous. In 1955 total pretax profits for the business was a million dollars. This gave a bonus pool of $300,000.00 to divide between the total work force of 205 men and 5 women. The split averaged $1428.00 per person, a tidy sum in 1955.

Chapter 13

A Good Year

1955

With the other businesses doing well, Alex and Nat started a construction company, Cascade Constructors. To gain practical experience Nat had worked summers, and for a year after graduating, with a large construction company out of Pittsburgh. That still left him a little skinny on job experience, so he and Alex hired a Job Superintendent with 30 years experience in heavy construction.

Also in 1955, Ben Dawson married a local girl, Marilyn Sanders. Two years later, following Ben's lead, Nat married a Morgantown girl, Alice Shaffer. During the ensuing years both men worked hard on improving and growing their businesses. Nat and his father modeled the management style of the Construction Company after the mining business, and it paid off in large measure. For a start-up company, Cascade Constructors started making money very early and was soon a big name in the industry.

Alex split most of his time between the mining and construction businesses, but still devoted a minor part of his schedule to the Timber Company. After the tragedy in 1951, the fifties turned out to be very good to the Dawsons.

At Dawson Mine #2, as Alex had promised, each year, 50% of profits was spent on improvements, and in 1957, half of one million in profits was invested in new facilities and equipment, which further improved production and safety. This allowed the Dawsons to further lower prices and attract more customers. The following year, 1958, each employee took home a bonus of $1900.00. At 1958 prices one could buy a new Chevy for $1900.00. The success of the mine and the miners infused considerable dollars into the Cascade economy.

On a clear and sunny Sunday afternoon in 1960, Ben and Marilyn Dawson paid a visit to the home of Ben's parents, Alex and Sarah. Ben's grandmother, Lucretia, who is now 85, also lives with Alex and Sarah. After an exquisite dinner, the family takes coffee to the front porch where they continue to catch up on each other's activities. Sarah has been busy with community projects, Marilyn is active on the school board, and the men, although they see each other most days, are usually too busy to get into family matters.

The three ladies have settled into comfortable chairs while Ben and Alex sit on an old walnut bench. After a few minutes of idle talk, Sarah asks the two younger family members her standard question, "Alright, you two, when do I get my first grandchild?"

Marilyn turns to Ben and in a manner that suggests anger, but which is, in fact, good-humored banter, says, "Ben Dawson, will you explain to this busybody that our family planning is a private matter."

Ben smiles and says succinctly, "Mom, It's a private matter." Then, Marilyn turns to her mother-in-law, a woman she admires very much, and continues, "Sarah, we've been trying for the past year, it just hasn't happened yet."

Sarah's face takes on a sad expression, but only for a moment, then it lights up. "Well, it will, dear," she says, "it will. Be patient and don't put a lot of pressure on yourselves, it will happen."

Ben changes the subject. Turning to his grandmother, Lucretia, he says, "Grandmother, Lu, you're without a doubt still the prettiest lady in these mountains."

Lucretia, never fully recovered from the loss of her beloved Robert, for the past few years has been showing increased signs of dementia. She smiles at Ben and says, incorrectly, "Oh, Alex, you're still full of it. You sound just like your daddy; he always said I was the prettiest girl in West Virginia."

Ben goes along. "Well, he was right, and you still are," he says. She blushes. Ben again changes the subject, turning to his father, he says, "Dad, I hate to talk shop on such a nice Sunday afternoon, but there's been something I've wanted to talk about and haven't been able to pin you down."

"What is it, son?"

"Well, you know the old fan houses from Number One are still standing, and I think, for safety reasons, we need to dismantle them and fill and cover the shafts."

Sarah and Marilyn take up another topic, but Lucretia, overhearing Ben's suggestion to Alex, panics. She now has Ben correctly identified and in a pleading voice, appeals, "Oh, Ben, you must never cover the Blackwater shaft! Robert will have no way out of the mine if you cover it up, that's his only way out, you see, you must never cover it up." Ben looks mortified. He has always realized that Lucretia has never accepted his grandfather's death, but he didn't realize that after all these years she still expects him to come home."

Ben does not quite know how to respond to his grandmother. Alex helps him out. To humor his confused mother, he offers, "Perhaps, Ben, you can come up with a way to solve the safety problem but still leave a way for dad to get out."

"Yes," responds Lucretia, "He must have a way to come home, Ben."

Ben recognizes the need to soothe his grandmother's concern. "Of course, Grandmother, we'll figure out a way, he says."

"Good," she replies, and pats his hand.

A few days later, Ben has a crew raze the Laurel fan house and fill the airshaft with shale and gravel from nearby Laurel Creek. But, before he addresses the Blackwater shaft situation, Lucretia's heart begins to fail and he, along with Marilyn and his folks, Nat and Alice, and other family members, is at her bedside as the end nears. In a delicate and feeble voice Lucretia asks Ben to come nearer.

"What is it, Grandmother?" He asks, leaning close and taking her hand.

"Ben," she pleads in a frail whisper, "You must promise me that you will never close the Blackwater shaft." She makes a barely audible coughing sound, then continues, "Promise me, Ben, that you will always leave a way for my Robert to come home."

Ben's eyes fill with tears. His parents, Nat, and the others lean closer to try to hear what Grandmother Lu is saying, but only Ben can understand her words. Alex does not need to hear, he knows instinctively what his mother is asking of Ben. Lucretia holds a determined look at her grandson's face. With a newfound clarity of voice and mind, and with startlingly penetrating eyes, she again appeals, "Ben, promise me."

The tears roll freely down Ben's cheeks, dripping onto Lucretia's lacy blue gown. He whispers, "Grandmother, I love you, and I love Grandfather, and I promise you faithfully that I will always keep a safe way for Grandfather to come home to you."

A smile slowly transforms her pale face into a picture of tranquility. She gives Ben's hand a delicate squeeze. With her eyes now closed, she whispers, "Thank you, Ben, thank you."

A few days after Lucretia's funeral, Ben has a crew at the Blackwater fan house. He supervises the crew himself, not leaving any chance of error by delegating the task. He has the men cap the top of the airshaft with two feet of concrete reinforced with #11 rebar. He leaves a 30-inch manhole opening with a cast steel cover immediately over the ladder. The ladder is still firmly anchored to the sidewall of the shaft. He covers the reinforced concrete slab with one to two inches of topsoil and distributes grass seed over the surface. He plants a young maple tree next to the covered slab. With grass and weeds growing around the manhole he figures it will remain unseen and forgotten. He figures that a man who needs to come up the shaft could easily lift the manhole cover and an inch or two of soil, thereby keeping the promise to his grandmother, that he would always maintain a way for her Robert to escape the mine. For Ben, the maple will always mark the spot.

Chapter 14

A Girl and a Boy

1968

Morgantown, West Virginia

It was several years before Ben and Marilyn finally presented Sarah Dawson with a grandchild. It was a healthy and squalling boy. Sarah was there with her son when the baby was brought from the delivery room at University Hospital. Marilyn and Ben named him, Colbert, but they call him, Cole. The people of Cascade thought it a fitting name for a boy from a coal mining town.

A year after the birth of Cole Dawson, another child is born to a mining family in West Virginia. Angelo and Theresa Valentini become the proud parents of a little girl. They name her, Nicola, after her grandfather, Nicholas. The place where this child is born is far different from the charming community of Cascade. The town of Glen Haven is almost as grimy as it was when Angelo was a boy. Nicola's parents do not have the wealth, nor wield the influence of the Dawson child's family, but she's just as loved.

It's in a coal company house, on the hill above those lifeless waters of Trout Run, that Nicola lives with her family, in the same house that her father spent his youth, although the house has been renovated somewhat since those days. Now, the home is insulated and there is running water and a septic system. Little Nicola is a sparkling diamond in Angelo Valentini's life. He adores his little girl. He has two sons, but there has been two generations since Valentini men have been blessed with a daughter and Angelo certainly considers his little girl a blessing. She has the same beautiful features as her mother, and her Poppa often says that God must have broken the mold after creating two such beautiful girls.

By the time Nicola enters school, in the seventies, conditions have improved substantially in the coal mining industry, even in the southern coalfields. Coal removal is now done with very large cutting and loading machines. Over the years, since the brutal and bloody mine wars of the twenties and thirties, the United Mine Workers Union, under the leadership of John L. Lewis, had won many hard fought concessions from the mine operators. Many years before, one of the critical victories of the miners was in the area of safety. The National Mine Safety Board had been formed and the danger in the coalmines, although still ever present, was substantially lowered. Unfortunately for Angelo Valentini, it was not lowered enough. His beautiful little Nicola is only eight years old when her Poppa doesn't come home from the mine one day.

They don't tell her how her Poppa is killed, that he was in front of the large cutting machine, replacing one of the hardened steel cutters, when the machine's operator inadvertently started the cutters rotating and moved the machine forward into the coal face. There was no room for Angelo to escape, and his calls could not be heard over the noise of the machine. They just tell Nicola that he was hurt in the coal mine like his father and his grandfather, and he went to heaven to join them. The people in the mining camps are a stoic lot, they have to be; life is too hard to be otherwise. But it is still heart wrenching for Nicola's mother and brothers to tell Nicola of her father's death.

Nicola doesn't cry when they tell her that her poppa went to heaven, nor does she speak. She's angry at her poppa for not coming home. They don't explain to Nicola why she can't see him and why his casket is tightly closed. She doesn't talk for two months and when she does resume speaking, she's not the same bright and exuberant little girl as before. She won't cry for another three years, won't flush away the pain with her tears, but by then, there is a deep and lasting anger in her life - an anger that will not go away.

Chapter 15

Cormorant

1982, Teheran, Iran

A man enters a dingy cafe, on a dirty street, far from the center of the city. Coming in from the bright sunlight, he needs a moment for his eyes to adjust to the dim light in the building. The man is a native Iranian, in his late thirties, with heavy brows and deep set, dark eyes, alert, piercing eyes that dart quickly about as he surveys the room. His face is rugged, but in a mysteriously handsome way, with sharp features and a three-day beard.

The cafe has a pungent smell. Aromas drifting from the dirty kitchen are sharp and peppery. The walls are a dull green, the floor a mixture of faded tiles that must have been an agglomeration of leftovers when they were placed there forty years before.

The Iranian's eyes finally find what they are searching for, a figure at a corner table in the darkened rear of the room. After another quick survey of the room, he walks to the table and nods to the figure. "Greetings Teriq," he murmurs as he pulls back a heavy red chair which has large chips in the paint, exposing the yellow coat beneath.

"Hello Omar. Welcome home; sit. May I get you a drink?

"Just coffee" The man called, Tariq, waves to a skinny man, in an apron, standing by a door to the small kitchen. "Two coffees," he orders. Then he returns his attention to the new arrival. "Ah, Omar, you look well, how long has it been, six months?" It's apparent from his appearance and his manner that Tariq is the older of the two, not by far, but older, and is taking control of the conversation.

"You joke with me Tariq, you know exactly how long it has been since you last met me here."

"Well, these days I am not always so sure of time. But, you're correct, my friend, it has been six months since we decided on a target date, and yes, this is it. So then, how was your trip, have you been successful, did you find us new people, Omar?"

"Yes, I think so. One in particular looks very, very promising. I have been working with a young fellow who is

111

a student at the University of Southern California at Berkeley. His mother is the sister of Saeed and Uday Ramadan, two younger brothers who were killed at the Embassy takeover in 79. She has been sympathetic to our cause since the early sixties. Papers were created to give her an identity as a widow whose Italian husband died in Milano in 1961. Our people got her into the US through Canada. Her boy is the illegitimate son of one of our people who was active on the Berkeley campus at that time."

Omar interrupts his talk when the skinny man brings two cups and a small ceramic pot to the table. Tariq pours the coffee as Omar continues. "The boy was born in 1963. He knows not his father; the man never provided any help. The mother was very close to her slain brothers and her anger is deep. Although living as an Italian American she has discreetly educated her son in the ways of her homeland and has infused into his mind an understanding of our cause. At the university the boy studies electronic engineering. I have been working with him very carefully for most of these six months now and I am positive that I have his trust. I am certain that he will, one day, play a vital role in our cause, not soon, but someday."

"Does he understand, Omar, that if he joins us he will be undertaking a very long and dangerous journey."

"He does, Tariq. More than that, he's extremely enthusiastic. I believe he will be a dedicated and humble servant. He's aware that without our financial help his mother would be under great hardship, perhaps even being discovered to have false papers. Also, his ability to continue his studies would be in jeopardy. He's a very bright boy with excellent marks. His hatred for the murderers of his uncles is strong; he was 16 when they were killed. For this reason, I believe I must be very careful and very patient. He's still young, only 19, but I will work with him closely over the course of the next few years in order to prepare him for an assignment well into the future."

"This sounds very interesting, Omar. You say he's studying electronics?"

"Yes, and with electronics training I think it would be very easy to get him into the American Navy. If he could get into their electronic warfare group, and with his intelligence I believe there is an excellent chance of that, he would be in a position to provide us with very unusual and valuable information on a global basis."

Tariq smiles. "Omar, I am highly impressed. With the growing ability of the Americans to capture worldwide communications, if things go as you suggest this young man could ultimately be in a position to provide information not only about American activities, but also about the devils across our borders."

Omar is very pleased that his superior is impressed. His face brightens as he replies. "Precisely, Tariq, but it's not a sure thing. It will take careful planning and special grooming of this boy. Also, I will need continued financing to help his mother. That will be the most important carrot."

"That will not present a problem, Omar. Spend as much time with this boy as it requires. Tell me of anything you need in order to succeed. Make of this boy a man with purpose. Make him a special advocate; one who is willing to die for our cause. But, as you say, be very patient, we must not rush this kind of endeavor."

"Yes, Tariq."

"Omar, what do you call this boy?"

"I have given him the code name, Cormorant," Omar replies. Tariq smiles. "Cormorant. The bird that swims under water. I like that," he says.

Over the course of several months Omar discreetly meets "Cormorant" on a regular basis. To the young man, Omar is a hero, a protagonist, and a champion; a fighter who has been under fire. Omar has described to the young man, in great detail, several incidents where Omar and his group have attacked US military personnel and civilians working on defense projects in Teheran. He also boasts about his action during the 1979 takeover of the US Embassy where the uncles were killed.

Omar recites, over and over, the purpose of his group, Citizens Mujahedin of Iran (CMI). The group was formed in Teheran during the early sixties by he and other college children of Iranian merchants. CMI seeks to counter what is perceived as excessive Western influence on the controlling regime in Iran. They seek to paint a picture, in Iran, of Americans as immoral, atheistic murderers. Following a philosophy that mixes Marxism and Islam, CMI has developed into the largest and most active armed Iranian dissident group.

Omar preaches that the CMI strategy of anti-Western activity and attacks on the interests of the clerical regime in Iran is working, that they plan to scale up terrorism against the United States both domestically and abroad and, most importantly, that they plan to get "Cormorant" positioned to play a major role in those activities. To the impressionistic young man, Omar is a god, a leader he will follow anywhere.

In 1985 "Cormorant" is ready to begin his adventure. He joins the United States Navy. After outstanding performance in a battery of psychological and aptitude tests, he applies for and is accepted into the Navy and Marine Corps Intelligence Training Center at Virginia Beach, Virginia. He is one of the brightest young men in the program.

Chapter 16

The Library

Early May, 1990

Morgantown, West Virginia

It's six o'clock on a Wednesday evening. Cole Dawson sits in a comfortable, old, green, overstuffed, chair in the student lounge of the downtown campus library, at West Virginia University. The library is housed in an old building, one of the first on the grounds. The walls are paneled in dark cherry. Wild cherry, native, cut and milled in Taylor County. The ceiling has an intricate pattern of beige plaster and cherry molding. It looks like something out of an old English castle. It's not a bright room. The lighting, which was originally by gas, was replaced with electricity in the late 1800's. It was updated in the thirties and is now in desperate need of upgrading again. The room has an old smell. A smell of old wood and old books. Old books have a unique smell. Not quite musty, not quite stale, just a, sort of, worn out kind of smell. Cole is in his senior year and like three generations of Dawson men before him; he will soon graduate from the school of Mining Engineering. Cole is a very well balanced young man, and exceptionally down to earth for someone from a family as wealthy as his is and with a mother who dotes on him. He has had a good life. He gets along extremely well with his parents. He and his father, Ben, have always been active together. They enjoy hunting, fishing, golf, diving; anything to get them outdoors. Cole is reading a book on earthen dam failures. His father has asked him to bone up on the subject because he foresees the need to construct a new containment reservoir at the Dawson mine complex.

Cole's attention is interrupted by the lively conversation of two girls seated behind him. One of them in particular, sounds rather passionate as she describes to her friend a subject on which Cole is reasonably well versed, mine accidents.

"But, you just don't understand! The coal operators in this state control the government, Jaime, and they do exactly as they please. Their actions cause the deaths of hundreds of men each year and in the process they make themselves rich. I hate coal operators, I hate them!" Cole winces at the comment.

The other girl responds, "How do you expect me to make a difference, though, my goals aren't the same as yours. I don't want to be a crusader; I just want to teach poly-sci at the high school level."

"But, there you are, you can make a difference. You can be a messenger. Think of all those lives you can touch, and your students can carry your message to the parents."

"But I don't have a message, Nicki. You have a message. Listen, I appreciate how you feel and I think what you want to accomplish is cool, very admirable, but don't impose your message of hatred for mine owners on me. When you become a congresswoman, you'll have the power to do something, I just want to teach."

The girl who Cole presumes to be Nicki becomes more frustrated. "Jaime, come on," she protests, "why can't you feel what I feel?"

Things grow quiet for a while, which disappoints Cole. He was beginning to enjoy the drama. He was also able to get a quick glance at one of the girls, but he doesn't know which voice she belongs to. What a knockout. He hopes she's the crusader - he likes her spirit. The talk resumes, but in a more subdued tone, and it's the crusader speaking. "Well, maybe you can at least help me find some information to support my argument. I need to find out how many men died in the worst West Virginia coalmine disaster in this century, and where it occurred."

Cole takes the cue. He turns in his chair and looks at the two girls. They are only a few feet away. It's his first good look at them. He's instantly attracted to the one with the dark hair, the one he got a quick glance at before. He sputters the words, "three hundred and sixty-two."

The girl with the dark hair looks up. "I beg your pardon?" she asks, much more softly than she was speaking before. She's looking directly into Cole's eyes. Her own eyes are

117

dark, but bright and inquisitive. *God, you're beautiful*, he says to himself, and he feels his face flush with delight that hers is the voice of the crusader.

He swallows hard and tries again: "There were 362 men killed in the Monongah mine explosion at Fairmont in 1907."

She looks teasingly curious. "How do you know that?" she asks with a smile, a terribly sensuous smile.

Shit! He's not prepared for that question. He would very much like to get to know this girl, and based on what he knows so far, it's not a good idea to admit to having anything to do with coalmines. *Think fast, Dawson, think --- -- "Uh, well, I just happened to read that somewhere recently and, it just kind of stuck with me, I guess."

"Oh," she remarks. Then after a short pause asks, in a most seductive voice, "Do you think, perhaps you could recall? It sounds like it may be a source that could help me." She finds this good looking, not so smooth, sort of funny man, interesting. She knows she can find the information in the library, or on the Internet, but thinks it may be a more exciting pursuit with his help.

He scrambles. "You know, I don't really remember where I read it, but, I have this friend in the mining school and I bet he could help us."

He gets up, walks around his chair to where the two girls sit, pulls up a straight back chair and sits on it in reverse, with his arms resting on the back of the chair. Looking directly at the dark-haired beauty, he introduces himself. "I'm Cole Dawson. If you're interested, I'm sure he wouldn't mind helping. His name is Fred Lockheart."

"Hi, I'm Nicola Valentini," she says, "and this is my best friend, Jaime Siebert."

Cole heard nothing after her name. He's utterly captivated by this girl. He nods Jaime's way and says, "Hi, very nice to meet you both," but did so without taking his eyes away from Nicola. Jaime is annoyed by this intruder who doesn't give her so much as a glance. She's remarkably pretty herself, and she knows it. She's tall and slender. Her body flexes almost erotically as she moves. Her hair is naturally red and its color is especially vivid against her light, yet radiant complexion. Her features are precise, and placed in a symmetry that is accurate to the tiniest millimeter. She says to Nicola, "Nicki, I'll be happy to help you find some stuff, they'll have all kinds of statistics in the library. You don't have to go to a guy in mining school."

But Nicola has no intentions of continuing research on her report without the help of this man called Cole Dawson. And she likes his name. She says it slowly in her mind, *Cole Dawson.* She takes in his appearance. Most remarkable is the smile, the tender, warm, honest, boyish, almost devil-may-care, smile. His sandy colored hair seems to fight with itself to stay in one place. It has delightful curves and waves and turns, and it tumbles in an unplanned array of locks, which seem to be seeking; seeking a place to find cover. A firm jaw and a strong neck establish a foundation for a kind and gentle and youthful face that is framed in soft angles reminiscent of Greek sculpture. Intense brows shield hazel eyes that have specks of amber and gold dust. His nose wrinkles when he breaks into that tantalizing smile. He sits with strong arms resting on the chair back and where he straddles the chair his thighs press against the fabric of his jeans. This and his broad shoulders give a message of strength and vitality.

She suddenly realizes that, just as she's studying him, he likewise explores her every movement and expression. She finds herself having difficulty holding eye contact, afraid that he'll see her blushing from the obvious attention he's giving. She shifts in her chair, looks at Jaime and responds to her offer. "But I think someone who has studied mining could offer insights that we may never think of, Jaime. And, since Cole is being so kind I think I would like to accept his offer of help."

"Whatever," Jaime sighs, in a failed attempt to act as though she doesn't care. She rises from her chair, pushing it back noisily and frowning, says; "I think I'll go to the house and study, it's too hot in here. How about you, wanna come with me?"

119

Nicola glances quickly at Cole, then back to Jaime. "I think I'll stay here, for a while. I'll see you later, okay?"

"Sure," Jaime says, without feeling, tosses her hair and walks away.

Nicola looks at Cole. "I think I've hurt her feelings," she whispers.

Cole looks bewildered. "But you didn't do anything," he offers.

Nicola is amused that he didn't pick up on Jaime's jealously. *Obviously*, she tells herself, *Jaime is jealous of the attention he's giving to me while he utterly ignored her.* She replies to Cole, "Oh, I think she feels I've been kind of ignoring her lately, but she'll be okay in a little while, so when do you think we can start digging up some stuff on coal mine fatalities?"

Cole pulls his chair a little closer. "Anytime," he says, "But tell me a bit about what it is exactly that you're after, give me some background." As Nicola begins speaking, Cole is transfixed with her beauty. Her skin is a creamy pearl white, her face framed in hair as black as, he muses, coal. Her hair is cropped short and kind of swept up in the back. Her face is a beautifully symmetrical oval with remarkably defined features. Eyes that are as dark as her hair have a smoldering flame deep inside that flickers almost imperceptibly, but he sees it. Her brows arch delicately over those exotic eyes. Her nose is straight, with just the right flair to the nostrils, and turned up ever so slightly. Her mouth is forbiddingly sensuous, with defining curves exactly where he thinks they should be. Her ears peek from under her hair like miniature white kittens peering from beneath a midnight sky. Above a gentle, but determined jaw line, glowing cheeks terminate beneath crests of elegant cheekbones. Her slender neck descends to a perfect transition with her shoulders. Her ample breasts have provocative curves and just a hint of cleavage escapes the opening of her blouse. Even where she sits, her body appears lithe and graceful and unremittingly proportioned.

Suddenly, he's aware that she's speaking, answering his

question, "and I'm majoring in political science, and I want to do a paper on the status of mine safety in the state and what I think can be done on the state and federal level, through legislation, to improve it."

He's close enough now to notice the fragrance of her cologne. The scent seems intertwined with the smell of fresh soap. The combined bouquet is heavenly. He wants to say, *God, you smell sweet!* But instead asks, "Why is this important to you?"

Nicola suddenly becomes passionate. "Because mine owners are greedy and have no concept of fairness or empathy toward the miners. They have no regard for their lives, they maintain horrible working conditions and if a miner is killed, their only concern is the fact that they have lost some production of their precious coal." Her dark eyes are filled with fire as she finishes.

Cole takes a deep breath. *Wow!* He thinks, *what gave her this picture of mine owners? Yes, some have been ruthless in the past, but this is 1990, she's back in the thirties. How can I tactfully find out what's pushing her button?* He asks, "Nicola, how do you come to have this opinion of mine operators?"

Her back stiffens. "I know, believe me, I know. They killed my father! And they killed my grandfather and my great-grandfather. My dad was the kindest, dearest, most loving father in the world. His death was so terrible. I never even got to see him."

"How do you mean?" he asks, sympathetically.

"I mean, I couldn't see him after the accident, after he died. They wouldn't let us see him, I, I really would rather not talk about it, okay?"

He's hurt her and he feels awful. "Sure, I'm sorry. I didn't mean to upset you, I'm really sorry."

Nicola regains her composure. "I'm okay now. It bothered me a lot when I was younger; I was eight when Poppa died and it was really hard, especially since I could not see him. Years later, the doctors told me that I never got closure, that it would have helped if I could have seen his body

121

afterwards, but apparently, he was injured so badly that they had to keep the casket closed. I was very angry with him for not coming back to me."

Cole can feel her hurt intensely. Her lovely eyes are on the verge of tearing and he feels responsible because it was his probing that upset her. He tells her again, "Look, Nicola, I really am sorry that my questions brought back those bad memories," then adds, awkwardly, "can I get you a coffee? There's a machine down the hall."

She reaches out and touches his arm. "That's sweet of you, yes, that sounds really good, but maybe we could walk downtown and get a cup at the Mugshot." *Oh my God,* she thought, *what an idiot I am, that's too forward.* But it seemed so natural to ask him that.

"Hey, that's great!" he beams, "and they have a strong brew that I really like."

Minutes later, with jackets donned, they walk toward the main street of Morgantown. She points to the book he carries and asks, "What's the book you were reading?"

"Oh, it's on dam failures." Thank God it's not one of his mine texts.

"Dam failures? Why a book on dam failures, are you studying fixing dams?"

He chuckles. "Well, sort of, I guess. I'm actually studying engineering and if one is going to design a good dam it helps to know what causes them to fail sometimes."

"I see," she says. "And what kind of engineer designs dams?"

"Uh, well, a civil engineer, I guess" he says. Then he thinks, *Aw shit! Why did I say it that way?*

"So you're going to be a civil engineer?"

He almost panics, *Oh God, I don't want to lie to her.* His mind races. "Well, not exactly, I, well, I may change, I'm just not sure yet."

"Oh, I guess I assumed you were a senior," she says as they arrive at a cross street and wait for the light to change, then looks up at him curiously and adds with a delightfully teasing laugh, "You look like a senior, but forgive me if I

122

make you older than you are."

He grins. "Uh, yes, I am, I'm a senior, but I, you know, I may go on to add some civil engineering courses to round out my schedule."

"Well then, what kind of engineer are you planning to be?" *Damn, she's relentless. How do I get out of this. I can't tell her yet that I'm a mine engineer and come from a long line of damned mine owners.* He stutters, "I've been kind of leaning towards a mixture of electrical, structural, geological and civil." *God! That was beautiful, and it's very near the truth.*

Just as they arrive at The Mugshot, but before they enter, Nicola stops and asks, "Are you sure coffee is okay, would you rather have a beer?" She's looking up to his eyes. At six feet even, he stands only a few inches taller than she. Her proportions are perfect, he thinks. And those eyes, those magnificently sensuous eyes. "Coffee sounds great," he says, softly.

"Good," she replies, and they enter The Mugshot. The coffee shop is a student hangout and it's noisy. They get two coffees, find a table in the back and resume their conversation. As they sit, she asks, "So, Mr. Cole Dawson, what does an electric, structure, geologist and civil engineer call himself, I know! An E-S-G-C Engineer, am I right?"

He laughs. "Well, not exactly." *Shit! I'm in trouble now; maybe I can change the subject.* "But let's talk about you. Did I hear your friend say you're going to be a congresswoman?"

"Someday, maybe. And when I am elected do you want to know what my first attempted law enactment will be?"

"Yes, I'd like very much to know that." *Whew, I think I'm in the clear.*

"My first proposed action will be a law that requires all men to be straightforward and honest in their discussions with women."

Now he sweats. *God, is she perceptive.* "Uh huh, okay," he half-smiles nervously. "Well, I guess that means we're back on the subject of engineering?"

She looks troubled. "I guess so. What's up, Cole? Somehow I get the feeling that you're not being completely honest with me. Are you a senior? Are you in engineering school? I know we've only known each other for, what, maybe 30 minutes? But if we should, perhaps get to know each other better; well for all I know you may be a serial killer." As she finishes, the troubled look is gradually replaced with a grin. *Wow, this girl comes right to the point, she doesn't keep you guessing. I really like that. I guess I'm done for, unless I lie,* he decides. He holds up his right hand, "Nicola Valentini, I swear to you, I am a senior and I am in engineering school and I am going to graduate in May, and I am not a serial killer, cross my heart," and he makes a cross on his chest. "And you're going to be a ---- ?"

Why am I drawn to this girl, she's a witch, or something. "A Structural Engineer," he lies. *Aw shit! Why not tell her the damned truth? Because, stupid, she'd dismiss you in a nano second, that's why, because she's totally against mine owners.*

She gives him a cheerful look, and says, "A Structural Engineer. That's good. I think I could like a Structural Engineer."

Cole has a myriad of thoughts careening around inside his skull. She likes him; he knows that. He likes her a lot, that's for sure. She's exceptionally bright and perceptive. She has a real hang-up about mine owners, bordering on paranoia. And he just told her a great big lie, something that he would never normally do. *I'm off to a great start. Ok, let's get away from this engineering stuff and find out more about her.* "Ok, now can we talk about you, Nicola? Like, where are you from and how did you get such a beautiful name?"

She blushes a tiny bit, and then smiles. "Thank you. My father named me. It's very Italian. Normally, in America, it would be, Nicole, oh, that's interesting; it's almost the same as your name, Cole."

He grins broadly. "I like that, Cole and Nicole. Sounds like twins, except, I don't think we'd pass as identical."

She scrunches up her nose a bit and smiles. "But I don't use

Nicole, no offense, but Poppa didn't like it if someone called me that, he felt that I should be proud of my Italian heritage."

"He was right, you should be very proud," Cole replied, "And I like Nicola better, it sounds more, you know, romantic like, or, continental." He says her name slowly, "Nicola Valentini. That's it; it's continental."

"Well, I don't know about that, but anyway, my friends call me Nicki," she replies with a cute little laugh. "And," she continues, "to answer the rest of your question, I'm from a tiny community in the southern part of the state, Wyoming County, I don't think you'd know the place, Glen Haven."

"Sure I know the pla-," he catches himself. Yes, he knows that the Headley family has a coalmine at Glen Haven, but she wouldn't expect him to know the place. He quickly shifts gears, --- "the place. I knew a guy in my freshman year that was from there." *Shit! Another lie.*

She looks curious. "Who was he, Cole? That would have been my senior year in high school and I don't know anyone the year before me who came here to school, I don't even know any boys from Glen Haven, at least none near my age, who went to college."

"Oh," he stumbles, "maybe it was one of those other Glen places, like, Glen Jean, or Glenwood, there are several of them, I must be thinking of the wrong one."

"Yes," she laughs, "there are a lot of 'Glen' places in West Virginia. How about you, Cole, where are you from?"

That was a close one! He's glad she changed the subject. "I'm from Cascade," he answers.

"Where's that?"

"It's a small town up in Preston County, not too far from Kingwood."

"Oh, I know where Kingwood is, Jaime and I went there with some other girls for the Buckwheat Festival last fall."

"That's cool," he says with a smile, "did you eat lots of pancakes?"

"We did," she laughed, "and then we had ice cream and cotton candy and a bunch of other stuff. Jaime got so sick, oh, it was awful! We had to wash out her sweatshirt to get rid of the smell before coming home."

As Cole laughs, she catches him off guard with her next question, "What does your father do?"

"I beg your pardon?" He pretends not to hear, stalling for time.

"Your father, mine was a coal miner and both my brothers work in the mine, what does yours do for a living? Is he a serial killer, too?"

"You have two brothers?" He asks, further stalling.

"They're my big brothers and they protect me from serial killers."

Cole laughs, and then seriously, says. "I hope they'll like me."

"I hope they will too, they can be very, very mean," she says with a sinister look.

He chuckles, and then soberly says, "I don't think Jaime likes me."

"Are you kidding!" She giggles. "Jaime would like you very much, if she knew you. She was just miffed because you didn't pay her any attention. She's not used to that."

"She's not?" He asks.

"Not a bit. She has boys chasing her all the time. Sometimes I worry about her, though."

He looks puzzled. "Why, why do you worry?"

She scrunches up her nose. "Oh, I don't know, just that, well, she seems to need attention. I think it's because she was so close to her father, he was in the military and they moved around a lot, so it was hard for her to make friends and she grew very close to him. Then, when she was very small, her father left, just left without so much as a goodbye to his little girl. She was crushed. I think it affected her self-assurance. Her mother remarried and Jaime's new stepfather was a cold man, showed her no attention. Now she seems overly friendly, to guys, I mean, so a lot of guys hang around her, and if she's had a couple of beers she gets, well she, oh, I don't think I should say anymore," and a sad look flows over her face.

They are both quiet for a moment, and then he asks, "Where in Wyoming County is Glen Haven?"

"In the middle," she says with a grin, then, "so what does your father do? And your mother, does she work?"

A way out of his problem pops into his mind. "My dad is in the lumber business, timbering and lumber. The Dawson Lumber Company." *There, that's the truth*, he tells himself, then continues, "We have a large tract of hardwood forestland and a sawmill. My mother doesn't work, but she stays very active trying to make Cascade the cultural center of the universe."

"Really!" She remarks with excitement, "I would love to visit your town some day." Then her exuberance fades and a look of disgust clouds her pretty face as she says, "Glen Haven is a mining community along Trout Run, a dirty little creek that carries acid pollution into the rivers. The water quality is supposed to be controlled, but the mine companies have too much influence and they get away with murder, literally murder, Cole." Her eyes again have the fire in them. She continues, her voice trembling with passion, "They've killed all the fish in the creek and probably half the fish in the Ohio, and the miners; they have killed so many poor miners. All mine owners should be put on trial like they do for war crimes."

Nicola spent the next two hours telling Cole how the mining companies had raped and pillaged the land and maimed and murdered the miners, and hampered opportunity for the young and took away the dignity of the old. She talked about growing up in the remote mountain area and how she promised herself as a young girl that she would overcome the hardship and one day make something of herself, and how she hoped to become a congresswoman and help the poor and struggling humanity in Appalachia.

She talked about how she studied so hard in high school, hoping for an academic scholarship, and she succeeded, and she was here in her junior year majoring in Political Science, and she was determined to make a difference in the world, and she worked a part time job to pay her rent. And, the

127

more she talked, the more Cole Dawson was drawn to her.

Finally, after finishing her second mug of coffee, Nicola looks at her watch. "Oh wow!" she exclaims, "It's after nine, where did the time go?" She looks at Cole. Her eyes suddenly seem somber. "I think I'd better go, Cole. I need to study and I promised Jaime I'd help her with a paper tonight."

He's amazed at how much her feelings and emotions are expressed in her eyes. "Do you really need to, Nicki? Can't we talk for a little while more, there's so much I want to know."

"But I've been doing all the talking," she complains with a smile. Then, continuing to smile, she says, "And I've learned so little about you! I just know you're a serial killer, that's why you were so mysterious about what kind of engineer you are and I still don't believe you're an engineer at all. You're probably an axe murderer who preys on innocent young damsels and, and you just called me, Nicki. I don't remember giving you permission to do that."

"I'm sorry, may I call you Nicki?" he asks with a grin.

"Only if you promise you're not a murderer," she replies with an impish expression.

"I promise, but, if I were an axe murderer, could I assume you're an innocent young damsel?" He asks with a wide grin.

"I am a damsel, I am young, and I am ever so innocent," she says, again with that impish smile that he thinks she should patent.

"So, can we stay and talk?"

"I would really love to, Cole, but I did promise Jaime. Perhaps another time?"

"Tomorrow?" He pleads.

"Maybe. Can we talk about it while you walk me home?"

He grins. "But I don't have my axe with me."

Over the course of the next three weeks Cole and Nicki see each other often. Nicki is busy with classes, homework and her job, so it's difficult for her to find a lot of time to spend with Cole, but they manage to squeeze in short meetings over a drink or sandwich, a movie, canoeing on Cheat Lake, Drinking Margaritas at the Chili Pepper. They thoroughly enjoy each other's company and they've both developed deep feelings for the other. Cole has almost told Nicki that he loves her, but hasn't. It can't be, it can't happen this fast, he tells himself. He's afraid to move too quickly, for fear of scaring her away, sensing that she has an unusually strong commitment to a career and may not want a long-term relationship at this time.

Also, since their first evening together, she has twice become overly emotional when discussing her home town of Glen Haven, and mining companies, and he's afraid that her feelings reach beyond what's psychologically healthy. This causes him concern because he has not yet figured out how to tell her that his family is in the coal business and is afraid that when he does, she'll be so overcome with emotion that there's no telling how she'll react. To complicate matters, he's lied to her. He wants to confess to his dishonesty, and he wants to do so before telling her how much he loves her, but being so unsure what her reaction will be, he's locked in indecision.

Nicki is convinced that she must be in love with Cole. During that first evening she was captivated by his smile, his warmth, his kind manner, his boyish charm, sense of humor, his strength, confidence and, yes, even his forthrightness, in spite of his obvious hedging on the "engineering" question. But beyond liking those qualities in him, she has a feeling that she can't describe. She's tried. She tried telling Jaime what she feels for Cole, but she couldn't find the right words. When she's with Cole she almost forgets all her goals and ambitions, just wants to be with him a little longer and she fights herself to regain control and discipline. She aches when she's not with him, can't concentrate for any length of time on any subject without his presence invading her thoughts, cannot imagine living a full life without him, but yet, she asks herself, can this be real? Can it happen this quickly? And he's not yet mentioned the word, love.

On a morning in late May, just two days before Cole graduates, he calls Nicki to ask if they could see each other that day. "Oh, Gosh, Cole, I have to study for a final and do some shopping, and I have to work this evening, but I so want to see you."

"So, can we squeeze in an hour?" He asks.

"I need to shop for groceries, it's my turn, maybe you could go with me?"

"Great, I love shopping with pretty girls, what time?"

"I promised myself I would study until three, how about then?"

Later, as Cole leaves his apartment, he takes his mail out of the box and carries it to his car as he struggles to get into a light jacket. As he gets into his car he places the mail in a tray of the console, just behind the gear selector. What he doesn't notice is, one envelope is boldly printed with the Dawson Colliery Company logo.

Three minutes later, he pulls up in front of Nicki's apartment. She waves from the window where she's been studying and soon is out the door and walking to his car. He reaches across and opens her door. As he does, his elbow pushes his stack of mail from the tray of the console. As Nicki gets in, he tries to reach the letters, which have tumbled to the floor of the passenger compartment. She says, "Here, let me do that," and quickly scoops up the letters. She holds them in one hand and as she reaches for the seat belt with the other she says, "If we hurry with the shopping maybe we will have time to grab a sandwich and have a quiet chat."

"You're the boss," he says, as he pulls away from the curb.

After fastening her seat belt, Nicki's eyes inadvertently drop to the stack of envelopes in her hand. There, on the top of the stack, is a business size envelope with the words, Dawson Colliery Company printed in bold type in the upper left corner and followed by an address in, CASCADE, WV.

Cole sees the envelope, sees her staring at it. "Oh lord, no!" he cries, and quickly turns toward the curb. "Nicki, let me explain," he pleads as he brakes to a stop. She looks at him briefly, and then her eyes drop back to the envelope and lock on the words, DAWSON, and, COLLIERY. How can she connect this? Cole and Dawson Colliery? Colliery, coal mining. Dawson and coal mines. Cole and coal mining. She's stunned! Oh God, please don't let it be! In a small, childlike voice, she moans, "No, nooooo."

He grips her shoulder firmly and again pleads, "Nicki, listen to me, let me explain!" But, she doesn't hear. Her thoughts have already flashed back to the large sign printed on the tipple in Glen Haven. In large, dingy white, block letters, it reads, HEADLEY COLLIERY COMPANY.

Deep within her consciousness, the picture of the sign fades and is slowly replaced by another scene. She sees a long, gray, shiny box with flowers draped on top. Standing beside the box her Momma cries. Someone says her Poppa died, that the Coal Company killed him. A very large man in a black, baggy suit and dirty, black, scuffed shoes, bends down to her, and with smelly breath, says, "I'm sorry you can't see your father, Nicola, we must keep the casket closed," and he points to the shiny, gray box. She asks herself; *is my Poppa in that box that the smelly man called a casket? The smelly man is lying. Poppa's not in that strange box. Why is everyone lying to me?*

From where she sits with her brothers, the box, the casket, looms above her. Her brothers told her she would get to see her Poppa here in this place, this strange old house, but where is he? The casket box appears to be tightly, ever so tightly closed. The sweet, sickening, overwhelming fragrance of flowers fills her delicate nostrils. She hates such a strong smell of flowers.

If her Poppa is in the casket box, why can't she see him? Is Poppa really in the casket box? When he didn't come home, her Momma said he went away to heaven, but that she would see him again, so maybe he is in the casket box? But, she wonders, *why can't I see him? Why does he hide in the big, gray, shiny casket box? Why does he hide from her at all? Has she done something bad? She must have done something very bad if her Poppa won't come home to her and hides in a box.*

Why is Momma crying? I will not cry, because if I cry it means I may never see Poppa again, so I will not cry. I will never cry. And I will not speak to any of them, because they lie. And, if I speak, maybe I'll cry, and I shall never cry, never will I cry. If I don't talk and don't cry, maybe Poppa will come home. I don't remember doing a bad thing...............

Nicki's world slowly begins to darken. It grows shadowy, fuzzy, murky, silent and morbid. In this world she sees her hand reach for the door latch. She lifts, and then slowly pushes the door away. She tries to move through the door, but something holds her shoulder. She wrenches it free and steps from the car, into the murkiness. She hears Cole's protests, his apologies, and his agony from far away. She walks away from the car, enveloped in this dark world that she has not visited for such a long, long time.

Chapter 17

Moving On

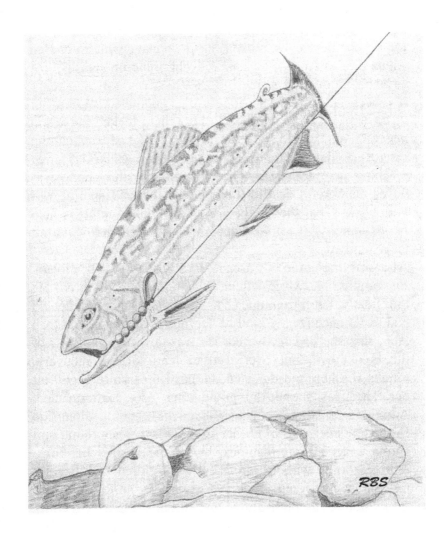

May, 1991

Cascade

The air is clear and brisk in the mountains as Cole steps into the quick waters of Cascades Creek. The hemlock boughs are heavy with early morning dew and they hang low over the water. Cole wears hip waders over khaki pants, a wool shirt, a fishing vest and an old, rumpled, red felt hat. It's been a year since he graduated and returned to Cascade. He agreed with his father, Ben that he should work in the mine for a year before he moves into a management role. Ben wants him to learn, first hand, all the mine operations, just as he had done a long time ago.

It's been a hard year since Cole graduated. After her discovery that Cole had lied to her, Nicki locked herself in her room and would speak to no one. Cole had tried calling her every day. She wouldn't return his calls. He tried reaching her mother, in Glen Haven, but the phone was never answered. He didn't know that Mrs. Valentini was with Nicki. That she had been called by Jaime to come help her daughter who wouldn't speak, wouldn't eat and wouldn't leave her bed.

After arriving home in Cascade, he still tried to call, in vain, for months. He wrote letters, which went unanswered. He did, finally, learn from one of his friends at school that Nicki had experienced some kind of nervous breakdown, and then later, that she had recovered. He was devastated to hear of the breakdown, but overjoyed to learn of the recovery. Finally, broken and dejected, he gave up trying to contact her. Then, last month, his grandfather, Alex Dawson died. Alex was 90, doing what he loved best, riding alongside Cascades Creek. His old heart just gave out. They found him sitting under a large hemlock, by the creek, after his horse returned home without him. His health failed rapidly after his Sarah had died, two years earlier. So, with Nicki weighing heavily on his mind and still grieving over the loss of his Grandpa, Cole figures a Saturday morning spent in his favorite trout stream will ease the pain. He cradles the rod in his arm as he cups his hands to his mouth to flood warm air from his lungs over his tingling fingertips. He listens intently to the sounds of the forest around him as he gazes up the stream, always eager to catch sight of deer, turkey, bear or any form of wildlife, which inhabits the wooded haunts that he loves. Despite the sounds of the tumbling water and the chirping of the ground squirrel that is setting on the old stump on the bank above him, he feels the quiet of the surroundings. There is no traffic noise, no ringing phone, and no voices.

He's thought, many times, about trying to find Nicki. He could try again to contact her mother in Glen Haven. But, if Nicki wouldn't return his calls, how would she react if he suddenly showed up. Perhaps it would drive her into another breakdown. She was so angry and disturbed when she discovered that he had lied to her, he wouldn't want to put her through that again. If she would only take his call, let him explain.

As he begins to feel the coldness of the stream migrating through the rubber boots he removes a small plastic box from a vest pocket and, careful not to spill the contents into the rapid water, opens the box and grips a shimmering object between thumb and forefinger. Returning the box to the pocket he tests the sharpness of the hook on the homemade brass spinner, one of a half dozen he made the evening before. The point of the hook will not drag across the surface of his thumbnail, proof of its sharpness. Satisfied, he ties the spinner to the four-pound test line.

The sun is now visible through the hemlocks at the bend upstream and the sight of it seems to take some of the sting out of his fingertips. The morning sun reminds him of the time he and Nicki spent a similar Saturday morning canoeing on Cheat Lake. He's angered that he cannot control his thoughts, they keep returning to her.

He has entered the stream thirty yards below a pool that he knows will be holding drift-feeding trout. The trout will be a few feet above the rock ledge over which the pool spills its contents. When he judges that he's a good cast below the intended target, he makes one final test of the strength of the knot that captures his spinner.

Looking at the knot, he thinks about the strength of his relationship with Nicki. Was it so weak that she would allow a minor indiscretion to tear it apart? Well, it must have been a mistake from the beginning.

He eyes the tail of the pool, fifteen yards ahead, and he can picture the trout lying there, patiently waiting at this strategic spot where the thirty-foot-wide pool is narrowed by the rocks to only four feet, funneling food to them. If the fish are there they will, of course, be facing upstream and unable to see his approach. If they are there? He knows they are there. The question is can he fool them?

Can he fool the trout as he had fooled Nicki. Why had he lied to her in the first place? Why did he not try to learn, early on, more about her passion against mine operators? Perhaps he could have intelligently argued against her bias and gradually changed her thinking.

He sends the spinner on its way and as it arcs above the water the trailing line catches the sun and resembles the trail of a miniature rocket. There is a small splash as the spinner enters the dining room of the wild brookies.

Raising the rod tip and snapping the bail closed in one motion, He cranks fast to keep the spinner off the bottom and moving rapidly toward the trout that he knows must now see it. In the simple mind of the fish, it's a streaking minnow that, for some reason, has left the safety of the rocks. The fish does not reason this; it simply reacts to the vision of something, which it believes to be food.

The needs of a trout are few. Cold water, oxygen and protein, and to this brookie it appears that protein is on the way. The trout makes no move until the final instant, when, with a quick hammer of its tail, it thrusts upward, timing the strike perfectly. At exactly the right instant, the mouth opens, forming a vacuum in the water that sucks in the artificial minnow. As the fish clamps down on the cold brass it's suddenly confused. Something is not right. The minnow is hard and has a strange force about it. The fish opens its mouth to expel this peculiar object that made an odd sound as his jaws closed around it, but even before it realizes that it cannot spit it out, its head is pulled sharply backward. Swiftly recovering, the trout thrusts forward and upward, breaking the surface of its domain, somehow instinctively knowing that in the other world above its own, there is a weird freedom in which it may be able to shake free of this terrifying force that it does not understand. But, the fisherman is too well prepared. The hook is sharp. The knot is solid and the drag is set perfectly.

The fish pulls hard against the drag as it bolts for the safety of its hiding place under the log at the upper end of the pool, but it's frightened and bewildered by the force that seems even stronger now, and it veers into the current, again trying vainly to free itself. It dives to the bottom and tries to rub the mysteriously hard object against the rocks, but it cannot maintain a proper balance and it's pulled over on its side.

The fish strikes out again for the far side of the pool and the safety of the log, but, its strength waning, it cannot pull directly against the drag. Another thrust upward into the other world, another dive to the rocks below. Again and again it breaks the surface in a desperate attempt to shake free, but to no avail. Its strength depleting, the fish finally surrenders. It now follows as the fisherman pulls it with the current.

It sucks cold water through its gills, frantically trying to get oxygen and regain some strength. One more try as it turns and pushes. No use. It's now totally spent and the invisible line guides it in. Cole bends down and gently slides a hand under the belly of the fourteen-inch, native brook trout, and lifts it from the water. He's not concerned that the fish will slip away, for he intends to release it for another time and another sportsman. For now, he simply wants to admire its beauty for a moment and relish the experience that he's about to complete. He removes the hook and holds the fish in the water for a moment with its head facing into the current to force water through its gills. Cole smiles as it comes to life and slowly leaves his hand.

The sun is now clear of the hemlocks above the bend and bounces golden rays off the wide stretch of slow water eighty yards upstream. The morning is spectacular. There should be a couple more brookies in the tail of the pool and before the fisherman again arcs the spinner through the clear mountain air he examines his knot to assure it survived the struggle with the trout. He feels refreshed, renewed and revitalized. As the brook trout survived its battle, he'll survive without Nicki. He will move on.

Chapter 18

Transmission

February 1998

The Pentagon, Washington, D. C.

Admiral Arland DeWitt, who fills the Navy's chair on the Joint Chiefs of Staff, rises to greet a visitor, Rear Admiral Douglas Thompson. Thompson heads up the Navy's Electronic Warfare Department. With the customary small talk out of the way, DeWitt gets down to business. "Doug, I understand you have something of importance to discuss. On such short notice I'm afraid I can't give you a lot of time, got a heavy schedule in front of me, so let's get right at it."

"Thanks for working me in, Arland, and I'll get right to the meat of it. I think you know that at our electronic research center in Idaho we have one of the world's top men in the field of Electronic Warfare, Dr. Heindrick Wagner?"

"Yes, I understand he's quite a character."

"Well, Arland, Dr. Wagner has developed a concept that we think will interest you."

"A concept?"

"Actually, it's more than a concept, it's been proven to work, although at a substantially reduced power, on a mockup in Idaho, but Wagner says that even at the low power his theory was proven, he's sure it will work."

"I'm listening."

"Wagner has developed a scheme whereby, in addition to strengthening our ability to capture electronic communication transmissions, he can jam a television broadcast anywhere in the populated world. By that I mean, anywhere that a satellite orbiting over the equator can transmit a signal in a direct line, and at the proper altitude, that takes in just about everything except the arctic. Further, he claims the system will give us the power to not only jam a TV transmission, but also actually transmit a signal powerful enough to override a targeted broadcast signal with our own signal."

DeWitt, while maintaining eye contact, is silent for a moment, then responds, "Let me make sure I understand what you're telling me, Doug. You're saying that we could target a broadcast of Saddam Hussein spewing lies to his people in Iraq and replace it with I Love Lucy?"

"Precisely. Or, with a live telecast of the President."

Admiral DeWitt is again quiet. Thompson can almost hear the gears turning in the head of the highest Naval Officer in the nation, then DeWitt queries, "The ability to jam their signal would be one hellava way to put a crimp in their propaganda, I see the merit in that, Doug, but if we send our own signal what keeps them from simply pulling the plug on their camera?"

"Nothing, Arland. But if I understand this thing correctly, our signal would be directed at their down line receiving antenna, be it tower or satellite mounted, which in turn relays the signal on down the line. By the time they figure out what the hell is going on, and redirect their antennas, or shut them down, we have our message out to the viewers."

"It sounds far out, Doug."

"It is far out, Arland, and it's complicated and it's not cheap. We would need to add to our existing satellite base and build an operations center in the mountains of West Virginia. But, you understand, at the same time these additional satellites give us this television capability they also dramatically increase our intelligence gathering ability."

"Why West Virginia?"

"Sorry, Doug, I don't have that detail yet. What I was hoping to accomplish at this meeting was getting you interested enough to allow me to bring Dr. Wagner in to explain it to you and to whomever else you would want involved. Also, and this part is a little fuzzy, Wagner says that if we approve this thing, once he gets it operational, it will be like a large experimental prototype that will allow him to develop an even more valuable system, something beyond intelligence gathering and propaganda purposes."

"Like what?"

"He won't tell me that, Arland. Wagner is a funny duck, you know how some of these brainy types are, he says his idea is still germinating and he doesn't want to embarrass himself until he's more sure it will work. He will only say that the TV signal over-ride program could be, in his words, 'A stepping stone to the control of other, more exotic mediums.' I know Wagner has been fooling around with some far out idea of his for a superconductor, something along the lines of turning hydrogen into a metal. If he can create a superconductor that would not require extreme cooling, well, the possibilities are mind boggling."

"For example?"

"Well, you understand that the current level of technology requires a superconductor to be cooled with liquid nitrogen to minus 126 degrees Celsius. That's just not practical outside the laboratory. However, Wagner tells me a metallic hydrogen compound would transmit electricity without resistance, or, super conduct at room temperature. He says that with such a conductor, transmission lines would not lose energy, computers would run faster, trains could be levitated, and, and this is far out, vast amounts of energy could be stored in magnetic fields."

"You're right, Doug, it sounds far out."

"Wagner also says metallic hydrogen could be used as fuel, because of its density, it could store large amounts of energy, which would be released when the solid phase is reverted to gas. Now, I don't know what the hell he has in mind, but knowing Wagner, I think there's something here, and it's big, Arland, real big! "

"Well, you better get him in here, Doug. I'd like to learn more about this."

Chapter 19

The Navy Calls

U.S. NAVY

September, 1998

Cascade

Ben Dawson, at age 68, has been phasing down his management activities as Cole, 30, takes over more of the day-to-day operations of the coal business. Dawson Mine #2 has been hugely successful from the day that Alex Dawson mined the first ton of coal. The unusual success has been due to the quality of the coal and the Dawson management style, which is remarkably employee oriented.

On a sunny Tuesday afternoon, Ben Dawson receives a visit from a representative of the United States Navy. The captain explains that the Navy wants to purchase 500 acres of Dawson land in Blackwater Valley. He further explains that the Navy wants to construct a high-security naval communications center on the site. Ben discusses the request with his brother, Nat and they both agree to sell the land to the Navy providing Nat can have the construction contract. After a week of hurried internal discussions the Navy agrees and the contract is awarded to Cascade Constructors on a cost-plus basis. The Navy's civil engineering department will closely supervise the job.

As far as the general public is aware, the communications center will be a standard microwave transmission installation for domestic military communications. However, known to only a few in the very highest levels of government, the facility, code named, Skywatch, will be operated by the Naval Security Group Command, (NSGC) a Signal Intelligence Operations (SIGINT) unit, which in turn, is under the direction of the National Security Agency (NSA).

June, 1999

Cascade

Nat Dawson arrives at the Cascade Constructors company offices on a sunny morning. "Good morning Jennifer," he greets the receptionist. "Good morning Nat. Be sure to see Margie first thing, she needs to talk to you." Margie is Nat's administrative assistant. "Okay, will do."

At 66, Nathaniel Dawson is still a handsome man, with broad shoulders, angular features, dark eyes under heavy brows and a strong jaw. His dark eyebrows accent his gray hair. He holds degrees in civil and electrical engineering from WVU. The Construction Company is a corporation, with the stock owned by Nat and his brother, Ben.

Nat finds Margie at the copy machine. "You want to see me this fine morning Miss Margie?"

"Oh, good morning Nat, yes, someone from the Navy CEC office called. They want to deliver plans for the new Navy communications center and brief you. They seemed to be in an awful hurry."

"O.K. Margie, I'll call them."

The next day a Navy Commander and two Lieutenant Commanders from the Navy Civil Engineering Corps arrive at Cascade Constructers. They are shown to a large conference room where Nat and two of his key engineers join them. After introductions, the Navy gets right to business. Commander Scott Wilson addresses Nat. "Mr. Dawson, it will be necessary for us to see some i.d. and the clearance papers of you and your men."

"Of course, Commander," Nat responds. As his engineers pull their wallets and produce identification, Nat pulls a folder from his brief case and hands it to Wilson. "Here are the clearance papers of each man in the company who your security people determined would be required to have them.

145

On top of the stack you'll find the three of us."

"Thank you Mr. Dawson," Wilson says with a friendly smile. He carefully studies the papers and the identification of Nat and his two engineers. "I believe these look to be in order, thank you. Now, if we may, I'll have Commander Marconi brief you on the plans, and please, ask questions as they occur to you, we don't want to miss anything."

"Well, I guess I have a question right off the bat, Commander Wilson," Nat says. "You introduced Mr. Marconi as Lieutenant Commander, but you just referred to him as, Commander."

"That's true Mr. Dawson, using full titles can sometimes be a little unwieldy. It's a lot simpler to shorten it, and in the Navy we always refer to the higher rank, which in the case of, Lieutenant Commander, would be simply, Commander."

"I see. Then it would be appropriate for us to call each of you, Commander?"

"Yes," replies Wilson. "But under Navy custom you would also be correct in referring to us as, Mister, but I have a hunch, Mr. Dawson, that you and I will be on a first name basis before we get far into this project."

"Well hell then, why wait, I'm Nat."

"Okay, Nat, that's fine by me, I'm Scott," and referring to the other two Commanders, Wilson says, "and this is Frank and Chuck."

Nat's two engineers volunteer, "I'm Jason" and "I'm Slick."

Wilson says, "I don't think I've ever met an engineer named, Slick."

Nat offers, "He used to be called, Archie, but he has most of the ladies in town chasing after him, so we think he's a pretty slick operator."

"I see," Wilson muses. "You know, Slick, you're sworn to secrecy regarding this project, am I going to have to worry about your pillow talk?"

"Hell, don't pay any intention to the old man; he's just sore that even with Viagra he can't get it up any more."

When the laughter ends, Lt. Commander Frank Marconi spreads drawings and specifications on the large table.

"Gentlemen, let me first take you through the site plan. Here you see the main structure, the communications operations building. Here is the barracks, the maintenance building, sewage treatment plant, water pump house, officers' quarters, laundry, mess hall and guardhouse. Perimeter fencing here, here and around here. Any questions about the overall site?"

The men shake their heads in unison. Nat noticed, however, that the site is to be situated in the area where he believes an old Dawson mine airshaft is located. He makes a mental note to check that later with his brother, Ben.

Marconi lays aside the site plan, exposing the next drawing. He continues, "The key structure on the site, the communications operations center, or in Navy language, op center, is a single-story building measuring 100 feet front to back and 172 feet in length. The walls are of reinforced concrete construction, two feet thick, without windows. The footers supporting the walls are 36 inches thick by twenty feet deep. The roof is also of heavy reinforced concrete construction."

"Pardon me," Nat interrupts, "Those are unusually heavy footers."

"Yes," Marconi explains, "They are safeguards against a potential tunneling entry.

"O.K." Nat muses, "I guess those would make it a little bit tougher to get through."

Marconi continues, "The left rear portion of the building is a large mechanical room which houses the main power distribution system, the emergency power generator, fuel oil tank for the generator, a twelve-inch curb around the base of the tank in case of leakage, emergency fresh water supply tank, and HVAC equipment. Here, we have stairs to a secure hatch in the roof. The roof is designed to support a helicopter landing. Here we have an eight-foot, heavy-duty steel, overhead door to the exterior, with a 48-inch high, loading dock. There is a door leading to the kitchen and an emergency evacuation door from the operations room."

Slick asks, pointing to the drawing, "You have an external

147

mess hall on site, but you also have a kitchen here in the op center?"

"Yes," Marconi continues. "The op center is to be an autonomous, self-sufficient unit, able to operate for 90 days without outside support. That's the reason for the emergency power and fresh water supply. The storage room, located here at the far end of the mechanical room, will hold food rations, cots and other supplies to sustain personnel for that extended period. The kitchen will be well equipped and will house a pantry and walk in freezer."

"I see," Slick responds.

Nat's other engineer, Jason, asks, "You're showing a 36-inch drainage catch basin here behind the generator. That's a pretty big catch basin, and I would think you would want it in the center of the room."

Marconi responds, "The Navy is a stickler for cleanliness. The entire floor has a gentle slope to that drain in order to allow cleaning the floor by hosing it down. We don't want the drain in the center of the room for a couple of reasons. It could present a tripping hazard and it could be an obstacle to the operation of a pallet truck. Supplies will arrive on pallets and be transported to the storage room. As for the large size, we've learned that catch basins tend to get forgotten, they fill up with dirt and sediment until the stuff exceeds the level of the outflow line, so we just play it safe and put in a big mother."

"I gotcha, that makes sense. I guess you guys have done your homework."

"We've built a number of similar installations and we've learned from each of them." Marconi replies.

The CEC engineers go on to review the remainder of the project. Since the op center will be operational seven days, around the clock, on rotating shifts, there will be two bunkrooms to allow personnel to catch forty winks if necessary.

Nat inquires about the housing, will the personnel be required to live on post? He's told that because of the highly secure nature of the Operations Center all officers and

148

enlisted personnel will be required to live on base, although they will have periodic leaves. Questions and answers continue for another half-hour until all points seem to be covered. Wilson wraps up the briefing with, "Well gentlemen, that's the plan. If there are no further questions regarding design, let's talk about a time line." After another twenty minutes of discussion and agreement on the fast track schedule for the project, the Navy officers depart. Nat returns to his office, where he places a call to his brother, Ben. "Ben, its Nat. You know that Navy job that I got the contract for, to build the com center on that land we sold them in Blackwater Valley; well, the Navy was just here briefing us on the plans, and looking at the site-plan it appears they have the building complex awful close, if not right over, the old Blackwater airshaft."

Chapter 20

There is silence on the line. Nat says, "Ben, are you there?"

"Yeah, I'm just thinking."

"Well, you better think real hard you old fart. Suppose the shaft is within the confines of the perimeter fencing, what do I do then, Ben?"

"Nat, I'll tell you once more, I promised her that I would never close off the shaft."

"Shit, Ben, this is stupid."

"Damn it, Nat, I didn't pick the site for this facility, the government did! Anyway, what's the problem, we'll secure it in such a way that it will cause no problem to anyone, and what the Navy doesn't know won't hurt them."

Nat argues, "But Ben, this is ridiculous, you're asking me to jeopardize the security of an important military facility, an action for which I could probably be shot, just to satisfy a promise you made to an old lady who's been dead for almost forty years."

Ben Dawson is drawn back to that time when he made the promise to a dying lady. It was a long time ago that he lost his grandmother. A long time since the tragedy that cost her the man she so loved. A long time ago.

"Ben, are you there?" Nat presses.

"Ah, yeah, I'm here. Listen, Nat, let me think on this for a minute, I'll get back to you."

"Ben, we need to figure out something quickly, the Navy wants to move on this."

"Okay, I'll be back to you within the hour, I need to think."

"Alright, Ben, don't let me down."

Two hours later, Ben's administrative assistance, Tracy, taps on his office door and enters. She hesitates for a second, then says, "Nat's here, says it's very important, you had your door closed, so I asked him to wait a minute while I checked with you."

Ben stands. "Good girl, but I'm not busy and I guess I was expecting him." He walks around his desk and follows Tracy to his doorway and finds Nat standing in the hall with an irritated look on his face. "Come on in, Nat," he says with obvious embarrassment in his voice, "Sorry, I got jammed up with phone calls," he fibs. They walk into Ben's office. Ben sits in a chair by a window while Nat slouches on a small couch.

Nat doesn't hesitate to get to the point. "Okay, what's your plan? You've had plenty of time to think about it, what kind of brilliant scheme have you come up with?"

Ben smiles. "That's a nice way to greet your old brother. No, 'Good morning, Ben,' or, 'How's your health, Ben?"

"Okay you old fart, how you doing?"

Ben frowns. "Having trouble pissing. Doc says my prostate's enlarged, probably gonna have to have a ream job."

Nat scrunches up his face, feigning agony. "Ouch! My pecker hurts just thinking about it."

Ben laughs. "Sure, I can tell I really have your sympathy." As he speaks, he takes a stick of gum from his shirt pocket, peels off the wrapper and shoves it into his mouth. He forms the wrapper into a little ball and throwing it at Nat, asks, "What do you think about this business that's going on between Israel and the Palestinians?"

As Nat spikes up a hand and catches the gum wrapper ball, he answers, "Hell, I don't know, I can't keep up with what's going on over there. I have enough trouble keeping track of what's going on around here," and he throws the ball back at Ben.

Ben bats at the paper wad with his hand and fires back, "Well what kind of citizen are you, that you don't keep up on what our friends are doing in other parts of the world?"

"What the hell is this, some kind of lecture on world affairs? I came here to talk about a problem we have and you start spouting questions about the damned Middle East, and who are these friends that you're talking about, the Israeli's? Hell, they don't mean anything to me, and as far as my standing as a citizen, I vote for the people who I believe can take care of world affairs and know how to handle all those loonies over there."

A wide grin spreads across Ben's face. He loves to pull Nat's chain. Always has. Nat goes on, "The way I figure it, there's a limit to how much one man can contribute to the betterment of society, whether it's the society of the community I live in , or the world I live in, and I've got my hands full trying to improve our town and our state. Shit, I can't keep up with the rest of the world. That's why I vote for a President who I think can handle the job."

Ben nods agreement. "What do you think of Bucklew, so far?"

Without hesitation, Nat replies, "I think the man's damn good, and he's got some character, some backbone, ethics, morals. He's got some things that had been missing in the White House for eight years."

"I think you're right, little brother, Yep, I think you're right, he's a strong man. Well, enough politics, to answer your original question, no, I've not come up with anything substantial."

"What! Well, what have you come up with?"

"Well, nothing, yet."

"Aw shit, Ben! I'm hanging out here, give me a break! We're talking about the Navy, Ben, the government, you know, those guys that seem to take national security a bit serious."

"Yeah, I know, the Navy. Well, Nat, I think you're missing the point. I made Grandmother Lu the promise! You were there, you heard her plea, I know it sounds silly, but I really meant it when I told her that I would never seal that shaft, and she believed me. You know I can't go back on my word. I was taught, and so were you, that a man's word is a contract, a binding contract, a promise from which he can only be released by the one who was promised, and Gramma Lu is not here to release me from that promise. Nat, I promised her as she was dying," Ben pleads.

"No, Ben," Nat appeals, "I didn't hear her plea, but I take your word for it, I know she did ask for your promise, and I know it's an important promise to you, but, do you agree that it compromises the security of this facility?"

"Hell no I don't agree! We can fix it so nobody knows about it except you and me, and I sure as hell don't plan to swim through miles of a flooded mine to steal a Navy computer, and, I don't think granddad's ghost will, either."

"What do you mean, fix it, Ben?"

"I mean, well, there must be a way that we can secure the opening to the shaft without sealing it, some way so the Navy doesn't know about it."

Nat is quiet, his head bent. After a long pause he volunteers, "Well, I don't know, Ben, it's awful risky, you know, of course, that the Navy CEC is going to oversee my work, they'll have engineers living on the job, how do I get around that problem?"

"Nat, we'll fix it. Let me come over and look at the plans."

"I can't do that, Ben, the plans are classified. They put us through a hellava background check in order to give me clearance to build this damn thing."

A long period of silence surrounds both men, till finally Nat quietly mutters, "Damn it, Ben, I swear I must be as crazy as you, but don't worry about it. I'll take care of it. I'll figure out a way, but I'll need you to show me exactly where the shaft is."

"That's easy," Ben blurts, with exuberance.

Nat turns to leave, then stops, turns back to face Ben and asks, "The prostate, not serious is it? I mean" - his words trail off.

Ben understands the question. "Naw, no cancer, just enlarged. We did a check with ultrasound, nothing there."

Nat looks relieved. "Good. Still, I do hurt just thinking about ol Doc Kotva running a big drill up your pecker."

"Get the hell out of here!"

A short time later, on an overcast morning, with dark and heavy clouds moving in from the northwest, Nat Dawson has a crew on the Skywatch construction site with laser instruments, laying out and staking the various building locations. He finds Ben's maple tree marker about twenty feet beyond the location for the rear wall of the op center. His plans show the inside of that section of wall being within the center's large mechanical room. He figures that he can more easily hide the airshaft if it's within the building rather than without, especially since the mechanical room is in that location. He studies the building plans more closely. "Wait a minute," he mutters to himself. "That 36-inch catch basin here in the floor of the mechanical room, with a six inch line running to the sewage main. If I could line up that catch basin with the opening to the airshaft, if I can convince the Navy that my test bores show more stable ground as we move further to the east, maybe I can make this work. I'll recommend we shift the building location 30 to 40 feet to the east and just enough to the south to line up that catch basin with the shaft opening."

That evening, Nat has Ben on the site where, within the week, he will start excavating. In the tall grass they find the manhole cover to the shaft. Nat has explained his ideas about moving the building and the use of the catch basin. Now he needs Ben's advice. "Alright Ben, tell me how I'm going to get this damn thing inside that building without my crew and the CEC guys flushing me out."
"Well, let me think for a minute, Nat."
As Ben scratches his chin for a long minute, staring first at the manhole cover and then off into space, then back at the cover, Nat can't contain himself. "You know what, Ben, If this isn't the dumbest thing I've ever done I don't know what is!"
"Just relax little brother, relax, it'll all work out, it'll all work out. Tell me, who will you have on this job that you can trust?"
"Oh no, Ben, I'm not going to pull anyone else into this. If we can't come up with a way for you and I to handle this ourselves, I'm pulling the plug on the whole damned idea. Besides, I don't want anyone else in this world to know how stupid I am, especially my men."
"Okay, I hear you. Well, let me ask you this, what's the size of that catch basin?"
"It's 36 inches in diameter, and roughly that long, made of reinforced concrete. But I wouldn't use a regular catch basin; it would have a reinforced concrete base. Instead, I'd order a three-foot length of reinforced concrete pipe with a hole for

a six-inch lateral drain. That way, we've got an open bottom, which we can place over the manhole cover. I'll tell the Navy that I couldn't get a regular catch basin on short order and that we'll construct a reinforced concrete bottom to the pipe, they'll buy that because of the rush. We disguise the manhole cover with a light wash of cement so it looks just like the bottom of a regular catch basin. The catch basin is going to be a heavy sucker, we'll need to set it with a backhoe."

Ben's face suddenly comes alive. "Alright Nat, here's what we'll do. You get on a dozer and shove some fill over the manhole. We'll mark the location. This area is a little low and you're eventually going to need a couple feet of fill anyway. Key all of your elevations off the top of the manhole. When your crew has the excavation and fill finished and you're placing the drain lines, save the catch basin for last. You and I will come out here during the night, dig a couple of feet to the manhole and set that 36-inch pipe over it. As you suggested, we put a light wash of cement over the cover. The following morning you move your guys, who were placing the drain lines, to another section so they don't notice that the basin has been set, and then you have the floor slab poured. When grandad's ghost wants to come up the shaft all he has to do is lift the man-hole cover, reach up three feet and lift the floor grate of the catch basin, and he's home free!" With that, Ben holds up his hands and says, "Hey, ain't I the smartest sumbitch you've ever seen?"

Nat slowly shakes his head. A slight grin creases his left cheek. "I don't know about that, Brother, but I can tell you that you're the strangest and most diabolical pecker-neck in these parts. Lord knows, I hope we never have to explain this to another soul. If the Navy finds out, they won't shoot us; they'll throw us both into the nut house."

Chapter 21

The Snake

September 11, 2001

Sarasota, Florida

On a sunny morning, in a small condominium, situated in the southern outskirts of Sarasota, Florida, a lone man sits before a television screen, a cup of thick, black coffee in his hand. The man is Iranian and is one of the key agents of the terrorist group called, Citizens Mujahedin of Iran (CMI), which is now a member of the Al-Qaida network. He's a tall, muscular man in his early forties. As he moves to the television to increase the volume, his movement is crisp and purposeful. His face is ruggedly handsome with features that are sharp and well defined. His eyes, set under heavy brows, are dark, piercing, penetrating, and cunning. His nose is straight and appears just slightly longish for his otherwise well proportioned face. His ears lay flat against his head. His squared chin is partially hidden by a short, rough beard that has a peculiar white streak running from his left cheekbone almost to the point of his chin. It gives his face an odd, lopsided appearance, but he prefers the beard because it covers a large scar beneath the white streak. As he watches the second plane crash into the World Trade Center tower, he sneers as he mutters softly, "Die, you heathens, you unholy cowards, die."

His speech reveals his long years of operating undercover in the United States. It's very American with a hint of a New Jersey accent. The man's name is, Yasin Ganji. Since "Cormorant" was recruited by CMI in 1982, the group has grown both in size and in the frequency of the acts of terror and violence against both U.S. and Iranian targets. Formed in Teheran during the early sixties, CMI initiated a bloody effort to counter what they perceived to be excessive American influence on the controlling clerical regime in Iran. Although the organization was originally started by a group of Iranian students, today CMI is made up of people with diverse ages and backgrounds and as leadership has changed the original objectives have become clouded. They only know that their lives are dedicated to the destruction of America. One thing they all have in common is that they have sworn their bayat, or complete allegiance to CMI and its purpose. Their targets in Iran are the Western sympathizers. Attacks there have been carried out by suicide bombers who target crowded locations which include women and children. They also pulled off the assassination of Asadollah Safari, the director of the Reza Prison. The group continues its terrorist attacks against Americans abroad and within the U.S. itself. They use a variety of methods to raise funds, some legal, some not. They also have members living under cover in various European locations.

Chapter 22

The Thinker

April 14, 2003

The Operations Center

Cascade Constructors has completed construction of the operations center and the Navy has begun installation of electronic equipment. The center is staffed by experienced personnel from other Navy warfare communication centers. Internally there are 48 Navy personnel and 6 armed Marine Detachment (MARDET) security personnel.

There are 29 Intelligence Specialists (IS), 9 officers, 6 administrative staff, and four kitchen and maintenance personnel. The group is made up of Cryptological Technicians (CT), Interpreters (CTI), Operators (CTO), Repairmen (CTR) and Maintenance Technicians (CTM). The distribution of rank in the group is, One E9 Master Chief, One E8 Senior Chief, two E7 Chiefs, three E6's, five E5's, six E4's, five E3's, and seven E2's. Five of the specialists and three of the administrative staff are women. This group is highly experienced and selected from the best of various Navy Electronic Warfare Installations around the world.

First in command is Captain Jeremiah Slade, age 39, married with two children. He has been transferred to Skywatch from a Navy Electronic Warfare Center in Yakima, Washington. Slade is a heavy-set man, but is muscular, not overweight. He has rugged, angular features, intense eyes and a strong jaw. He almost looks out of place in the neat and trim uniform of the Navy. His blond hair makes him appear younger than his age.

Second in command is 37 year-old Lieutenant Commander Tony Marino. He has been transferred from a communications site in Puerto Rico. Marino is unmarried, is a slender, but powerful man who obviously works out regularly, unlike Slade whose powerful body was assigned to him by his genes. Marino is a handsome man with a pleasing smile when he exposes it, but that is something that happens infrequently. He has a dark complexion and very dark hair. His eyes often flash a look of curiosity as he listens to one talk. His manner is pleasant and unassuming. There are also two Lieutenant Grade Officers, three Lieutenant Junior Grade Officers (JG), and two Ensigns; all Linguists who are experts in various foreign languages. Two of the JG's are women. The actual operations room, referred to as, The Shop, is a highly secure area. None of the Navy personnel are armed. Outside the op center the base is supported by a contingent of 36 naval personnel and secured by a 12 man MARDET.

In the dining room, over lunch, Slade is perusing a Time magazine as Marino walks up. "Hi captain, mind if I join you?"

"Hey Tony, how's it going, by the way, how are you and the MARDET coming on the permanent security plan, I'd like to get it wrapped up real soon."

As Marino sits, he replies, "We were held up for several days waiting for the instruction manuals on the voice recognition systems, but we have those now and I'm waiting for Lieutenant Carducci to give me an inventory of computers and monitors that qualify for destruction in case of a security breech. He promised me he'd have that this afternoon. It's the last piece of data we need and I can plug it into the plan within ten minutes, so we should have the finished plan on your desk this evening, Captain."

"That's great, and Tony, you can drop the 'Captain' crap when we're alone. My Name's Jere."

"Thanks Captain, er, Jere."

Slade opens his magazine again and drops his eyes to it, but instead of reading, he puts a question to Marino. "What's your read on Carducci?"

"Sir?"

"I mean, how good do you think he is, technically?"

"He's gotta be the best electronic intelligence guy I've run across, Cap, I mean, Jere."

"I concur with that, he has certainly impressed me with his technical ability. What's your read on him as far as his character, disposition, you know, and his temperament?"

Marino ponders Slade's question for a moment before responding. "He's a bit of a loner," he begins, "but otherwise he seems to be an okay guy. You know how some of these electronic geeks are, a bit different."

"I guess," Slade says, dryly. "There's just something about the guy that I can't put a finger on."

Marino finishes chewing a mouthful of cheeseburger before responding. "I think he'll work out, he's just a geek, that's all."

"I hope you're right, Tony, he certainly has the skills we need."

Slade returns to the magazine. Suddenly, he becomes more animated, stabbing a page of the magazine with a forefinger. "Here's an interesting piece of trivia, it says here that between 1991 and 1996 there were 9767 visas issued to students from middle eastern countries which are on the State Department's list of governments that support terrorism. And, get this! One of the guys convicted of the World Trade Center bombing held a lapsed student visa, can you beat that, we've got close to 10,000 possible terrorist sympathizers running around our damn school campuses!"

"That's hard to believe," Marino replies with little expression.

"Yes, I think it's damned strange that we let in so many kids who have been brainwashed into thinking that Americans are a bunch of murdering sons-of-bitches." Suddenly, Slade slams the magazine down on the table and rises from his chair. "Well, I gotta get back to work," he offers. He starts to leave, then stops and turns. "Oh, Tony, I had mentioned to you earlier, one of the scientific brains is coming in to direct the startup of the transmission and data collection system, I got a call this morning, he arrives tomorrow. This guy is supposed to be one of the top physicists in the world. He's coming in from one of the Navy's Electronic Warfare Research Labs, they won't tell me where. His name is Dr. Heindrick Wagner."

"How long will he be with us?"

"Good question. They hedge on telling me that. I have a

hunch it will be for quite a while."

"Is there anything you need me to do to prepare for him?"

"Naw. Just be available when he arrives. We both need to get to know him; he'll be working very close with us for the next several weeks. I've got a lot of questions, I'm sure you do too. He's scheduled to arrive around ten in the morning. Be prepared for anything, they tell me he is quite a thinker; a deep, deep thinker."

"I'll be on hand sir."

The following morning Dr. Wagner arrives by automobile. Wagner does not fit the image one would normally have of an intellectual and a genius. He's slightly rotund, nattily dressed, with a somewhat roundish, jolly face, sparkling eyes, close-cropped hair, a goatee, and younger looking than his 73 years. He's greeted by Captain Slade in the COM center lobby. Slade extends his hand. "Good morning Dr. Wagner, I am Captain Jeremiah Slade, it's indeed a pleasure to have you with us."

Giving Slade a hardy handshake, Dr. Wagner replies, "Thank you, Captain Slade, the pleasure is mine. I must say, this is most remarkable country here in the mountains; it's quite beautiful. I know it well from the topography maps and our three-dimensional model, but they hardly convey the reality."

"I certainly agree," responds Slade as he escorts the Doctor to a conference room. "I was surprised, Dr. Wagner, to learn that you were arriving by automobile, I assumed you would be coming in on a chopper."

"Oh no, Captain, I never fly by helicopter. Those pesky things have a nasty habit of falling out of the sky. Are you aware that a helicopter rotor has a finite life; that it will ultimately fail due to certain fatigue points?"

"No sir, I was not aware of that.

"It's a fact. The rotors are supposed to be changed after a specified number of operating hours, but sometimes things that are supposed to occur, don't occur, and then things that should not occur, like a machine falling out of the sky, do occur. They try to tell me that since they have made great advances in the science of materials from which they make the rotors, it's no longer a problem, but I still read about them falling out of the sky. No Captain, I never fly in a helicopter."

"Well Doctor, you have given me something to think about."

"That's the right attitude, Captain; think hard on that. By the way, do you know that the brain burns more calories when you're in deep thought?"

"I guess I never thought about that, Doctor."

In the conference room, Slade motions the doctor to a chair and asks, "May we bring you some coffee or a soft drink?"

"A cup of tea would be fantastic, if you've got it."

"I think we can arrange that." Slade picks up a phone and directs someone on the other end to bring the refreshments, which he had earlier specified, but with the addition of a pot of tea. He then rings Marino and asks him to join them in the conference room.

"Dr. Wagner, the officer that I just asked to join us is Lieutenant Commander Tony Marino, the second in command at Skywatch. He'll be here in just a moment. We are both quite interested in learning more of the theory behind the systems that we'll have operating here at Skywatch. Along with the technical staff we expect to be given abundant training in the operation of the amplified transmission and signal acquisition system, but I would like to know more about the theory and the physical principles underlying the system."

"Well, my boy, I'm sure there are some things I will be able to explain, and there are some things that I will not. You see, there are some facets of the physics business that even those of us in the ball game have difficulty explaining to each other."

Slade looks confused, but as he's about to ask the doctor another question Marino steps into the conference room. He's introduced, by Slade, to Dr. Wagner. With hardly a skipped beat the doctor continues. "Let me put it this way Captain Slade. Suppose I discovered an entirely new color, unlike any in the color spectrum as we know it. And suppose I have a marble in a box and that marble is of the new color that I have discovered. The box is locked and I have lost the key. Now, you ask me to describe the color of the marble. I cannot say that the marble is sort of yellowish brown, or that it's a cross between blue and red, because it's a totally new and different color. It's not a combination of the primary colors that we know, and there are no words in our vocabulary that I can use to describe the color of my marble, so, you see, I would have great difficulty describing my new color in a way that you could envision it."

The doctor continues. "Now, some of the concepts involved in this business of sending ultra powerful electronic signals into space is somewhat akin to me trying to describe my imaginary new color. I have the concept in my mind, but there are not words in our vocabulary that I can use to explain it. We work, of course, with mathematical equations, but even if you're a very capable mathematician those equations are extremely difficult to comprehend because of their length. So, some of this business I think I can explain, some I cannot, and some of it my superiors would not allow me to explain. Now, perhaps you can ask me a question."

"Alright," says Slade. "Why is this particular location, Blackwater Valley, in rural West Virginia, essential to the program? The com center sits here on the valley floor and the antenna towers are set up in an array that systematically increases in elevation over the course of forty-three miles."

A serious look forms on Wagner's face. "The fact is, Captain, the location is essential to the success of the project precisely because of the position of the surrounding mountains. Yes, the towers are erected in a geometric array with a progressively increasing elevation. A signal, aimed at a Navy satellite, transmitted from a dish here on the roof of Skywatch, beginning at an elevation of 1200 feet, will reflect from tower to tower, each time increasing in elevation and each time being amplified, or boosted, until the signal leaves the final tower at an elevation of 5000 feet.

The mountain, on which the last tower stands, is 4705 feet above sea level and the tower reaches another 295 feet into the air. When the signal leaves the last tower it will be 2000 times stronger than when it left the dish on the roof and will be closer, in elevation, by almost 4000 feet, to the first relay satellite."

Wagner sips his tea, then continues. "In addition, the added elevation results in a further horizon, thereby extending the horizontal distance to the first satellite, which, in the end, reduces the number of required satellites by one, saving the program about $170,000,000. Also, though a minor factor, never the less, important, the mountain air is cleaner, less pollution from automobiles, thereby giving less resistance. Another minor factor, the way the towers are dispersed through the mountains brings less attention to them, they appear to be ordinary microwave towers and less likely to be considered important military targets. In the end, this precise location allows us to generate the most powerful signal. A signal so powerful that we will have the capability to not only jam a television broadcast anywhere in the world, but perhaps more importantly, to override any broadcast signal with our own. In effect, we will have the ability to kidnap, if you will, any enemy transmission antenna, be it ground or space based."

Slade shakes his head in wonder, then asks, "Dr., Wagner, If elevation is important then why not place Skywatch in the Rocky Mountains where you could gain substantially greater altitude than here in the eastern mountains?"

"That's a very good question, Captain, a good question. Now you're getting into an area that is more difficult. Let me just say that it involves the earth's electromagnetic field at this latitude and longitude. I cannot say more than that."

"Dr. Wagner," Marino asks, "This whole program seems to be an extremely expensive one. Is it really worth that much as an anti-propaganda tool?"

Wagner tilts his head back and gazes at the ceiling for a long moment, takes a sip of tea, returns his eyes to the ceiling and looks as though he's totally lost in thought. Marino is about to speak again when the Doctor drops his gaze and in a very quiet voice says, "You understand, I must be very cautious in what I say. I must balance what you need to know in order to do the very best job you can do, with what an unfriendly country could do with this kind of information about our total capability."

Wagner again pauses, obviously caught in an internal struggle, weighing options, visualizing circumstances, contemplating the effects of anything he might add to what he has already said. Then he continues. "I will only say this, and mind you, this will be the end of this discussion. If we are successful in our effort to establish the ability to dominate the world's television signal transmission facilities, then perhaps this can be a stepping stone to the control of other, more exotic mediums."

Slade and Marino sit quietly, both minds searching for the meaning in Wagner's words. Slade has other questions, but doesn't know if this is the time to pursue them. He decides to gamble one more. "Doctor Wagner, on another topic, the guts of the primary signal booster is a superconductor, but I don't know the material. It's not super cooled, it works at room temperature. Based on the literature that I have studied and from the spec sheets that I've read on the booster, I'm guessing that there has been some kind of breakthrough in the area of creating metallic hydrogen. Is that possible? Has our technology reached that level?"

Wagner looks genuinely startled. "That, Captain, is a subject of which I definitely am not free to discuss; now, could I bother you for another cup of your wonderful tea?"

After two months of equipment installation and start up, under the direction of Dr. Wagner, Skywatch is operative. Captain Slade and his superiors plan what is purported to be a reception for the Chairman of the Joint Chiefs of Staff, Four-Star General Bruce Maddox, the Navy Joint Chiefs representative, Admiral Arland DeWitt, and the head of the Navy's electronic warfare department, Rear Admiral Doug Thompson. In reality, the intent is to give the General and the Admirals a demonstration of the satellite control system, but not wanting to overplay the importance of the communications center the military arranges for the visit to be set up as a promotional effort by the State of West Virginia. Attending the reception, unaware of the real purpose of the General's visit, will be the Senator from West Virginia, Robert Burke. The reception is planned for August, 2003.

Chapter 23

To the Mountains

Skywatch

Blackwater Valley

Washington, D.C.

On an extraordinarily hot and humid Washington, D.C. morning, Senator Robert Burke strides into his office. Burke is a tall man, thin, silver hair, with an angular, but yet, softly featured face, a kind and warm face, a face that breaks into a smile very easily, but a face that shows years of fighting the diplomatic battles that comes with the business he's in. It's odd how his face has so many lines yet remains youthful, vibrant, and vigorous. He greets his administrative assistant, Margaret. "Good morning you beautiful lady, I'd give you a kiss, but that could get me in trouble in this town."
"Oh, go for it Senator, I need to write a book and make lots and lots of money."
With a sparkling and ornery twinkle in his eye he fires back, "I'd probably try, Maggie, if Doris didn't own a big gun that she knows how to use. It's fear of her that keeps me in line!"
"And you better stay there, you dirty old man."
Maggie has been with the Senator for over thirty years and is one of the few people who could call him old without offending him. Burke stands over his desk looking at the day's agenda that Maggie had placed there the night before. He notes that the first item is a reminder to make arrangements for an upcoming trip to a new Navy post in West Virginia. He pushes an intercom button and asks Maggie to call Nicola Valentini and ask her to join him.
Nicki has been a member of Burke's staff for three years, the first year as an Administrative Assistant and the past two years as Burke's Legislative Director. She was recruited shortly after she obtained her Masters Degree in political science from George Washington University. Burke was highly impressed with the recommendations for Nicki that he had received from his friends at GWU. She had worked long hours at a full time job while going to school evenings to get her Masters. Her performance was impressive and she seemed totally inspired and dedicated to improving the well

being of the people of her home state. He felt that his interview with her, prior to his asking her to join his staff, was remarkable. She was poised, articulate, responsive, inquisitive, open, attractive and tastefully dressed. He marveled that this young lady came from the coalfields of southern West Virginia.

As Legislative Director, Nicki's duties are broad, but are primarily geared towards monitoring the legislative schedule and making recommendations to Burke regarding the pros and cons of particular issues.

Nicki enters Burke's office. "You asked to see me, Senator?"

"Good morning, Nicola. How did you manage to get through all that damned humidity this morning without losing one bit of your freshness?"

She blushes. He always makes her blush. "It is a bit nasty out there, Sir, and so early in the day. It kind of makes you want to be alongside a cool stream up in the mountains."

"Well now, it's very interesting that you say that, you must be reading my mind, because that's exactly what I need you to do, go up in the mountains."

"Sir?"

"Nicola, On August 15, I need to pay a visit, along with General Bruce Maddox, the Chairman of The Joint Chiefs; Arland DeWitt, the Admiral of the Navy, and a few other folks, to a new Navy communications center in northern West Virginia, near a place called, Cascade. I'd like you to go out there and make whatever arrangements are necessary to assure that General Maddox, Admiral DeWitt and their people receive the absolute epitome of attention. I would also like you to travel there with me, on the 15th, along with, perhaps another staff member, or two, to make sure things go well."

Nicki is startled at the name, Cascade. She knows that name and she's stunned to hear the sound of it. It's a mining town, a squalid, grimy, mining town. It was Cole's home, and the Senator wants me to go there. She turns pale. She hasn't been in a mining town for years. Not since her breakdown. Can she do it? Can she manage being in a mining camp again? She falters, takes a step backwards. Burke reaches for her. "Nicola, are you okay?"

She takes two steps to a chair and grips the back of it for support. "I, I'm fine, Senator. I'm just, I'm just surprised, I guess."

"Surprised?" Burke looks bewildered.

Nicki, somewhat recovered, straightens. "Confused, perhaps confused is a better word, I guess. It's just that, just, isn't Cascade, is that not one of those dirty little mining camps? I beg your pardon sir, but why would the Navy want to be located in a place like that?"

"Well, for a variety of reasons," Burke says, not convinced that she's all right. "Nicola, would you like a glass of water or, something? You look pale."

"No, I'm fine, Senator, I'm okay now, really."

Burke looks relieved. "Well, if you're sure. Now, why would the Navy select Cascade? Because the military seems to think that the location has some kind of strategic importance. In any event, we've got them there and it's great for the state. Now, Maggie has put together a packet of information to get you started. I'd like you to get on this real soon so that we don't miss anything." He pauses, looks a little pained as he adds, "Nicola, I know this sounds like a job for someone lower down the pole, but this is very important to me. Maddox is not going to simply fly in, doff his hat and fly out. He tells me, confidentially of course, that this trip is sort of a pain in the butt, a kind of public relations thing, and he would like to use it as an opportunity to get a little R & R. You know, a few days of relaxation, so he wants to arrive early. Now, I really want to have all these guys come away from this thing with a highly positive image of our West Virginia, so I'm asking a pro to take care of this for me."

"Well, Senator, I hope I'm up to the task, I don't expect to have a lot to work within Cascade."

The Senator winces, then, with a wink, says, "You may be in for a surprise, young lady, and by the way, the General likes trout fishing."

Friday, July 21

After an evening perusing the information in the packet, prepared by Maggie, Nicki had a tormented and sleepless night. She started the following day by contacting the offices of General Maddox and the Mayor of Cascade. She made arrangements to fly into Morgantown, West Virginia and spend the night at a hotel there, adjacent to the airport. The Mayor's assistant recommended she make lodging arrangements at a local inn, called, The Pierpoint, but unsure of the quality of accommodations available at an "inn" in a mining town in the coal fields, she opted to stay in Morgantown, at least for the first night.

In Cascade she's to be met by a group made up of the Mayor, a Chamber of Commerce representative and the manager of the contracting firm that constructed the communications center. When she has finished her calls she sits with her elbows on her desk, her chin in her hands, thinking, Cascade, Cole Dawson. I wonder if he's still there.

She spent all day Saturday and most of Sunday working to put her current projects in order and developing assignments for her assistants. This is a busy time for her and she can ill afford to take the time away from Washington. She has mixed feelings about this trip. She still fights the morbid feeling she gets, just thinking about a mining community and she's extremely nervous about the possibility, however remote, of running into Cole Dawson. Again, she sleeps fitfully, and then her flight into Morgantown was delayed, putting her into the hotel after midnight.

Chapter 24

Welcome To Cascade

Monday, July 24

Morgantown, West Virginia

Leaving the hotel, in her rented car, on a beautifully clear morning, Nicki finds her way to Interstate 68 and heads east. With the previous sleepless weekend, she worries about being alert enough to do her job well as she meets with the people in Cascade. But, as she drives, she sees a sky of vivid, noble blue with a generous sprinkling of fluffy white clouds drifting to the south and she's buoyed by the sight. She convinces herself that it's going to be a magnificent day and she will get the job done. Twenty miles before her, running in a northeast-southwest persuasion, is the majestic backbone of Chestnut Ridge, twelve hundred feet higher than the roadway she travels.

She was told by the Mayor's office that Cascade is a forty-five-minute drive from Morgantown. After crossing Cheat Lake and Chestnut Ridge Mountain, at a place called, Bruceton Mills she turns south off of I-68 and finds herself on a typical, winding Preston County road. She feels just a bit of nostalgia driving on this kind of road, a road unlike those congested arteries that surround Washington.

She stops for gas and looks again at her map. She wants to be sure of her way, not wanting to get lost and arrive late. She prides herself on being timely for appointments.

Back on the road, as she gets closer to her destination, she begins to feel the anxiety again. The fear of going through another depression haunts her. As she approaches the fringe of Cascade from the northeast, she passes a side road, where a sign reads, Dawson Colliery Company, Mine #2, and an arrow points in the direction of the road. As she passes the sign, her stomach suddenly feels queasy. She pulls to the side of the road and gets out of the car. She gazes back at the sign. She tells herself to remain calm, relaxed. It's just a sign, just a name. But the picture of the Headley Colliery Company sign appears in her mind. Then, the large man in the black baggy suit, and she smells his putrid breath. *"I'm sorry you can't see your father, Nicola, we must keep the casket closed.*" Holding her stomach, she walks quickly around the car, into the grass, bends over, and vomits. She feels dizzy, and the terrible, morbid feeling threatens her. She straightens. No, I won't let it. I won't fall into that place again. She turns to the car and, retrieving her purse, finds a tissue and wipes her mouth. She suddenly becomes aware of the sound of rushing water. She turns from the car and only now notices the beautiful, clear water of a mountain stream, splashing and tumbling over a thousand smooth rocks. She walks toward the stream, carefully down the bank, to the edge of the quick water. She bends and dips a clean tissue into the cold water, then puts it to her cheek, then her forehead, her chin and throat. She repeats the process twice more. I'll be fine. I have no fear now. I understand what triggers this feeling. It's all behind me, I'm fine.

She gazes at the water, the clear and sparkling water. It smells fresh, and clean. It's not discolored by mine drainage, acid runoff. Not like, Trout Run.

A few minutes later, she passes a colorful sign that reads, Cascade, Welcome to Our Town. As she enters the outer edge of the town, she sees no ramshackle houses; no grimy cabins perched on barren and blackened hillsides. The homes are modern and tidy, with green lawns that are manicured. The streets are well maintained and lined with beautiful trees. She's overwhelmed by the beauty and seeming prosperity of the small town. As she continues she sees signs of culture that she has not before seen in the more rural areas of the state. There's a concert center, a beautiful park overlooking a rushing waterfall, modern schools with spacious grounds and an attractive main street business district. She sees none of the dirt and grime that she has always associated with mining.

To her right she sees a beautiful, old brick building with a large front porch. Her jaw drops when she reads the sign in front of the terraced stone walls before the building, The Pierpoint Inn.

This cannot be a mining town. It simply cannot be. I must have driven through some kind of time warp on the way here, or crossed into a parallel universe. This is unlike any mining town I have ever been exposed to.

So this is the hometown of Cole Dawson. Cole; how many times has she thought of him? How many times has she cursed herself for being so emotional and chasing away the only man who ever truly touched her inner soul? How many times she had wanted to contact him, and now, she's here, in Cascade. Now that she has thought about it, the town is as he had described it. But, when she learned about his family owning the coal company she, well, she just lost sight of everything else and plunged into a deep depression.

Continuing on, she finds the town square. Huge maple trees shade the square. A fountain pushes a huge column of clear water into the air. The fountain is surrounded by park benches occupied by an odd mixture of silver haired men leaning on canes and a couple of young suits with computers on their laps. She assumes the suits to be lawyers, for she has noticed the County Court House across the way.

On the western edge of the square, across the street, is the town hall. In front of the building, she pulls into an angled parking space facing the square, locks the car, then, as an afterthought, looks around to see if anyone saw her lock it, somehow feeling guilty about the act. Satisfied that she escaped with the dirty deed undetected, she crosses the street and ascends the sandstone stairs to the town hall.

The building is of red brick. The brick somehow has the appearance of being old, but yet, not so old. Not that Nicki would know the difference, but the bricks used to construct the building twenty years ago, when it replaced the original burnt out wooden town hall, were made using the old molding technique. Most modern day bricks are extruded, giving them a more flat appearance with sharper corners. Molded bricks give a building so much more character. Few companies remain who make bricks the old fashioned way, and one of them is located in the eastern panhandle of West Virginia.

In the office of the Mayor, a young receptionist introduces herself as, Patti, and tells Nicki that the Mayor is expecting her. Patti leads Nicki to his office and introduces her to Mayor Aniston Pierpoint. The Mayor is a fellow she guesses to be in his fifties. He has a mop of thick brown hair with tinges of gray at the temples. He's a man of medium height with friendly gray eyes sitting beneath bushy brows, generous jowls and a middle that suggests he spends too much time sitting at his desk.

"Miss Valentini, I am very pleased to meet you. Welcome to Cascade. I hope you had a pleasant drive from Morgantown."

"The drive was beautiful Mayor, and it made me just a bit home sick."

The Mayor looks surprised. "Home sick, you mean you're from this part of the country?"

"Well, not exactly this part of the country," she says with a smile, then frowns slightly as she continues. "I spent my youth in a small mining town in southern West Virginia, Wyoming County."

"Oh, I see. Then you're a Mountaineer, so I understand what you mean about the drive making you home sick. The mountains here are a bit like those downstate, more distinct, parallel ridges, but similar. Of course, here, we're right on the Allegheny front, which gives us the long mountain ridges to the east and the more irregular hills to the west."

"I'm not totally familiar with the different kinds of hills and mountains, Mayor, when I was a kid I just wanted to get out of them. But, now I have to admit, I do feel a twinge of nostalgia."

"This country does grow on you, Miss Valentini. The mountains, trees, tumbling waters and the friendly people - I wouldn't trade it for any place on earth."

"I can certainly understand how you feel, Mayor, and please call me Nicola."

"Thank you Nicola, and please call me Aniston. Well young lady, I have made arrangements to meet the others at the General Pierpoint Inn, up the street. I hope you're hungry, the food there is sumptuous and generous."

They walk the short distance to the Inn. A large flagstone walk leads through a closely manicured front lawn, past huge oak trees and up stone stairs to a wide front porch, lined with rocking chairs. As they enter the Inn through a heavy, maple plank door, Nicki feels as though she has stepped back in time. The inn is at least 200 years old with wide, pine plank floors that show the many years of wear. There is generous use of Cherry paneling and molding on the walls and ceiling. From the lobby, a large, curved staircase with ornate carvings leads to an upper level. An old-fashioned hotel desk dominates the right side of the room. To the left, a large archway opens into a sitting room, which houses a massive stone fireplace and a generous sprinkling of comfortable old furniture, including two large oak rocking chairs standing before the hearth. The fireplace is of native sandstone. Nicki imagines what it would be like to sit in one of the rocking chairs in front of a roaring fire on a snowy winter day. One can almost hear the room whisper, "welcome, welcome."

"This is breathtaking!" Nicki exclaims. "What a wonderful place. And the Inn provides lodging?"

"Oh, it certainly does, and the rooms are more of the same of what you see here. Before you leave we can show you some of the rooms if you'd like."

"I would love it, Mayor, or, I'm sorry, Aniston."

"Fine, we'll surely do that. I think you'll also like our little museum of civil war relics, and the gardens out back."

"Aniston, I presume, since it's the, "Pierpoint" Inn, that you have a connection?"

"Yes, the Inn has been in my family since my forth-great grandfather bought the land from the town's founder, Robert Dawson and built it in 1792."

"Dawson?" She asks as she lifts her brow.

"Yes, both the Pierpoint and the Dawson families go back a long way, as a matter of fact, you're about to meet a Dawson, let's go on into the dining room."

Chapter 25

An Invitation

Nicki's heart skips a beat, she's "about to meet a Dawson." Can it be? No, impossible, it couldn't be Cole.

Pierpoint leads Nicki through the sitting room to a large dining room, again abundantly furnished with antiques. The furniture is an eclectic mix, but is predominantly cherry. Crystal and china pieces join several old portraits adorning the walls.

As they enter the dining room, two men seated at a large round table rise from their chairs. One is a young, dark haired, good-looking man in his mid 30's. The other is an older, distinguished looking man, in a rugged sort of way. He reminds Nicki of Paul Newman. She finds herself disappointed that neither man is Cole Dawson. Pierpoint introduces the two men.

"Jeff, Nat, I would like you to meet Miss Nicola Valentini." He introduces the younger man first, "Nicola, this is Jeff Lewis, the President of our local Chamber of Commerce, and this is Nat Dawson, owner of Cascade Constructors."

With greetings out of the way, Nicki is seated between Pierpoint and Dawson. She looks across the table at Jeff Lewis and then at the Mayor. "Gentleman I must tell you that I am wonderfully impressed with your town. It's beautiful, clean, picturesque, and it's certainly different from the area downstate where I grew up. My understanding is that the economy here is based primarily on coal operations. Is that not correct?"

Jeff Lewis responds. "Yes, the coal mine does account for the largest portion of employment here, however there is still a significant amount of timbering going on in the area, and of course, Nat's company gives the local economy a good infusion even though many of his projects are not local. There is a fair amount of positive impact on the area from tourism. We have skiing at Snowshoe, not far to the south, in Pocahontas County, white water rafting just to the west on the Cheat, one of the finest rafting waters in the east, the National Forest with it's hiking, hunting, and fishing supports various outfitters. Then, of course we have many smaller businesses, which grew up around the mining and timbering operations in this part of the state."

Nat Dawson interjects with a smile, "And we have a new Navy facility."

Nicki turns to Dawson, "And I guess that's why we're all sitting here, and I'm very happy, Mr. Dawson, that you, a local business owner, won the contract to build the COM center. Tell me; doesn't the Navy normally construct their buildings using their own civil engineering group?"

"Good question, Miss Valentini. As a matter of fact, the Navy does normally use their own group to design and supervise, but the construction is often done by private, civilian contractors."

"I see." Nicki pauses, then, while she has Nat's attention, she continues, "Mr. Dawson, with all due respect to the Mayor and Mr. Lewis, I have a question for you, as someone whose job does not include the promotion of the town. I must admit that Cascade is nothing like I expected. I had assumed that, since it was a mining town, it would have the appearance of the coal town where I spent my youth, why is it different."

"I guess we operate a little differently than the average bear, Miss Valentini."

"How do you mean?"

A mild look of embarrassment flows over Nat's face. He rubs his chin in contemplation, but before he speaks, Pierpoint jumps in, "The cat seems to have Nat's tongue, Nicola. What he's trying to say, and is too humble to say it, is that his family is responsible for a very unusual and highly successful mining company. One of several kinds of Dawson businesses that have not brought prosperity to just the Dawson family, but also to the folks who work for the mine and the community in general."

"I see," Nicki says in a soft voice as she looks at Nat. He blushes. She continues, "At the university, in Morgantown, I knew a Dawson from Cascade."

Nat regains his composure. "Well, let's see, I'd judge that you may have been in school about the time that Cole was studying mine engineering."

"Why, yes, it was Cole, Cole Dawson. Is, is Cole a relative?"

183

"Cole is my nephew, my Brother Ben's boy. So, you know Cole, well isn't that something."

Nicki feels a mysterious shudder run up her spine and a tingling at the nape of her neck. *This is Cole's uncle, shall I dare be so bold as to ask, Oh, well! Why not.* "How is Cole, is, is he, is he in town? Does he live here?"

Pierpoint and Lewis look on with interest as Nat seems to warm to this woman. Nat hears something in her voice, and sees something in her eyes, that suggests there was more than just a casual acquaintance between her and Cole.

"As a matter of fact, he is in town, and yes, he lives here, lives out my way. Cole's been fixing up the farm where my parents lived, his grandparents, Alex and Sarah Dawson. And you know what! On Monday nights my wife and I usually have dinner with Ben and Marilyn. Ben and I usually play a little poker after dinner and I think I remember Cole saying he might stop by this evening to try for some of my cash. Why don't you take dinner with us and perhaps you'll get to see your old friend."

Nicki suddenly feels her knees weaken, her face flush. She had said nothing about Cole being a friend. Her composure is a bit shaken. "Oh no! I couldn't impose, it, it would be an imposition, oh, I guess I already said that. Ah, no, just tell Cole that I said hello."

Now, after Nicki's obvious befuddlement, Nat is convinced there is, or was, something more between she and Cole. The Cupid in him takes command. In a kind and almost, fatherly manner, he says, "Nonsense girl, you'll tell him yourself. If you want my help in making the Senator's visit a fruitful one, you will honor us with your company at dinner. I'll be here at six to pick you up, you're staying here at the Inn, I presume?"

Nicki studies his face, his kind and intelligent eyes. Back in control of her emotions, she tilts her head and says, with her patented impish smile, "Well, since you put it that way, for the Senator's sake, I guess I had better accept. And, as a matter of fact, I do plan to check into the Inn."

Pierpoint motions to a waiter who has been hovering in the

background, waiting for a break in the conversation. "Why don't we have some lunch and talk about what we can do to impress a United States Senator and some very important military people."

After lunch Mayor Pierpoint and Jeff Lewis spend the afternoon showing Nicki the town and surrounding area. They brief her on some history of Preston County and suggest various points of interest. They discuss security and Nicki tells them that a marine security group will be contacting them to make those arrangements. They have her back at the inn at five o'clock.

Chapter 26

No Time for Marriage

The Evening of July 24, 2003

Nicki had hoped for a brief rest before Nat came for her, but at precisely six o'clock the desk clerk calls telling her that Mr. Dawson is waiting. As Nat stands with his hands in his pockets studying an antique civil war print on the wall of the lobby, Nicki appears at the head of the stairs. She's wearing a periwinkle blue sun dress and black, strap sandals. As she descends the stairs, Nat is struck with the thought that she's one of the loveliest women he has ever seen. A simple pearl pendant compliments a graceful neck. Her raven black hair causes her skin to look particularly delicate and creamy. In her hand she clutches a small purse and a sweater drapes over her arm. At the foot of the stairs she extends her hand. "Mr. Dawson, I certainly enjoyed our planning session earlier today and I realize that I forgot to thank you for your substantial input."

"You're most welcome, I'm pleased to be involved, and can you please call me, Nat. Mr. Dawson was my grandfather."
"Alright, Nat, and I am, Nicki."
On the ride to Nat's home, after some initial small talk, Nicki asks the question that has been on her mind since her meeting with Nat earlier in the day, a question she wanted to ask when Nat had invited her to his home to see Cole, but she could not muster the strength to ask it. In a voice so soft she can hardly hear herself, she poses the question. "Does Cole have a family?"
Nat doesn't hear, "I'm sorry, what was that, my hearing isn't what it once was, it's hell to get old."
"You're not old, not at all old, and I was just muttering, nothing important."
Nat thought he heard, "family". He looks at her and asks, "Are you married Nicki? Not that it's any of my business, just curious about the status of someone as pretty as I've seen in a long while, next to my Alice, of course."
"Of course." She responds. "No, I'm not married, I guess I haven't had time for marriage."

"Well, I expect that will surely please Cole!" Nat says, delightfully.

"Why, Nat, I am beginning to wonder about your motives."

"Hell, Honey, my motives are on my shirtsleeve, Cole needs a good women."

Her chest tightens. She asks, "Then, he's not married?"

"No, Cole hasn't married yet. Came close to finding the right girl once, according to his mother, but that was some time ago, don't know what the story was, never asked, and as you say, you haven't had time for marriage, I guess Cole would say the same. He's been awful tied up with running the mine since Ben phased down. A couple of girls in town are trying to pin him down, but haven't yet. You know what, if he finds out I've been talking about his social life he'll kick my butt from here to Wheeling."

"I won't tell."

After a seven-mile ride, Nat turns off the main road, proceeds through a gate and up a winding gravel drive for another half-mile. At the end of the drive, on a bluff overlooking the serene Cascades Creek valley, sits a rustic cedar and limestone home. The house is large but not ostentatious. It's not quite what Nicki expected. She assumed that a man of Nat's position in the community would live in a house that made a grander statement, perhaps even, baronial.

"Well here we are Nicki. This is what we call home."

"It's a beautiful home, Nat," she says with genuine sentiment.

As they walk towards the house Nat pauses to show Nicki the view of the valley. "It's so peaceful," she says.

Nat, in a sentimental voice, says, "I love it here in the mountains, wouldn't want to live anywhere else in the world."

They start again for the house, up a stone walkway. "Ours is a comfortable home, Nicki. We don't need a real fancy house, we don't do a whole lot of upscale entertaining. Besides, we don't want our folks to think we're any better than they are."

"Folks?" Nicki queries.

188

"I mean, our employees. Somehow it doesn't sound right to call them that. They are so much a part of the business, hell, they run the business, and I'm just a cheerleader of sorts. It's something that Ben and my father taught me. He pauses. What I mean to say is, well, you know, I learned an awful lot from my father and my grandfather, but I also learned from my brother Ben. Ben has a special knack for getting along with people, a special way, something he was born with I guess. Anyway, I think some of Ben's style has rubbed off on old Nat. The way he runs the mining business, the way he relates to his people, I guess you could call it his management style, whatever it is, it works, and I have learned that. So, I try to run the construction business the same way." They arrive at the front door. "Well girl, let's go on in and see what Alice has in mind for supper."

Meeting the two of them at the front door is an attractive woman with light brown hair, streaked with gray, striking green eyes, a few wrinkles, but a creamy complexion, a sprinkling of freckles, and a broad smile. "Welcome to our home, Miss Valentini, I'm Alice. It's so nice to have a visit from a friend of Cole's."

"I'm happy to meet you Alice, and please call me, Nicki. Does your husband often bring people in for dinner at the last minute? "

"As a matter of fact, he does, Nicki. But, bless his heart, he does at least give me a phone call most of the time. Come in and sit, what can I get you to drink, or would you like to freshen up a bit first?"

"No thank you, I'm fine for the moment. A glass of wine would be wonderful if you have that."

"Yes we do. And old man, Nathaniel, how about you?

"I think wine sounds just about right, and I'll open a bottle. Nicki, would you prefer white or red?"

"White, thank you."

As the ladies sit and chat, Nat goes into the kitchen and returns shortly with a chilled bottle of Chardonnay. As he pours the wine, Nat hears a car coming up the driveway. "Must be Ben and Marilyn," he says.

As they approach the house, Ben turns to Marilyn, "0h honey, I think I forgot to tell you. Nat called to say that they are having some extra company for dinner. A young lady, who was in to see Nat about setting up a trip for Bob Burke; evidently knew Cole in college, so Nat invited her to join us for dinner. Nat was trying to track down Cole to make sure he was coming over for cards as he had indicated he might." Marilyn has a confused look on her face. "Well that's strange, what's the girl's name?"

"Don't know. He didn't say."

Chapter 27

A Dropped Coffee

Driving a black pick-up truck, Cole Dawson negotiates a winding road on his way to Nat's home. He wonders about the odd tone in Nat's voice when he had called him earlier that day. The Monday night poker game was something that Nat and Ben did on a regular basis, and Cole would join them only occasionally, but Nat made it sound as though the game couldn't go on tonight without him. He seemed insistent that there was something important he needed to discuss. It sounded important enough that Cole broke a dinner date with Matti Carlisle, a woman he has been dating regularly. Matti was pretty upset when he told her that he had to meet with Nat and Ben about something very important.

The group having finished dinner, they retire to the back deck for coffee, Nat and Ben lean against the deck railing, talking quietly, while Alice and Marilyn, both of whom have taken an instant liking to Nicki, sit chatting with her in the fading light at the end of the deck.

Nicki has been fielding questions, very carefully and tactfully phrased questions, from the two ladies, about how close she and Cole were when they were at school together. She has told them that she and Cole were good friends, but didn't expand on that. As nervous and excited as she is about the prospect of seeing Cole again, she doesn't want to admit, even to herself, that there is more to what she's feeling than just wanting to see an old friend again, but she aches to see him, all the while terrified of how he might react at seeing her again.

While the ladies chat, Nat says to Ben, "Cole had a date with Matti tonight, but I convinced him to break it and come over."

Ben looks surprised. "Why'd you do that?" he says, too loudly. The ladies look his way with curiosity.

Nat says, "Hold it down!" Then proceeds, "I just told him there's something real important we need to discuss."

Ben's surprise turns to confusion. "You mean you didn't tell him about the girl being here?"

"Nope."

"Why the hell not?"

"Cause I was afraid he might not come, and, well, I was real impressed with this girl, Nicki, real impressed, Ben, and I think there was something strong between her and Cole. You know how Cole acted when he came home from school, all down in the mouth, no spirit, like his heart was broken. Well, I think it was this girl, and I think they must have been real tight. Whatever happened, it broke the boy's heart."

Ben smiles. "What the hell are you, some kind of Cupid, or something? And you seem to know my boy better than I do."

"You know how much Cole means to me, Ben, he is like my son, too, and I'd give my life for him."

Ben places his hand on his brother's shoulder. "I know that, and I know Cole would do the same for you."

"Besides, Ben, the Carlisle woman is just after his money, you know that."

"Yeah, I expect you're right, but don't you think Cole can see through that?"

"Are you kidding? When did Cole become some kind of super male who can see through the wily schemes of a woman? Hell, she has him snookered three ways from Sunday."

Ben lowers his voice even more. "What makes you think this?"

"Well, he's seeing her pretty regularly, I'm told. If he wasn't seriously interested in her, don't you think he'd spread himself around? Hell, he could have all the nookie he wants, if that's all he's after. No, I think he's beginning to think about settling in with someone, maybe marrying."

It's almost dark as Cole arrives at his uncle's home, parks his truck and walks to the house. He knocks on the door as he enters, shouting, "Hello, is old Moneybags at home?"

"Out on the deck," Nat answers.

As he passes through the kitchen, Cole stops to pour himself a cup of coffee, then moves through a back door to the deck. "Hello son," Ben greets.

"Hi Dad. Hi Uncle Nat, I hope you got a good price for that Navy job, because I'm feeling awful lucky tonight."

Noticing the ladies, he walks toward them. "Hello my lovelies," he says with enthusiasm. Only then does he realize that there is someone else with his Mother and his Aunt, but in the dim light he does not recognize the person. It's a woman. She seems familiar. Nicki stands, and as she does, light from a window illuminates her face. She says, "Hello, Cole."

It was at the same instant that he saw her face that she spoke. The recognition from both sight and hearing converge on his mind in an electrifying jolt that, for a moment, paralyzes him. He stops in his tracks, dropping his cup. Shards of china tumble through splashes of coffee across the boards of the deck, but he doesn't notice.

"It's me Cole, it's Nicki."

"I know," he mumbles, but he seems unable to move, unable to bring together a consensus of his senses. It's Nicki, the person who has dominated his thoughts for ten years. He has thought of her almost daily, dreamed of her at night, tried to put her out of his mind, lived with the agony of believing that she hated him. And she's here. It's Nicki. He hears his voice, almost a whisper, from far away, "Nicki, is it really you?"

"Yes, Cole, it's me." The shudder again moves up her spine, just like it did earlier that day.

"But, how, why, where have you been, how are you here?"

She starts to speak, but can't. She clears her throat and this time succeeds, "I've come to Cascade to make arrangements for a visit by Senator Burke."

He heard Cascade, and Burke something, but it didn't register. He stammers, "Burke, Burke who?"

"Senator Burke. I work for Senator Robert Burke of West Virginia."

"Oh, of course, Senator Burke." He begins to regain his senses and composure. He steps toward her, not noticing the crunching of pieces of the broken cup beneath his shoes. "Uh, what do you do for him, what kind of work?"

Cole's mother feels a strong catch in her throat and a welling up of an emotion she hasn't felt for a time. Her suspicions are confirmed; she always felt that Cole came home from school broken-hearted. Tears form at the corners of her eyes. Alice Dawson has a very different feeling; she's delighted. She also sees and feels the love between these two young people. It's blatantly apparent and she's enchanted. Ben and Nat are each quietly appraising the scene before them.

Nicki has lost all awareness of those on the deck other than the man in front of her. All the love that she felt for this man, the love that lay dormant, the love that would not fade regardless of how hard she tried to bury it, all that love was suddenly rediscovered in this moment. It welled up in her breast, flooded her consciousness, and impacted her soul. Cole now stands close. She smells his cologne, the brand she gave him in college. In a voice barely audible she whispers, "I'm the Legislative Director in his office."

From her chair next to where Nicki had been seated, Alice Dawson stands. "Cole, sit here next to Nicki. It appears you two have a lot of catching up to do. I'll get what we'll need to clean up this mess that you've created and another cup of coffee for you."

"I'll help," says Marilyn Dawson as she leaves with Alice. Ben and Nat follow the women into the house, leaving Cole and Nicki alone on the deck.

"Thanks Aunt Alice," Cole says as his family leaves. He sits on the edge of the chair vacated by Alice. He turns the chair to face Nicki. He looks at her for a long moment. She feels herself blushing and finds it odd. Finally, he speaks. "How have you been, Nicki?"

"Just fine, Cole, I've been just fine. My job keeps me very busy, not a lot of spare time on my hands, so I've stayed out of trouble," she jokes, "And how about you?"

"Oh, I guess I'm okay. The company keeps me pretty busy. I've been trying to get into trouble, but I can't find anybody to help me do that!"

"I doubt that very much, Cole Dawson. I bet there are a lot of women in town who would love to get into some mischief with you." She hopes not.

"Maybe one or two, but I'm not serious, real serious, yet, about anyone." His mind searches, is he lying to himself? What about Matti? Is he not serious about her? Be careful, he tells himself. Don't start off with Nicki again, by telling a lie. "I have been dating a gal, a local woman, on a somewhat regular basis."

"Oh." Nicki murmurs, without betraying emotion. What does he mean by; yet, and regular?

"Yeah, but I don't think it's going to go anywhere. There's never been anyone come along that could make me for-" oops, he almost said; forget you. He recovers with; "Uh, that I could get solidly interested in." He's suddenly aware that he couldn't love Matti, at least not in the way that he loved Nicki, once. No, he couldn't still feel this strongly about Nicki and be in love with Matti. But before he starts moving too fast with Nicki, perhaps he should try to get an idea of her feeling. He doesn't want to make a fool of himself again. But a thought rockets through his mind, hell, why would she be here if she were not still interested?

Nicki's heart actually skiped a beat, she feels it thumping in her breast. He almost said; forget you, Nicki. He hasn't forgotten what they once had. He still cares! "Cole," she offers, "I regret, very much, my behavior back then, back at school. I acted so foolishly."

"Nonsense, Nicki, you reacted naturally, as one would when discovering they'd been lied to."

"I've thought a lot about this over the years, Cole. I've come to the realization that you were only trying to protect me from myself. I had such a warped view of reality. You tried to get past that and I wouldn't listen."

"Maybe we've both grown a little since then, Nicki."

"I hope that I've grown, Cole. I hope that I have."

He smiles, then changes the subject, "So you work for the Senator, do you like it?"

She remembers how she was once warmed by this smile, and is comforted that she still is. "I really love my job, Cole, and I like it in Washington. I have a lovely apartment in Arlington that I share with Max."

Oh God! She lives with a guy. Taking all the courage he can muster, he asks, "Max?"

"My dog. He's a Yorkie. He's adorable, Cole, and he's such good company for me."

Thank you, Lord, Cole acknowledges his appreciation. Then he asks the big one. "Is there anyone other than Max to keep you company?"

"I do have many good friends in Washington, friends of both gender, but no, Cole, no one in the sense that I think you mean."

His smile returns. "I'm glad."

She asks, coyly, "And the 'regular' gal, anything serious?"

"It may have gotten to be, but no chance of that now," he says, almost implying a promise.

"Then I'm glad too," she says, with a twinkle in her eye and that wonderful little impish twist to her smile.

There's a pause in their discussion. They are both excited about the direction of the conversation. He finds himself delighted that she's not involved with someone. She's intrigued that he's also apparently uncommitted.

Cole moves on. "Tell me, Miss Valentini, just what does a Legislative Director do?"

She nervously runs her hands across her thighs, smoothing her dress. "Oh, I have a group of people who kind of keep track of current legislation, and sort of study it carefully to determine the good and the bad features. Then we make suggestions to the Senator as to how he may want to react to it, and then I do a bunch of other unimportant things."

"And you're here in Cascade to do something for the Senator?"

"Yes. He's making a trip here, actually, I'll be traveling with him, in August, to host a group of military people at the new Navy Operations Center that your uncle Nat has constructed and I am doing a, well, a sort of preplanning visit to get a flavor for the location. The Senator considers this a highly important visit and an opportunity for our State to present some of its qualities."

"I see," he says.

197

She asks, with a devilish grin, "So tell me, Cole, did you graduate from Structural Engineering School?"

He drops his head to his chest then slowly lifts it to look directly into her eyes. "I'm so, so sorry, Nicki, no, I took my degree in Mining Engineering."

"I sort of assumed that," she says, with an honest and sincere smile.

Just then, Ben opens the door and calls, "Phone call for you, Cole."

"Can you take a message, Dad?"

"I think you better take it, son."

"Will you excuse me, Nicki? I'll just be a second."

"Of course."

Cole walks into the kitchen where Ben stands, holding the phone. "It's Matti," he says.

Cole takes the phone. "Hello."

The woman's voice oozes with concern. "Cole, was there a problem? Is anything wrong, anything that I can help with?"

"No Matti, it's nothing that involves you, it's a, well, it's a business matter involving Senator Burke and some of his people."

In the most sultry and earthy voice she can muster, Matti goes on, "The Senator? Why, that doesn't sound serious enough to take you away from your little Matti, I had planned a special treat for you tonight. Can I still see you, later?"

God, she sounds sexy. "I don't think so, Matti. I, I'm afraid we'll be kind of late."

"But I'm going to be here all night Cole, and I really do miss you. Can't you stop by? The time makes no difference."

Not knowing how to tactfully refuse, Cole simply says, "Perhaps, I'll call you later."

Returning to the deck, Cole pulls his chair closer to where Nicki sits. He reaches out and takes a hand that has been busily smoothing her dress. He squeezes it and asks, in a supremely gentle voice, "and how long do you think it might take for you to get this, flavor for the location, that you were talking about?"

198

She holds his gaze, returns the squeeze. She thinks that it may take a long, long time for her to get familiarized with the area. "Well, the Senator wants me to explore what kinds of activities are available to keep a General entertained for a few days. I guess how long it takes me to do that will depend on how much help I get from the locals."

Cole's eyes sparkle as a smile invades his face. "Would you consider me a local who may provide some of that help? I know all of the places that will turn on the average American General. And I happen to have a break in my schedule," he lies.

His smile is contagious and her own smile answers it. "Yes, I believe you could do very well as a tour guide, Mr. Dawson. Are you sure you can spare the time? I need to do a rather rigorous investigation." She doesn't mention that probably the only interest the General will have is in fishing.

Cole cannot believe what is happening. He's sitting with Nicola Valentini and she's smiling that beautiful smile. And, in all likelihood, they are going to spend the next several days together. Obviously exhilarated, he replies, "It will take a monumental effort to adjust my busy schedule; allow me three minutes to do that in the morning and I will then be at your service, but, actually we shouldn't wait until morning, this important assignment calls for action now. Why not start tonight with a margarita down at the inn?"

Her eyes get a little misty. "You remember, I like Margaritas," she says, very softly.

Over the margaritas Cole and Nicki relive their time together at college. They talk about how the few weeks they had were the best time either of them had ever experienced. They laugh about how they would meet between classes for a quick hot dog, just to be able to spend five minutes together. They agree that the Pierpoint Inn Margaritas are not even a close second to those at The Chili Pepper. When the lounge closes at midnight, they move into the sitting room where they each sit in old rockers, in front of the dark fireplace and chat for another hour. Nicki tells him how, if there were a fire in the fireplace, she would curl up on the rug and fall fast asleep. He offers to build her one. "No," she laughs, "I'm sure you can build a great fire, Mister Dawson, but I'm really so very, very tired, and I want to be well rested for my tour guide in the morning, shall we call it a day?"

"I hate to leave, Nicki," Cole says.

"And I don't want you to, but," and she leaves her words hanging, not knowing how to finish. No, she doesn't want him to leave, but she also doesn't want to do anything that may give him the wrong impression, and she wants some time alone to collect her thoughts before they will be together again tomorrow, and she's totally exhausted.

"May I at least walk you to your room?" He asks, taking hold of her hand.

"Yes you may," she says, sweetly.

On the walk to her room, Cole suggests she get a long night's sleep and that he will pick her up at ten o'clock the next morning, after spending some time at his office clearing his schedule. He suggests she not wear business clothes, but something more casual. As they arrive at her door, Nicki gives him her key and he unlocks the door. He turns to her, takes her right hand, turns it palm up, places her key in it and closes her hand around it. Without releasing her hand, he says, "Hold very tightly to that, my Lady. Otherwise, some scoundrel may steal it and find his way into your chamber."

She lifts her face to look into his eyes, and with a tired, but warm smile says, "I have so much enjoyed this evening, Cole, it was wonderful. Being with you again has been a magical tonic and I thank you for that. I'm excited about spending tomorrow with you."

"And I with you," he says softly, and squeezes her hand. She enters the door and turns, continuing to look into his eyes as she slowly closes the door and whispers, "Good night."

Returning to his truck, Cole picks up his cell phone and dials Matti. "Hello," she says, with a sleepy voice.

"It's Cole, did I wake you?"

"I guess so, what time is it, are you coming over?"

"No, Matti, I've got a real busy day coming up, I'd better get home and hit the sack."

Chapter 28

The Guide

At ten o'clock Cole strides into the lobby of the Pierpoint Inn, whistling a Beatles tune. The young lady at the desk, who obviously knows him very well, as does everyone in town, greets him with, "Why, Mr. Dawson, what makes you so merry this morning?"

As he steps up to the desk, Cole winks at her and replies, "Darci, my little lovely, you're looking at the luckiest man in the county. No, the luckiest man in the world."

"Well, it shows, Mr. Dawson, would you like me to call Miss Valentini's room?" Darci said, with a knowing look.

He looks genuinely puzzled. "Now how do you know that I'm here to get Miss Valentini?"

Not wanting to disclose that the word passed through the staff that Cole was with Nicki until very late last night, Darci fibs with a mischievous grin, "A little bird told me."

Cole returns her grin. "Then you should ask that little bird for the number to the lottery because it certainly must be clairvoyant, and yes, I'm here for Miss Valentini."

Soon, Nicki is descending the stairs with a greeting, "Good morning, Cole." She wears a white skirt, white sandals and a yellow and white blouse. Simple pearl earrings adorn her ears. She carries a straw tote bag. She's well rested and looks radiant. Her cheeks are rosy, her eyes sparkle and there is a marked robustness in her step. He thought she had been beautiful the day before, but she looks so much more alive now. He quickly walks to the base of the stairs to meet her and as he does, he almost gasps the words, "Nicki, you look, you look, my God, you're beautiful!"

She blushes noticeably, "Thank you, sir."

As they leave the inn and start down the walk, Cole is startled to see Matti Carlisle walking toward them. Eying Nicki suspiciously, she says, "Cole, darling, I see you've started your busy day," with a strong emphasis on 'busy'.

Cole winces at the, 'darling'. It's not a term that Matti normally uses. "Hello, Matti. What brings you to the Inn this morning?"

Now ignoring Nicki, she replies, "I'm meeting a client, a

Navy man whose moving to town, showing him the old Nichols place. I missed you last night, Cole. I waited up real late, you know."

"I'm sorry about that, Matti. Let me introduce you to a friend of mine, Nicki Valentini, we went to school together. Nicki, this is Matti Carlisle, the lady I told you about last night."

Nicki extends her hand. "Hello Matti."

Matti weakly accepts Nicki's hand, then says, coolly, "So you were Cole's important discussion last night."

"I'm sorry?" Nicki replies, with a look of bewilderment.

Cole interrupts, "I had a dinner date with Matti last evening, Nicki, and I broke it when Uncle Nat conned me into coming over to see you."

"Oh." Nicki responds, as the bewildered look turns to one of understanding, and she smiles at Cole.

Matti takes on a hurtful look. "You lied to me, Cole. You said you were talking to someone about a Senator, or something."

"That's true, Matti. Nicki is an aide to Robert Burke."

"Who's he?"

"The Senator, Matti, the Senator."

"Oh."

Cole looks sincere as he tells Matti, "Look, Matti, I'm sorry if I misled you, but Nicki and I do have business to conduct and we need to be on our way." With that, Cole takes Nicki's arm and walks her toward his car, a black Cadillac STS, which is parked at the curb.

Matti stands on the walk, with a pouty look on her face, as they walk away.

After seating Nicki, Cole walks around the car, gets in, turns to her and says, "I'm sorry about that, Nicki."

She smiles. "You don't have to explain."

He looks at her seriously. "I do have to explain. I won't let us get into a situation where you may think I'm lying to you again. I'll never be dishonest with you again, Nicki, not like I was when I lied about our coal business, never. Last night's phone call, at Uncle Nat's, that was Matti. I told her I was talking business. What I didn't tell her was that it was with a beautiful woman."

Nicki blushes. Cole goes on, "She asked me to stop by her place when I was finished. After I left you, I called her, told her I had a busy day today and was going home to bed. That's it, Nicki, and there's no longer anything between she and I, I promise you that."

"But Cole, I don't want you to feel obligated to tell me this, it's your own business."

He takes her hand. "But I want it to be your business too."

She looks genuinely moved. "You're so sweet. And I respect you so much for your honesty. I promise you, also, that whatever the future may hold for us, I will always be candid with you."

He places her hand to his lips and softly kisses it. Then, playfully says, "Dawson Tours at your service, Miss, what can I show you?"

"Well," she replies, looking suddenly full of zest, "the Mayor and Mr. Lewis showed me the town yesterday and some of the countryside. We developed a plan to welcome the entourage when they arrive, so the only remaining thing I need to do is work up a plan for the leisure time of the General. Now, let me see, in my research I learned that, besides trout fishing, he enjoys golf, shooting trap, whatever that is, and horseback riding, yes, he loves horses and is quite an accomplished rider, western style. Do you think you can find us places to do those things?"

Cole breaks into a wide grin, "Why, Lady, you have just made our task very easy, we can do all of those things at my place, except for the golf."

"We can? Your place?" Nicki asks with an astonished grin, "Even shooting trap?"

"Even shooting trap," he laughs.

"That's wonderful, and then we can probably work out a plan for him pretty quickly, do you think?"

As Cole starts the car, he says, "I think we can make the General very comfortable at my place, I'll need to get it cleaned up a little, but I think we can provide him a very enjoyable stay."

"But Cole, I don't want to impose on you, he would love to

stay here at the Pierpoint, I'm sure."

"Well, let me see," Cole deliberates. "We could put him up here at the Pierpoint for the first night, so he could enjoy the experience of the inn, and then arrange golf at Lakeside Country Club, over on Cheat Lake, or at the Wisp at Deep Creek Lake, both are great courses, especially the Wisp, it's the more challenging of the two. Do you know how well he plays?"

"I was told he has a seven handicap, whatever that means."

Cole whistles! "A seven, huh, okay, I think we may want to set him up at The Wisp, that will give him a test, but we'll look at both places, talk to the managements and you can decide between the two of them. Why don't we take a ride over to Deep Creek, check out the Wisp, have lunch on the lake, at McGuinty's, then drive over to Lakeside to check it out, and depending on the timing, perhaps have dinner at the Club."

Even before he finished speaking he can tell from her smile that she agrees with his plan, so he puts the car in gear and pulls away as she affirms that his plan is excellent.

On the drive to Deep Creek Lake, which is located across the line, in Maryland, they enjoy remembering their times together at school. Cole asks, "So how is your friend, Jaime, these days, are you still in touch?"

Nicki looks sad. "No, I haven't seen her for awhile. We remained in contact after school. I was working in Washington. She was working for a modeling agency in New York where she made a great deal of money, then she moved to Arlington, said she was taking a break from work and just wanted to spend some time with me. Then the strangest thing happened." She pauses for a long moment, as though she's trying to frame her next words.

"What, what happened?" Cole asks.

"Well, in the beginning, after she came to Arlington, we were spending a lot of time together, really enjoying each other's company again, just like in school. Then, one evening we were at her apartment when her phone rang and she asked me to answer it. It was a man, not so unusual, but he sounded strange, kind of business-like, you know, and he evidently thought I was Jaime, and he said, "It's me, can I see you this evening?" Well, I called Jaime to the phone and she agreed to meet this man. She sounded very hesitant, at first, then, she agreed to meet him, and Cole, I could tell they were agreeing on a hotel."

Cole reaches over, pats her hand and says with a grin, "I wouldn't be too concerned. I have a hunch she's been to a hotel room with a guy before."

"No, it's not that, not just that. This was an older man. Not old, but older. You know, you can tell. And then, a few days later, we met for lunch at this place down town, a little cafe where we had a table out front, and this big Lincoln pulled up to the curb. A man got out and came directly to where we were sitting and said to Jaime, "Can you break away for a few hours? He'd like to see you." Well, she made a flimsy excuse about some kind of interview for a photo shoot, and left with him. Cole, it wasn't the same voice that was on the phone, and how did this guy know where to find her?"

Cole shakes his head, "That is strange, and sounds spooky. Maybe Jaime's a spy," he laughs.

Nicki pokes him in the shoulder, "Oh, you're still impossible, Cole Dawson. But, I'm serious, I'm worried about her. I'm afraid she," and her words trail off.

"What, afraid she's what?"

"In business for herself," Nicki blurts out.

Cole looked puzzled. "What do you mean? What kind of business?"

Nicki scrunches up her nose. He loves it when she does that. "Well, not really a business kind of business," she says. "Do you follow me?"

Now his puzzled look turns to bewilderment. "Well, ah, I guess not," he says.

She looks directly at him and says, sadly, "I think she must be a paid escort."

"Wow!" He blurts out. "Really?"

"Really. In school she was kind of promiscuous, well, not kind of, she was. I worried about that a lot, but I never expected her to end up doing what she does. She was living very well, making a lot of money modeling, I thought. She's very pretty, you know. I don't know how she got into this other thing. And I'm going to have to be very careful, I can't risk continuing our friendship, you know, with me working for the Senator. If the media were to find out it could taint him, and that would be horrible. I need to stop having contact with her, at least for now, and I feel very guilty about that, she needs my friendship."

"I understand, absolutely, but there's no reason for you to feel guilty," he assures her. "But don't you think you should confront her about it, find out if your suspicions are correct?"

"Oh Cole, I'm afraid to do that. If she wanted me to know I think she would have told me, I don't want to embarrass her."

He nods. "Yeah, I guess. Well, what else is new? Your mother, how is she?"

"Momma died, Cole," she says, very softly. "Five years ago."

"Aw no. Lord, how? Aw gosh, I'm sorry Nicki."

"It's okay. It was hard for awhile. You know, the thing with you and I, then Momma, now this business with Jaime, It seems that I am being tested."

Cole truly hurts for her, especially since his actions contributed to her trials. "Gosh, Nicki, I hope I can make things up to you, make up for my foolishness."

"Don't be silly, Cole, you didn't do anything wrong. Let's change the subject, okay? Tell me more about where we're going, the Wisp, is that what you called it?"

The rest of the drive to the Wisp was spent with Cole describing the passing countryside and Nicki telling him about her experiences working for the Senator. They also talked about Cole's management of the Coal Company and how the mine and the town had prospered since his grandfather had started the present mine, the second mine developed by his family. He talked about the explosion that had killed his great-grandfather and the closing and sealing of the mine. He described how the workers for the Dawson mine participated in the profits and that last year's bonus averaged $20,000 per employee. She couldn't believe it. "Cole, you're kidding, twenty thousand dollars, each?"

"Yep, twenty. It was a good year."

"My God, Cole," she said with widened eyes, "that's unbelievable. The Mayor alluded to the fact that your family had done very well for the community and its people, but I had no idea."

Cole looks embarrassed. "It's really not that big a deal, it's something that my grandfather instituted, and I think my dad encouraged him. I know dad certainly followed in granddad's steps. The Dawson's always did well for the town, but I think when granddad started the new mine and the bonus plan, things really took off."

"Why, Cole, I am really, sincerely impressed with this, and the town, Cascade is certainly not like the mining towns that I have experienced."

"This is what I wanted to tell you back in school, Nicki, to explain that all mine owners were not greedy bastards, but I couldn't figure out how to do it. Of course, now I know that I should have just said it and made sure that you understood, but I was kind of immature then, I guess, and afraid of losing you, which, of course, I did, my stupidity costing me our friendship." As he finished they arrived at the entrance to The Wisp.

"Cole, you were not stupid, it was I," Nicki says as Cole stops in front of the resort office.

"Well, whatever, Miss Valentini, I just hope that maybe I can talk you into giving me another chance, but, we're here, let's see what these folks can do for the General."

The rest of the day was a whirlwind of activity. Their long discussions with the management of the Wisp ran into lunch and by the time they drove back to West Virginia and went through the same process at the Lakeview Country Club, over dinner, then returned to Cascade, it was after ten o'clock when they entered the Pierpoint. "Could the tour guide buy the lady a drink to cap off a great day?" Cole asks.

"Just one," she replies with a weak smile. "I am so tired, you wore me out today. I thought after such a good rest last night I could go forever, but I guess I was more run down than I thought, so, just one, okay?"

He grins. "Just one and then we tuck you in for the night."

An hour later, when he opened her door and again put the key into her hand, he held both her hands tightly. He wanted so much to go into her room with her. He ached with the desire to hold her, to love her, but he was also afraid to push too fast. And, he's sure that she's tired and that concerns him.

He says to himself, *tomorrow, Miss Valentini, you will not escape my clutches, but for tonight, I'll settle for a small kiss.*

"Any chance," he asks, "of a guy getting a good night kiss?"

She responds with a warm, sincere, loving smile and, moving closer to him, raises her face. Her lips part slightly. They are moist. He bends to meet them with his own. His kiss is soft and tender, not passionate, but sensitive and caring. She's warmed and touched by his tenderness and thoughtfulness. She knows that if he pressed she would surrender to him, but he respects her and she loves him even more for that. *"I do love him. I do love him so very much,"* she says to herself.

The following morning at eight o'clock, Cole pulls up in front of the Pierpoint in his pick-up truck. He's dressed in faded jeans and a red plaid shirt. He had suggested to Nicki the night before that she wear jeans if she had them. He's whistling again as he enters the inn. Darci smiles and says, "Shall I call her?"

"If you would be so kind, my sweet lady," he says, smiling broadly.

Within minutes Nicki is waving as she comes down the stairs. This morning she's wearing tailored jeans, short, black boots, a black sleeveless scoop-neck sweater and carrying a black cardigan over her arm. She wears a fine gold chain with a tiny cross, around her neck.

Cole seems transfixed. She smiles as she reaches the bottom of the steps and he meets her there with, "How do you do it?"

"Do what?"

"How do you look so much more beautiful each time I see you? I don't think it's possible."

"Oh, you're just full of it," she laughs, as she gives him a hug.

Cole suggests they have breakfast in the dining room and talk about the day's plan. As they do, Nicki again suggests that having the General use Cole's place is too much of an imposition. Cole reassures her. "Nicki, If he's the outdoor type, as it sounds, he will be wild about my place. He can fish the greatest trout stream in the east, five miles of pure, wild, waters full of native brook trout, all to himself. He can shoot his heart out, and I've got some great horses, he can ride for a month and not use the same trail."

"Well, if you're sure," she concedes.

"Nicki, this is great, we'll head right out to the farm and I'll show you what I mean. I brought my truck just in case we need to go off-road to show you the real Preston County."

A short while later, breakfast finished, they are in Cole's truck and as he pulls away from the curb his heart races at the prospect of taking Nicki to his farm. What a great day! What an absolutely fantastic day! Nicki looks at him with smiling eyes and flushes as she recognizes the boyish enthusiasm that charmed her so much in the beginning.

Soon they're driving up a long, winding grade on a road lined with hemlocks as they travel southward, out of town. Cole explains that they are driving up the base of Davis Ridge, a mountain that Cole's great, great grandfather, Tom Dawson, had inspired the West Virginia legislature to rename for a young soldier who had saved Dawson's life when they had both fought in the civil war. "They were in the cavalry, Nicki, and he was shot and wounded by a Confederate sniper. Then, before the sniper could reload his rifle and finish what he started, Granddad's buddy, a fella by the name of Matt Davis, put a bullet into the guy's heart. Later on in the war, Davis lost his life. Ol Tom Dawson never forgot him. My grandfather told me the story many times when I was a kid."

"That's a wonderful story," Nicki replied. "How did Tom Dawson talk the government into doing that, renaming a piece of geography?"

"Well, he owned the mountain, I guess that was part of it, and he was a pretty influential guy, all the old Dawson's were. They settled this part of the country way back in the old days."

"How far back?" She asked.

"In the late 1700's," Cole went on, "The first was Robert Dawson. He had fought in the revolutionary war and was given a large piece of land in Maryland; they did that for veterans of the war. The higher the rank of the vet the bigger the chunk of land. Anyway, Robert Dawson traded his patent on the land in Maryland for this land that we're driving on right now, about twenty thousand acres."

Nicki's jaw dropped. "T w e n t y t h o u s a n d a c r e s!" she exclaimed.

"Yep, twenty thousand."

Nicki could not imagine one person owning 20,000 acres of West Virginia. She looked quizzically at Cole and asked, "How long did he keep it? Did he sell any of it?"

"Oh no, he never sold any, split it between his four kids, 5000 acres apiece. Then, one of those four left his 5000 to my great, great grandfather who then bought 3000 more acres from an uncle. Most of the 20,000 is still owned by Dawson descendants. The 8000 that was my great, great grandfather's is now owned jointly by Dad and Uncle Nat. Of course, I own the small piece that the farm sits on, 500 acres."

Nicki is overwhelmed. It's becoming apparent that the Dawson's must be very, very wealthy. An obviously very successful mining company, a lumber operation with thousands of acres of timber, and a construction company.

"Cole," she says, in the form of a question, "Your family must be very wealthy, it didn't strike me that way from the time I spent with them last evening, they seemed so, so normal."

"They are normal, Sweetie, they are very normal."

The fact that he called her, Sweetie, does not escape her. It warms her to think that he's becoming so familiar once again. But, she's still reeling from this new information, this new insight into Cole's past life; that he's from what must be an extremely wealthy family, but remains so down-to-earth, so unpretentious. She's drawn even more to this man who has so affected her life for the second time.

"Well, anyway, as I was explaining, this is the base of Davis Ridge and we're now about two miles out of town and about five hundred feet higher. Just ahead, the road levels out and follows along the side of the slope. Off to our right, across the valley, that's Laurel Mountain. Cascades Creek tumbles down the valley between Davis and Laurel Mountains, drops about a hundred and fifty feet a mile, pretty spectacular, you'll soon get a close look."

"Oh Cole, it's such beautiful country."

At this slightly higher elevation the hemlocks have thinned a bit and the forest becomes more of a mixture of hardwoods, white pine and spruce. Cole explains how the Dawsons have managed the growth of timber for over two hundred years, how they have done selective cutting and replanted species that grow better in this particular environment. He refers to some areas of the forest as, microenvironments, where a combination of elevation, soil and moisture conditions provide particularly strong growth for individual species. The road winds between patches of thick evergreens, gleaming silver beech, shaggy hickory and towering oaks.

"It's truly an enchanted forest," Nicki marvels.

In a short while they turn off the hard road and travel down a tree lined lane with rolling meadows gently falling away to their right. Several sleek horses graze in the distance. A little further on, they cross a stone bridge where a brook tumbles down the hill from their left, under the bridge and over moss covered rocks into a clear, deep pool that is restrained by a stone impoundment. Before them spreads a scene that appears to have been lifted from a storybook.

There are barns, stables, sheds, and fenced pastures holding a variety of horses and a large, old stone house. There are fences of stone and of split rails and there are wooden gates. There is a large stone well behind the house with a genuine wooden bucket hanging under a windless. An old copper weather vane, a horse, atop the largest barn, turns slowly in the breeze. Two colts frolic in a pasture beside them.

The farm is the same one built by Tom Dawson and later occupied by Cole's grandfather, Alex Dawson. It's largely unchanged from the way it was built a hundred years before. Nicki is enchanted. This girl who grew up in a dingy mining camp and has lived in urban apartments since leaving home, is spellbound. "Cole, it takes my breath away, what a wonderful, magical, Oh Cole, I'm speechless."

"I thought you'd like it," he says with a delighted grin as he stops his truck near the house, at a point where they have a good view of the lawn as it falls away to the creek below. The waters of Cascades still tumble over huge boulders a hundred yards down the sloping lawn. The crashing water seems to be trying, heroically, to escape its jangled channel. Beyond the creek, to the northwest, the rolling foothills still create a magical setting for the majesty of Laurel Mountain as they did when Tom Dawson stood in this spot. "I use the original house," Cole continues. "I built a nice cabin of hemlock and stone just up the creek a couple of hundred yards, It makes a really nice guest house and I think will work well for the General's stay. It has three bedrooms and there's even a bunk house behind it, so I figure, assuming that he'll have some kind of security contingent with him, it should accommodate them very well. We'll go on down and take a look at it in a minute, but first I'll show you my old place."

"Cole, this place is so, it's so, you, it fits you so perfectly, everything about it."

As they get out of the truck, Cole says, apologetically, "I hope you don't find the house too much of a mess. I have a cleaning gal come in every once and awhile and I did a little picking up this morning, but I'm afraid the old place reflects the life of a bachelor."

"I'm sure it looks just fine," she comforts him.

They climb the front steps, but before they enter the house, Nicki turns to look at the view from the porch. The summer color of the rolling hills of the valley are various shades of green, but generally of a darker hue. Beyond, the steep rising slopes of Laurel Mountain have a hint of blue. As the mountain rises in the distance, there are tiny spots of red where some of the old maples have already, in late July, taken on some fall color due to a dryer than normal summer. Nicki is mesmerized by the spectacle.

As they enter the house through a large, solid oak plank door, her eyes are first drawn to a magnificent stone fireplace. The stones are of limestone and sandstone with a sprinkling here and there of shiny, black coal. "I guess old Tom was proud of his coal discovery," Cole says as he describes the fireplace to Nicki. Huge hemlock posts and beams support the structure and wide, knotty hemlock planks form the walls. The floor is laid with pine boards that have a reddish cast to them. The wear patterns reveal the softness of the old pine. The interior of the house reminds Nicki of the main lodge at the ski resort of Seven Springs, where she and Jaime went skiing with friends one weekend.

Chapter 29

The Four-Poster

As Cole shows Nicki through the house he points out that much of the original furniture of Tom and Elizabeth still remains in use. Upholstered pieces have been replaced over the years, but most of the original wooden tables, hutches, cabinets, beds, armoires and such, still remain. A large chestnut bed graces Cole's bedroom. He explains that the bed is over two hundred years old and belonged to Robert Dawson, the original Dawson settler. During those two centuries the wood has taken on a satin patina that Nicki finds to be of incredible charm. "Cole," she coos, as she slides a hand across the edge of the large headboard, "This is the most beautiful piece of furniture I've ever seen, it's absolutely remarkable, I'm running out of superlatives to describe this day, this place, this home, how happy you must be to live here."

He gives her a winsome smile and replies, "but it's been a lonely place, Nicki, and a lonely time."

"Well shame on you for keeping such a wonderful place all to yourself, you should have found someone to share it," she tells him, not meaning it at all.

He steps close to her, places his hand to her cheek, then raises it to her forehead where he gently moves a lock of hair that has fallen from its natural place, then says softly, "Perhaps I have."

Realizing where they are, in his bedroom, Nikie raises her hand to his, gently grasps it, pulls it down to her side and then leads him from the room as she chides, "I don't trust you, Cole Dawson, come, show me the rest of the house."

Finished with the tour of the main house, Cole takes her on a quick tour of the grounds around the house, then suggests they return to the truck. "But I haven't seen it all," she protests, "I want to see the stables and the horses, I want to pet the horses."

"We have lots of time for that, come, I want to show you something." They return to the truck and he takes her back up the lane toward the stone bridge. Just before the bridge he places the truck in four-wheel drive, turns off the lane

217

and proceeds up the hill alongside the tumbling brook. They follow the brook for a quarter of a mile up a fairly steep slope. The brook tumbles and cascades over rocks and ledges on its way to the pool below and ultimately into the rushing water of Cascades. Soon, Cole's truck levels out on a large shelf that sits at the base of a sheer rock face, which rises straight up for a hundred feet. Water falls from a notch at the top of the ragged cliff and mists as it descends to a large pool at the base. From there, it forms the brook which they followed up the hill. "It's magnificent," Nicki whispers. Cole stops the truck, facing the waterfall. "Let's get out here," he says as he opens his door, then walks around to her side.

He leads her to their right, forty yards, where they stand on a large rock ledge. The valley spreads out below them, the farm buildings hidden by an outcropping of spruce covered rock. He stands behind her, with his hands on her arms, just below her shoulders and turns her slightly so that she's looking up the valley between the mountains. They can see forever. The sound of the falling water, in the background, plays a soothing melody of contentment, serenity, tranquility. He draws her close, her back against his chest. Close enough that his face is in her hair. He speaks softly into her ear, "Wouldn't this be a wonderful spot for someone to build a home?" She turns and buries her face in his chest.

She clings to him, tightly. She says nothing for a long time, just presses her body against his. Then she lifts her face to look into his eyes. Her eyes are moist. Her large, beautiful, dark eyes with the tiny flames. She tries to speak, "Cole," but he puts a finger to her lips and says. "Don't say anything, I want to show you the rest."

"There's more?" She sighs, "What more can there possibly be?"

"I want to show you my hiding spot, my own secret hiding place where I can escape when the whole world seems to press in on me, it's a special place, I think you'll like it."

Soon they are back in the truck and driving past Cole's house, heading towards the creek below. Once at the creek, the lane turns and follows the creek upstream through large outcroppings of rock and huge, huge hemlocks. Giant, moss covered hulks of fallen trees accent the cathedral-like appearance of the forest, darkened by the canopy high overhead. "I've never seen such large trees," Nicki marvels. "This section is virgin forest, never been timbered," Cole tells her. "These trees are hundreds of years old. Most people have never seen a virgin forest. The forests of the eastern mountains have been logged for two hundred years, about every thirty to sixty years, but this has never been cut. It's just the way Robert Dawson found it in 1785. You notice that there are no small trees or undergrowth, the sun cannot reach the forest floor, so nothing new can sprout except where an old tree has died. Can you imagine how difficult it must have been for the old lumbermen to cut down one of these monsters, with hand axes and saws, it's hard for me to fathom."

Cole's eyes sparkle as he talks. Nicki is tickled and warmed by his enthusiasm. The boyish quality that she fell in love with years ago. "It's unbelievable, remarkably unbelievable," she says. Soon, Nicki sees a building appear from the trees ahead. It's a log cabin setting among the trees, just above the creek. As they get closer she sees a moss covered stone chimney climbing one side of the cabin. A porch almost hangs over the creek. This must be the cabin that Cole told her that the General could use, and, it must be his hiding place. He stops the truck and turns to her. "What do you think?" He asks.

"It's too much! You just keep coming up with all these wonderful, remarkable creations, I don't know what more to say, it's just, this is a perfect hiding place, Cole. I can see how you can shut out the rest of the world in a place like this."

"Come see the inside," he playfully orders.

The inside of the cabin is just as quaint and rustic as the outside, something out of a 1920's outdoor magazine. It has a smoky, woody smell with comfortable looking wood and leather furniture. Old guns and hunting and trout fishing equipment hang on the walls. He shows her the bedrooms, also with rustic furnishings. The large bed in the master bedroom is made of debarked and varnished pine poles and covered with an old fashioned quilted comforter. Cole grins from ear to ear. "I've been working on the cabin for years, off and on," he says. "It was first built by Alex Dawson, my grandfather. It kind of went unused for a long time after he died. Isn't it the neatest place you've ever seen?"

"Yes, it is, it's without a doubt the most wonderful place I've ever seen," she laughs, catching his excitement.

"Okay," he says, "What can I get you to drink, there's soft drinks, beer and white wine sitting in the spring and there's red wine in the springhouse. Sorry, I don't have the stuff to make a Margarita, I was gonna get it in town this morning, but forgot."

"I shouldn't, this early, but this is a special day, how about a glass of red wine?" she asks with a warm smile.

"Okay, you take a seat on the porch and enjoy the surroundings while I get a bottle from out back, how about a Merlot?" he asks as he moves toward a back door.

"That would be wonderful," she replies over her shoulder as she strolls toward the front door. Once on the porch she feels a little coolness coming from the water. It's a bright and sunny day, but with the heavy forest shade and the cool water of the creek, coupled with a slight breeze, she feels a chill, so she walks back inside the cabin to get the cardigan that she threw across a chair when they first entered. As she picks it up she happens to glance out a window and she sees Cole emerge from the darkness of a small stone building, which is tucked into the bank to the side of the cabin. He has a bottle of wine in his hand. He looks at the label, shakes his head and ducks back into what must be the springhouse. He does the same thing twice more before he evidently finds the bottle he's looking for. It's a small thing, she thinks, but it gives her such a warm feeling to know that he wants the wine to be just the right selection. He closes the old wooden door to the springhouse and steps back into the cabin. He finds her standing there, cardigan in hand, looking at him. His hair, as usual, tumbles in a hundred different directions, and a piece of cobweb, from the springhouse, hangs from his ear. "Oh, I thought you were on the porch," he said. She smiles. "You're so sweet; I think I'm going to cry." A crooked smile, a confused, crooked smile overruns his face. "What, did I do? Why am I sweet?"

"You just are, that's all, you just are."

The confusion fades from his smile, but the smile itself doesn't and as he walks to a drawer to get a bottle opener he says, in a very business-like way, "Well, Miss Valentini, I don't know why you think I'm sweet, but it certainly is a good sign, because it means that you and I are operating on the same wave length."

"I hope so," she says softly.

He now has the corkscrew in hand and reaches into a cabinet for two wineglasses. Retrieving those, he suggests, "Shall we sit on the front porch?"

On the porch, Nicki puts on the cardigan and they sit in rustic, bent hickory chairs that face one another. To the side is a small table where Cole sets the wineglasses. The sound of the water tumbling over rocks nourishes the tranquil atmosphere. The air is pure and sweet and fresh. Sitting here, in this place, with this man, Nicki feels contentment, freedom, fulfillment. She feels as though she has found a part of herself that has been lost for a long, long time.

Cole looks at Nicki as he works to open the wine. She's looking at the water. A tender breeze lifts a lock of hair that has somehow escaped its station. She brushes it back into place with a delicate hand, a gentle hand, the hand of a real lady, he thinks. She turns and catches him staring at her. She blushes. And it's an honest blush, no pretense. There is no pretense with this woman. He pours their two glasses. He hands Nicki one of them and picking up the other, he says, "I would like to offer a toast."

She smiles and lifts her glass. He hesitates, seems to almost choke up, but quickly recovers. Nicki can almost see a moistness to his eyes that was not there a moment ago. With an almost imperceptible break in his voice, he says, "To discovery, I toast discovery. I have discovered a treasure that was once in my grasp, but was lost to me. Now that I have been blessed with rediscovery of this treasure I pray to God Almighty that I shall never lose it again." And he touches his glass to hers.

As Cole spoke the words, tears formed in Nicki's eyes. Now, one slowly trickles down her cheek. Her lips part, but words do not come at first. When they do come, a brief moment later, her voice trembles. "I too lift my glass in a toast to discovery, and I too have re-found a wonderful prize, an elegant prize that has been mostly lost to me, but not completely, it's always been in my heart." And she touches her glass to his, and they each sip the wine.

Cole starts to speak, but she puts a finger to his lips and says, "Don't say anything, let me, I need to tell you why, Cole, why I pushed you away."

"There's no need, Nicki, no need to say anything."

"Oh there is, Cole, there is." Now the tears are streaming down her face. "I need to say it, to explain, to say what a foolish and crippled person I was. Since the moment I saw you the other evening I've wanted to explain. And I always wanted to contact you when I got out of the hospital, but by then so much time had passed and I was afraid, afraid you had forgotten me and probably found someone else, and -"

Cole interrupts her, "Hospital? What? What do you mean hospital?"

She looks genuinely confused. "The hospitals, in Morgantown, and then in Pittsburgh, I thought you knew!"

He looks totally flabbergasted. "No, no I didn't know you were in the hospital. Why, why were you?" He pulls his chair to hers until their knees touch. He takes a clean, white handkerchief from his pocket and begins to dab at her tears as she answers. "I lost a whole year of my life. Something just went all wrong. I thought I was a little girl again, I had visions and was confused, thought my poppa, my father, died all over again. I didn't eat, was in a deep depression. Oh, Cole, it was horrible. The doctors told me that somehow the discovery that your family owned a coal mine triggered something that caused me to finally realize that my father was dead, that I never fully accepted that he was gone, that I had such intense, deeply held anger, and that something just snapped."

Cole shakes his head slowly. "And I did that to you, Nicki, I did that to you."

"Oh, Cole, no, no, it was not your fault, Darling, it was not your fault." She pauses to wipe her nose with his hanky, not even realizing what she had called him, but he didn't miss it. With nose dutifully daubed, she continues, "Nor was it mine, I know that now. But it took over a year for me to get well, to understand what was behind it all, and by then I thought I had lost you, you never came to see me."

Cole grips her shoulders. "But Nicki, I tried! I tried constantly."

"I know, my sweet, I know. My mother told me years later. She was angry, and so was Jaime. They thought it was your fault, but it wasn't, and you must never, never feel that it was. What you did was natural, after all, you were dealing with a nut case," she grins, now almost finished with her sobbing.

Cole looks at her for a moment, her nose red from her rubbing it with the hanky, her eyes still wet from the tears. He thinks she's the most adorable creature in the world. "Do you know what you called me?" he asks.

"Called you?" she repeats.

"Yes, you called me, darling, I like that. But you know what, I don't think I ever told you my real name."

"Cole is not your real name?"

"It's Colbert!" he says, as he feigns a serious expression.

She puts her hands to her mouth, her eyes laugh. "Cole is short for Colbert?"

"It is."

"But I like it!" She squeaks.

"You don't need to. You'll probably never hear it again," he quips. Then he reaches out, puts his hands on her shoulders and stands, pulling her up with him. He slides his hands down her arms, then moves his arms around her, pulling her to him. He holds her in a firm embrace. Tears well up in his eyes. In a husky, but soft whisper, with lips close to her ear he appeals, "How did it happen, Nicki? I would have come for you in a heartbeat, my precious, if I had thought for a single moment that you still cared. I thought you hated me for lying to you. God, how I've missed you."

Nicki, through her own tears, which reappeared with his, looks up into his eyes and says in a delicate, fragile voice, "I have been a fool. A complete fool for all these years. I have wasted so much of our precious time. How can I ever make it up to you?" She buries her face in his chest.

He moves his hands to each side of her head and gently lifts it until they again look into each other's eyes, and says, "I love you, Nicki, I love you so much."

Tears flow from her radiant eyes and the tiny flames still flicker deep inside them. She trembles with excitement. Her heart pounds. "I love you my dearest, my most precious darling, I love you," and her lips rise to his.

The passion they both feel in the kiss is overwhelming. It feels the same as it did ten years before only a thousand times more electrifying, exhilarating, intoxicating, arousing, and, natural, so very, very natural, meant to be. Their lips are meant to be together, gently pressing, softly sliding, exchanging moistness, searching, exploring. She relinquishes to him the totality of her being, in this kiss. He wills her to accept that he will always protect her, in this kiss. They both express an unfathomed love, in this kiss. He lifts her in strong arms as her own arms lock around his neck, carries her to his room and gently puts her on her feet beside the bed. His world, his special hiding place, is now almost complete.

She slips off her shoes as, slowly, between kisses, he tenderly removes her sleeveless sweater, exposing the creamy skin of her shoulders and back. Releasing the back of her bra, he slides it off her shoulders, then swallows hard as her voluptuous, sensuous breasts are revealed. Leaning forward, he gently kisses one, then the other. As he does, he delicately lifts her onto the bed, her head gracing a fluffy pillow. He unsnaps the fastener of her jeans, and as she raises her bottom slightly, he slides the jeans down her legs and drops them to the floor. Hesitating; feeling he may be taking her willingness for granted, he does not remove her panties. He kicks off his shoes, removes his shirt and pants, tosses them aside and lowers himself to the bed beside her. She pulls him to her, presses his face to her breasts and sobs softly. He lifts his head and with a concerned expression, looks deeply into her moist eyes. "What is it my sweet – have I assumed too much?"

"Oh no, not at all. It's just that, it's; it's just that you are so considerate, and I've missed so many years of not having this intimacy with you. Please, my darling, make love to me."

For the remainder of the week, before Nicki returned to Washington, she and Cole spent every hour together. On Sunday night, when he put her on the plane, he promised he would call twice a day until she returned in two weeks with the Senator. As they kiss goodbye, he holds her close for a long moment, then says, "After you get this business with the General's visit out of the way, we need to have a serious talk about our future. Do you think you could be happy here, in Cascade? I know your career is important to you and I respect that very much, but there is so much you could accomplish for the underprivileged if you were based right here."

Her impish smile appears. "Why Cole, that sounds as though it could be some kind of proposition." Then she pinches his cheek and adds, "Perhaps, by the time I return you could be a little less ambiguous."

He gives her a sheepish grin and replies, "Okay, I'll try to do that, but promise me you'll think about it till then."

"I promise," she says with a more serious tone, "I promise."

Chapter 30

The General

August 1, 2003

The Pentagon

Four Star General Bruce Maddox stands towering above his desk. He's a large man. Not large in the sense of being overweight, but tall, broad shoulders, heavy arms and legs, a powerful man. He's in his late fifties. His face is somewhat rounded with a chin that juts forward. His steely green eyes sit beneath heavy, reddish brows. Above straight lips is a nose that is too small for his face, and his hair shows the gray from many years of handling the stress of one crisis after another. He gazes off into space, lost in thought, his brow creased with concentration. Suddenly, he leans forward and picks up his phone. He punches in a set of numbers. On the other end, a woman's voice answers, "Yes?"

He tries to speak softly into the phone, difficult to do, because of his deep and raspy voice. "It's me. Sorry I haven't been in touch sooner, there's just too damned much going on."

"That's okay. It's nice to hear from you."

He clears his throat, and then continues, "I'd like to see you again, if I may. Next week I need to be at a place called, Cascade, in West Virginia. I'll be staying at an Inn called, The Pierpoint. I have an adjoining room reserved for you, on the 8th, under the name you used last time. Can you make it?"

The woman's voice is provocative. "Of course," she says, "and I'm excited, really."

"Good. Now you'll need to be very careful, I'll have some people with me and, of course, I don't want my wife to know, not just yet."

"I know the routine, no need to worry."

Maddox breathes deeply, and then says, "I'm really looking forward to us getting to know each other better."

"As am I, It's been too long," she suggests.

"See you then," he says, and punches the "end" button.

Nicki's Office

The direct line on Nicki's phone rings. She glances at the clock, and then smiles as she lifts the phone to her ear. "This is Nicola Valentini."

The voice on the line causes her to feel no less excited than she did when he called the day before and again when she left him at the airport two days ago. "Did you dream about me last night?" he asks.

"Of course I did, But I dreamed you were with another woman and you took her to your hiding place," she teases.

"Not a chance. God, I miss you Sweetie," Cole replies.

"And I miss you, my darling; I can't wait to see you. I'll be arriving with the Senator on the 14th. We should get to the Pierpoint around six, and you have made sure your parents are going to join us for dinner, right?"

"They certainly are," Cole replies, Dad balked at the idea, said it was Uncle Nat's show, but Uncle Nat and Aunt Alice made him promise to come."

"That's great, honey," Nicki says. "The Senator is anxious to see the four of them again; he says it's been too long since he has seen the Dawsons. Cole, it's amazing how much he knows about your family, I can't believe I've worked for him for three years and never discovered how close he is to your dad and Nat."

"Actually, Granddad was much closer to the Senator," Cole replies. "He and Burke used to do a lot of trout fishing together, Burke loves to fly-fish and he's crazy about our stretch of Cascades Creek."

"Well, I can't blame him," Nicki says. "And by the way, I have firmed up the plan for General Maddox. He'll arrive on the 9th, at ten o'clock, on his personal helicopter. I have assured him that the world's greatest trout fishing guide will meet him, is that okay?"

"Absolutely, I'm looking forward to it."

"But there is a slight change from what you and I discussed,

Darling. For some reason the General wants to stay at the Pierpoint instead of at your cabin, I can't understand why, I think he would love the seclusion in the woods."
"That is odd," Cole replies. "But I guess he has his reasons, maybe it's some kind of security thing."
"I suppose you're right. Now, can I depend on you to make the Senator very happy by taking really good care of the General?"
"I have a hunch that Maddox may never want to return to Washington. He'll be eating his fresh caught, pan-fried trout on the cabin porch one day and then on the golf course the next, where with his handicap he'll most likely take some money from me, Dad and the Mayor. He's going to love it down here."
"You're a sweetie," Nicki coos. Then, in a more serious voice, says, "Well, my darling, I must get back to work."
"Okay, I'll call you tonight," he promises as they end the call.

August 8, 2003, 7:00 P.M.

The Pierpoint

Cole sits at a table, in the dining room, with his father, his Uncle Nat and the Mayor. They have been discussing, over dinner, the arrival of General Maddox and the upcoming event at the new Navy site. Cole excuses himself to go to the men's room. As he walks through the small reception area he notices a very attractive woman at the check-in desk. She's a redhead, a tall, slender, curvaceous, redhead. As he passes, she glances at him. He sees recognition in her eyes, and at the same instant, he also recognizes her. He stops in mid stride, turns to face her, and utters, "Jaime, Jaime Siebert?"
Jaime looks away, to the desk clerk, then back to Cole. She stammers, "Cole Dawson, my God!" The woman behind the desk looks at Jaime with a questioning expression. Jaime had just signed the register as, Joleen Summers.

229

Cole nervously runs his hand through his hair. Jaime was not his most favorite person, and since learning that she lied to him about Nicki not wanting to see him, that feeling has intensified, and, her profession, if Nicki is correct, wow! "So, good gosh! What brings you to Cascade?"

The woman behind the desk looks even more confused. Jaime senses that. She turns to the woman and says, "I gave you my professional name, I'm a model, and I don't use my real name, you know, when I'm working." The woman behind the desk smiles and nods, "Of course, and I'm not surprised to learn that you're a model, you're so beautiful, honey."

"Thank you," Jaime says, nervously, but sincerely. Then back to Cole, "I'm, well, I'm here to, ah, to check out the area for a shoot, we have a shoot coming up soon, and, ah, we need a small-town setting."

"I see," Cole replies. *She is obviously lying. Why would the model be looking for the site? That would be the producer's, or the photographer's task.* "So how long will you be in town?"

"Oh, not long, not long, just a few days."

"Well," Cole stammers, not knowing quite how to address a professional escort, "maybe I'll see you around town," and he walks away, toward the rest room. As he does, his mind searches for an answer. She's obviously lying about being here for "a shoot". Or is she? Maybe Nicki had it all wrong, maybe she isn't a call girl. Maybe she really is a model. She certainly has the looks for it. Naw, that doesn't add up. Nicki's probably right; Jaime's here on business. If so, with who?

As Cole turns into a hallway, Jaime takes her key from the clerk and starts for the stairs. Her mind races. Shit! Of course, Cascade. This is where Cole lives. Why in God's name did He have to pick Cole Dawson's hometown for a rendezvous?

A few minutes later, as Cole returns through the reception area, he stops at the desk. "Margaret, I'm curious, what did Miss Siebert give as her professional name?"

"Now Cole," she teases, "you know I'm not supposed to reveal what's on our register, but its, Summers, Joleen Summers. Where do you know her from? She's so pretty!"

"She used to go with a friend of mine, in school, at Morgantown," he answers with a smile. Then, "What room is she in, Margaret?"

"Cole Dawson, you naughty boy, you know I can't tell you that!" Then, with a devilish look, Margaret relents, "She's in room 12, at the end of the hall."

"Uh huh," Cole utters with a serious tone. Then, "Oh, by the way, Margaret. I'll be bringing a military man in tomorrow, a famous General from Washington."

"I know, Cole, isn't it exciting!"

"Yes, it is, Margaret, I expect, more than you know. Uh, when I bring him in, and he will have some security people with him, I don't want to waste his time checking in and all that. I'd like to just go ahead and take him and his people directly to their rooms, uh, can you tell me which rooms they're in?"

"Why, of course, Cole. But you know the secret service was already here to check us out?"

"Why no, I didn't know that."

"Oh yes, they went over the place like they were searching for old Robert Dawson's ghost, looked into every nook and cranny."

Cole rubs his chin, "I didn't realize they did that for a General. I guess it's because he's the Chairman of the Joint Chiefs."

"Well, whatever," Margaret continues, "Yes, we can go through the formalities of checking him in with one of his assistants, I suppose he will have an assistant, don't you think?"

"Yes, I expect he will have an assistant, maybe two or three, and it sounds like he'll also have some secret service guys with him. So which rooms are they booked into?"

"Well, let's see. The General is in room 14. And they booked all the other rooms on the upper level, all ten, except for the one that Miss Summers is in, of course. But, you know what's funny, they said they weren't going to use all the rooms, just don't want anyone else using them, isn't that strange?"

"Yes, a little. Okay, well, perhaps I should do a quick check of the General's room, even though the secret service already did, you know, just to double check, make sure everything is all right."

"Certainly, that's probably a good idea, what with Eleanor's eyesight being what it is, she may have missed something. I'll come along."

A minute later, Cole and Margaret are in room 14, next to Jaime's room, 12. Cole's suspicions are confirmed. Rooms 12 and 14 are adjoining, a bolted door between them.

August 9th, 2003, 11:00 A.M.

Cole, Nat, Mayor Pierpoint and a few others, greet General Bruce Maddox as he steps off a Blackhawk helicopter that has landed in the high school soccer field. Traveling with Maddox are two staff assistants and three secret service agents. After getting the group set up at the Pierpoint, Cole, Ben and Nat take the General straightaway to Lakeview Country Club where, with the vista of Cheat Lake in the valley below, and an indigo sky above, they trade dollars for eighteen holes. The next morning, at Cole's cabin, they bust clays until their shoulders can take no more, have lunch of country fried steak, prepared for them in Cole's kitchen, by the cook from the Pierpoint, and spent the afternoon fishing Cascades. The General vows, to Cole, that he plans to bring his army and capture all of Preston County, particularly the portion that holds Cascades Creek.

That evening, with Ben and Nat having left, and after a dinner of pan fried brook trout, as he and Cole sit alone on the cabin porch, sipping brandy, Maddox says, "Cole, my boy, there's something I'd like to ask. It's a personal thing, but I'm an excellent judge of people, and their character, and

I think I can trust you to keep a confidence."

Cole swirls his brandy in the glass as he looks quizzically at Maddox. "What is it, General?"

Maddox takes a sip of the brandy, savors it for a moment, swallows, looks directly into Cole's eyes, and says, "I have my daughter with me, she's staying at the Inn, and," he clears his throat, "and after getting a look at this place of yours, I think she might be more comfortable and enjoy herself more if I take you up on your original offer and she and I spend the rest of our stay here. It's very private here and it would give her and me a chance to get to know each other a little better."

Whoa! Cole is taken aback. He has grown to genuinely like the General, but now has a problem accepting the fact that Maddox is traveling with a hooker and all the while has been talking about his wife and kids, and how much he adores them, and how rough it's been on his wife being married to a military guy. Now he wants to pass Jaime off as his daughter? *Oh well, Nicki wants me to make him happy.*

"Sure, General," he says, "I'd love to have you stay here, and I'm sure your daughter will find it to be a very relaxing spot."

"That's mighty good of you, Cole. But, you understand, we'll need to keep it kind of quiet, for her security, you know."

"Of course, and there's plenty of room for your security guys up at the main house."

"That's kind of what I figured," Maddox says, with a wink of his eye.

Cole nods, then, wanting to change the subject, points his brandy glass at one of the secret service agents who leans against a tree, out by the General's car. "Are you sure we can't offer your guys something to eat or drink?"

"Naw, they're fine. They get along, one of them probably went into town and brought something back. I'm not supposed to worry about them, just kind of pretend they're not around, hellava job; I wouldn't want it."

"I guess," Cole muses.

"There's one other thing," Maddox continues.

"What's that?"

"The dinner we're supposed to have on our last evening, before I have to get back to business. You know, with the Senator and the others."

"Yes?"

"Well, would you mind too much if I begged off. I really do enjoy this spot, and just between you and me, I sure do get my fill of politicians, you know what I mean?"

"I do, General, I know just what you mean. Sure, why don't you plan on spending some nice quiet time with your daughter for the remainder of your time here; just you, your daughter, and the trout. I'll send someone out to do the cooking for you."

"Cole, you're going to spoil this old soldier."

Chapter 31

The Snake Has a Plan

Near Cascade

As the sun sinks behind Laurel Mountain, darkness comes quickly to the thick forest along a remote, gravel road, five miles south of Cascade. A small green sedan pulls off the road and onto the remnant of an old logging lane. It stops behind a pickup truck which is parked thirty yards inside the cover of the forest. The outline of a heavyset man appears in the cab as the headlights of the sedan envelop the truck. The driver of the sedan is the Iranian, Yasin Ganji. Both drivers get out of their vehicles and meet at the rear of the pick-up. Ganji greets the driver of the truck. "It's good to see you again, Ahmad, how are you?"

Ahmad, also Iranian, in his thirties, is a portly man of medium height, but appears unusually agile for his weight. He has a squarish face with a wide nose and full lips. Heavy lids make his eyes appear sleepy, but this is deceptive, as they are ever alert. He returns the greeting. "I have been better, Ganji, but I'm tired of traveling and staying in hotels. It has been very difficult since the great victory in September; we've had to stay on the move and the stupid American public is much more curious now. It would be nice to have a little farm somewhere to relax for a while. Perhaps, if I perform well, you will allow me to do that one day."

It's clear, from the conversation that Ganji is in charge. "You were not destined for that kind of life, Ahmad. Allah decided long ago that yours was to be a life of adventure and service. Look at some of your recent accomplishments; smuggling Kakashnikov rifles on camel caravans to our friends in Palestine, sneaking explosives to our men in Yemen, teaching the Sudanese how to make bombs right under the noses of the authorities and giving cover to our comrades who brought the plane down in Pennsylvania. Yes, Ahmad, yours is the life of adventure, you would not be happy doing anything else."

"Perhaps, but it would be nice to have an occasional period of rest, I'm feeling too old for my years. Maybe, if I make it through this thing alive, I will take a sabbatical."

"Ahmad, that is no way to talk, of course you will make it through alive, you're too good to die. Yes, there is risk, but we have faced danger many times." Pointing to the white streak in his beard, he asks, "Do you remember how I got this? Of course, there is danger."

Ahmad sighs, "But you survived the knife of the American marine; this is a little different, and unlike our brothers who died in the planes, I am not ready to depart this life - there are things I want to do."

"Trust me, Ahmad. I think we have a good chance of success, and I, like you, am not yet willing to sacrifice my life unless there is no other way. If I am dead then I can no longer fight the Americans and that is what I live for. Since the strike by our brothers, in September, we have the infidels scared to death.

Ahmad's wide eyes glisten in the moonlight as he listens to Ganji's preaching. Ganji is his hero and he will follow him anywhere.

Ganji continues, "But, enough of that, now, listen to me; I don't believe the American President will be willing to sacrifice the lives of the country's highest ranking military officers plus a United States Senator, so I believe we can succeed, and if we do, then yes, my friend, you may take your sabbatical, it will be well deserved. But, if we die, Ahmad, you will be remembered forever as a hero; is that not worth taking a bullet?"

Ahmad does not look convinced. "I suppose, Ganji, I suppose."

Ganji smiles, "Good, now, tell me. Ahmad, have you lined up the full complement of men; ten, including yourself?"

"Yes. It was easy to get our men into the country through Canada before the September attack. Also, I recruited two men from our group in New York. I have been working on this for several months, Ganji, and I think I have good men."

"You're sure they are all solid, each one has your trust?"

"All of them have tasted blood, Ganji, they are the best and they are willing to die for our cause, if necessary, as am I, I guess."

"Good! I am proud of you, Ahmad. It's quite possible that we may lose one or two of them in the initial effort, and, there is always the possibility that none of us will survive this venture, but I assure you, Ahmad, even if we die, the world will long remember that we were here."

"This sounds like a very dangerous mission, Ganji; Generals and a Senator. Is it time for you to let me in on our objective?'

"Yes my friend, it's time." Ganji pauses to light a cigarette. He does it slowly, very deliberately, then continues; "Our objective, Ahmad, is a large one. We have been planning this for over two years now. We intend to set up the Americans so that we can demand the release of our friends who are to be executed for helping us attempt to blow up the American military barracks in Panama. Although the bomb did not detonate, our friends killed three American soldiers before being taken prisoner. As a result, our men are heroes and to let them die at the hands of the Americans will not be good for our recruiting efforts. They have both been very brave to hold their tongues and not implicate the rest of us. We must obtain their freedom. It's not good for our cause to have the world learn of their execution; and additionally, with this plan we will have a tremendous opportunity to show our strength to the whole world. Allah will be pleased."

"Go on, Ganji."

"On August 15th, there will be an entourage visiting the new Navy Operations Center near here. One of them will be General Bruce Maddox, the Chairman of the Joint Chiefs of Staff. Another will be Admiral Arland DeWitt, head of the Navy. A third will be Rear Admiral Douglas Thompson, head of the Navy's Electronic Warfare group. With them will be some staff assistants and a security detail of secret service agents. There will also be a United States Senator, Robert Burke and some staff members, including a women.

There will also be some guy from the civilian company who built the complex. We are going to take them, along with the entire crew of the operations center, hostage."

Ahmad's face turns very somber. In a low, guttural tone, he mutters, "Holy shit, Ganji! You do not want me to have my sabbatical!"

Ganji takes a long, slow draw on his cigarette, inhaling deeply, then slowly blows the smoke into the night air. He levels his gaze directly into the worried eyes of his comrade. "Relax, Ahmad. My plan is a good one. We have a man on the inside. He has been there for many years. We recruited this man when he was a student many years ago. He has been in the American Navy for 15 years and many times has supplied us with valuable information, much of which we have sold to interested people for a great deal of money. Much of our work has been financed through the sale of the information he has passed to us."

Ahmad is not convinced. "How well do you know this man, Ganji?"

Ganji takes another, slow draw on his cigarette, carefully trying to give Ahmad the impression that he, Ganji, has complete control of the situation and confidence in the man on the inside. He speaks through smoke that curls up from his lips. "His control, Ahmad, was passed to me from our friend, Omar, seven years ago. He has rank and he's trusted. He's fully trained in the operations of this new communications center."

Ahmad is relieved to learn that the inside man was taught by his old friend. He's a little more comfortable. He asks Ganji, "Why do you stress his knowledge of the operation, do you plan for him to do more than get us inside?"

Ganji's face becomes alive for the first time. Even in the darkness, Ahmad sees the gleam in Ganji's eyes. "Ah, Ahmad, you're clever, my friend. Clever and very perceptive. Yes, he will do a great deal more than get us inside. Ahmad, the capability of this new communications center is unbelievable! We will be able to televise to the whole world our control of the hostages, and if the President does not meet our demand, the world will witness their slaughter."

"I don't understand, Ganji."

"I will explain, Ahmad, with your patience, I will explain." He takes a quick puff and exhales rapidly. "Our man on the inside, we will call him, 'Cormorant,' first saw the potential of this operation when he learned of the Navy's plan for this facility and volunteered for service in it. It seems this communications center, in addition to gathering electronic intelligence, has the ability to transmit a very powerful television signal to any location in the world. When we learned of a possible visit by high level military people the idea for this exercise began to form. Now, here is the beauty. Once we have taken command of the center and the hostages, we will up-link to television satellites around the world a live telecast of our takeover, and if our demands are not met, the systematic assassination of our hostages."

Ganji continues. "Our plan is a simple one, to prove our determination to carry out our objective, we will kill one of the key hostages each hour at the top of the clock. Although we know that the policy of the United States is to not negotiate, we believe that with the lives of the two highest ranking military officers in the nation at risk, also a U.S. Senator, and with a demonstration of our resolve through the systematic disposal of a hostage each hour, killings seen on live television by millions of people around the world, the President of the United States will meet our demand and release our friends."

Ahmad responds, "I hope you have a plan to get us out, Ganji?"

"Of course; first, we will be assured of the release of our comrades by seeing it take place on television. Once they are in the air, headed for asylum in Iraq, we will put a hold on killing our hostages until they are landed safely. Then we demand a helicopter. With the General, the Admiral and the Senator as hostages, we will fly to an airport at Morgantown, less than 15 minutes by chopper. There, to show our good faith, and to make things simpler for us, we will release the Admiral and the Senator. Then, with the General remaining as our hostage, they shall have a military jet take us to Iraq. The jet shall have in-flight refueling capability. Once in Iraq, assured our comrades are safe, we will allow the General to return with the jet."

"I don't know, Ganji, it sounds difficult, highly risky. The transfer from the chopper to the jet, that could be a very dangerous time."

"Of course, it's risky! But I have it covered. My plan assures that if any of us are killed the General will automatically be killed in return."

Ahmad is not convinced. "But will the Americans know that, that the General's death is guaranteed?"

Ganji becomes irritated. He starts to shout, but catches himself and lowers his voice. "Yes! They will know, they will know from our television broadcast. Ahmad, what is our business, if not the business of risk? We are pledged to do whatever it takes to bring down the Americans in the eyes of our people. If necessary, death is a part of our commitment to that end."

"But, if we fail, it will be a great impediment to our cause."

Ganji's expression becomes serene. "Ah, but that is the beauty of this plan, Ahmad. Even if we do not succeed in forcing the Americans to turn over our friends, we are willing to sacrifice our lives for the opportunity to televise, to our countrymen, the killing of the American hostages. Will that not be a supreme achievement, the slow and systematic slaughter of very important and powerful Americans. It will prove to the world our ability to humble the superpower, the atheistic and immoral murderers who plan to dominate our homeland and the world. They will talk about us for years to come. We will be heroes, Ahmad, heroes."

"Perhaps, Ganji, perhaps." Ahmad looks at the ground. He's quiet for a long while. Ganji says nothing more, then Ahmad breaks the silence. "I don't think they would give a second thought to losing the Senator, the other two, maybe."

"But, think about it, Ahmad, including the three of them we

will have more than thirty hostages in total. If need be, we will kill them all. Remember, we will have the American Government in a position that is totally unfamiliar to them. Can you imagine the pressure on the President of the United States when the whole country, actually the whole world, watches live television as one by one, the Americans are slaughtered? Remember, the picture cannot be censured, it will be before the world in all the bloody detail."

Ahmad is not convinced. "Perhaps, but never under estimate the Americans, Ganji. They are adventurous people. It's in their blood. They are the children of adventurers who left their homeland to find something better, and they have the, how do they call it? The pioneer spirit, which binds them together when there is adversity. It seems as though the more you push an American, the more they push back."

"Ahmad, you disturb me. I think the Americans are converting you, but I give you this one, what you say is true. Just remember, my old friend, here we have a different situation. It's unprecedented. When the killing begins there will be unbelievable pressure on the President and his people to save the lives of our prisoners. The families of the hostages will watch their beloved ones on the television screen, can't you picture it, Ahmad, and can't you see the mother of a young Navy boy as we press a gun to his head! When have the American people ever before been in such a dilemma? At least within memory of most, Never! The Americans are slaves to the TV. And when they see the blood begin to flow they will demand that the President act."

"Ah Ganji, I wish I were as sure as you."

"Trust me, my friend."

"O.K., but give me more comfort, Ganji, let me hear the full plan, in detail."

Ganji lights another cigarette before he answers. "I will tell you, Ahmad, but first, tell me that you have obtained the vehicle and necessary arms?"

"Yes, with some difficulty, but it's done. The weapons I got from the Chinese in New Jersey, and the truck from a military surplus dealer in Baltimore. We have given the truck good repair and new paint, it will do the job.

"And the Navy uniforms?"

"The uniforms were a little more difficult. I think we were in every Army, Navy store in New Jersey. They are not all perfect, in your early briefing you told me the men will be in the truck and probably not seen anyway, is that still true."

"Yes, Ahmad, but yours must be very authentic."

"Do not fear, Ganji, mine is good, I will look better than the Admiral."

"Very good, Ahmad, very good."

Ganji pulls a folded paper from inside his shirt, unfolds it and lays it on the bed of the pickup truck. With a penlight he illuminates the paper and begins to explain his plan. "I trust, my friend, that you have studied your copy of this layout of the base and are familiar with the location of the gate?"

"Yes, I've got that well memorized."

Ganji drops the cigarette, which he had just lit and scuffs it in the dirt with his boot. He takes on an air of authority. "Okay, then here is my plan."

The paper Ganji places on the truck is a hand drawn layout of the base and a detail of the operations center. He sweeps a finger around the perimeter of the drawing as he explains. "There will be four marine guards patrolling the perimeter fence. At the gate there will be two guards. The total marine detachment numbers 36. Twelve are on duty at all times, six outside and six inside the operations center. The General's entourage is scheduled to arrive by helicopter at 1:00 in the afternoon. Thirty minutes later the General and his group will be in the operations room for a demonstration of the system. This demonstration will take one hour. Some of the secret service agents, we don't know how many, will wait outside the operations room with the marine guard. Of the other agents, some will probably wait outside the building, or perhaps in the dining lounge along with the staff assistants, we don't know. Cormorant was successful in getting myself and Taha Sahaf papers as Navy officers. He also got us authentic uniforms. You, Taha and I will be in the truck. We will arrive at the gate precisely thirty minutes after the General's entourage arrives at the site. I will have a man positioned to observe their arrival, he will have a radio to alert us. When we arrive at the gate, the guards should not be too suspicious since we will be in Navy uniform and driving a Navy truck. On the truck we are supposed to have several large crates of electronic equipment. But, instead of equipment, your men will be in the crates."

"But Ganji, what if they want to inspect the crates?"

"That will not happen. Cormorant will have previously alerted the marine guards to the arrival of the equipment. I will have documents, given to me by Cormorant, representing the transportation papers for the equipment. He also will have told the guards that he wants to talk to us by phone in order for us to give him a password. That way, he can personally assure that he's at the loading dock when we arrive, that there can be no error in that regard. To avoid any possibility of the gatehouse guards suspecting something and alerting the operations center, we will need to take them out. This is another reason for the phone call to Cormorant. I will go into the guardhouse with the guards to make the call. While on the phone, I will say that I am missing one of the documents. I will call for you to bring it to me. That gets us both inside the guardhouse. I will try to distract the guards by putting down the phone and asking them to check the papers, pretending that I'm uncertain of something. Then, we kill them."

"How?"

"Knives, Ahmad, knives. And we must time it perfectly and do it simultaneously, and it must be done quickly, we know how to do that. We will then proceed, with the truck to the loading dock and overhead door at the side of the Operations Center. Cormorant will open the door. Are we together so far?"

"I'm with you, Ganji"

"Good. Now, here is a diagram of the Operations Center." Ganji lays another paper on the truck. "The marine guards are stationed so, one in the foyer, one in the lobby, one just outside the Operations Room and one here in the mechanical room.

"What kind of security lock is there on the door to the Operations Room?"

"You are getting ahead of me, Ahmad. It's a combination retinal and fingerprint scanning system, but that is not a problem. When we arrive at the loading dock, Cormorant will open the overhead door. You and Taha will use a pallet truck to unload the crates. I will give Cormorant a pistol with a silencer, it will be hidden within a document folder. He will make a reason to talk to the marine guard who is stationed in the mechanical room, and will kill him. If there is anyone else in the mechanical room at the time, Cormorant, you, or I will need to take them out immediately and quietly. We will play that card when the time comes."

"I understand. After we secure the room then I will let my men out of the crates?"

"Yes, Ahmad, and you'll have ten men, right?"

"That's right, ten."

"And those men will have our weapons?"

"Yes."

"Good. Now, we will group them in this way. One man at the door to the kitchen, one at the door to the operations room, eight at the door to the corridor leading to the main entrance to the operations room."

"But, why not go in through the door from the mechanical room where there is no longer a guard, Ganji?"

"Because that door can only be opened from inside."

"But, we could blow the door."

"Ahmad, you're a fool. There are six armed and superbly trained men in the area of the main door to the operations room and the lobby, but they are in a compact area. We cannot give them time to spread out, we must surprise them and take them out quickly."

"I see." Ahmad replies, but then questions, "only one of our men at the door from the operations room? He will not be able to control a bunch of guys coming out that door when you go in the main door."

"Ahmad, sometimes you make me crazy. Do you think I have not worked this plan over and over and over. None of the Navy personnel in the operations room will be armed, it's not permitted."

"Why not?"

"The Navy always uses a marine detachment for security. The Navy people who work in facilities such as this are not trained in the use of firearms and are not permitted to carry them."

"That is stupid!" Ahmad exclaims, with a twirl of a finger at his temple.

"Maybe stupid, but true, and to our advantage. Now, no more mindless questions. Back to the eight men at the door to the corridor. Four of them will have their weapons in boxes. Cormorant will lead them up the corridor, past the guards and to the conference room. As you see here on the sketch, the conference room is just across the corridor from the guard station. Once in the conference room, the men will remove their automatic weapons from the boxes. They open the door and shoot the two Marines and the three military police. It should be very easily done. At the sound of the shooting the remaining four men will storm up the corridor. One will stop at the door to the lounge to cover the occupants in that room, the man at the kitchen door will have entered through the kitchen to cover them from that side. We now have seven men in the corridor, and this is the tricky part. It will be up to the three men from the second group to quickly move into the lobby and foyer to take out the guards there. The first four men will be responsible for getting into the operations room."

"And how do they do that , Ganji?"

"Cormorant will step out of the conference room and open the operations room door. He will actuate the retinal scan and finger print scan systems controlling the door, our group of four, assuming we still have four men alive, will burst into the room. Their first action, once in the room, is to neutralize the computer operators. These operators are instructed to destroy their computers if the security of the room is lost. They actually have fire axes at hand to accomplish this. Ahmad, they must be prevented from destroying those machines."

"I understand."

"Once that room is secured we will rig the door in an open position so that we do not need Cormorant to open it again if we need to do that, this is important, do you understand?"

"Yes, Ganji."

"We kill whoever is necessary in order to preserve the equipment." Ganji reiterates.

"I understand." Ahmad says, with mild annoyance.

"You're losing patience with me, Ahmad, but I cannot over emphasize the importance of saving the equipment, because in the excitement we are not going to know which pieces are necessary for us to make the television broadcast, so we must save it all."

"You're right, Ganji."

"Good. Now, once we have the equipment secured, we separate the hostages into two groups. The General and the Admiral will remain in the operations room. The others will be herded into the dining room. The Senator will be brought to the operations room along with one of his underlings. All will then be bound with duct tape. Our men outside will be rounding up the administrative and other personnel."

"Why do you want one of the Senator's underlings, Ganji?"

"I may want that person to be the first to die, to demonstrate what will happen to the important leaders. A woman would be preferable, people don't like to see a woman die, especially the way this one will die."

"How is that?"

A smile contorts the face of Ganji, a venal, a demonic smile. "It will be a surprise, Ahmad, my special surprise. But, we are not finished, while we are securing the hostages we will need four men to fill the lobby with furniture, desks, chairs, whatever, we want to slow any potential charge through the front door. The only other way in is through the overhead door, which cannot be opened from outside, and the roof hatch, which likewise is secured on the inside. If they try to come in through any entrance, we will have time to slaughter all the hostages."

Ganji folds his drawings and returns them to his pocket. He places his hand on Ahmad's shoulder and grips it firmly. His eyes flash as he bids farewell. "I will see you in five days, my friend. Get plenty of rest between now and then for we will need to be strong and tenacious for a long time without rest. In five days, here, at this spot." Ganji walks toward his car, then stops and turns, "One more thing, Ahmad. Make sure your men shave their beards and do not carry their Korans with them; we must be very, very careful. The marine security groups who guard sites such as this one are very good at what they do."

Chapter 32

The Knife is Sharp

August 15th, 2003, 12:00 Noon

It's raining as Yasin Ganji arrives at the meeting place in the woods. Already there is Ahmad and his men. They arrived during the previous night in a pick-up truck, a van and the fake Navy truck. The rain is not heavy, but it's steady and the sky doesn't appear to relent. "Bless the rain!" Ganji cackles as he emerges from his car and approaches the green truck of Ahmad. "The guards at the gate will be less motivated to check us closely." He gives a wave of his hand to Ahmad. "Are you ready, my friend, ready for our adventure?"

"We are ready, Ganji," he replies solemnly.

"Good, let's prepare for it, I would like to check the weapons before they are distributed."

"Yes, Ganji, they are assembled in the van."

As Ganji leans into the van, he carefully inspects the weapons and ammunition. He picks up a container of ammo, frowns and asks curiously, "Ahmad, are these tipped with explosive projectiles as I asked?"

Ahmad looks distressed. He replies nervously, "Ah, no Ganji, they are solid, metal jacketed bullets, the Chinese screwed me and I, I didn't discover it until yesterday."

Ganji is furious. "Damn, damn, damn, damn! Ahmad, these will not kill effectively, they will pass through the American dogs without an immediate kill if they do not hit a vital spot! Damn! Why did you not check sooner?"

"I am sorry, Ganji," Ahmad replies. His drooping eyelids seem to hang to his chin.

Ganji continues to rant. "These bullets are for wounding, not killing. We don't want to just incapacitate our enemy, we want to kill them!"

"I know, Ganji, I know. But my men are good marksmen and they will make sure of many hits."

"I hope so, Ahmad. Damn it! I hope so."

While Ganji and his men prepare for their attack, an Air Force Sikorsky Black Hawk helicopter flies over the

Maryland countryside, on its way to Skywatch. The air is clear and the Black Hawk flies at 150 knots until it reaches the Allegheny Mountains and runs into the rain. The pilot reduces speed to 75 knots, but is able to maintain the schedule filed in his flight plan. The chopper carries the two Navy Admirals, DeWitt and Thompson, two staff assistants and two secret service agents. At precisely one o'clock, the chopper descends to the roof of Skywatch. Already in the op center is General Bruce Maddox and his contingent, and Senator Burke, Nicola and Nat, who arrived by auto minutes before.

At 1:30, the rain still falls, only now, heavier, as Ganji and his group, dressed in navy uniforms, pull up to the gate at Skywatch.

"As Cormorant said, there are two guards," Ganji mutters. A marine sergeant steps to the open door of the gate house as Ganji rolls down the window of the truck and squints his eyes against the rain. Not anxious to get wet, the marine yells from the door, "State your business mister?"

Trying to sound as American and navy as possible, Ganji shouts back, "Delivery. We have some equipment to deliver, Pal. You're supposed to be expecting us."

The marine steps back into the enclosure, shuffles through some papers, says something to the other marine guard, a corporal, then returns to the door. "Okay, bring your documents inside. The Commander also wants to verify your identity, so you need to talk to him on the phone in here."

Ganji smiles. So far, the plan is working. He gets out of the truck and, hunkering under the rain, takes three quick steps to the door of the gatehouse. Inside, handing his fake documents to the marine, Ganji swears, "Damn, it's wet out there."

The sergeant makes no comment as he takes the papers. Ganji leans against the frame of the open door. After a moment, the sergeant looks up from the documents. He has been trained to ask questions. "This says you're bringing this equipment from Baltimore?"

Ganji, trying not to look puzzled by the question, answers, "Yeah, Baltimore."

"What time did you leave there?"

Ganji quickly tries to calculate the travel time from Baltimore. "Uh, this morning, around eight."

The sergeant looks curious. "Took you only five and a half hours to drive from Baltimore in this rain?"

"Yeah, I guess that's what it was, left there at eight."

"Un huh," the sergeant mutters as he studies the papers. Ganji begins to feel just a bit nervous about the guards demeanor. Does he suspect something?

"Well, I guess your docs look okay. You need to talk to the Commander, I'll dial him for you." The sergeant picks up a phone and dials three numbers. After a moment he speaks. "Commander, Sir, the delivery you're expecting is here. I'm going to put the driver on the line as you requested." He hands the phone to Ganji. Ganji speaks into the mouthpiece, "Sir?"

To make the ruse sound legitimate, Cormorant puts a few simple questions to Ganji who answers them as the marine guards listen to his replies. Then, Ganji turns to the sergeant and says, "he wants information that I've left in the truck, I'll have my buddy bring it in." He stretches the phone cord as he takes a step toward the door and calls to Ahmad, "Johnny, bring me that packing list in the yellow envelope."

The sergeant steps to the door. "No, he stays in the truck, I'll get it," he says.

Alarmed, Ganji thinks, *Shit, no, I need Ahmad in here.* Thinking quickly, he quips, "Stay dry Sarge, let Johnny brave the storm."

"No, I'll get it," the sergeant says as he steps out into the rain and opens the door of the truck. He reaches a hand inside the truck and Ahmad, a quizzical look on his face, places a yellow envelope in the marine's hand.

Returning to the shelter, the sergeant hands the envelope to Ganji who still holds the phone in his hand. Fumbling to remove some papers from the envelope, Ganji stalls as he tries to think of a way to kill the two guards without Ahmad's help, the help he had planned for and counted on.

Seeing a large bottled water dispenser, he asks, as he puts the phone back to his ear, "May I have a cup of your water, Sergeant?"

The sergeant nods to the corporal, who removes a paper cup from a stack and begins filling it with water. Ganji speaks into the phone, "I have the packing list in front of me now, Sir, but I see something here that I think the sergeant here should see." As the corporal steps up to Ganji with the water, Ganji lays down the phone, turns to the sergeant and hands him the packing list.

As the sergeant takes the papers, Ganji turns to the corporal and reaches for the cup of water with his left hand, but as the corporal releases the cup to his hand, Ganji relaxes his grip and drops the cup.

As the sergeant looks at the papers, and the corporal watches the cup of water splash to the floor, Ganji reaches inside his shirt with his right hand and removes from a sheathe strapped to his chest, an eight inch knife with razor sharp double edges. In a smooth, calculated, practiced motion, he whips the blade across the throat of the startled corporal, who still watches the bouncing paper cup.

Even as the knife blade leaves the throat of the corporal, Ganji has his eyes on those of the sergeant, looking for the sign of recognition, of realization that he has been duped, but he has his blade twisting in the sergeant's chest before the realization comes, and instead of comprehension, the sergeant's eyes suddenly show confusion, puzzlement, then anger. He grabs Ganji's hand and the hilt of the knife, and tries to force the knife from his breast, where it has nicked his heart and sliced into his left lung, but Ganji presses hard.

The corporal, grasping his throat with both hands, a throat from which volumes of blood courses in measured gushes, slumps to his knees, trying to determine if he has any chance of surviving his wound.

Losing the battle with the knife, the sergeant lets go with his right hand and reaches down for his pistol, but Ganji anticipates the move and has his own left hand on the pistol when the sergeant's hand gets there. The sergeant, now losing strength rapidly as his heart leaks vital blood and his lung collapses, tries to strike Ganji with a clenched fist, but Ganji easily ducks as he pushes harder on the knife.

The corporal falls forward on his face as the blood in his brain is depleted of the life-giving oxygen that kept him conscious; kept him alive.

The sergeant still battles. Even with Ganji's twisting blade in his lung and a hole in his heart, the heart will not stop beating, though a good portion of the blood it pumps leaks into his chest cavity. He maneuvers a leg behind Ganji's legs and throws his weight forward. Ganji, surprised at the marine's endurance, is caught off guard. He stumbles backward and goes down. As he does, his leverage is lost and the knife pulls free. At the same time he loses his grip on the sergeant's pistol. The sergeant rolls to his right and comes up on his knees, coughing blood, but still alive, his pistol in his hand. Ganji rolls on his side and is startled to be looking into the barrel of the pistol.

Ganji reads in the sergeant's eyes that he is about to pull the trigger, that his brain is about to send that very message via his nervous system to the right forefinger.

But before the message arrives at the finger, the sergeant's eyes go blank as Ahmad crushes his head with a heavy tire iron. The brave marine falls heavily to the floor and Ahmad quickly leans over him and slits his throat.

Ganji slowly gets to his feet and grips Ahmad's shoulder. "Ahmad, you saved my life."

As Ahmad wipes his blade on the uniform of the dead sergeant he speaks softly, but urgently, "We must move quickly, now."

Ganji nods as he wipes the blood from his own knife and returns it to its sheathe.

Returning to the truck, they proceed to the loading dock of

the Operations Center. As they back the truck toward the dock and the large overhead door, the door begins rising. A navy officer, a Lieutenant Commander, stands in the open doorway as the wind blows rain on his trousers. Ganji stops the truck short of the dock, where Ahmad and Taha get out and open the rear doors of the truck. Then, Ganji backs the truck against the dock bumpers, turns off the engine, gets out and walks up a set of steps to a heavy, steel personnel door, adjacent to the overhead door. Ahmad and Taha follow close behind. The commander opens the door and gasps at the sight of Ganji. The front of his uniform is covered with blood. He whispers to Ganji, "Shit, Ganji, you're covered with blood! Stay outside, the guard stationed by the op room door will see the blood." Only then did Ganji realize that the marine sergeant's blood was all over the front of his uniform.

"Okay," he responded, also in a whisper. Then, turning to Ahmad, "Ahmad, you and Taha go inside, I will wait here until the guard is eliminated. Once inside, the commander gives Ahmad a serious look, "Hurry, get the crates off quickly, there's a pallet truck there," he says, pointing to an orange hydraulic pallet truck sitting by the door.

The marine guard by the op room door has been watching and yells to the commander, "Everything okay, Commander?"

The officer waves at the guard, "Fine, everything's fine, except these guys are trying to get me all wet. Its pouring out there."

The guard looks satisfied and relaxes.

As Taha hurriedly positions the pallet truck under one of the crates, the commander nervously glances at the door leading to the corridor and at the guard stationed at the operations room door, then whispers to Ahmad, "The pistol, do you have the pistol?"

Positioning himself so that the commander is between he and the guard, Ahmad slides a Beretta automatic pistol, equipped with a silencer, from a leather document case. *So this is the one called, Cormorant,* Ahmad considers, as he passes the pistol to the commander.

As the guard is distracted by watching Taha roll the first crate off the truck, Cormorant places the pistol inside a manila folder. He then walks toward the guard, and in a friendly voice, asks, "Hank, can I bum a cigarette?"

The guard smiles as he reaches into a pocket, "Hell, that's not fair, Commander, I'm not allowed to light up and you're asking me for a smoke."

"I'll make it up to you," Cormorant says with a smile.

As the guard extends a hand, which holds a rumpled pack of cigarettes, Cormorant deftly slides his pistol from the folder, and before the guard has time to react to the gun pointed at his head, a bullet tears into his brain. He drops to the floor as though his legs were chopped from beneath him.

As Taha takes a pry bar and begins to remove an end panel from the crate, Ahmad opens the door to allow Ganji to enter. As he does, five men step from the opened crate. After dragging the dead guard's body away from the op room door, Cormorant, who appears more nervous than he actually is, approaches Ganji. Ganji looks at him and says, in a reassuring tone, "Relax, everything is going well."

Cormorant frowns, "The General was early and you are late, we need to move quickly."

Taha opens the second crate and the remainder of Ahmad's men step into the mechanical room. They quickly distribute weapons to Ganji, Ahmad and Taha.

Ganji calls the men together and, speaking very quietly, quickly reviews the plan as Ahmad watches the doors. "Men, as I briefed you earlier, the guards are stationed so; one in the foyer, one in the lobby and one in the corridor outside the operations room. However, we should find some secret service agents in there, probably stationed with the guard at the door to the operations room. But this is speculation, they could be anywhere. They will be civilians in dark suits, and heavily armed. Now, we will group this way; one man, you," and he points to a short man with a pointy face, "at the door to the kitchen." Then he places a hand on the shoulder of a husky, squat man, "You, at the door to the operations room, and the rest of you at the door to the corridor. The four of you who have your weapons in the boxes will be behind the commander here," he says, pointing to Cormorant. "Ahmad and I will be right behind you. Now, let's go."

With everyone in position, Cormorant opens the door to the corridor and walks through. Two men, carrying a box between them, follow close behind and two more men, carrying an identical box bring up the rear. As the five men walk past the door to the dining room, Cormorant glances inside. He sees Senator Burke among the group of men and women who make up the visiting party, but who were not permitted in the operations room for the demo. Also, the op center's administrative staff is in the room mixing with the guests. As Cormorant's group proceeds, a secret service agent steps into the corridor from the guard station at the op room entrance and inquires, "What do you have there, Commander?"

Cormorant points a thumb over his shoulder and replies, "A couple of crates of spare parts just arrived. They go into the op room, but I'll just place them in the conference room until your folks leave."

The secret service man nods and steps back as the group passes. Three other secret service agents, and a marine guard, stand with him. The men carrying the boxes follow Cormorant into the conference room. There, they are surprised to find another secret service agent, seated by a large table. The agent looks curiously at the boxes as Cormorant directs the men to place them on the floor in the corner. Looking at the agent, Cormorant says, "Spare parts, just arrived. I'll have them taken into the op room after the demo, for your people, is completed." The agent nods, gets up, walks to the door and glances across the corridor at the other agents. Saying nothing, he turns back toward the room, but continues to stand in the doorway. Still clutching the folder that holds his pistol, Cormorant searches his mind for a way to handle this unexpected turn. His thoughts are interrupted as the agent asks, "You plan to leave the stuff here?"

"We can't leave it," Cormorant responds, "it's highly secret spare parts that must be watched until we get them into the op room, we'll have to stay with them."

"All of you?" the agent asks.

Cormorant decides he must make a move now. The agent is acting suspicious and time is wasting. "Yes, these men," he points to his men to get the agent to direct his eyes their way, "need to," he reaches his hand into the folder and grips the pistol, "open the boxes now," and he fires, from five feet away, into the agent's chest." The agent, although having taken what will prove to be a fatal shot to the heart, dives into the corridor and shouts to the other agents there, "He's shooting - he's got a gun."

As the four terrorists scramble to get their weapons out of the boxes, Cormorant steps to the doorway and fires several shots at the secret service agents and the marine across the corridor, as they are getting their own weapons ready to return fire. Then he turns to his men and yells, "Shoot through the wall - here," and he points to the wall opposite the corridor and the guard station where the agents and the marine are located. All four men open up with their automatics. In seconds, the wall, constructed of plasterboard and sheet-metal studs, is pulverized by the blazing lead.

At the sound of the shooting, the other four terrorists burst from the mechanical room into the corridor, Ganji and Ahmad behind them. The first man darts into the dining room as the others dash up the corridor. As they do, a marine steps into the corridor from the lobby and looks to his right, toward the sound of shooting, and sees the secret service agents and the marine crumpling to the floor in a cloud of vaporizing blood. The lead man in the rushing group of terrorists opens fire and catches the marine in the legs, but as he goes down, the well-trained marine turns toward the terrorists and as he hits the floor his automatic is blazing at them. The lead terrorist goes down, several rounds in his upper chest, but the others open fire and the marine is nearly decapitated by the fusillade of projectiles. Reaching the door where the marine just went down, one of Ahmad's men ducks through the door, but the marine guard, stationed in the foyer, opens fire and kills him instantly with several rounds penetrating his chest and shattering his spine.

Inside the op room, at the sound of shooting, all heads turned toward the main entry. General Maddox turns to Captain Slade. "How secure is this room, Captain?"
Slade has an intensely worried look on his face. "Those are very secure doors. The auxiliary door cannot be opened from outside and only one man outside this room can access the security on the main door."
"And who is that?"
"Commander Marino, Sir."
"Where did he go, Captain? He was here with us a while ago."
"He went to receive a shipment of equipment in the mechanical room, sir."
"Well, it sounds like he got a little more than he bargained for. Do you have any weapons in here?"
"No sir, we don't."
"Damn!" Maddox thunders, "then I think we're in a bit of a bind, because it sounds as though whoever is out there shooting, if they get past the guards they'll blow their way in here."

Cormorant peers around the door frame of the conference room. Across the corridor from him, the secret service agents and the marine lie in a mangled heap. He shouts to Ahmad and Ganji, "We're clear here."
Ganji shouts back, "There's at least one more standing, in the lobby."
The marine is actually in the foyer. He stands waiting at the door between the foyer and the lobby, his weapon at the ready. Then, he makes a foolish mistake. He leaves the foyer

where he had the protection of the heavy concrete exterior wall, and where he could have opened the door to allow outside help into the building, and rushes into the lobby where he takes a position by the door leading to the corridor. A short hall, no more than five feet long, separates him from the terrorists. Ganji hears him enter the lobby. He motions to Cormorant to shoot through the wall separating the conference room and the lobby. Cormorant nods.

Placing his four men in a line, facing the wall, he directs them to fan the wall with lead. The roar of the four automatics is deafening in the enclosure of the conference room. The wall is quickly riddled, literally blown away. As the smoke from the gunfire, and the white dust from the plaster, settles out, the tormented body of the marine is revealed, covered with white dust, which rapidly turns crimson.

The terrorist, who had originally darted into the dining room, fired a short burst into the ceiling and shouted to everyone inside to get onto the floor. The terrorist stationed at the kitchen door did the same. One of the women screamed. Senator Burke shouted, "What the hell's going on here - who are you sons-a-bitches?" Nat Dawson grabbed Nicki's arm and quickly pulled her down. "Do as they say, Nicki, get down."

The first terrorist, the short one with the pointy face, shouts, "Face down, on your bellies, hands where we can see them." With horrendous sounds of gunfire reverberating from outside the dining room, Nicki, a terrified look on her face, lies down on the cold, tile floor, her hands under her face. Pointy Face shouts, "Everyone down, quickly, and I want to see hands." Nicki takes her hands from under her face and stretches her arms before her, palms down. She rests her left cheek on the cold floor. Nat does the same thing beside her, but with his right cheek to the floor, he faces Nicki. "Don't worry, girl, we'll be alright." He tries to console her, having no idea what the hell is going on.

"No talking," Pointy Face shouts as the gunfire continues.

As the terrorists in the conference room shoot through the wall and kill the marine in the lobby, the bullets continue through the wall of the dining room and through the air, inches over the prone hostages on the floor, and, just missing Pointy Face who jumps backwards into the doorway to the corridor. The terrorist who stands in the kitchen hits the floor as the bullets ricochet off the kitchen equipment.

"Jesus!" Burke shouts, "They're going to kill us all!"

Then, the shooting stops, as suddenly as it had begun.

Exactly thirty-one seconds have transpired, since the first shot sounded, as Cormorant steps up to the op room door. He places his eye to the retinal scanning device and his right forefinger to the fingerprint scanning unit. The door is immediately opened by a hydraulic actuator. Cormorant steps aside as Ganji is the first to rush into the room, Ahmad and the others right on his heels.

Captain Slade is shouting to several technicians to trash their machines, but it's too late. There are too many weapons pointing at them.

"Everyone on the floor, face down," Ganji screams, "Now, now, quickly."

As most of the group, some confused and frightened, some angry, complies, Ganji bellows, "Ahmad, secure the door in the open position."

Maddox and Slade still stand. Ganji glares at them. "Don't be foolish, Gentlemen, do as I say, get your bellies on the floor."

They do not move. Without taking his eyes off Ganji, Maddox says to Slade, sarcastically, "I guess that door was not as secure as you thought, Captain."

Slade spits out the words, "They've forced Commander Marino, somehow, to open the door."

Maddox turns his glare back to Ganji. "Who are you? What do you want?"

"Don't be coy, General. Please follow my instructions. I don't want to hurt you unnecessarily, at least not at the moment, please, on the floor."

"I asked who you are," the General demands, angrily.

"You will learn that soon enough, General. As soon as we secure this place." Then he turns to Ahmad, "Have him put down before I lose my patience."

Ahmad walks to within four feet of the General and levels his weapon at his legs. "I would do as he says, General. You will serve our purposes even with your knee shot out. Ganji has a very short fuse, you see."

Maddox slowly lowers his large frame to the floor. Slade follows.

"Good," Ganji shouts. Then, in the voice of one used to giving orders, instructs Ahmad, "Now, we separate the hostages into two groups. The General and the Admirals will remain here in the operations room. Also, bring the senator here. Handcuff them to chairs. The others, take them to the dining room. Bind them with the duct tape." He looks at his watch. "We made very good time, Ahmad, very good time."

"But we lost two good men, Ganji."

"Yes, we did, Ahmad, two good men. But, they will be heroes, my friend, heroes. You can be proud."

"I will save the pride until the end, Ganji."

Only 23 minutes have lapsed since the time Ganji's group entered the gate. Outside the op center, no one on the post is aware of what has taken place. Ganji orders his men to drag the bodies of the dead Marines and secret service agents into the mechanical room. The bodies of his own men he has placed in the conference room.

With General Maddox, Admiral DeWitt, Admiral Thompson and Senator Burke separated from the other hostages and secured to chairs with handcuffs, Ganji keeps them in the operations room where he plans to maintain his own position. The remaining hostages he holds, under guard, in the dining room.

Satisfied that everything has developed according to his plan, he calls Ahmad and Cormorant to his side. He notices that Ahmad has blood on his sleeve. With a look of genuine concern he inquires, "Ahmad, you're hurt?"

Ahmad holds out his arm and with a sad look, replies, "No, Ganji, it's the blood of my men. We carried them to where they rest in the other room."

Ganji tilts his head and looks hard at his friend, his eyes showing a mixture of sadness and anger. In a tone of consolation he says, "My compatriot, I too, am saddened at the loss of our comrades, but we all knew the price could be high. Let us try to complete our mission without further loss, but, Ahmad, if we lose more of our comrades, yes, even if you and I die, remember, we will take many of these American dogs with us. And, our accomplishment here will be long remembered in our beloved homeland, Ahmad, long remembered."

Ahmad straightens his shoulders, lifts his head, and takes on a distinct demeanor of determination. "You are my leader, Ganji. I will follow you anywhere, you know that. I am sad, yes, but I am ready for whatever tomorrow holds, now, tell me, what is our next move?"

Ganji smiles. "Good! I am proud of you, and of your men." He turns to Cormorant, places a hand on his shoulder and tells him, "You're a true hero, my friend. To have devoted these many years of your life to our cause, and to have conceived of this plan, you may be very proud. Now, if we are remarkably clever, and if we receive some help from Allah, perhaps we can prove successful in our bid to free our friends and send them home." Regardless of the praise from Ganji, Cormorant's face shows little emotion as he replies, "I am just doing what I was born to do, Ganji."

Turning again to Ahmad, Ganji quietly commands, "Now, I want to see the other hostages. I want a woman, and I hope we can find a beautiful woman. Americans especially dislike seeing a beautiful women molested."

Ganji and Ahmad walk into the dining room where the hostages are being seated in plastic chairs, their hands and feet bound with duct tape. Their faces reveal a variety of expressions. Captain Slade looks mildly curious. Nat

Dawson looks madder than hell. Nicki looks frightened and small. The rest of the hostages range from looks of pure terror to teeth clinching anger. Nat and Slade sit next to each other. Slade has been looking around the room to see who is missing. He realizes the MARDET Marines are missing. He also realizes that Commander Marino is missing. He mumbles, "Bastards." Nat leans over to Slade and whispers, "I concur with that, Captain." One of Ganji's men hears the exchange and shouts, "No talking, keep quiet!"

Ganji directs his men to slide the chairs of the eleven female hostages into a row at the front of the group. He paces before the line of women, carefully surveying their faces. "Good afternoon, ladies," he says in a mockingly kind voice. Some of the women are crying. "There is no need for fear," he continues. "If your President uses good sense you will not be harmed in any way and tomorrow you will tell your friends about your adventure and you will laugh with them." One of the women completely breaks down in uncontrolled sobbing. He stops in front of Nicki and turns to face her. He looks at her long and hard, a slight smile bending the white streak in his beard. Nicki's body shakes. He stands with feet wide apart, his hands in his pockets, as he studies Nicki. He muses softly, "You my lovely, are an exceptional specimen. Yes you are, a truly exceptional specimen." A tear slowly rolls down Nicki's cheek. "What is your name, my beauty?" He asks.

She doesn't answer, just quietly sobs.

Still smiling, Ganji goes on. "Here now, did I not just tell you that you have nothing to fear, that is, if your great president is the wise man that I think he is. Do you think your president is a wise man, my dear?"

Nat is furious. He can contain himself no longer. His chair is positioned near the front of the group of hostages. With flashing eyes he sneers, "You're a mighty brave man you son-of-a-bitch, picking on a helpless woman. What are you after, anyway?"

Without changing expression, the smile still intact, Ganji shifts his eyes to Nat. He studies him while Nat glares. Ganji speaks slowly. "You're an old man, is that why you're so obstinate, because you think I will not harm an old man?" Nat figures that if he can draw the attention of this lunatic away from Nicki then he may forget about her. He spits out his words, "You think I'm an old man, take off this tape and I'll show you how an old man can whip your ass you crazy sack of shit."

Ganji continues to be almost unflappable, almost. The smile, although still holding position, takes on a barely perceptible slackening. He turns to Ahmad and pointing to Nat, orders, "Take the noisy one to the back of the group where he will be less of a bother." Then he turns back to face Nat. "Your ploys will not deter me from my plan, old man. You see, there is a difference between you and I, and that is why I will be successful. Even though you insult me with your blasphemy, I will not harm you, because that is not my plan, and I will work my plan without being deviated by your pesky insults."

Two of Ahmad's men drag Nat's chair to the back of the group of hostages, at the far end of the dining room, near the door to the kitchen. As they release their grip on his chair, one of the men sneers at Nat, "He may not harm you, but I am not so kind." He draws back a heavy arm and punches Nat hard on the back of his neck. The blow paralyzes Nat momentarily and his head flops onto his chest. He's dazed, but not hurt seriously.

Ganji shouts at the man. "You fool! I will tell you when you're to use force. Get away from him. Listen to me, we will not be distracted by the ranting of a fool. When we draw blood it will be carefully thought out and I will order it, only Ganji will order it, do you understand?"

The man growls, "Yes Ganji."

Ganji turns his attention back to Nicki. "You see, I want to harm no one. If I have to harm someone it will only be because your president is not a wise man. Again, do you think your president is a wise man? Why, of course you do, at least, you should pray that he is. If he is, you will live, my lovely lady." Then he turns to Ahmad. "She's the one for my little demonstration, Ahmad. Bring her to the room with the important ones."

As she's taken into the operations room, Nicki sees Maddox, DeWitt, Thompson and Burke, in that order, left to right, on a makeshift stage, made of four sturdy tables placed side by side. The four are handcuffed to the chairs in which they sit. Nicki is placed on the end, at Burke's left. The stage is centered on the west end of the operations room. Cormorant has placed a television camera and a large monitor before the group. The camera is directed at them. The monitor is positioned in front of them so that they can see the screen, their images in full view. Ganji, satisfied with the arrangement, stands before the group. He looks very calm, but serious. This is the moment he has waited for. The moment for which he has planned with excruciating detail. He has a feeling of supreme power. He speaks to Maddox. "General, you're a very, very intelligent man, and, you are, without doubt, a brave man, but I wager that you're also a man with a large ego. Having your image broadcast on television is certainly not new to you -" Maddox interrupts, "Who the hell are you and what are you after?" But Ganji, without breaking stride, goes on, "No, you have been seen by millions. You're a star by any standard."
Maddox challenges again. "Cut the bull, what's your purpose?"
Ganji continues. "But I am going to make you a super star. Do you think you'd like that, being a super star on television? It takes a big ego to be the most powerful military man in the world, you should like super star status, don't you agree?"
Maddox grits his teeth. DeWitt bellows, "You think you're pretty important, you and your shabby cohorts, you can't pull this off, whatever the hell you have in mind, it won't work."
Ganji smiles and the white streak bends. "Listen to you, Admiral, listen to you. You sit there securely bound to a chair while I have control of the most sophisticated

electronic warfare installation in the world and you puff out your chest in indignation, saying my plan will not work. But, it's working, don't you see, it's working." DeWitt says nothing. Ganji looks at Admiral Thompson. He asks, "And you, Admiral Thompson, another brave man, I know, I have studied your record, I have studied you all very carefully, do you have anything cute to add?"

"Go to hell," Thompson mutters.

Ganji turns to Senator Burke. "Senator?"

Burke smiles. "You also are a very intelligent man, my friend, a very clever individual, to pull off a stunt like this. You must be congratulated. I suppose you're about to tell us what you have in mind, and, my old nose tells me that you're also about to tell us who you are."

Ganji laughs aloud. "Ah ah! Now here is a true diplomat, yes, by God, oops, pardon me, I forgot, I no longer need to play games with who I am. I mean, by the pure love of Allah, you're a true diplomat, Senator. I say that, I, Yasin Ganji, say that."

During this entire exchange, Nicki has been quiet. Her tears have dried and the look of fear has diminished somewhat, but only because she's trying to hide it from Ganji. She is, in fact, terrified.

"Yes, it's time, Senator, time to enlighten you all." Ganji replies. He rolls a desk chair from one of the computer stations and positions it in front of the group. He sits, leans back in the chair and says, "I will do just that, Senator, I will do just that." He takes a long, thin cigar from his pocket and lights it. He spends five minutes weaving a tale of the CMI adventure and how the exploits of his group have worked to convince the people of Iran that Americans are immoral, atheistic, gun toting murderers and how the western influence in his homeland is steadily being diminished.

Burke interrupts. "My understanding, Mister Ganji, is that the youth in Iran are wearing Levi's jeans."

For the first time Ganji looks irritated. He snaps at Burke, "Enough words, it's time to get on with my plan. Then we will see, Senator, how many young Iranians will be wearing

Levi's in the future." He calls to Ahmad. "Bring the collars, Ahmad, let's see what the good Senator thinks of our designer collars.

Ahmad carries a plastic box and sets it on the platform before Burke. From the box he lifts a metal object that is shaped like a ring, about eight to ten inches in diameter. One side of the ring is hinged. He climbs onto the platform, walks behind Burke, opens the hinged ring and places it around Burke's neck. He then closes the ring and threads an odd looking padlock through holes in the two ends of the ring. He snaps the padlock shut.

Ganji laughs. "There you are Senator, your own designer collar, and you won't find anything like it in Iran. He then places identical collars and locks on Maddox, DeWitt and Nicki. However, he does not put one on Admiral Thompson. Thompson is wondering why, when Ganji, who stands behind them with his hands on his hips, says, "Do you all know what is so special about your new collars? You'll like this," he says with a hearty laugh, "They explode!"

Nicki turns white. She whimpers, "Oh noooooo."

"And another special feature of your beautiful collars is that they are secured with handmade locks made by my uncle in his small shop in my home village. It is of a design that dates back many, many years and serves a distinctive purpose in our village. You see, it is intended to keep the شیاطین away. In your tongue the word is - demons. Now don't you think that is appropriate?" Thompson glares at Ganji and spits out the words; "You're damned crazy!" and then asks, in a gruff voice, "Why haven't you put one of those damned things on me?"

Ganji's face bends into something between a smile and a sneer. He says, "I have another plan for you, Admiral. But first, we need to tune into the world." He turns and calls to his agent, Cormorant. "It's time to start our broadcast."

268

Chapter 33

A Global Broadcast

2:20 P.M.

Ben Dawson is in his den Watching CNN News when the screen suddenly goes black. Then, seconds later, the screen comes to life again as the camera slowly pans a group of men, three of them in uniform. Then, the image of Senator Robert Burke appears on the screen and Ben says, "What the hell?" He's stupefied. He calls to Marilyn. "Hey Honey, come in here, Bob Burke's on TV, I think they must be televising the tour of the Navy's facility at Blackwater. Maybe Nat's gonna be on camera." As Marilyn Dawson enters the room the camera has panned to Nicki. After focusing on her face for a brief moment the camera slowly zooms out and an image of the group of five hostages fills the screen. Marilyn Dawson looks at Ben curiously and asks, "Where are they Honey? And why are they in those chairs like that? What's going on, Ben?"

As Ben is answering, "It beats the hell out of me!" a man walks in front of the camera and begins speaking. "Good afternoon ladies and gentlemen of the world, welcome to our show. Let me introduce myself. I am Yasin Ganji of CMI, a Mujahedin of Iran. The five people you have just seen on your television screen are; American Four Star General Bruce Maddox, the Chairman of the Joint Chiefs of Staff; Admiral Arland DeWitt, who fills the Navy Chair on the Joint Chiefs; Rear Admiral Douglas Thompson who is in charge of the American Navy's Electronic Warfare Department; the United States Senator from West Virginia, Robert Burke, and a very beautiful young lady who assists the Senator."

Beginning to feel a sense of foreboding, Marilyn Dawson has her hand to her mouth. She asks Ben again, "Ben, what's going on? What's that thing around Nicki's neck?"

Ben now has a worried look on his face. He answers, "I don't know, Sweetheart, I don't know."

The camera has now zoomed in on Ganji. His face fills the screen. He's thoroughly enjoying himself before the camera. A smile, a sinister smile, spreads across his face as he resumes. "These five people, along with about fifty others, are my prisoners, you see. A short while ago a very heroic group of CMI agents and myself took control of a highly secret Navy Installation located in the State of West Virginia. This is where we are broadcasting from, the beautiful Allegheny Mountains. It's too bad we can't show you a view of the mountains, they're actually quite breathtaking, but that's not on our program today."

"My God," Ben hisses, "They've got Nat in there!"

2:30 P.M.

An assistant in the office of the Secretary Of Defense in Washington, receives a phone call. He quickly switches on a television set and tunes to the CNN channel just as Ganji says, "I am hoping that someone out there will tell the president of the United States that I would like to speak with him. Also, it would be appropriate for someone in the Capital to begin taping this telecast, if you're not already doing so, because, you see, I am going to be giving the President some very important instructions and it would be sad if those instructions are not clearly understood."

The defense department aide grabs a phone. As he's dialing, another aide bursts into his office and breathlessly sputters, "Are you watching it?"

"Yes, what the hell is going on?"

"He's got the Chairman, my God, Bob, he's got the Chairman, and DeWitt and some others."

The aid, called, Bob, looks incredulous. He shouts, "who, who the hell is it?"

"He calls himself, Gangee, or something like that, we've got to get the Secretary, call him, call him now!"

Within minutes, the Secretary of Defense, Jacob Arbogast, is on the phone with the President of the United States, Adam Bucklew. The President is at the U.S. Embassy in London where, at the moment, he's with the Ambassador. It's 7:40 P.M. London time. "Mr. President," Arbogast begins, "Do you have access to a television set?"

"I suppose so, Jake, what's up?"

"Mr. President, we have a hostage situation at the new electronic warfare center in West Virginia. You need to get someone to tune in to CNN for you, while I brief you on this thing."

Noting the urgency in Arbogast's voice, Bucklew asks to be taken to a television set. A few minutes later, he and the Parliament members are watching Ganji as he says, "So there you have it, Mr. President, I will expect your call. Let me assure you that we are not here to play games. My prisoners, that you see here," Ganji points to Maddox and the others, "will die if you do not release our comrades. And here is my schedule. The young lady, and I am told her name is Nicola Valentini, will die at midnight tonight. Senator Burke will die at 1 a.m. Admiral DeWitt will die at 2 a.m. General Maddox will die at 3 a.m. To prevent their deaths, you simply need to release my comrades."

The President is still on the phone with Arbogast as he watches Ganji's performance. He notes that Ganji didn't include Admiral Thompson in his schedule. "Jake," he asks, "what's he after?"

"The two guys who blew up the barracks, the two that we have scheduled to be executed next month."

Bucklew pauses, then asks, "What do you recommend, Jake?"

"Give me thirty minutes, Mr. President, I'll call you back with a plan. Meanwhile, assuming we make contact with this guy, think about who we should have make the call."

"I'll do it myself," Bucklew says.

"Do you think that's wise, Mr. President?"

"Yes, with the whole world watching this damned thing I don't want the people to think I'm a wimp by delegating it to someone down the line, yes, I'll do it myself."

Arbogast hesitates, then, "You understand sir, and I don't mean to presume that you haven't considered this, if you negotiate with him directly you don't have the ability to maneuver by claiming you don't have the authority to make a final decision; you, of course have the final word."

"Yes," Bucklew says, "I know it's a negotiation no-no, but in this case I'll just have to work around that problem."

"As you wish, Mr. President, but obviously I don't want you to make the call until we have a plan in place."

"All right, Jake, take the 30 minutes, I'll stay right here," the President says, reluctantly, and returns his attention to the television and Ganji.

As Ganji melodramatically describes how the metal collars on each of his victims are filled with an explosive material, he slowly walks behind the five hostages. While continuing his speech, he stops behind Admiral Thompson and takes out his pistol. He raises the pistol toward the back of Thompson's head. Senator Burke, who followed Ganji with his gaze, opens his mouth to warn Thompson, but Ganji already has the barrel of the semi-automatic pistol an inch from Thompson's head. He squeezes the trigger and the pistol barks. Thompson's head falls to his chest. Burke lurches against the side of his chair and makes a strange, grunting noise as he's splattered with blood and fragments of bone and brain tissue. Nicki screams. Maddox utters, "Aw shit, no!" DeWitt gasps, but says nothing. Thompson's body slumps in his chair. Blood pours from a gaping hole in the left side of his forehead where the bullet made its exit.

Ganji retraces his steps to the front of the group, faces the camera and says, "You see, Mr. President, just in case you had any doubts, now you know that I am serious. In addition to several of your boys who we killed while making our entry, you now have a dead Admiral on your hands."

Bucklew gasps at the man on the screen, "You crazy son-of-a-bitch!"

Ganji continues without pause. "Each of the explosive collars, on my hostages, has a timing device, and I will give you a close-up of the display." He motions to Cormorant and the camera zooms in on a digital display attached to the collar, which encircles Nicki's neck. It reads, 09:07:34, and the seconds are ticking off. "You see, President Bucklew, you have a little more than nine hours to free my friends, or the pretty Miss Valentini will lose her head." Nicki moans, a small sound, at first. Then it escalates into a more pronounced peal of the word, "Noooooo. Please, noooooo." Then, in a soft, tiny voice, "Cole, I love you."

"Ah ah!" Ganji exclaims with glee. "The little lady has a lover. So much the better. Are you watching our program, Mr. Lover? Won't it be fun to watch as your sweetheart's pretty head explodes?"

Senator Burke jerks violently at his handcuffs. His face is purple with rage. Veins bulge from his forehead as he screams, "You rotten, filthy bastard! Bastard! Bastard! Bastard! Baaaaaaaastarrrrrrrrrrrrd!"

Ganji simply smiles, appreciative to Burke for making the scene more dramatic, then turns serious as he resumes speaking to the camera and the President. "Call me soon, President Bucklew, and I will give you instructions about releasing my friends. Trust me, the American people do not want to see this young lady die," and he points to Nicki.

In a conference room, at his office in Cascade, Cole Dawson is watching Ganji's show. Through clinched teeth, he curses, as the woman he adores followed her expression of love with a tormented, groaning sound. His chest heaves with anger and emotion unlike anything he has ever felt before. His mind races as he tries to grasp hold of the situation. He wants to rush from his office, go over the mountain to Blackwater and crash through the walls of the place that holds his Nicki, but how, what, what can I do, he asks himself. He can't seem to focus on a clear thought, and his body seems paralyzed along with his mind. *A plan, I need a plan, there has to be a way to get to her, there must be a way, God, give me a way to reach my Nicki.*

Ganji resumes talking to the camera. His speech continues to be directed to the President who, Ganji assumes, is watching by now. If he's not, then Ganji knows the substance of what he's saying will be relayed to him. "And it would be very foolish for your military to try to enter this building. The front entrance is barricaded to slow down an attempt at entry. The large overhead door through which we entered has been welded shut by my men. The hatch from the roof is small, only one person at a time could enter through it, and we have it well guarded. So, you see, before your people could gain entry we will have slaughtered all our prisoners. And, one more thing. We are not afraid to die. In fact, our mission may prove even more successful if we are slain in the process of eliminating your top military brass. So, you see, my friend, we will succeed one way or the other."

Cole Dawson's phone rings. He doesn't hear it at first. It continues ringing. His mind races, I have to get to Nicki, somehow, I have to get to her. Suddenly, he realizes the phone is ringing. He picks it up and stammers, "Yes?"
"Cole, it's your dad. Have you seen it?"
His anger building, Cole answers Ben Dawson. "Yes, I'm watching it now. Dad, I've got to get over there, I've got to get to her."
In a confident and steady voice, Ben says, "Listen carefully son. The government will not give in to these people. The United States does not give in to terrorists who hold hostages, period, end of story. And if the military busts into that place, well, I expect we'll lose your Uncle Nat and Nicki. But I think I know a way, Cole, I think I know a way in."
Cole doesn't fully understand what his father is saying. "What do you mean, a way? A way inside?"
"It's a long shot, son, but, yes, I think I know a way in. Now, I need to make a couple of phone calls; while I'm doing that I want you to get a crew of men and start blasting through the concrete that seals the portal of old Number One."
Cole is bewildered. He asks, "The old mine, why, Dad? Why the old mine? What's it got to do with this thing?"
Ben's voice is urgent. "Just do it, boy, just do it. Bust in there. The mine's our way in. I can't take time to explain, just get started."
As soon as Cole is off the line, Ben dials the number of an

275

old friend in Florida, who used to scuba dive with he and Cole. His friend answers. Ben says, "Fred, this is Ben Dawson."

"Ben, why you old fart, how you doing? Been diving any Florida caves lately? Hey, have you seen this crazy thing on the tube?"

"Yeah, and that's why I'm calling, Fred. I think I know a way we can get a team of SEALS into that communications center."

"What! Have you been sniffing glue, Ben? That's gotta be one hellava secure building, and from what I've seen, they'll kill a lot of our people if we start busting into the place."

"But that's why I think my idea will work, I know how to get in quietly, and if your SEALS are as good as you've always told me, then I think they can take those bastards out without losing any of our people. Look, I don't have time for a lot of explanation, Fred. I'll give you the scope of my idea and fill you in on the details later. Here's the deal, the site of that COM center was bought from us Dawsons. It sits over an old airshaft that goes down about 60 feet to an old flooded mine of ours. I think we could lead a SEAL team through the mine and up the old shaft, into the building. Now, don't ask me a lot of questions, I know it sounds impossible, but I think it can be done."

Fred sounds incredulous. "How long has the mine been flooded, Ben?"

"About fifty years."

"Jesus, Ben, it's probably all fallen in!"

"I don't think so, old coalmines have been pumped out before and restarted, there may be some places where it's fallen in, but if there is, there's probably a way around the fall. Look, Fred, we just don't have time to go into it, trust me, I think it's doable. Now, you're an old SEAL. You guys remain buddies forever; can you call one of your cronies in the Navy and get a team here soon?"

"Hell yes!" Fred says, with an air of supreme confidence, "I know there's a team standing ready in Baltimore, but there could be a hitch, Ben."

"What's that?"

"Delta Force."

"Delta Force?" Ben questions.

"The government's counter terrorism group. It's run directly by the defense department. It's so secret they don't even acknowledge that it exists. DF is probably already in the air out of Fort Bragg. They may not like the SEALS horning in."

"Hell, Fred, they won't have the kind of guys we need for this, will they?"

"Not in my opinion, but I'm not running their show. Let me make some calls, Ben. I think you have something, I mean, with your coal mine entry. One way or another let's try to get some guys into that mine."

At 3:10, precisely thirty minutes after the President gave Arbogast thirty minutes to call back with a plan, Arbogast calls. "Mr. President, we need more time. The Skywatch building is too damn secure, we haven't figured out how to get in without compromising the hostages. Can we have another hour?"

"Damn it! Jake, Okay, call me in an hour."

"Thank you, Mr. President, but in the mean time I think you should have someone call this guy, Ganji, and try to stall for more time, I think we're going to need it."

"All right, Jake, I'll call him within the hour, I want to think about it for a while, you know, talk to some of my people here."

"Of course, Mr. President."

4:05 P.M.

The Op Center

A red phone rings, on a desk central to the operations room. Cormorant answers it. He motions to Ganji and calls, "It's the President!" Ganji slowly walks to the phone. Knowing the President is watching, he doesn't want to appear in any

277

hurry. He takes the phone from Cormorant and places it to his ear. "This is Jasim Ganji."

"Mr. Ganji, this is Adam Bucklew."

"Yes, President Bucklew, may I call you Adam?" Ganji asks with a sneer.

"No, you may not. I hold the office of President of the United States of American. You're talking to the office, not the man."

"I see," Ganji says slowly. "So I am talking to an office, so be it." He says the word, office, as though he's spitting out something vile. "As long as the office gives me what I want I will speak to the office and not the man."

Bucklew asks, matter-of-factly, "What are you after, Mr. Ganji?"

"You hold two of our friends, Mr. Office. You're planning to execute them. Our friends are heroes in Iran and it would be a shame for Iranian heroes to die on American soil."

Ignoring Ganji's childish attempt at ridiculing his position, the President plays along. "On whose soil would you like them to die, Mr. Ganji?"

Ganji laughs, "Oh, you are funny, Mr. Office, I like that. I like a sense of humor." Then he scowls, "They shall not die, that is my demand. If you want to save your people who are here, in my hands, you will release our friends." Ganji directs Cormorant to zoom in on Nicki. "Take a close look at the young lady. Do you think your people will enjoy seeing her head disappear?"

By now, most television sets in the world are tuned to CNN. Calls have been placed to CNN headquarters from the White House demanding that the broadcast be stopped. CNN explains that they have no control other than to destroy their dish receivers and if they were to do that it would take months and millions of dollars to replace them. Besides that, they explain, if CMI was able to take over CNN transmission capability, then they could do it to any other television broadcasting entity in the world.

As a result, the broadcast continues and people around the

world are glued to their televisions. A family in Iowa, whose son is a specialist at Skywatch, watches the telecast in shock. They are tortured with the thought that the military will try to storm the Op Center and their son and brother will be killed by Ganji's men.

A cafe in Leon, France, empties as the patrons rush to find a place with a television set. At the Lanesborough Hotel, in London, where President Bucklew will spend the night, the President's security personnel work to bring the building under more rigid security.

Senator Burke's wife quietly sobs as she watches her husband who is furious at his helplessness. The wife of General Maddox is hysterical, her son, a military man, stationed in Germany, tries to reach Pentagon officials to ask them to negotiate, knowing there is little chance of succeeding in his request. In a bar, in Camp Verde, Arizona, men make bets as to what the President will do. The drama is beginning to shut down the country as people stop working to watch it unfold. Washington, D.C. is paralyzed.

In the Op Center, Ganji's conversation with the President continues. Bucklew speaks. "Midnight, tonight, is not enough time for me to get your people released. I am out of the country, I need more time."
"No, Mr. President," Ganji replies, now more serious and less playful. "Midnight gives you ample time to initiate procedures necessary to give them their freedom and have them on an airplane. Their release and the departure of the plane must be televised on network news. If they are on the plane by midnight, I will reset the timers on my hostages to allow time for my friends to arrive safely at a destination which I will give you, once they are in the air. When they arrive safely, at their destination, I will give you instructions on the departure of my comrades and me."
The president grimaces. "It's now 4:15, West Virginia time, give me time to discuss this with my people, I will call you back in one hour."

"Fine, Mr. President, talk to your people and press them for a plan to rescue Maddox and the others, but understand this, they cannot be saved. If your military tries to penetrate this building, my hostages, all fifty of them, will be shot. One other thing you need to know. When I leave this building, the device around the neck of General Maddox, who will accompany me out of your country, will contain a radio controlled trigger that will detonate his explosive collar if my breathing were to stop for more than ten seconds, so, don't try to set up a plan to take me out once we leave this building. Let me assure you, we have very capable electronic technology, very capable."

4:20 P.M.

The President's phone rings. It's Jake Arbogast. "You're late, Jake, the President says, impatiently."
"Yes sir, Mr. President, but we have some good news and I was trying to get some detail on it."
"What is it?" Bucklew urges.
"Sir, we think we have a way into the Skywatch building."
"I don't understand, Jake, you told me it was damn tight."
"Well, it should have been, Sir, but the security had evidently been breached accidentally when the facility was constructed, I don't think you want me to take time to explain the details. I'm not sure I fully understand them myself, but my people tell me they believe a team of SEALS could have a good chance of saving most of the hostages."
"How good a chance, Jake?"
"Don't know yet, sir. We're going to try to get the SEALS there as quickly as possible to review the situation and report back."
Bucklew grits his teeth. "Jake, I'm not going to release those two bastards, you know I can't do that, they killed 43 of our boys when they blew that barracks. And this bastard wants me to televise their release. I don't want the world to see those guys walking, even if we just fake it to gain time, so work hard on this thing with the SEALS. Give them whatever they need."

"That's already happening, Mr. President."

"Good, that's real good, Jake." Bucklew is about to end the phone conversation when he has an afterthought. "Jake, this guy, Ganji, says that when he leaves the op center he's taking Maddox as his hostage and he has some kind of device that will sense any cessation of breathing on his part, and if we were to kill him it would trigger the explosive collar around the neck of Maddox."

"Okay, Mr. President, I'm with you."

"Well, what I'm reaching for, here, Jake, is this; we need to try to figure out some way to incapacitate this bastard without stopping his breathing, and render him unable to hold his breath. Do you follow me?"

"Yes sir, I follow you."

"So, as a backup, it may be a good idea to get someone working on that?"

"But Mr. President, my understanding is that Ganji won't leave the op center until he sees his guys get off a plane in Iraq. You're not suggesting there's a possibility you'll agree to do that, are you?"

"No, I won't, but maybe there's some way to fool him into thinking we released them, then when he leaves with Maddox, maybe we could neutralize him in some way."

"I'll get some people working on that, but I don't think we'll be able to fool this guy."

"I know it's a long shot, Jake. Okay, keep me posted."

5:15 P.M.

Viewers from around the world watch as Ganji answers the red phone. On the other end, "This is President Bucklew. I need more time." Bucklew figures he will continue to stall as long as he can. "My people tell me I cannot release your people without an o.k. from the Panamanians. It seems they also lost some people during your attempt to blow up the barracks."

Ganji's cool demeanor begins to fade. "Bullshit! We both

know you're lying. I will not give you more time. I know you're simply stalling in order to figure out a way into this building without the loss of my hostages. I repeat, you cannot do it. It will take you too long to penetrate. They will all die. Trust me on that, and trust your military who has told you the same thing. Midnight, Mr. President. And if you continue to stall I will move the schedule up one hour, they will each die an hour earlier, the woman at eleven o'clock, so, cut the crap, President Bucklew, cut the crap!"

Bucklew doesn't back down. "Tell me, Mr. Ganji. Why do you risk the lives of all your men to save just two people?"

Ganji regains some composure. He's slightly flattered that the President of the United States, without question the most powerful man in the world, power that Ganji would give anything to have himself, asks him to describe his purpose. Making sure the camera is on him, he repeats the President's question to the millions of people watching. Then he answers. "Let me pose a question to you, President Bucklew, why do you take time to consider how you will save the people here? Why are their lives important to you? Is the answer not, because you're a principled man? Is it not, because this General and this Admiral have devoted their lives to protecting their country and its ideals? Well, President Bucklew, I also have certain principles and ideals. And my friends have devoted their lives to our cause."

Bucklew, knowing that no reasonable person will buy into Ganji's answer to his next question, whatever that answer might be, asks, "And what is that cause, Mr. Ganji?"

Without hesitation, Ganji takes the bait. "To prove to my countrymen and to the world that you Americans are immoral and godless murderers and my country should cut-off relations with you."

"Oh, and you intend to accomplish that by killing our innocent young people and our very noble Officers? How, Mr. Ganji, does your murdering our people demonstrate the immorality of Americans?"

This time Ganji hesitates, thinks about his answer. Did he slip-up in referring to the desire of CMI to influence Iranian relations with the western world? Did he make a mistake? His face now flushed with anger, Ganji shouts; "Don't cloud the issue with your rhetoric, Bucklew. It's clear that my Iranian countrymen want the release of our brothers. That is our most pressing mission at the moment. I will discuss philosophical views at another time." He hangs up the phone and says, into the camera, "Call me when you have worthwhile information about the release of my friends, Mr. President. You now have less than seven hours to save the young lady.

5:30 P.M.

Skywatch

The outer perimeter of Skywatch is surrounded by West Virginia State Police, while the area inside the fence is secured by the FBI and the government's elite counter terrorism group, Delta Force, out of Fort Bragg. Delta Force was in the air within minutes of the Secretary of Defense being notified of the takeover at Skywatch. Marine Colonel Jesse Grimes is in charge. Grimes has just finished reviewing, with Ben, a blueprint, faxed from the Pentagon, of the interior of the Skywatch building. Ben describes how he and Nat modified the catch-basin design to allow access from the airshaft into the mechanical room. Grimes scratches his head and proclaims, "I think your idea has a chance of working, but I'd sure like to know how in the hell you guys managed to rig your little secret entrance and compromise the security of a top secret military facility, and do it right under the noses of the Navy's engineers."

Ben answers, "It's really a long story, Colonel, maybe we can talk about it over a beer after we get our folks out of there."

"If, we get them out, Mr. Dawson, if. And, if you're not in jail."

"I've already taken that gamble, Colonel," Ben says, "and

right now, I'm damn glad I did."

"I can give you no argument there," says Grimes, then continues, "I think we're finished here, Dawson, so why don't you get over to the mine and see how they're doing at getting it opened up."

"I'm on my way," Ben replies.

Chapter 34

SEALS in the Air

5:45 P.M., 10:45 P.M. Greenwich time

Lanesborough Hotel, London

At his hotel suite, the Presidents receives a phone call. It's Jake Arbogast. "Mr. President, I have good news. The Marine Colonel with Delta Force, at the Skywatch perimeter tells us he believes the plan will work. A SEAL team is in the air now. We'll get back to you after we hear from the team leader, but the preliminary word is that we have a good chance."

"That's great, Jake. What do I do in the meantime?"

"I think you should call Ganji and tell him the release is being implemented. He may be less vigilant if he believes he's succeeding."

"Good idea, Jake, I'll let him sweat a while longer, then I'll call."

8:45 P.M.

Skywatch

Colonel Grimes has ordered the electrical power to the op center turned off. By so doing, the back-up power generator in the op center automatically starts. Grimes figures the loud noise from the generator will cover the sound of the SEALS coming up the shaft, loosening the old manhole cover and removing the heavy cast iron grate from the catch basin.

Over the mountain, Cole's men have removed the concrete, which sealed the portal of Dawson, Mine #1. The SEAL team has arrived and has been briefed, by Ben, on how the interior of the coal mine is laid out. They have also been carefully briefed by one of Colonel Grime's men on the interior layout of the op center. They study the location of each room, the corridors, interior and exterior doors, and the equipment in the mechanical room.

The leader of the SEAL team, Lt. Commander Linden Pell,

has agreed that Cole should lead the SEALS through the mine. The logic behind that decision, as explained earlier by Ben to Colonel Grimes, is that none of the SEALS have ever been in a coal mine and that even though Cole has not been in this particular mine, his thorough familiarity with mine interiors will permit him to lead the SEALS around any obstacle that may be present in the main haul way, on the way to the Blackwater shaft.

Pell briefs Cole on the equipment that he will carry. That done, he raises the question of Cole carrying a weapon. "Cole, in the briefing given to me during the chopper ride here I was told that you're not willing to lead us through the mine without your being armed, that right?"

"That's correct, Commander; if I'm going in with you I sure as hell don't plan to go naked."

"I understand, Cole. I'm told you're experienced in the use of conventional sporting arms, that right?"

"That's right, most types of long arms and hand guns."

"Okay. Now you must understand, Cole, your job is to lead us to that airshaft. You're to stay back once we are in the building. Me and my guys will handle things once you get us there. You're going in armed only as a precaution to protect yourself. Understood?"

"I'm making you no promises, Pell, I have an uncle and a girl that I love very much being held in there by those bastards!"

"Now hold on, Cole. We're going up against a bunch of experienced shooters who are crazy enough to take any kind of wild-assed chances. This is not going to be a rabbit hunt, now we have to have an understanding here!"

Cole's thoughts churn as he considers Pell's words. I know where this man is coming from, but if he thinks I'm going to sit on my butt with Nicki in harm's way he has another think coming. He tells Pell what he wants to hear. "Whatever you say, you're the boss."

"Good." Pell says, relieved that Cole has come to his senses. He continues, "Are you proficient in the use of a semi-automatic pistol?"

"Yes Sir, I own a 9mm Glock."

"That's great, and, by the way, we can do away with the "Sir" business, you're a civilian, how about you just call me, Pell?"

"I can do that, Pell."

"Good. Now, I don't suppose you've had any experience with an automatic weapon, so let's just leave it at the pistol, okay?"

"As a matter of fact, I have had a little experience. One of our guys, at the company, has an old Thompson that we've taken out to a quarry near here; I've got a fairly good feel for it."

"Pell didn't expect that. He's silent for a moment, then. "Okay, not that we expect you to have to use these weapons, as I said before, you're to stay in the background once our guys get inside the op center, but just in case things don't go entirely as planned, I'll let you carry a Colt M4A1 Carbine. It's a shorter, more compact version of the M16A2 rifle and was specially designed for U.S. Special Operations Forces. I'll give you a quick demo when we finish here. You'll have four spare clips in your pack. You'll also carry an M11 Sig Sauer P-228, four extra clips and a knife. This is our standard carry pistol. It's small, light, durable and accurate. Any questions?"

"None," Cole replies.

"Okay. One other thing, have you ever seen a man shot?"

"No I haven't," Cole replies.

"Well, it's not like in the movies. When you shoot someone they don't get flung back five feet and fall down dead. In the heat of a gunfight, with adrenalin flowing, a man can be hit and not even know it. He can be shot in the heart and be eight seconds from blacking out and still be pumping lead at you."

"I'm aware of that, Pell. It's something like shooting a deer. Its heart can be shot away and it will still run a hundred yards. It's dead, just doesn't know it."

"Precisely. Keep that in mind, if you hit a guy, unless you hit him in the central nervous system; that is, the brain or spine, he'll probably still be capable of shooting back. Okay, let's move on to the dive equipment. Now I know you're an experienced SCUBA diver, but for a dive of this duration you're going to have to use one of our rebreather rigs instead of the compressed air rig that you're accustomed to."

"I understand, Pell. Tell me, how long can we stay under on a rebreather?"

"I'd say a man your size, operating under the stress that you're going to experience with a dangerous dive such as this, will consume about 1.2 liters of oxygen per minute. The Mark 15 rigs that we're using will hold about 604 liters at 3000 psi; that will give you about 500 minutes, or just over 8 hours. However, that could obviously change quite a bit depending on your level of exertion and stress, as I'm sure you're aware. To play it safe, I suggest you assume you have no more than six hours supply of gas. That should get you back out if there is any problem."

Cole nods, "I hear you."

"Good," Pell replies. "Now let me tell you something about the Mark 15. Under ordinary circumstances I would not permit you to make an extended dive with a rebreathing rig without a hellava lot of training, but, unfortunately, we don't have the luxury of time, so, you get the two-minute version and I'll be right on your tail all the way in. If you get into any kind of trouble I think I'll be able to handle it."

Cole nods, "I understand."

Pell continues. "The Mark 15 is a closed circuit, mixed gas rebreather that re-circulates your respiratory air. At each breath, your exhaled air passes over a moisture trap and then through an absorbent bed where the carbon dioxide is removed. It next passes over the oxygen sensor and -----
well, crap, you don't need to know all that bullshit. Here's the bottom line; if you have a problem with your rig it's not a simple procedure to buddy-breath with a rebreather. Assuming you wouldn't have experience with it, and due to the nature of this little adventure, we're not using full face masks; I brought rigs with separate masks and mouthpieces. That will make buddy-breathing doable, not simple, it's still

tricky because of the dual hoses, but it's doable. If you have to do it, you get behind me, your face right at the back of my head. I'll remove my mouthpiece, pass it over my head to you, you take two breaths and pass it back. I take two breathes and, so on. Again, it's not as simple as what you've been trained to do, but it will work if you keep your cool. When we get in the water, we'll make sure you get it down pat." Pell continues briefing Cole on the Mark 15 as the rest of the SEALS begin the process of donning their wet suits and preparing equipment. Pell and Cole go to the base of a hill nearby where Pell quickly takes Cole through the basics of the Colt M4, after which Cole fires a number of short bursts at a corrugated carton, gets his questions answered and satisfies them both that he can handle the weapon.

Back at the mine entrance, Ben explains to Pell that the crew, which opened the entrance, checked for accumulation of methane gas. No gas was found between the portal and the flooded part of the mine. Years before, after the explosion, the water pumps that kept the mine free of water had been shut down and the greater part of the mine, being below the prevailing water table, had filled with water.

Cole, Pell and seven SEAL team members board two pickup trucks that will take them into the mine, down the sloping main haul way, about a quarter of a mile to the point where the water begins. Ben drives one of the trucks.

Years before, the rails had been salvaged from the main haul as far in as the water, and the trucks have no problem traversing the mine. Arriving at the beginning of the flooded area the men scramble out of the trucks and after a check of equipment, begin putting on the Mark 5's, dive masks and flippers.

Pell addresses the group. "Men, this is a new one. I've never been in a coal mine, let alone one that's filled with water, but you've all made cave dives and this can't be that much different. As you know, Cole, here, is an experienced Mine Engineer as is his father, Ben Dawson." Pell shines his light on Ben, who nods to the group.

Pell continues. "Now, Cole has never been in this mine, but Mr. Dawson was quite familiar with it when it was operating a long time ago, and he has reviewed the blue prints very carefully with Cole. Our objective, the old airshaft, leads up from one of the two main tunnels, the one which they call the air course. The old air shaft is about three miles in. Now, we're standing in what's called the main entry, or main tunnel for hauling the coal out. Once in the water and on our way, at some point, to be determined by Cole, he's going to lead us across into the air tunnel. We'll proceed up the air tunnel to our target, the airshaft. If for some reason we find the main tunnel blocked, there could be a way around the blocked section, and again, that's where Cole comes in. It's his job to find us a new route. Is everybody clear so far?"

"Sir?" One of the SEALS asks, "Why don't we just start out in the other tunnel, the air course tunnel, according to the map of the mine isn't it just the other side of these crossovers we were passing on the way in?

Cole answers the SEAL, "That's right, we call those, breakthroughs, and the air course is just the other side and running parallel with this, the main haul. However, the main haul, here, still has track down and that gives us something easy to follow for most of the way in. When I figure we've reached the airshaft, I'll take us across to the air course and the shaft."

Another of the SEALS, with a serious look in his eyes, asks, "Sir, as we were coming in on the truck I saw a lot of coal dust on the ground. Once in the water do you think we'll stir it up and give ourselves a visibility problem? I got into trouble once when a lot of bottom sediment stirred up. I don't want to have that problem again."

"That's a good question." Says Pell; "Cole, what do you think?"

"Ben interjects, "I think I can answer that for you." He walks over to the edge of the water, squats and shoves a hand in the water and shakes it vigorously. "See, it won't stir up. The coal dust is hydroscopic. That means it absorbs water. And, it's of fairly high density; that is, it's fairly heavy, so it settles out of solution quickly. We call it, Bug Dust. It's the residue from the cutting machines, kinda like sawdust from a sawmill. I don't think it will give you a problem."

The SEAL who asked the question shows a satisfied look and says, "Thank you, Sir."

A SEAL who appears to be older than the others asks Pell; "Sir, if we get separated from Mr. Dawson, are we sure our beacon will guide us out, seeing as how he describes the innards of the mine as being somewhat of a maze? "

"Yes Sentowsky; the beacon will be on a frequency that cannot penetrate earth. If you hear it, it's coming only through the water. Even if you take a different passage than what we take in, it will guide you out."

Sentowsky nods toward a younger man beside him who was obviously the originator of the question.

"All right men," Pell says, "It's nine-twenty. I figure we should be at the airshaft in two hours if we don't run into any problems.

Let's get in the water, but before we start on the way, give Cole and me a chance to do a little buddy breathing practice. If any of you care to give a hand I'm sure Cole won't mind."

With helpful tips from the entire team, Cole masters, to a degree, the technique of buddy-breathing on a Mark-15 RB.

"Alright, it's time we go, let's get at it," Pell starts to group his men along a safety line, Ben Dawson wades into the water to his son and puts a hand on his shoulder. "Cole, I wish I were going with you."

"I know, dad."

With a breaking voice, Ben continues, "Now, son, don't take any unnecessary chances." But even as Ben speaks the words, he knows that his boy will do whatever it takes to get Nicki and Nat out safely. And because of that, he's afraid for his son. He squeezes Cole's shoulder and with pure warmth, that only a dad can feel, says, "I love you, Boy."

"You don't need to worry, dad, we're going to do this thing. And I haven't said it for awhile, but, I love you too. You just try to keep mom from worrying."

"Hell, I haven't told your mother about this. She'd knock me

from here to Sunday if she had any idea what we're up to."
Pell interrupts. "We better get moving, Cole, it's 9:23."
"Right, I'm ready," Cole says, and he moves into deeper
water.

Chapter 35

The President Takes a Call

9:30 P.M., 2:30 A.M. Greenwich time, London.

While on his encrypted phone, linked to the Whitehouse, President Bucklew is interrupted by an aide who says, "Secretary Arbogast is on your hotline, Sir." Bucklew punches in a code to another line on the phone. "Where do we stand, Jake?"

"They're in the water, Sir. They're in the mine, on their way. Started six minutes ago. ETA inside the op center is 11:30."

"Good," Bucklew says, then follows with, "I've been thinking, Jake, maybe we should go ahead and fake the release of those two guys. Maybe I'm being overly sensitive about that being televised. After all, it would only be for a few hours before the truth would come out that we didn't really let them go. It could buy us some time, several hours, at least."

"Let's keep that in our vest pocket, Sir. I'll arrange for it, but we won't go through with it unless the SEALS fail, what do you think?"

"That'll be cutting it awful close, Jake. We're only two hours away from the young lady's death, what's her name, Nicola something?"

"Valentini, Sir, Nicola Valentini. She's an aide to Senator Burke."

"I don't want to lose her, Jake. The American people don't want to lose her."

"We won't let her die, Mr. President."

"Okay, keep me posted."

"I'm afraid we'll have no news until the SEALS are on the inside and can make radio contact," Arbogast responds.

"All right, let me know when that happens," Bucklew says, "I'm going to call our Mr. Ganji, now."

Bucklew presses the disconnect button on the phone and hands it to his aide. "Get Ganji on the line, Billy."

Thirty seconds later, Billy motions, "He's on the line, Mr. President."

295

Planning to continue stalling for time, while also trying to lower the level of vigilance within Ganji's group, Bucklew takes the phone. "Mr. Ganji, this is President Bucklew. After lengthy discussions with my people, I have decided to release your cohorts. However, I have a condition."

On the television screen, Ganji faces the camera and replies, "Condition? I am the one who sets the conditions, President Bucklew, you're not in a position to give me conditions."

"Never the less, I have a condition," Bucklew continues. "I don't want the release of our prisoners broadcast on live television."

Ganji grimaces, "That is not possible. I need to see my friends board a plane. Otherwise, I have no assurance of their release. It must be a military plane capable of in-flight refueling. The plane will take them to a destination, which I will give you, once the plane is in the air."

Bucklew continues, "There must be some way that I can give you that assurance without their release being broadcast. You need to give me some room here, you know our country has a firm policy of not capitulating to a hostage situation and I have the entire nation that I must account to and they'll have my scalp over this as it is."

Ganji wrongly senses a weakness in the Presidents voice and his confidence inflates. "Your scalp is not my concern, Bucklew. You will allow the world to watch the release of my comrades or they will watch as your friends get their heads blown off."

Chapter 36

Whatever It Takes

Trouble:

A state of mental distress
A condition of disorder
A condition of malfunctioning
A cause of disturbance, or pain

August 15th, 2003, 9:35 P.M.

The Flooded Mine

Cole Dawson suddenly snaps back to the present time, breaking his thoughts free of stories about the Dawson family as told by his grandfather years ago. He and the Navy SEALS continue the swim through the cold, clear water of the old mine. Cole is calm. He's under control, has purpose. But with the black walls of the old mine seeming to close in, he's again faced with the need to keep his mind occupied. He thinks of Nicki, his precious Nicki. How in the world did she get into this mess? What combination of events? What random circumstance? Where did her life make the turn that placed her in this danger? Was it his fault? Hell no, it's not his fault or Nicki's - it's those sons-a-bitches above.

9:40 P.M.

Cole feels somewhat secure carrying the pistol and automatic rifle. Having used firearms all his life, the quick rundown on the M4 came easy. But, they really don't expect him to be in a situation where he has to use the weapons, he's only to lead them to the airshaft. Lead them to the airshaft and then stay in the rear. Easy said - can he do it? It will depend on the circumstances, he tells himself. Then, an image of Nicki's face, ashen from fear, flashes across his mind. *Damn it, Pell can't hold me back, I'll do whatever it takes.*

10:15 P.M.

Just ahead, Cole sees trap door number two. It's closed. He finds it curious that the explosion that killed all those men so long ago did not blow out the air door. Probably because the pressure dissipated throughout the vast labyrinth of the mine and up the airshafts, he surmises. Cole and Pell have to struggle to open the door, but it opens, and moving through the door, the group continues the journey into the interior of the earth.

They move no more than fifty yards when Cole feels three quick jerks on the safety line; he turns. Two of the SEALS seem to be communicating with sign language. Bubbles have appeared at a scrubber connection on the rebreather of one of the divers, indicating a gas leak. Pell briefly joins the two men, and then swims to Cole. He points to one of the divers, points to his own mouthpiece and shakes his head. He again points to the diver with the problem and to a second diver, then points toward the mine portal, the opening of the mine. Cole understands. One of the divers is having problems with his gas supply and must go back. His dive buddy will return with him. That leaves Cole and only six SEALS.

10:30 P.M.

The SEAL with the gas leak and his buddy begin swimming back to the safety of the mine portal. If the diver's equipment fails completely he will still be able to buddy-breathe with the other diver, assuming the second diver has no equipment problems of his own. Before the two men are out of sight Cole and the six remaining SEALS resume their journey into the bowels of the old coal mine.

10:35 P.M.

With a gas leak in a rebreather and two of the SEALS having to return to the portal, Cole wonders if the odds are against him and the SEALS. There are at least eight to ten armed men in the op center, perhaps more, according to what they were able to determine from the television footage being broadcast by Ganji. Pell figured the team of eight

SEALS could carry off the rescue because they would have the element of surprise. Now there are only six against ten or more. Not good odds, Cole speculates. But, he decides, *we have no other option, no other choice.*

As they continue their course through the old mine, Cole's thoughts turn to Nicki. How different both of their lives would have been had they not had that stupid and childish break-up back in college. They would have children by now and instead of being caught up in this mess he'd be home to watch over them and Nicki. That was a comforting thought, taking care of Nicki and some kids.

Ahead, a form gradually takes shape. It's a motor, sitting on the tracks with a string of loaded coal cars behind. As the men approach, Cole takes a close look at the motor and wonders what happened to its operator when the explosion occurred on that unfortunate day so long ago. With Nicki's passion about the harm that mine operators have wrought on the miners for years, who would she blame for the deaths of all those men? Was it the fault of a Dawson, or was it caused by a careless miner, or a freakish accident that could be blamed on no one? Only the Good Lord knows, he decides.

The group has moved through two trap doors now, five to go and number 3 is just becoming visible in the beam of Cole's lights. They reach the door and again position themselves to swing it open, but this door gives them a problem. It seems to be jammed, the wood swollen from the water, it doesn't want to open. Being weightless, it's difficult to apply force. Cole plants his feet against a rail crosstie and pulls hard. Pell joins him. Together, they are only able to force the door open about thirty inches, but that's enough. Cole squeezes through and the others follow.

Before they make another forty yards, Cole is shocked to see, looming ahead, a huge pile of rock blocking their path. At some point in time there has been a fall. A large section of the ceiling has fallen, creating a jumbled wall of rock. As they get closer he sees an opening on the top left side of the blockage. The opening appears to be large enough to pass through. It appears to be a distance of about 15 feet to the other side.

Cole thinks through the situation; 'Should we proceed through this restricted area, or backtrack to a break-through into the old air course? I know what the conditions are in front of me; I don't know what they are on the other side. When the mine was operating, I'm guessing the main haul was better maintained then the air course, I think I'll gamble that it's in better shape now, as a result of that. Yeah, I'll take them through.'

Cole waits while Pell also assesses the situation, moving the beam of his spotlight through the narrow tunnel. They look at each other and give a thumbs-up sign. Cole starts through. His rebreather rig scrapes the ceiling in a couple of places, but he makes it though. Pell follows and emerges on the other side with Cole. The third man is about half way through when a hose bracket on his rig wedges between two rocks. He's jerked to an abrupt stop. He tries pushing himself backward but his rig is hung up tight.

Pell returns into the small tunnel to assist. He takes his knife from the sheath on his leg and tries to pry the bracket free of the rock, but he cannot find enough room between the rig and the rock above and he's afraid the knife may slip and cut a hose. He attempts to squeeze past the trapped man to try working behind him, but he can't get past. He returns to his first position. He plants his knees against a rock and pushes hard on the equipment, but it's jammed too tight, it won't budge. He pauses and looks hard at the situation. If he uses too much force he fears the rocks will break loose from the ceiling and fall on the diver, bringing more of the roof with it. He can't get the other men past the man who is stuck. The diver has only an inch or two of clearance below his chest and belly, not enough room for him to get his hands in to release the buckles and free his back pack. Pell figures he can cut the straps to release the diver, giving him freedom to move backward through the opening to the remaining four SEALS. It's only a distance of several feet and for a SEAL

301

to hold his breath until he can reach the other divers and buddy-breathe would be a piece of cake. That gets the man to safety, and then Pell can try to free the rig.

Through sign language, Pell explains his plan to the trapped diver. With the diver's agreement, Pell cuts the harness. The freed diver moves out of the rig, but still has his mouthpiece gripped in his teeth. The hoses from his mouthpiece to the gas rig stretch tight. After taking a deep breath from the mouthpiece, he releases it and begins moving backward through the small tunnel. Once outside, he assumes a position alongside his dive buddy who removes his mouthpiece and hands it to the freed man. They pass the mouthpiece back and forth, each, in turn, taking a lung full of life giving oxygen.

With the man out of the dive rig, Pell moves back into position to try to remove the snared equipment. As he grips the rig, he braces his legs against the rocks on his left and the solid wall of the mine on his right and gives a hard, twisting jerk and the dive gear falls free. He prepares to take up the gear and move through the tunnel to get it back to his companion, figuring he can jury rig the severed straps, but, without warning, the rocks on which the rig was snared, fall. Barely missing Pell's head, the rocks falls hard on the rebreather rig. Then, smaller pieces of rock start falling and Pell, afraid that more of the roof will fall, quickly backpedals out of the hole. Even as he does, the entire roof section, where his comrade had been trapped, gives way. Pell barely breaks free of the hole before it's completely closed off by falling rock, his team on the other side.

Thankful that Pell was able to escape the falling rocks which blocked any chance of the remaining SEALS to join them, Cole considers trying to find the next break-through to the air course and trying a circuitous route to reach the men and lead them back, but considers that it would take too long and use too much air. Besides, the men would probably be on their way back out of the mine, and there is no guarantee that he could find a clear way to them. As he ponders the drama unfolding before him, the numbers run through his head, "Two good guys; ten bad guys. Not good odds!" Pell swims up to Cole. With dive masks inches apart, the two men look into each other's eyes for a long time. Cole makes the first move. He points to the H & K strapped to his body, points to his breast, points to Pell, and gives a thumbs up, in affect saying, "It's you and me against the bad guys, Lt. Pell, let's go get them!" Pell smiles with his eyes and returns the thumbs up. They direct their lights down the rails toward the far airshaft, and kick.

As they continue through the blackness toward the airshaft and Nicki, it's just the two of them now. Two determined men. One, a warrior doing his job. The other, a man desperately in love. With the other SEALS having been turned back by the equipment problem and the cave-in, it's up to Cole and Pell to save Nicki, Nat, General Maddox and the others. But, they have arrived at a trap door, which simply will not give. Cole realizes that they will have to circumvent the jammed door by circling through the old air-course. He motions Pell to follow as he swims back in the direction from which they just came. He travels roughly eighty feet before coming to the first breakthrough, on their left, to the airway passage. There, the trap door stands open. Pell follows him through the passage a short distance to the airway. There, they make a left turn, then proceed for two hundred feet to another breakthrough, on their left, which leads back into the main haul.

As they swing into the breakthrough, Cole suddenly comes up short. In the twin beams of his lights, a skull looks up at him through large, black eye sockets. Cole gazes at the fully intact skeleton of a miner as lays face up, where life was snuffed out a half century ago. A hard hat lies, open-side up, beside the skull. Cole pauses, briefly, to look down at the remains, four feet below him. The miner, most likely was someone who was related to a family still living in Cascade. It occurs to Cole that these remains could be taken out, and through DNA testing, the miner's identity could be determined and his family could give him a proper burial. Then, the thought leaves him as quickly as it came. He must move on, he must hurry, he's losing precious time. As Pell moves past the skeleton, a cold shiver slides down his spine.

The trap door in the next breakthrough opens easily. Cole and Pell move silently into the main haul once again, where they make a right turn, now beyond the jammed door and once more heading further into the innards of the old mine, swimming side by side. They make no more than twenty yards when Pell, having gotten close to the mine roof, is jerked to an abrupt stop as he catches part of his rebreather rig on a jagged piece of steel. It's an old bracket that held the power cable to the roof and it had evidently been damaged at one time. Pell's gas supply is suddenly operating sporadically and Cole sees tiny bubbles coming from one of the gas fittings. Cole indicates to Pell what is happening and Pell nods in acknowledgement. He is still getting enough air to continue, but at a reduced pace. He gives Cole a thumbs-up and a sign to go slower.

The two of them then set out again, this time avoiding the roof and trying to relax and maintain a smooth rhythm. Being forced to go slower brings more mental stress which also seems to cause the two of them to breathe a little harder.

They make their way through several more trap doors, when, to their right, in a small room off the main haul, they see the old pumping station, just as it showed on the blue prints. In another hundred feet they should find the break-through to the air-course and the old Blackwater airshaft.

Cole feels a lump in his throat. They're getting close to the shaft and the danger involved in the rescue they are about to attempt now begins to sink in. Somewhere above them, in the navy's operation center, trained killers will pull out all the stops in an effort to stop him and Pell. The two of them are out-manned and out-gunned. He's never killed a man before and if he is to be successful in saving Nicki he may have to kill several men within the hour. Is he up to the task? Does he have the grit? Will his aim be accurate? He vigorously shakes his head to stop the questions. He must stay focused, think of only one thing. Whatever he must do to save Nicki he will do. *I will save her,* he tells himself, *I will save her.* Suddenly, he feels short of breath. He realizes his thoughts about Nicki are causing anxiety and forcing his body to use more oxygen. Pell stops, and looking directly into Cole's eyes, asks a question with his own eyes; *Are you okay?* Cole nods and gives a thumbs-up. Pell nods in return and touching his mouthpiece gives a thumbs-up which Cole takes as assurance that Pell is getting enough air, at least for now. The two suck air and kick forward again and within minutes both see what appears to be an opening ahead to the right.

As they are about to turn into the breakthrough they suddenly come up short. The breakthrough is blocked with a huge stack of timbers. Cole immediately realizes that the breakthrough had wrongly been used as a storage area for a supply of roof support timbers. *Son-of-a-bitch! Now what? We'll have to keep going to the next breakthrough to cross over and then backtrack to the air shaft.*

With the timbers blocking the breakthrough, Cole signals to Pell what they must do. Pell nods and they immediately strike out for the next breakthrough. As they swim, it suddenly occurs to Cole that, perhaps, back in 1951, the miners had also used the next breakthrough for storage of timbers, and perhaps the one after that. He grabs Pell's arm and stops swimming. *Shit! We can't take a chance on the forward breakthroughs, we'll have to backtrack and cross over through the last breakthrough before the pump room. How can I explain this to Pell?*

He doesn't try. He takes Pell by the arm and pulls as he reverses course. Pell looks confused, but Cole's actions are very definite and Pell knows he should follow. As they pass the breakthrough with the stored timbers, Cole points to the timbers and then points with a jabbing finger back in the direction from where they just returned. Pell understands; *the forward breakthroughs may also be blocked with stored timbers.*

10:58 P.M.

They swim past the old pump room, now to their left, and continue on toward a breakthrough that Cole knows was clear when they had passed it on their way in a short while ago. As they continue swimming, Cole looks at Pell's gas, or, air supply gauge. With all the air Pell had expended helping to open jammed trap doors, struggling to help the trapped SEAL at the rock-fall, circumnavigating a jammed trap door, back-tracking, and leaking gas, his supply is running critically low. It's now Cole who signals to slow down. They must conserve air, even though they are behind their estimated schedule. Ahead is the breakthrough which he's been looking for and they move easily through it, and turn left into the air course. Cole's heart starts beating faster, knowing that they are close to the old air shaft. A tug on his arm reminds him to follow his own advice, but he can't, not now, not when they're this close. He thrusts hard with his flippers and Pell keeps pace. Suddenly, Cole points ahead and gives a thumbs-up. There it is, looming before them, overhead, the opening to the airshaft. Cole is overwhelmed with relief as he sees the concrete base and the galvanized steel wall of the shaft rising above. Swimming below the shaft, the beams from Cole's lights fall on the steel ladder fastened to the wall. His light beams follow the ladder up. About thirty feet above, the light reflects from the surface of the water.

Arriving at the ladder, Pell does a quick check of their gear and weapons. As he is checking the equipment, the beam of Cole's light catches a reflection from the ladder. He moves closer. To his astonishment, a gold watch hangs from the bottom of the ladder, four feet above the floor. The chain of the watch is looped around the rail, then back around itself, with a decorative fob holding it in place. He looks closer. A diamond and gold tie tack is fastened to the chain of the watch. Cole shakes his head. How in the world - who could have placed this here? He gently removes the chain from the ladder and carefully places the treasure in a zippered pocket. Turning to look at Pell, he sees him pointing up. He nods. They rise toward the surface. At the surface, they move to the ladder and each clings to a side of the ladder as they remove their masks and mouthpieces. They tentatively sample the air. It smells dank, but not unusual. Cole quickly whispers, "If there's methane gas you won't smell it, it's odorless, so we'll keep the mouthpiece handy for a minute. If you start to feel anything unnatural, shove it back in." "You got it." Pell replies, also in a whisper.

11:15 P.M.

They remove their flippers, leaving their feet protected with their dive suit boots, and let the flippers sink. As Pell removes his rebreather he says to Cole. "This rig only has a short time left on it; minutes maybe, so we may as well dump it. If we can't get through that manhole up there, like your dad says we can, we've bought the farm."
Cole nods in agreement. They drop the rigs and they rapidly sink to the bottom of the shaft.
Pell shines his light up the ladder and says, "Looks like this is where the fun begins, Cole, are you up to it?"
With a catch in his throat, Cole replies, "I'm ready".
"I think I might have to get out of your way and let you have at them," Pell says with a grin, then continues, "But it's important that you remember something. I am trained to kill, that's the business I'm in. You're not trained to function in a combat situation, Cole, and that's exactly what we have up there. There is going to be a firefight and if we are to come out the winner, I need two things. One; a hellava lot of luck. Two; I need you to do exactly as I say. Understand?" Being this close to the danger, Cole suddenly feels a wave of

anxiety flow up from his diaphragm to his throat. But he gets the words out. "I understand; you're the boss."

"Ok, we're clear on that." Pell looks at his watch; "It's eleven-twenty-one. We've been just under two hours getting in." Pell moves the beam of his spot light to the concrete ceiling over the airshaft, the ceiling that is actually the bottom of the concrete slab that was put into place by Ben Dawson, forty years before. Moving the beam of light towards the ladder, Cole sees a round opening immediately above the ladder. About two feet up that opening he sees the bottom of a cast iron manhole cover. "Just like your dad said, Cole, there's the manhole. That's our doorway, let's get through it and get this job done."

Pell checks each of their weapons and ammo. Satisfied that everything is in battle order, he clips his spotlight to his belt in order to free both hands and starts up the ladder, Cole right behind. The top of the ladder ends at the ceiling, leaving another two feet up through the manhole to the cover.

When Pell reaches the top of the ladder he plants his feet firmly on a rung of the ladder, holds the top rung with his left hand and braces his right hand on the side of the man-hole away from the ladder. Both men clearly hear the noise of the power generator in the mechanical room above. Pell kills his light and then reaches up to the manhole cover and pushes. It doesn't move. Moving up two more rungs on the ladder, he positions his upper body in the 30-inch manhole, his head inches from the cover. With both feet again planted firmly against a ladder rung, he presses his back against the side of the manhole and gives the cover a hard thump with both hands. The heavy cast iron plate pops free, as small flakes of concrete and liquid fall in Pell's face. Light appears around the perimeter of the cover. Pell whispers, "We're in!"

As he lifts the heavy cover out of its seat and leans it to one side, a wet, sticky substance dribbles from the cover. There's not enough room for the cover to stabilize against the wall of the 36-inch diameter pipe, which was used as the catch basin. Pell swears, "Son of a bitch, the cover won't stay upright." He tries again to get the cover to set on the narrow, 3-inch ledge between the 30-inch opening of the slab and the 36-inch diameter of the catch basin, but it won't stay.

"Cole," he whispers, even though the noise of the generator would hide his voice. "It's gonna be a tight squeeze up through this thing, there's not a lot of room with this cover against the side. Make sure your piece and your gear are as close against your body as you can get them"

"O.K. just get your ass up through there," Cole says through clinched teeth.

Pell looks at his watch. It's 11:27. He whispers to Cole, "We have 33 minutes."

"Go!" Cole demands.

Pell squeezes his shoulders through the hole where the cover sat a minute before, moves his feet up two more rungs on the ladder and looks up at a cast iron grate above his head. He suddenly jerks back down as he sees a face peering through the grate. As he stabs a hand toward the pistol on his belt, he realizes, even in the dim light, that the face has dead eyes. He again pushes his body upward until his head is no more than two inches from the grate and the dead marine whose body lies upon it. He hesitates. Cole whispers, "What's happening?"

"There's a dead guy on the grate," Pell answers in a sad, but angry voice. As he does, he realizes that the sticky substance that coats his face and upper body is blood.

He presses his hands against the underside of the grate. "I hope this damn thing isn't stuck," he mutters, and pushes. With a feeling of great relief, he is able to move one side of the grate upward about three inches. Lowering the grate back into its seat, he shoves his fingers through the openings in the grate, grips tightly, pulls his legs up, plants his feet on the ledge surrounding the old man-hole, and prepares to lift the grate and the body. "Okay, you bastards, the party is about to begin."

Chapter 37

What's Happening?

11:27 P.M., 4:27 A.M. Greenwich time

London

President Adam Bucklew is awakened by an aide. "Secretary Arbogast is on the phone, sir," the aide says, softly. Bucklew rises quickly to a sitting position, rubs his eyes; looks at his watch. Bucklew is a man who prides himself on his ability to maintain a calm demeanor in any situation. He's a practical man, strong and firm in his beliefs. He has a fervent love for his country and its people. He is in his late sixties and just a tad wider in the middle than he was when in his forties. He's just under six feet tall with broad shoulders and straight-up posture. He has a square jaw, high cheek bones, a straight nose, a moderately pronounced brow over piercing; no, stabbing dark eyes. Eyes that seem to look through you and convince some part of your consciousness that he is stronger and wiser than you are. And yet he has a gentle and considerate manner and a passion for improving his effectiveness as the leader of the free world. There's an intangible quality inside that gives him a commanding presence in any social, business, or political situation. He is a leader of the first order.

He takes the phone. "Yeah, Jake. What's happening?"

"We're not sure, Mr. President. A lot has been going on. First, two members of the SEAL team had to return because of equipment failure. Then, there was a cave-in, which blocked the passage of five others. As those five men were on their way out of the mine, they met the original two who were headed back in with another civilian, a guy who knows the mine."

Bucklew rises and begins to pace as he asks, "Who, Jake?"

"I don't have much on that, Sir. His name is Ben Dawson. They tell me he's an experienced diver and also knows the interior of the mine, and can get the SEALS around the blocked passage of the mine. He's our only chance, now, Mr. President."

311

"What about the other SEAL, Jake, weren't there eight in the team?"

"Yes Sir, there were. Two men made it through to the other side of the cave-in, Commander Pell and the civilian, Cole Dawson. We don't know their status sir. They were on the other side of the section of mine where the cave-in occurred. We think they're both okay. Also, only two divers carried radios and they were among the seven who returned. We won't have radio contact, Mr. president, even if Pell and Dawson get inside."

Bucklew stands and motions for an aide to turn on the TV.

"Jake, we have 30 minutes till the girl dies, if Pell makes it inside it's just he and the civilian until the other guys get back in there, is that what I'm hearing?"

"Yes sir, Mr. President," answers Arbogast, who then hears an explosive, "Shit!" through his phone, then adds; "There's one other detail you should know, Mr. President."

"I hope it's better news, Jake."

"I'm afraid not, Sir." Arbogast clears his throat before continuing. "Ben Dawson, the replacement guide, he's 72 years old, Mr. President."

"My God!" declares, Bucklew, as he runs a hand through his ruffled hair. He stops pacing and grips the back of a chair with a strong hand, lifts it into the air and throws it, crashing, against a wall as he sputters, "Damn it to hell, why can't this world gain some normalcy?"

He slowly walks to the chair, lifts it, and places it on its three remaining legs. He grimaces, embarrassed at his loss of control. *Why, he asks himself, why do old wars and old hatreds persist? Hell, most of these terrorists probably don't have a clear idea of what they're fighting for, or who, or why. They're brainwashed by some fanatic who, unfortunately for the rest of the world, finds himself in a position of power and persuasion. Why can't we learn from history? When the "wall" came down and the cold war ended - and we kicked ass in Iraq, it looked as though we, at last, had an opportunity for some peace. Then we have those damned lunatics fly into the WTC and the Pentagon, and now this, shit!*

He moves back to the couch and slowly lowers his tired body into its soft folds. As he does, from somewhere in the back reaches of his mind, some words take form; *History is a nightmare from which I'm trying to wake.* "Who said that?" he asks himself out loud, then, "It was Joyce," and he silently repeats the words of the author, James Joyce. *History is a nightmare from which I'm trying to wake.* "Well, Joyce sure had it nailed."

11:30 P.M.

Above the Flooded Airshaft

Raising one side of the grate, Pell carefully eases his head up just enough to look into the room. He finds himself looking at a blank wall, just a few feet away. Twisting his upper body, he lifts the opposite side of the grate and looks in that direction. "My God," he exclaims in a whisper. Several more bodies lay on the floor, a few feet from where he peers out from under the grate and the dead marine. Some of the bodies are in uniform and some in civilian clothes, dark suits. Blood covers the floor and has flowed to the drain.
With impassioned anger flooding his emotional underpinning, Pell lifts the entire grate, and the marine's upper body, and surveys the entire perimeter. In front is the blank wall. To his left the same. To his right is the interior of the mechanical room and, behind him and to his right, the huge diesel powered generator; its piercing whine blocking out all other sound. Beyond the bodies of the dead men, the room opens into a broad, clear area. It looks just like the blue print.
Very carefully, Pell moves the grate and the marine, to one side. A large blob of congealed blood plops down on his thigh. A chill flows through his body as he watches the blob slowly slide off his leg and fall away. His anger swells. He removes the H&K that has been strapped to his body, places

it on the floor in front of him and placing his hands on the rim of the basin, pulls himself up and out of the hole. He picks up his H&K and carefully surveys the surroundings as Cole climbs out, his head and dive suit splattered from the blood. He appears as bloody as the dead marines. Crouching, Pell squeezes between the wall and the generator to a position between the generator and a large fuel tank. The tank is surrounded by a raised curb, about twelve inches high, designed to catch the diesel fuel should the tank leak. Cole follows closely behind. Motioning for Cole to stay put, Pell inches his way between the generator and the fuel tank, pulls a small mirror from a pocket, and carefully positioning the mirror at the outer edge of the fuel tank, surveys the mechanical room. He sees one man, a short, but husky, powerful looking man. The man stands guard at the door, which leads from the Operations Room. An automatic rifle leans against the wall, next to the man.

Pell moves back to where Cole waits. "I see only one man," he tells Cole. "He's guarding the door to the op room." Remembering, from the plan of the mechanical room, that beyond the fuel tank is a water tank, a large heating and air conditioning unit and finally, a large rubbish hopper, Pell says, "Let's move up between the wall and the other equipment, I need to check for more bad guys at the far end, get a look at the door to the kitchen and get closer to that guard."

A minute later, with the two of them positioned behind the HVAC unit, and satisfied there are no other terrorists in the mechanical room, or the kitchen, as far as he can determine, Pell whispers in Cole's ear, loud enough to overcome the noise of the generator, "The guy guarding the door is evidently supposed to make sure no one comes out, and probably to alert the others if there's an effort from outside to penetrate through the overhead door or the roof hatch. He's not looking this way, I think I can get a bead on him without him seeing me." Cole nods. Pell hands his H&K to Cole. "Hold this for me." Cole takes the weapon and Pell pulls his P9 pistol from its holster. He retrieves a Dalphon silencer from a secure pocket and attaches it to the P9. He eases forward between the HVAC unit and the rubbish hopper. Raising the P9, he aims just above the ear of the guard, who stands 30 feet away. He squeezes the trigger and the man, his central nervous system invalidated, instantly falls to the concrete like a sack of potatoes.

Pell quickly retrieves the man's automatic weapon and moves back to where Cole waits behind the HVAC unit. They then swiftly move to the door of the kitchen, Pell with his silent P9 at the ready, Cole carrying the dead man's weapon. Seeing no one inside the kitchen, they crawl inside to a position beside a serving counter, above which is an opening to the dining area. Using his small mirror, Pell surveys the dining room. The hostages are bound to chairs with duct tape. There are two terrorists guarding them. The guards are at the far end of the dining room, beyond the hostages. Pell whispers to Cole, "There are two bad guys standing guard over 40 to 50 hostages. They have automatic weapons. If we can take them out and get their weapons, we can arm three men from the group of hostages."

Cole responds. "Do you see my uncle? He's an older guy, gray hair."

Pell eases the mirror up and again scans the group. He sees a man in civilian clothes matching Cole's description. "Yes," he tells Cole, "he's at this end, very close, not five feet from the door over there." Pell points to the door that leads to the dining room. The door is ten feet to their right.

Cole says, "Let me release him, he's an exceptional man with firearms and he's a natural leader, he can select two more men."

Pell considers Cole's suggestion. He knows that the Navy hostages do not have Navy training in firearms, except, perhaps, the Captain, what was his name? Slade, yes, Jeremiah Slade. Pell is extremely impressed with Cole up to this point, and decides to gamble on his judgment. "Okay, crawl in behind your uncle and cut his bonds. Take the dead guard's piece with you, here, I've taken it off safety, it's ready to fire. Leave it with your uncle. Stay as low as possible. With that large bunch of hostages in chairs, above you, you should remain unseen. Make sure your uncle knows he's to stay put until we take out those two bastards. Leave your automatic here, I'll cover you."

Cole nods, then crawls to the door, where he pauses and takes out his knife. As he slides through the doorway on his belly, one of the hostages, who is in front of and to the right of Nat, is startled to see him and jerks his head Cole's way. Cole quickly puts a finger to his lips. The young Navy specialist relaxes. However, Nat saw the man's reaction. As Cole slides to a position behind Nat, the Navy man gives Nat a slight smile and a very subtle nod towards Cole. Nat then feels a hand grip his left wrist and feels the sensation of a blade slicing through the tape, which binds his wrists. Knowing he must not show movement, Nat keeps his arms in place. Cole then slides forward, alongside Nat's chair to reach the tape around Nat's ankles. Only then does Nat realize who is freeing him.

Nat is totally bewildered. How in the name of heaven did Cole get in here? After cutting the tape surrounding Nat's ankles, Cole motions for Nat to stay put and shows him the automatic weapon at his feet. He puts a finger on the trigger, then jerks it away and pretends to blow on his finger, indicating that the automatic weapon is hot, ready to fire. Nat gives an almost imperceptible nod. Having been watching Ganji's show on the television monitor, Nat knows precisely what's going on. He wants to tell Cole about the bomb around Nicki's neck, and the short time she has, but he cannot risk it with the guards watching. Before he can decide what to do, Cole is gone, as he eases his way backwards, on his belly, into the kitchen.

11:32 P.M. 4:32 A.M. London time

In the President's suite the television screen comes to life and a close-up of Nicki is on the screen. She looks pale, drawn, exhausted, and her eyes have a conspicuous look of fear. On the explosive collar, which surrounds her neck, the timer display reads, 00:28:10. Somewhere behind the camera, Ganji is saying, "I'm afraid your government is going to let you down, Miss Valentini."

Bucklew sits down heavily on the couch, the phone to his ear. "Son-of-a-bitch!" he mutters. "Jake, we've got to do something!" he shouts into the handset. "Get the release started. Get the networks on it, all of them. Get those sonsabitchs on a plane and in the air, we should have already done it, damn!"

"Yes Sir. You must call Ganji, Sir. Tell him the release is about to take place."

A minute later, Ganji is on the line. Bucklew speaks, "We'll give you your friends, Mr. Ganji. We'll have them on a plane shortly."

"Shortly, Mr. President? Shortly? You have less than 28 minutes to have them in the air," Ganji says with a strange, twisted smile that bends the white streak in his beard, "or the lady dies," and then, in a throaty, guttural tone, adds; "as the whole world watches."

11:40 P.M. The Op Center

While Cole was freeing Nat, Pell was watching a dining room television monitor which sits forward of the hostages. On the screen is an image of General Maddox , Nicki, and the others on the platform, strange devices around their necks. Then the camera turns 90 degrees and focuses on Ganji. He fingers a key, an old brass key, which hangs from a thong around his neck, and talks about how only he can remove the bombs from his hostages. As the camera made the turn to Ganji, Pell was able to determine precisely where, in the op room, Maddox and the others are positioned. When Cole is again at his side, Pell says, "I know where your lady is," and smiles.

"Where?" Cole demands.

Pell explains where they are positioned and the fact that they

317

are on some type of platform. Cole looks at his watch. It's 11:41. He looks frightened for the first time. He tells Pell, "We've only got 19 minutes."

"All right," Pell says, "here's the plan. I'm going to blow the door to the op room. I want you positioned by the door that leads from the mechanical room to the main corridor. When I blow the door, you go into the corridor to the doorway of the dining room and take out the two guys who guard the hostages. Get their weapons in the hands of two good guys. That gives us five guns. Now, we don't know how many other bad guys there are, or where they are, but I suspect some are guarding the main entrance at the lobby. Try to keep them pinned down and if you can get inside the op room to help me, so much the better. O.K.?"

Cole nods, "O.K."

They move quickly across the floor of the kitchen and into the mechanical room. Then, with Cole in position at the door to the corridor, Pell places an explosive charge on the door to the op room and takes cover behind a set of stairs that lead to a roof hatch. The explosion blows a huge hole in the door where the latch had been and the door swings open, on its hinges, amidst thick black smoke. In the next instant, Pell is through the smoke and the door and catches Ganji, Ahmad, Taha and Cormorant dashing for their weapons. Making the critical assumption that any man moving and not bound, is a bad guy, Pell opens fire on the nearest man. Taha falls face down and slides, on his belly, across the tile floor, leaving a path of blood. His already dead body comes to a stop with his head against the butt of his automatic rifle, where it leans against a computer cabinet.

As Taha was falling, Pell swung his weapon on Ahmad and squeezed the trigger. Two rounds rip through the right side of Ahmad's head and exit the left side amidst a cloud of blood and brain tissue.

Ganji had left his weapon lying on the platform that held his hostages. It was behind the Senator. Pell sees him going for it, but can't shoot for fear of hitting Burke and the others, so he swings on Cormorant, who has, by now, his weapon in his hands and is trying to get into position to use it. As Pell fires at Cormorant, Ganji drops to the floor behind the tables holding the hostages and fires, under the tables, at Pell. Both Cormorant and Pell are hit. Cormorant with one bullet through his abdomen, another barely creasing his head, and Pell with both legs shattered. Cormorant struggles to find cover in the maze of computer stations. Pell goes down behind a bank of heavy, metal cabinets, but quickly spins around and fires at Ganji as he dashes from his position behind the tables to find better cover. One bullet rips through Ganji's right arm and he drops his automatic rifle which slides across the floor before him. Another bullet pierces the muscle of his right buttock, but it's a slight wound. He dives for cover behind some equipment and finds himself beside Cormorant, who lays face down, his pistol with the silencer beside him. General Maddox, from his position on the platform, sees Ganji pick up the pistol. Maddox, fully aware that Ganji may turn the pistol on him, none-the-less yells to Pell, "He's got a pistol, son. His right arm is useless, but he's gotten the pistol off one of the others."

Pell waves at the General from his cover, "Thanks, Sir, I appreciate that."

Ganji does, in fact, aim the pistol at Maddox, but then lowers it. He sneers, "That would be too easy, General. I prefer that you lose your head." Then he yells at Pell. "It's no use, you have no legs. I will stay right here, and along with the whole world I will watch them lose their heads."

And the whole world hears Pell answer, "You're wrong about that you slimy bastard, I'm gonna blow your frigging brains out and get that key."

Ganji cackles, "Oh, so you know about the key. You must have been watching my little show. I'm sorry, sonny, but you'll have to crawl if you want to come and get the key, and if you come this way, I'm afraid I'll have to kill you."

When Pell blew the door to the op room, Cole had stepped through the other door, into the corridor and ran to the open door of the lounge. Leading with the barrel of his H & K, he swings into the room and opens fire as the two guards who, confused for a moment by the sound of the blast, now scramble to reach their weapons. Cole kills them both, then returns to the door and watches the corridor as he yells to Nat, "Free a couple of guys and get those guns."

As Cole entered and started shooting, Nat had grabbed his automatic and now rushes forward to Captain Slade's side. He yells to Cole, "Throw me your knife!"
As Cole reaches for his knife, a man appears running down the corridor toward him with his automatic rifle blazing. Bullets rip at the doorframe. Cole drops the knife, kneels, shoves his H & K through the door, points it up the corridor and fires blindly. The Iranian falls face down, his body sliding to a stop directly in front of Cole.

Nat runs to the knife at Cole's feet, grabs it and returns to free Slade. Cutting him free, he gives Slade the knife and yells, "Get another man," then takes a position beside Cole. Cole yells, "You watch the corridor, I'm going through the kitchen and into the op room."
"Nat yells and points to Cole's arm, "Cole, you're hit!"
Not realizing he was wounded, Cole takes a quick look at his left arm, then moves it. "It's okay, I'm going."
"Wait," Nat yells, "The one they call, Ganji, he has a key hanging on a cord around his neck, it's to the lock on an explosive collar around Nicki's neck. She only has about fifteen minutes!"
Cole shouts back, "I know," and rushes away, through the frightened hostages, toward the kitchen.
Nat looks into the corridor as three more terrorists appear. They rake the doorframe with lead as he ducks back in. He shoves his piece around the door and fires two bursts up the corridor. As he fires, two of the men slam through a doorway to the left, the ladies rest room, one of them hit, the other man to the right, into the conference room. The one in the conference room is also hit. As Nat fires another burst to

hold them down, Slade and a young Navy man join him at the door.

Cole, moving into the mechanical room, then to the door of the op room, the door that Pell blew out, takes a position to the side of the door. He yells, "Pell, you O.K.?

Nicki's head jerks upright at the sound of Cole's voice. "Cole?" she murmurs softly. "Oh, Cole, is that you? How? Oh dear God, please don't let him get hurt."

Pell yells back, "Stay there for now, I have one live bad guy in here and he has cover. So do I. Right now, it's a draw. I have three down and I think they're dead, but I'm not certain about one of them. I think the live one is the head honcho, Ganji, the bastard with the crazy stripe in his beard."

Ganji yells from behind a bank of computers, where he has taken cover, "It's too late, pigs, the girl will die in 14 minutes. If you try to reach her, I'll kill you."

"Pell yells to Ganji, "You're wrong you son-of-a-bitch. I'm going to smoke you."

11:45 P.M., 4:45 A.M. London time.

The President and several key aides have been watching the television screen as the camera remains focused on Nicki and the other hostages. The microphone picks up the sounds from the room as Pell yells, "I'm going to smoke you." Staccato pounding of automatic weapons can be heard in the background as Nat and Slade shoot it out with the Iranians who are pinned down in the rooms off the corridor.

Marilyn and Alice Dawson listen to the same sounds as, tormented and frantic; they watch the TV in Marilyn's study. All over the world, people watch and listen as Cole, shielding himself from the open doorway, yells into the op room, "Where is he, Pell, where are you?"

"He's on the north side, behind some equipment, I think. I'm on the south side, behind some cabinets. Ease your head around the door and you'll see me."

Cole peers around the doorframe, which sets in the thick, reinforced concrete wall. He sees Pell. Pell waves and points to his legs, which are bleeding and obviously broken.

Cole hears more automatic weapon fire from the corridor where he left Nat and Slade. "Hang in there, Uncle Nat," he says, softly.

But Nat has taken a hit. A bullet has pierced his left side in the lower abdomen. The same bullet, after passing through Nat, hit the young Navy specialist in the hip. He lies helpless next to where Nat slumps against the wall, beside the door, where he has maintained position. Slade is across the corridor in the men's restroom where he dashed moments before. The men's room is next to the ladies restroom where two of Ganji's men took cover and fired the burst that caught Nat. Now, Slade points his captured automatic at the wall between the two restrooms, and pulls the trigger. He fans the wall in an S pattern with fiery, full jacketed, lead projectiles. The bullets tear through the plasterboard and sheet metal studs and riddle the two men on the other side. Outside the op room, one terrorist remains, the wounded man in the conference room.

Cole, now knowing Ganji's approximate position, looks into the op room at Pell, and signals that he's about to dash into the room. Pell motions for him to come ahead. As Pell eases his weapon around the cabinets and rattles off a burst of fire to keep Ganji occupied, Cole rushes into the room and takes position next to Pell. Pell says, "We've gotta flush out that son-of-a-bitch, we're running out of time to save your girl."

"I know," Cole responds. "Tell me what to do."

Pell winces as he moves slightly to try to ease the pain in his legs. He's bleeding badly. Cole says, "I've got to get tourniquets on those legs."

Pell shakes his head, "No time, we gotta get that bastard. I'm gonna send a couple of bursts his way, you circle around to the right and see if you can find a position to nail him. I think he only has a pistol."

"Okay," Cole agrees.

As Pell rattles off a couple of short bursts, Cole rapidly crawls through a maze of racks supporting electronic gear and computer workstations. Peering around a desk, he sees blood on the floor. The blood trails off in the direction where he believes Ganji to be hiding. He slithers on his belly, following the trail until it disappears around the corner of some type of large electronic apparatus. It's the metallic hydrogen super-cooler of Dr. Wagner's beam accelerator. Carefully easing around the strange contrivance, Cole sees a small portion of Ganji's shoulder and a partial sole of a shoe, protruding from behind the other end of the super-cooler. Ganji obviously kneels there. Cole knows he has a shot at the shoulder, not a killing shot, but a shot. Once, when he was a kid and hunting deer with his dad, he had a brief opportunity at a huge buck, but only a small portion of its neck was exposed. He passed on the shot, waiting for a better one. It didn't come. His dad said, "Son, when you have a shot, take it."

He slowly works his automatic into position, aims at the bit of shoulder, and squeezes the trigger. A short burst of rounds explode from the H & K, then nothing, the piece is out of ammo. But one of the rounds caught Ganji's shoulder and spins him around. For an instant, the two men stare at each other, twenty feet apart. Ganji, his face distorted with rage, raises his pistol as Cole ducks back behind his cover. Even as he does, Cole is certain he hears the "click" of the hammer fall on an empty chamber. In that instant, that fraction of a second, when Cole's brain logged the click, then compared the sound to similar "clicks" stored in his memory bank, it registered; empty chamber. In that instant, Cole, knowing that time is running out for Nicki, decides to gamble. In one motion, he slides his own pistol from the holster on his waist and leaps from his cover with the pistol belching. He catches Ganji with two rounds as he struggles with his wounded arm to insert another clip into the pistol. Ganji dodges again behind the hydrogen cooler, but now seriously wounded by five bullets, two of them Pell's. Still on his feet, he runs through the maze of equipment in the op room, heading for the door to the mechanical room. Cole runs to the end of the super-cooler and fires two more rounds at him as he's zigzagging through the equipment, but misses. Ganji pauses once, fires seven wild rounds and then strikes out again for the door to the mechanical room. Cole yells to Pell, "He's coming your way, Pell, shoot."

Pell, weakened now from pain and loss of blood, is slow to react, and he sees that Ganji is running between him and the hostages. He holds his fire. As Ganji clears the hostages, he's almost to the door. Pell fires a string of scalding lead from an awkward position. Ganji is hit again and seems to go down as he disappears through the door. Pell calls to Cole, "I hit him Cole. I think he's down."

11:54 P.M. The Op Center

Back in the dining room, Nat is getting woozy from the pain and loss of blood from the wound in his abdomen. Slade, who is pinned down in the men's room, across and up the corridor fifteen feet, yells, "How you doing, Nat, how bad are you hit?"

Nat scowls. "It hurts, damn it! But it's not gonna kill me. How many more do you think there are, Slade?"

"I don't know for sure, but I think, only one. He's in the conference room. He's hit, but evidently not bad. He's got a good bead down this corridor, and I'm pinned down here. I'd like to get into the op room and help those guys, a hellava lot of shooting going on in there, but I don't think I can make it from here to you without taking some lead."

"Well," Nat says, "we're gonna have to do something. By my watch, Nicki's only got about six minutes."

Slade calls back. "Alright, you cover me if you can, I'm gonna make a break for your door. Shoot low, okay?"

"You got it," Nat says, as he grimaces and rolls into position. He eases his automatic around the frame of the door, aims up the corridor and starts shooting. As Slade breaks from the restroom and runs toward the door where

Nat lays, a bloody man steps from the conference room, directly into the corridor, with his automatic rifle belching fire and lead. Nat kills the man almost instantly. Almost, but not before Slade takes two rounds in the legs and falls into the doorway beside Nat.

Back in the op room, Cole cautiously approaches the door to the mechanical room, the door through which Ganji disappeared. As he passes in front of Nicki, without taking his eyes from the door, he says, "I'm gonna have you out of that thing in a second, Nicki." She answers, softly, almost in a whisper, "Whatever happens my darling, I love you and I am so proud of you."

DeWitt and Burke give Cole words of encouragement as he passes. Maddox says, "You've got less than five minutes, son."

Untold millions of people from around the world are transfixed as Cole passes in front of the camera, which is still trained on the hostages. They have heard the entire drama of the earlier gunfight between Pell and Ganji, Ahmad and Cormorant, and the current fight in which Cole is now engaged.

Cole reaches the door to the mechanical room. Figuring the only chance he has of quickly determining where Ganji hides is to expose himself. He yells to Ganji, "I'm coming, you son-of-a-bitch!" Words that are despised by Ganji.

Cole runs through the door, heading for the space between the HVAC unit and the rubbish hopper, forty feet across the room. As he does, Ganji steps from his position behind the water tank and fires twice, missing both times. The third pull of his trigger returns a click, but it cannot be heard as the generator still roars, just behind Ganji. Although Cole didn't hear the click, he knew from Ganji's motions that his gun was empty. He slides to a stop just before the rubbish hopper, turns and fires several rounds at Ganji from 25 feet. Three slugs smash into Ganji as he turns and runs. He makes it as far as the pile of dead bodies, which lie grotesquely behind the generator. He falls over the bodies, to the floor.

He finds himself looking down, through a large, round, dark hole in the floor. He takes from around his neck the cord that holds the key. As Cole approaches, Ganji, blood running from his mouth, gasping for breath, almost dead from nine bullet wounds, holds the cord over the open mouth of the catch basin. Cole raises his pistol and shouts, "Don't do it!"

As Cole aims his pistol at his head, the white streak in Ganji's beard, now stained red with his blood, twists, as a pained, demonic grin materializes on his face. "The death of your lover and the military pigs will make me a martyr, my friend," he says, and his hand releases the cord.

As the key falls to the water below, Cole screams, "Noooooooooo!" And empties his pistol into Ganji's head. He then jerks Ganji's body away from the catch basin and starts to position himself to drop through the opening and down the dark shaft to the water below.

Chapter 38

A Brass Key Will Not Float

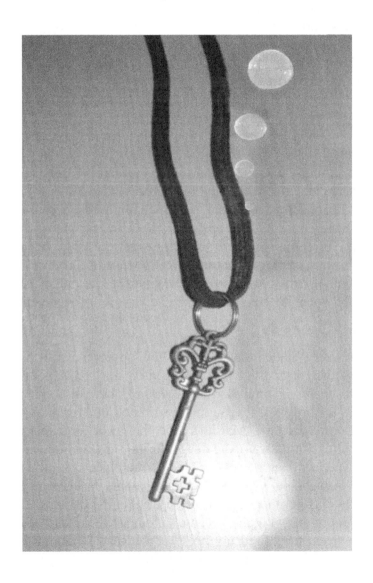

11:56 P.M.

Back in the corridor, Slade, his legs bleeding, crawls towards the door of the op room. Nat, bent with pain, holding pressure on the wound in his side, tries to assist him. They reach the door, which has been secured in the open position by Ganji's men. Slade calls, "This is Captain Slade, what's the status in there?"

Maddox shouts, "Come in, we need help, we have a man down." At the same time, DeWitt bellows, "Here Captain, quick, we need help!" Pell shouts, "This is Commander Pell, Navy SEALS, It's all clear, Captain, but we could use some help." Burke shouts, "We need the key, the goddam key, to Miss Valentini's bomb, we need the key!"

Nat, knowing that Nicki's time is just about up, hurries inside. He calls, "Cole, where are you, boy?"

Nicki motions with her head to the mechanical room door and screams, "Nat, Cole's out there, please help him!"

From his position, where he's relatively immobile because of his shattered legs, Pell answers, "He's in the mechanical room, come this way. He's trying to get the guy with the key." Nat heads for the sound of Pell's voice. He grabs Pell's H&K and then forces himself, despite the burning pain in his abdomen, to run through the door of the mechanical room.

Meanwhile, Slade crawls inside the op room. Half way across the room, sprawled in an aisle way, in a pool of blood, he sees Tony Marino. "Marino!" he calls out, and crawls toward him, leaving his own blood in streaks on the tile floor. Reaching Marino's side, he feels for a carotid artery to get a pulse. As he does, Marino stirs, and opens his eyes. He stares at Slade, mumbles something indistinguishable and eases a hand to his head, where a bloody channel marks the trail of a bullet. Slade says, "I'm real glad to see you alive, Tony. I assumed they held you in here. When they fired up the TV broadcast, I figured they were forcing you to operate the equipment."

Marino, looking dazed, says, "Yeah, Captain, that's right." Slade then notices movement of something that is clutched in Marino's other hand. Before it fully registers that it's a knife, Marino, with a grimace on his face and with barely enough strength, plunges the knife into Slade just below his sternum. A look of astonished surprise freezes on Slade's face. Stunned, it takes a second before he realizes what just happened. He grabs the hilt of the knife with both hands and pulls it free. But the damage is done; the blade has sliced inward and upward into the right ventricle of a brave man's heart. Captain Slade will never see another sunrise.

11:57 P.M. The Flooded Airshaft

In the water of the old airshaft, below where Cole Dawson has just killed Jasim Ganji, a brass key, attached to a rawhide cord, drifts downward through the water, twisting and turning, gliding deeper into the chasm. The rawhide undulates in a serpentine fashion as it resists the weight of the key and resists gravity's tug on the mass of the brass. Suddenly, the key glistens as it's caught in a shimmering beam of light. Then, a strong, gloved hand encircles the device that represents the only chance of saving the life of Nicki Valentini.

As Cole is about to drop into the airshaft, he sees several beacons of light beneath the surface of the water below. The entire airshaft glows as the lights draw nearer the surface of the flooded shaft. As one of the lights breaks the surface, a hand also appears, and in it, a shiny brass key reflects the light of Ben Dawson's dive lantern.

11:59:18 P.M.

Within seconds Cole is in the water beside his father and shouts; "The key, dad, give me the key!" Another few seconds and Cole is scrambling up the ladder. Clear of the culvert and manhole, he sprints into the op room, jumps on the platform behind Nicki; grabs hold of the vintage padlock that secures the explosive collar around her neck. He shoves the key into the lock and turns. The padlock springs open. He quickly slides it out of the collar and tosses it aside, but before he can remove the collar, he hears a strange voice bark a command as a burst of automatic weapon fire tears into the ceiling. "Hold it right there, mister. The bomb stays on the lady."

Dumbfounded, Cole looks toward the voice. Cormorant, or, Marino, rises from behind a computer station, an automatic weapon in his hands. Blood oozes from his head wound and a huge crimson splotch stains the side of his white uniform. He commands, "Step away from the girl," and points the weapon toward Cole

The world is watching, as Cole stands motionless behind Nicki. The timer on the metal collar around her neck reads, 00:00:14.

Cole frantically searches his mind for options. There are none. He and Nicki will die, either from the bomb or from the weapon pointed at them by Marino. *Hell, I won't let Nicki die by having her head blown off.* He jumps in front of Nicki to shield her body with his own and jerks the collar open. At his move, Nicki takes in a deep breath, expecting a burst of gunfire to take both their lives. And, there is a burst, the staccato barking of automatic rifle fire resounds throughout the op room as Cole, in one motion, swings the collar wide on its hinge, slides it from Nicki's neck, and with 3 seconds on the timer, heaves it as far as he can toward the other end of the op room. As the bomb flies through the air, Cole, still shielding Nicki with his own body, waits for the stabbing bullets in his back. The bomb falls between metal cabinets toward the floor and explodes in a fiery concussion with a force certainly powerful enough to decapitate a young lady. Cole, still fully expecting pain and death, leans over Nicki, his arms wrapped around her. But there is no pain, just silence. Nicki's lungs suddenly expel the breath she thought would be her last. It comes in convulsing sobs as Cole continues to embrace her. He slowly turns to look toward the gunman behind him. He sees Tony Marino's riddled body, on the floor, jerking, as it convulses in death. Standing in the doorway of the mechanical room, a hurting Nat Dawson slowly lowers Pell's smoking Colt M4. As he does, his brother, Ben steps to his side and helps him ease his tired and punished body to the floor. Then, several SEALS arrive at the doorway, guns at the ready, but the job has been done.

Billions of people are glued to televisions, watching as Cole returns his attention to Nicki. He buries his face in her breast and he, too, now sobbing, trying to find his voice, cries, "I was almost too late; I almost lost you."

The billions watch Senator Burke let out a deep breath as his body begins to tremble, then convulse in relieved sobbing. Admiral DeWitt, his face contorted with rage, yells at the dead Marino, "You sonavabitching traitor, go to hell! Go to hell and rot there!" Then they watch General Maddox, who had been rigidly erect in his chair, slowly slump into a relaxed posture. Turning to look at Cole, who still embraces and comforts Nicki, he quietly declares, "Cole, I don't know what to say. I've been in some tight spots. I've seen a lot of brave men die and I've witnessed heroic actions, but I'll be damned if you guys didn't just pull off the most remarkable engagement I've ever seen." Then, he turns to one of the SEALS and asks, "You suppose you fellows could get some medical help in here and then get us out of these damned contraptions?"

Epilogue

Mid October, 2003

The mountains that surround Cascade are clad in a symphony of color as the autumn leaves reach their peak. In stark contrast to those vivid hues is the brilliant white of Nicki Dawson's wedding gown, as she and Cole are applauded by family and friends who wait outside the Methodist Episcopal Church, the same church where Tom and Elizabeth Dawson married, almost 130 years before.

Included in the well-wishers are General and Mrs. Bruce Maddox and a large delegation of Military brass, Senator and Mrs. Robert Burke and a contingent of political figures, and most of the town's residents. Somewhat to the dismay of Cole and Nicki, most of the country also watches as the major networks televise the event. During the few weeks following the Skywatch incident, Cole received over 300 letters proposing marriage, but Nicki teased that the proposals that she received beat his number by a factor of 10.

Nicki's bridesmaid was the former Jaime Siebert. She now goes by the name of Jaime Maddox. Her father, General Maddox, spent many years trying to find his daughter after her mother had taken Jaime and left him. Her mother had lied to Jaime, telling her that it was her father who had left, that he didn't care about either of them. Her mother remarried and as the years went by Jaime had forgotten her real name. But the General found her, and they met several times, secretly, because the General's wife was not aware that he had a daughter from a previous marriage, and the General felt he needed time to prepare her for it. But, as men often do, the General misjudged his wife's understanding and compassion. She was delighted to meet Jaime, and the two of them have become very close.

Both Cole and his uncle Nat are recovering nicely from their bullet wounds. The doctors cited the fact that the bullets didn't expand, or mushroom, as the prime reason the wounds were not more serious.

As he watches Cole and Nicki enter their rented limo, Nat Dawson turns to his brother and says, "Ben, I've been thinking a lot about that whole business in the op center, and one thing keeps going round and round in my mind."

What's that, little brother?"

"Well, the fact that you arrived when you did, just as the key was drifting down, right into the beam of your light, right into your hand. Can that be just coincidental?"

Ben rubs his chin. "Nat, I wouldn't tell this to another soul in this world, not even to Marilyn. She'd think me crazy," he clears his throat before continuing, "But, as I got to the shaft that night, I looked up and could see light from the open manhole above. I reached for the switch on my light to turn it out, not knowing who might be up there, and I couldn't turn it off, Nat, I couldn't turn the damned light off. And then, and this is the strange part, it seemed as though a force of some kind turned that light straight up, right where I didn't want to point it, and there was the key, shining in the beam. I thought, this is strange, a key floating down through the water. I just reached out and wrapped my hand around it. And it almost vibrated in my hand. I had this overwhelming feeling that I had to get it up there as fast as I could. It was a strange experience, Nat, very strange."

After a pause, Nat asks, "Are you thinking the same thing as me?"

"Don't know what to think, brother. I just don't know."

As the limo drives away, Ben reaches into a pocket of his tux and pulls out a gold pocket watch. It's a Longines, with an engraving of a brook trout on the front cover. He flips open the cover, checks the time and says, "They're right on schedule, and the reverend wasn't as long-winded as normal." Nat, standing next to him, places a hand partially over his mouth, leans toward Ben's ear and whispers, "I gave him a hundred-dollar bill, told him there'd be a mate to it if I didn't have to sit through one of his standard weddings."

Ben grins at him, "You sneaky Peckerneck!"

Nat retorts, "Hell, somebody has to take charge around here." As he speaks, the sun reflects multiple colors from a large diamond, which anchors his scarlet tie. If one were to look closely, on the gold backing of the diamond they could clearly see the engraved initials; R.D.

Shortly after the marriage of Cole and Nicki, the people of Cascade initiated steps to build a memorial to the military men who lost their lives during the takeover of Skywatch. President Adam Bucklew plans to dedicate the memorial. Also planned for that ceremony is a special presentation, by the President, to honor Cole, Nat, Ben, Commander Pell and, posthumously, Captain Slade, for their heroism.

The End

A coal mine explosion that occurred on May 19, 1902 near the community of <u>Fraterville, Tennessee</u> took the lives of 216 miners, either from the initial blast or from the after-effects, making it the worst mining disaster in the state's history. The cause of the explosion, although never fully determined, was likely due to the build-up of <u>methane</u> gas which had leaked from an adjacent unventilated mine.

This note was found with one of the bodies.

Ellen, darling, goodbye for us both. Elbert said the Lord has saved him. We are all praying for air to support us, but it is getting so bad without any air. Ellen I want you to live right and come to heaven. Raise the children the best you can. Oh how I wish to be with you, goodbye. Bury me and Elbert in the same grave by little Eddy. Goodby Ellen. goodbye Lily, goodbye Jemmie goo Horace. Is 25 minutes after two. There is a few of us alive yet

Jakee and Elbert

Oh God for one more breath Ellen remember me as long as you live. Goodbye darling

About the Author

Russell Blair Savage was born and spent his early years in a grimy coal mining "camp" in West Virginia during the late 1930's and 1940's. The "camps" were small communities huddled near the entry to the coal mine, so the miners could walk to work. The houses were crude, without running water, central heat, or insulation. Clothes were washed by hand and hung on a clothes line to dry. After drying, it was necessary to shake the clothes to remove as much dust as possible. Dust that settled on them from the dirty air. The "slag dumps" where unusable lumps of poor quality coal were piled, spontaneously combusted and constantly burned and smoldered, giving off a toxic smoke heavy in various chemicals and carbon particles. Despite the disadvantages of those early years, Savage became a successful Vice President in a leadership position for an international manufacturing company. His job required international travel and extensive writing. When he retired he turned to this experience to write and publish.

He published two books about the history of his Savage ancestry which, in America, dates to 1607 at the first successful English settlement, Jamestown, Virginia. These books were the result of years spent searching through old documents in court houses and archives in several states from Ohio to Virginia. In the process Savage discovered that his is the oldest continuing family name in America. These books are titled, SAVAGE IS MY NAME and SAVAGE IS MY NAME – PART II. In addition, Savage has published 12 GAUGE PADDLE, a book of true short stories about his many years of hunting, fishing, Scuba Diving and other adventures.

Savage has published other books about family members and distributed them to relatives around the country. He has also published two children's books explicitly for his grandchildren.

Made in United States
Orlando, FL
23 August 2023

36376063R00192